A young Wehrmacht soldier in the last days of the war, tries to save as many lives as he can at Auschwitz by joining the SS and becoming a secret resistance fighter.

From one of the darkest chapters in history comes the extraordinary story of courage and hope.

THE CITIZEN OF AUSCHWITZ

an unexpected resistance

KYMBERLY HASTINGS

ISBN
978-1-958690-60-4 (Paperback)
978-1-958690-61-1 (eBook)

Dedicated to Moe

A veteran of World War I and II.

Graduated

West Point

Class of 1923

TABLE OF CONTENTS

PART 1

PART 2

PART 3

THE CITIZEN OF AUSCHWITZ

March 28, 2022

The love God gave us, bonded us and gave the strength in these very dreadful times to help those in need.

PART I
ECHOES

CHAPTER ONE

BERLIN

Late August 1939

"Their unexpected arrival has really taken me by surprise?" Geir informed his Aunt Margit.

"And quite frankly I feel like I'm being made to stand in a brisk wind under a sign advertising the Adlon Hotel. And this sign is swinging back and forth like a pendulum clock, getting ready to fall on top of my head—"

"Oh, Geir, please," said his aunt, shaking an admonishing finger at him. "Wipe that worried look off your face. And get ready to meet Hedy and her mother in an hour, for our luncheon engagement. "

"At the Adlon Hotel. Berlin's finest and named for Kaiser Adlon— wouldn't you know. A place *you* only set foot in when you're delivering your sewing. And *me*, when I'm delivering Hayim Glick's tailoring. Which, as we both know, is a place far too rich for people like us who run this boardinghouse, making me continue to wonder why Hedwig Ritter, or *Hedy* as she's called, and her mother Greta Birnbaum are traveling all the way from Switzerland just to see us."

"Something we can ask ourselves after they leave."

"But don't we have a duty to ourselves to ask them why they're here?" he challenged her.

"Since after all, Hedy's the step-daughter, of my American-Jewish father who never claimed me."

"Still, he sends me checks for your well being every month in these bitter times. Money now that my beloved Wilhelm's dead, we need more than ever." She laid a gentle hand on Geir's arm." So don't let your bitterness show a lack of gratitude or compassion."

"Not easy to do," he countered, patting the letter in his pocket he'd written to Hedy. It explained everything. Although he seriously doubted he was telling her something she didn't already know. *Because what it comes down to is my being rejected by my father. A pain that's been difficult for me to endure, because it's meant such emptiness.*

"Listen to me," Margit said, pulling his attention back. "Maybe I shouldn't tell you, but Hedy's mother asked me in her last letter if there was a young woman in your life."

"A young woman," he repeated with some astonishment. "Why do you suppose she'd asked that?"

"Probably because you're at the age of falling in love."

"And what did you tell her? That there was no one. Since even with Daniel's money, we had the responsibility of keeping this boardinghouse in good shape for the owner and his tenants, so we'd have decent place to live. Or otherwise, we stood a good chance of ending up in these dangerous times, in an apartment in the slums of Berlin."

"I cut the details and simply told her you had two friends, Volker and Charlotte Bandt, who were brother and sister—"

"And that Charlotte and I often joked about getting married, "Geir cut in, "but not to each other. And now, with war brewing, these times are much too uncertain for us to seriously consider finding the right person and doing something like that."

"Indeed they are. "Margit agreed, her brows coming together. "Even if I do find it peculiar Greta asked me if you had a girlfriend."

"Definitely. Since as of now, our place in this world is certainly not enviable, and is a question that raises another question." His shoulders stiffened. *'Especially considering the pictures I've seen of Hedy lately,' he thought about saying. 'They're enough to take a man's breath away. A rare, young woman with the beauty and electricity of a cinema star.'* So, why was Hedy's mother asking Margit if he had a girlfriend? Was Hedy pregnant and needed to be married? *Probably was.* And with him being the unaccepted family member, then on short notice, he was possibly the most logical person they could come up with. *Since over the years, in every letter Margit has written my father she's enclosed pictures of me, informed him I've learned English, and need to be taken to America.*

"I think Greta and my father have found the perfect way to use me."

"*Use* you?" Margit questioned, tilting her head to one side. "Why on earth would you say that?"

"Simply that I'm suspicious plans are being made as we speak, for me to marry Hedy because she's pregnant."

"What!" His aunt jerked back like she'd been struck with an SS man's swagger stick. "Now you don't *know* that, Geir."

"True." He gave a slightly bitter laugh." But I have ever intention of finding out." And once again he patted the letter in his pocket.

Obviously too startled to suggest he not mention it, Margit took a sharp breath before reminding, "We need to leave within the next ten minutes but first, I have to go back upstairs and put on another blouse, since I just noticed the one I'm wearing has a spot on its sleeve."

"Then by all means do it," Geir said, reaching in his jacket to withdraw the letter. "No reason not to look your best."

And watching her, he waited until she was on the staircase before he opened the letter. "An uncontrollable display of emotion I detest," he grumbled at what he'd written— 'Like I'm doomed to a life of despair. But given the circumstances, I feel it's something I need to get off my chest. "

Then, he began reading it for the fifth time:

My dearest, Hedy,

As I'm sure you know by now, I'm vulnerable. But considering I've only laid eyes on my father once, since he left me as an infant with my Aunt Margit, why wouldn't I be? And then, when I finally did see him, he didn't recognize me because I 'd just turned ten.

'The American Herr Daniel Birnbaum,' someone at the front door announced as he headed up the steps of one of Berlin's most impressive homes... beautifully silhouetted with its grandeur stabbing the darkening evening skyline.

My Uncle Wilhelm, who was hiding in the shadows, pointed at him. 'That large, prominent-looking businessman dressed in the elegant tuxedo is your father, Geir. So go introduce yourself...' Which I immediately stepped forward to do. However, when I opened my mouth to say who I was, no words came out. So he just stared at me. "Isn't it a little late for a young man your age to be out alone at this time of night? he asked me. But before I could answer, he turned and went inside.

'Didn't he recognize me from the pictures Aunt Margit sent him?' I asked my Uncle Wilhelm.

But he told me there was a glow on the light-filtered porch, and the autumn moon had a cloud cover, which probably made it difficult for him to see me plainly.

Even so, I cried all the way back to the boardinghouse, with my uncle holding me. 'Now remember, Geir, your aunt and I love you. And we're looking after you. Having even got you Aryan-Christian papers that declared you a bastard, before adopting you. So you have nothing to fear with all this hatred for Jews that's developing.'

Of course under the circumstances, adopting me was the right thing for my aunt and uncle to do. But even so, my father was a wealthy, American Jew— or a Hebrew he liked to say—who'd fought in the Great War. So why couldn't I go to America with him?

'He was just one of the many soldiers occupying Berlin,' my uncle would point out. 'But when he met your Aunt Margit's beautiful younger sister, my mother Noelle, he fell in love. And even though he was suffering from shell-shock, they were rarely apart. With their affair resulting in you. But then when she died from an infection a month after you were born, he refused to look at you. Since her doctors believed the infection had occurred because she was still very weak from giving birth.'

'Take the baby to America.' My aunt later told me she'd begged my father. But he'd refused.

'He's a bastard, and I'm a Hebrew. So, I don't have to take him to America and give him citizenship. Although, he is your nephew and you've had five miscarriages—which seems an excellent reason to look on my son as a blessing. Meaning that if you keep Geir, I'll send you a check each month to get you through these lean times in Germany.'

An offer my Aunt Margit had no choice but to accept.

My Uncle Wilhelm, who was a former schoolteacher, had injuries from the Great War and was often in pain. So he and my aunt ran a ramshackle, boardinghouse for an owner who paid them only when they had tenants. 'Hopefully, the owner won't close this place and throw us out 'Margit would say. 'Even if I do still have a few people who hire me— when they can afford it— to sew for them. And, thankfully, my dear Wilhelm is able to tutor students whose parents always pay him.'

Still, the older my uncle got, the weaker he got. But by that time I was old enough to do many of the things that were difficult for him to do... I continued my schooling but shortly before I finished, I got the opportunity to become an apprentice to a Jewish tailor, Hayim Glick. He'd made uniforms during the Great War and lived close to us. But his son had left for America, leaving him and his wife shorthanded. So, three days a week after school, I worked under Hayim's direction for a small wage.

Now, here I am, Hedy, waiting to meet you. My father's step-daughter. You're the only other child in his life, and he didn't adopt you either. Yet, you and your mother were German-Aryans, and he got you both American citizenship. Even though the three of you did eventually leave New York and take up residence in Switzerland.

"Much of my husband's business is in Europe," Greta had written in a letter to Margit. "And Hedy's in school in Switzerland here and loves it."

That was five years ago and now, Hedy, I look at your pictures and see a beautiful, grown woman with porcelain skin.

It still surprises me my father married a widowed, German woman. But then in a letter your mother sent my aunt, there was a sentence in it where Greta hinted that she and Daniel were perfect for each other because they'd always love someone else. Which I'd like to think if he did love someone else, it was my mother. And that was the reason he'd stayed away from me.

Am I right or wrong? I trust if you know, you'll tell me.

Yours,
Geir Gallen
P.S. Hopefully, I'm not being used.

"I'm ready, Geir," Margit called down the staircase.
She clutched the blue-flowered handbag that matched the flowers on the hat she wore, to cover her silver hair." Do I look all right?"

"You look fine. But me—what do I look like? And even if I feel like one, don't say a frightened rabbit."

"Enough! Our purpose is to make a good impression. Which means we mustn't let our feelings get in the way."

"Something I'm trying my best not to do, "Geir said, swallowing his pride.

An hour later Geir was pacing back and forth outside the Aldon Hotel's dining room, waiting expectantly with Margit, for Greta and Hedy to make their appearance.

"I can't imagine what's keeping them," said Margit, a distraught look on her face.

"I can. They've changed their minds."

"And didn't send word?"

"Wouldn't surprise me. Since anything's possible when you consider the rupture between our families."

But he and Margit need not have worried because a minute later Greta and Hedy were stepping from the elevator into the lobby. "Sorry we're late, but I had two phone calls," Greta informed them." One was from my cousin, Dr. Frank Rath, whom I used to help balance books, as well as his other hospital paperwork when I was living in Switzerland, and he was living here. Then, the other call was from my husband.

"Does he know you're meeting us?" Margit asked.

"Not yet. But I'll call him back after we eat."

The concierge stepped up and greeting Greta and Hedy warmly, steered them toward a white-covered table in the hotel's dining room.

'*Your beautiful like your pictures,*' Geir wished he could tell Hedy as he followed behind her.

She was turning the head of every guest in the place. And a sudden surge of something more than physical desire made him feel prosperous and proud with the feelings she was stirring in him. *Definitely a young woman a man would be honored to be seen with. Even if I suspect her beauty makes it appear she's unapproachable.*

A brief moment passed, with a silence hanging between them before she spoke. But when she did, he was caught off guard by the vibrancy of her voice. "Good to meet you at last," she said, shaking his hand. "And to inform you that your lovely name, Geir Gallen, is one sure to bring sighs."

Words completely unexpected after all these years of his grief from his father's rejection, making him sorry he hadn't bought some flowers for her. But since he hadn't, he took her hand and drew it to his lips. A reaction that caused an eager look to flash in her green eyes. Was her look a subtle way of flirting with him because she had ulterior motives? Could be.

But for now it didn't seem to matter as he admired the way the sunlight, streaming through the dining room's windows, bathed her wavy, chocolate-colored hair in a reddish-gold light. *That like her perfume and beautifully shaped lips covered in red lipstick, makes her compelling in a sensuous manner. Since she's the kind of woman a man rarely meets. A great beauty who doesn't appear to have the arrogance of one.*

The *maitre'd* showed Greta a bottle of French wine, and she nodded. 'We're fortunate you stock such a quality wine," she said, smiling as he uncorked it and poured it for everyone.

Her smile widened as she turned to Margit and Geir. "I'm certainly pleased to meet the two of you at long last."

She was wearing a small hat and pink suit Geir immediately recognized as a Chanel— the Queen of Paris— from the pictures of her pinned on the wall in Hayim's tailoring.

The hat matched her suit, with its elegance calling attention to her smooth, ginger -colored hair and the diamond earrings dangling from her ears. "Would you like the salmon?" she asked.

" I hear it's delicious, having been flown in from Scotland."

Geir looked up from the menu with an air of reluctance. *'Because we're people who belong to an inferior class, and we're dining with* you— *a member of the upper class— then it's only proper we take you up on your suggestion,'* he opened his mouth to say—but didn't. Since immediately he felt guilty at having such an bitter thought.

However, once the salmon arrived they all devoured it. "We're acting like people who haven't eaten in a week," Hedy teased with a playful grin. "But wait until you taste the *apfelstrudle* and apricot dumplings."

It was a perfect complement to their meal, and when they finished Greta asked Margit about the boardinghouse. "Do you have many tenants these days?"

Margit looked down, blotting her mouth with her napkin. "Only the three Schroders—Otto, Hugo, and Fritz. The retired fellows Daniel claims to know. However, with all the soldiers in Berlin, the owner of the house is talking about selling it. Because he insists his house is a Christian establishment and won't allow any taking of tobacco or alcohol on the premises, other than a little beer and wine." "Which must make it difficult to find tenants," Greta remarked tersely.

"It does. Considering our country's still quite *ferel*." Margit's face hardened for a moment. "But in a different way from the days of the Weimar Republic. And I have a framed, newspaper article my husband gave me during those days, that advised us to take a look at the nightclubs in the city. So we'd remember the Germans lost the war."

"Yes," Greta agreed. "And I've also read that during this time women, dressing as men, performed in those nightclubs. Alongside girls, who were dancing with their naked backsides showing—" She stopped and turned to Geir. "But you never saw those clubs, did you?"

"No—which was a blessing."

"So all those flashy girls wouldn't have interested you?"

"Not in the least." He frowned." Because I'll be content to settle for one girl to love and spend the rest of my life with."

"You impress me, but tell me, since education can give you a decent life why didn't you not attend the university? Your aunt wrote you had good report cards, and my husband wrote back saying he'd support you if you wanted a higher education. So what kept you from doing it? Was it the political system in the universities?"

"What else?"" He lowered his voice. "Because there was no academic freedom."

"Your aunt mentioned something about *that* in a letter she wrote me."

"I would have liked to have studied economics but doubted I would have gained the knowledge I was seeking, with all the misinformation the Nazi party line is circulating about the—" "Jews," Greta broke in mid-sentence. "And how we lost the war because of them."

"Exactly."

"Daniel got himself some Aryan-Christian papers because of the business he does in Europe—but getting back to the Wehrmacht. What will you do if they draft you?"

"I'll have to go. Which would surprise me because so far there're more men volunteering for it, than they're drafting. And I don't have an impressive job, which seems to flag their attention and gets a young man drafted." One corner of his mouth lifted slightly. "Plus, I graduated before I was required to do the service for several months of working on a farm or in a coal mine— like those poor unfortunates who are still in school are being made to do."

"And you weren't in Hitler Youth either, were you?" Greta asked.

"Not quite sure how." He shrugged. "But my friend, Volker, and I managed to escape being in it."

"Then I commend you both." She brightened, raising her wine glass to Geir's and clicking it against his. "And I know my husband has said he'll cut your aunt's funding when you turned twenty—"

"—which I did this month."

"Something Daniel mentioned but still—" A silence passed as she gazed at Geir with a soft smile. "In light of the unpleasant circumstances in this country, I'm going to see the money 's continued. And provided the owner's willing to sell it, I'll purchase the boardinghouse."

"What!" Margit gasped, complete surprise on her face.

And Geir, taking a deep breath, wished he had something better than the table to lean on to steady himself. "News we certainly weren't expecting to hear."

"I know. But Daniel and I are pleased to do it for you. Even if he does fear that if Germany goes to war, the house will probably be bombed to rubble."

"Mama's got an excellent business head on her shoulders," Hedy said with a gleam of pride. "And my step-father's been able to make some sound investments because of it. So she's willing to chance it."

*'Taking chances like that impresses me, '*Geir wanted to say. *'And reassures me that your not pregnant by some unknown rogue... With you and your mother here in Berlin to pressure me into a fake marriage, so your reputation will be protected.'*

Then Hedy caught him off guard, by filling her wine glass and suggesting they go sit in the courtyard next to the garden. "There's something I want to show you, Geir," she remarked in her silky voice, before putting her small, shoulder-strap bag across her chest."

He had no idea what that might be, but he quickly filled his wine glass and followed her.

"And by the way." She turned, a bright alert look in her eyes. "I checked the meaning of your lovely name before I came and learned that Geir is Norwegian and means *spear*. And Gallen is French and means *cheerful* or *high-spirited*."

"So does that make me a high-spirited spear? Or getting speared by me *cheerful* —as vulgar as it may sound?"

"If it were anyone other than you, a vulgar meaning might be implied but you—"

"I'd like to think I'm not."

"Don't worry, you're not.'

In the warm courtyard the air was fragrant with the pink and white roses in the garden. And when she led him over to a small table with two chairs close to it, he quickly pulled one out for her.

"What do you think of this hotel?" she asked. "Do you like it?"

"I might if I stayed here," he said, turning toward the garden. "But since I'm only here when I'm delivering for Hayim's tailoring, I can't really say."

"Ah-h the tailor shop. Do you enjoy working in it?"

The question challenged him, making him curious why she needed to know? "There are other things I'd rather do," he replied politely. "Though with the uncertainty of the times I'm hardly in a positive to object working for Hayim, but what is it you want to show me?"

"This." She reached into her shoulder-strap handbag and pulled out a sketch of his mother. "Once I see a face I can sketch it. So I looked at a picture Daniel had."

"Photographic memory," he said, taking it. "Now that surprises me."

She gave him a meaningful glance. "My sketching or the picture?"

"Both. Since memory like that is something few people have."

"I suppose. Which was good for me because Daniel *does* keep your mother's picture well hidden."

Geir suddenly felt cold. "What I would expect from him."

"Still, I think he loved her."

"If he did, then why not *me*? He should have taken me to America, you know."

"I know." She lightly touched his hand. "Which is why I'm here."

"To take me to America?" he asked in a slightly sarcastic tone. "It's a little late, don't you think?"

"What some are saying. Even though I came of age two weeks ago, so I can marry you and give you the American citizenship you deserve."

Astounded, he just stared at her. "D...did I hear you correctly or am I imagining things?" He faltered, thinking about adding, *'Do you really feel more concern for me over the American citizenship than my own father?'*

"You heard me," she said, patting his hand.

Once again he feared she might be pregnant. "But why?"

"Why *what?*"

" You'd do something like that for me?"

A trace of light shone in her eyes as she reached into her handbag again.

"Because your extraordinary smile puts my heart in my throat. And like my mother, I believe a woman should go where her heart takes her." She handed him a framed photo of himself.

"And I realize you're a handsome man with your compelling, gray eyes and dark hair, but your smile is so genuine that I've never seen one like it on another human being. It lifts my spirits. Which is the reason I make a point of keeping your picture close."

Hearing talk like that from such a desirable young woman was something he would have never believed possible. But did she really mean it? Or was she just saying it because she was pregnant and needed someone to marry? A question he knew better than to ask her. Yet, under these unusual circumstances there were other questions he could ask her which, hopefully, would enable him to learn the truth.

"Was I your first crush?"

"Not really. But when I saw the photo of you —all grown-up — everything changed.

And of course, I did know a lot about you from the letters Margit sent."

He stared at the framed photo of himself. "If I were to marry you, Hedy, would it be a real marriage or one we'd have annulled after several months? Since we don't exactly know each other very well."

"That's something that would be up to you. But know this, I've walked away from a good many men because none I've never met had a smile that could compete with yours."

The enormity of what she was saying made him consider the obvious: he really had nothing to lose by marrying her... *I've everything to gain... No—it's selfish of me to think like that.*

'I'm confused,' he wanted to say. *'Considering this is the first time a woman has thrown herself at me in this way'.* So naturally more questions

surfaced. "These are perilous times, and should the need arise, it'll be hard to get Margit and me out of the country."

"It probably won't be easy. But mother and I are certainly willing to give it a try."

"So your mother knows what you're planning?"

"She brought me here because she knows how much I love your picture. And how badly I wanted to meet you. "Her eyes glistened in the sunlight. "Considering the greatest attraction I've ever known for a man, is the way I feel when I look at your picture." "And you're not confused, like me? Between this attraction thing and the first time you've come across it."

"Not in the least but why, are you?"

"I just fear as time passes we might forget about each other."

"I'd never forget you. Even if the war took you from me. Which — God forbid—it won't."

His gaze met her vibrant, green eyes. "You're a temptation hard to resist. So I could never forget *you* either—especially after that citizenship offer. Though he did consider asking her if she felt sorry for him. But then, after giving it more thought, he decided to let the matter drop. *Obviously she recognizes my emotion, because she's looking at me as if in pity. But then if I marry her and can't leave the country, I'd be the ideal choice for a pregnant girl without a husband, would I not? Of course, the marriage would be brief—no sex—and after a month she'd return to Switzerland. So why not marry her? Since Greta and my father are going to keep sending Margit money.* "Do you want to get married, Hedy?" "To you?"

"That's what I'm offering."

"For the citizenship?"

"I suspect with the clouds of war approaching it might be too late for me to get the citizenship. And even if it weren't, I'd have reservations about using someone to get it."

She took both his hands in hers. "Geir, I don't know what you think of me, but I'm beginning to suspect it's not very flattering—"

"It's not."

"Then tell me."

He couldn't face her so, he handed her the letter. "Read this. And if I offend you, then maybe you'll understand why your visit here has raised some questions with me."

Acting anxious to gain more insight into what he was telling her, she quickly opened the letter and began reading it.

Watching her, he sank back against his chair. Feeling so uneasy that he became aware, to his chagrin, he was nervously tapping his foot.

"It doesn't surprise me you feel like you do," she remarked, after she finished reading the letter. "And that I have plans to use you. But rest assured, I don't."

"If I feel that way, then perhaps it's because everything you've told me— particularly about my picture— has amazed me."

"So I imagine you're trying to make sense of it. And probably think I'm pregnant and need a quick marriage,"

Better she said it than me. "That thought has occurred."

"But you're wrong. I can barely take my eyes off you. And if war does come, then I might never get to know you—which would be something I'd always regret. And if you feel like marrying me for the citizenship is wrong, then I could possibly take a month off from my nurse's schooling, in order to spend time with you at the boardinghouse. So that way, we can get to know each other better."

What man wouldn't love getting to know such a gorgeous, young woman? Especially since clearly she's unaware of her own beauty... just as she seems unaware that Germany's war mongering Fuhrer could be the undoing of both of them.

"Hedy, you impress me as a woman most men wouldn't have difficulty loving. Which gives me reason to suspect that if we do spend a month getting to know each other, then it wouldn't surprise me if we end up getting married."

"And you wouldn't want that?"

"I would if war wasn't brewing. But in these unstable times you could wind up being stuck with me in this very dangerous city. Plus, if I get drafted—"

"I'll take my chances. So humor me. But if we do get married and Mama and I can't swing it so you can get your American citizenship or move you to Switzerland, then I say life is short so take your happiness where you find it."

Since something about her made him feel extremely good inside, he'd have to agree. And for time being he lost a hold on his senses as his thoughts of this coming war seemed to vanish.

CHAPTER TWO

Geir put his letter back in his pocket as Hedy rose from the table. "Don't you think we should go tell Mama and Margit what we're planning?"

Her face was now very close to his, making it difficult to know who moved first. But once their arms were around each other, his spirits soared as her slenderness rubbed against him in her black and white polka-dot dress. And with a sudden impulse, his mouth descended on her lips which— to his embarrassment— brought applause from everyone in the courtyard.

"Wrong place, Hedy, I should have known better."

"I disagree. It just confirms what I've been thinking all along about us being right for each other."

"Still, I should have respected you and been more discrete. And besides Volker's father warned us at an early age that in this city, a young man kissing a girl in public, could get him in trouble with the police. And now, most likely, the military."

"Geir—*hush*."

"Not about to." He grinned as they took their wine glasses and walked across the courtyard into a hall, with two wingback chairs and a table. Luckily, the only people in sight were in the courtyard.

"Have you kissed many girls?" Hedy asked, taking a seat in one of the chairs.

"Just Charlotte Bandt, my neighbor," he said, also taking a seat. "But only once."

"Were you in love?"

He shook his head. "She just wanted to kiss me to see what it would be like. Since she described herself as unattractive and doubted she'd get many kisses."

"But she liked your kiss, didn't she?"

"No. She said I needed to read a book like she had, on how to do it better."

"And did you read one?"

"Oh. Yes. "But never kissed her again because without money, I really had no business getting involved with anyone."

"But *me?*"

"Things are different between us. And I don't mean the money." The thought continuing to strike him hard where she was concerned. "Since we've been getting along so well I'd almost forgotten about the great financial gulf between us."

She ran her hand soothingly over his shoulder. "Don't worry about it, I have a trust fund—"

"But a man should support a woman."

"And in the future I'm sure you will. But for now, in these dangerous times, listen to me and concentrate on what I said earlier about happiness."

Margit had always told him that if he wanted to get along with a woman, he should show her respect by listening to her. Something he most assuredly was doing Hedy. And also, he should learn what she liked and disliked and give her presents such as flowers and chocolates. "You continue to amaze me."

"Good." Her joy was apparent. "And I thank you for the big smile that my world now has on it, "She leaned closer to him. "But reflecting on your many hardships, I would like to know how you developed such a magnificent smile."

"Margit and Uncle Wilhelm," he answered, breathing hard due to the attention Hedy was giving him. "Even with all the hardships they encountered, they loved and respected me. And never took it out on me and beat me, like some parents did their children. So the only thing I could do for them was to be cheerful and pleasant. Hoping in some way I was making their lives happier."

Hedy took a sip of wine. "You know something. I have a theory about German parents beating children. Want to hear it?"

"Of course," he said, suspecting it had something to do with the "*Sieg Heil*" shouting and outstretched arms. *The Great War's bitter lesson.*

"Well—" A moment passed as she sipped her wine again. "After the Great War times were so very bad in Germany, people were doing anything to survive. And often this fear and frustration made them take it out on their children. So, showing no mercy, they beat them violently. In fact, my mom told me about a family with seven children and if one child got out of line the father whipped them all. So that meant the children got a whipping almost every week. With such cruelty breeding a lack of empathy, which could easily have attracted male children, who were treated like that, to join the SS when they grew up. "She stared fixedly at the people in the courtyard before adding, "Because the SS appears to take delight in showing no mercy to those they're ordered to torture or kill."

"How well I know," said Geir, the thought cutting through him. "Since I was brutally beaten once."

"By the SS?" she asked, shocked.

"No," he said, still tormented by the memory." A school teacher. When I was twelve years old for accidentally tearing a page in a book, about the *Fuhrer*."

"That must have been terrible."

"It was. But what was even worse was this teacher wouldn't accept my offer to pay for it. *'Our Fuhrer will not allow his future soldiers to exhibit such clumsiness,'* he informed *me*. *'So you must be punished.'* And after school, he took his cane and commenced to whack me across the buttocks so many times I lost count."

"Heavens!" Hedy shouted. "I can't believe it— but what'd your uncle do?"

"He tutored me, Volker, and Charlotte after school. And was coming on foot to get us, when Volker ran down the street and informed him what was happening—"

"And then?"

"My uncle burst into the school, grabbed the teacher's cane, and held it over his head. 'If you ever strike my nephew again I *will* kill you,'" he told him.

"The teacher then explained I had dishonored the *Fuhrer* by being clumsy and tearing a page in a book about him. An action that couldn't go unpunished."

By now Hedy was furious. "Your uncle should have struck that teacher."

"I know, but it wouldn't have been wise. Because he told that teacher he hated the Reich and the *Fuhrer*. Words that could have got him arrested and carted off to God knows where. Which, lucky for us, they didn't."

"Something that amazes me."

"My feelings exactly. With Margit writing my father about it."

"Now that's interesting," Hedy said, appearing to ponder it. "Since that's one of her letters I never saw, but what'd Daniel do?"

"Sent some extra money to Margit that she gave to me."

Hedy shook her head. "Nice. Though I doubt it was enough to compensate you for all the pain you suffered."

"It wasn't. Considering, I still have nightmares about something similar happening to me."

He paused briefly. "Although it did reinforce the love Margit and Wilhelm had for me —with Margit crying when she doctored my cuts. And later, as I sat between them on the sofa listening to the radio, they had their arms around me like sheltering wings."

"Sheltering wings?" She raised a brow. "Sounds like you're a writer."

"My plans and my dreams." His eyes on the letter which was now on the small, round table between them." I've written a book of poems. And I'm in the middle of writing a play I call, *The Sorrows of Destiny*. With the scholarly Otto Schroder, one of our tenants, being my mentor. He's written several plays, which to his regret, none were staged because of the controversy they might generate."

"Impressive— to say the least. But getting back to the money Daniel sent you. What'd you do with it?"

"Insisted Margit, Wilhelm, and I go out to dinner at a fine restaurant."

"And the three of you enjoyed it?"

"Absolutely." In fact, we even ordered ice cream to complement our dessert. Then as a surprise, they gave me one of the Great War bi-plane model kits I'd been admiring—"

"Geir," Margit suddenly interrupted, standing in the middle of the doorway between the lobby and the hall. "I was starting to worry about you with all this sudden commotion at the desk."

He grabbed his letter off the table and slipped it inside his shirt pocket.

"You two have been gone quite awhile, "said Greta, edging forward.

"I know, Mom," said Hedy. "But we're getting to know each other better—like I said I wanted to do."

"Then I guess you're making plans to stay at the boardinghouse?"

"Till mid-September."

"Your daughter strikes me as having a strong belief in the giving of love," Geir asserted with a smile." Something most people have lost in this angry world."

Greta reached in her purse and removed a telegram. " I'm glad you feel that way, because I just received this from Daniel. And he's telling us to get back to Switzerland at once! With his sources saying that Germany could go to war with Poland any minute."

Immediately, Hedy grabbed Geir's hand "But what about his citizenship, Mom?"

"Unless he can go to Switzerland with us, it's a little late."

"Which hopefully he can, " Hedy remarked. "But since we're not there yet, I'm afraid for him."

Her eyes met his disparagingly." Even If we are both of age and can marry without anyone's permission."

"And you'd marry him without knowing him?" Greta asked, shaking her head in disbelief.

"Exactly, like history reports the mail-order brides did."

"But you've an American passport like me. And if war comes, and you don't get out of Germany, then there's no telling what the Germans will do to you."

Hedy regarded her with a serious look. "I'm not worried. Daniel will get me a fraudulent German passport."

"Please," Geir uttered, feeling flustered. "It's best if you do what your mother says and go."

"I felt something like this would happen," said Margit. "Which is why I begged Daniel in my letters to take Geir to America."

"Something about which my husband eventually had pangs of regret about not doing,"

Greta informed her. "Having admitted to me he'd made a mistake. Part of which he blamed on being shell-shocked and the asthmatic condition he developed." Then as if thinking about it, she stood there a moment without moving, before continuing, "And later, when he wanted to come for Geir, he didn't. Because regardless of what you wrote in your letters about taking him to America, he realized it would have broken your heart."

"Which it would have,"Margit said, teary eyed. "And what would have become of me and Wilhelm would have been a pain, that nevertheless, we'd have found a way with which to deal."

Geir gave Greta a long stare. "After the Great War the enemy was never really crushed. So surely Daniel could have done something about my citizenship before the Reich took over."

"He talked about it. But decided if Germany went to war, the Americans would get into it.

And if you were an American citizen, then the Americans would draft you and send you back over here because you spoke German."

"So now we're facing Armeddon," said Hedy, also teary eyed. "But no matter. Since if you and Margit heard the applause in the courtyard, then it seems from the kiss Geir gave me there, we share a passionate intensity. So—*please*—Mom, help me with my wedding and getting my fraudulent German passport."

Greta turned to Geir. "We're here because she's had a crush on your picture for several years.

Telling me she can't imagine life without it."

"But if I put her in danger, then what—"

"I'll take my chances," Hedy broke in, blinking back her tears. "And if the world truly is about to end— like I've said— we must take our happiness where we can find it."

Greta looked at her with a heartbreaking sadness. Making Geir wonder if she wasn't reminded of another time when a letter she'd sent Margit had mentioned that after only a few days of marriage, the Great War had taken Hedy's father from her to fight in a foreign land.

"Mom," Hedy went on to add, "from everything I've heard and read we have some very dark days ahead of us. So who knows if we'll live through them or die trying?"

The words seemed to cut through Greta. "Only God, "she replied, lowering her head as if quite aware of how their world was changing. " And while I don't doubt the truth of your words, I'm still uneasy when I think you're marrying someone you don't know."

"But, Mom," Hedy persisted. "I've read nearly all Daniel's letters from Margit, which he keeps in an open box in his office. And all they talk about is Geir. So I feel I *do* know him."

Immediately, Geir shifted his attention from Hedy to Greta. "Your daughter's offer to marry me to give me American citizenship, says a lot about her."

"So that being the case, Mom, how quickly do you think we'll be able to get married?"

There seemed no respite from her determination.

"Soon—in view of the coming war," Greta replied, clearly not able to restrain her daughter's wishes. "Which means if you can get the license right away then maybe, less than three days—" Her hand trembled as she looked down at Daniel's telegram she was still holding.

"Good." Hedy perked up. "Because if we act fast there's a chance before Geir gets drafted, we can take him to Switzerland with us."

"And I'm anxious to go," he said, draping an arm around her. "But Margit has to come with us."

"Yes. However, if I do, Geir, what about our three tenants? Someone has to look after them?"

"Then we'll find someone," Greta answered before Geir could.

Margit was obviously puzzled. "So your still planning on buying the boardinghouse?"

CHAPTER THREE

"I'll have to wait and see. But right now, we have to put the plans in motion for Geir and Hedy's wedding."

Hedy stared anxiously into her mother's eyes. "And since we've got a clock ticking on us, we'll need to hurry."

"Of course, but where Daniel's concerned—"

"Is what?" Hedy asked. "That he's probably expecting us to be on the next train to Switzerland."

"Those were our travel plans," said Greta.

Not sure quite how to phrase it, Geir let a moment pass before he asked, "Then why can't we be? I mean I'm not drafted yet, so there's no reason I can't vacation in Switzerland. And as far as our three tenants, the Schroders, there's no reason they can't come with us."

"That's a great idea," Hedy replied. "Since Daniel appears to know them, and they write saying they treat you like uncles. "She turned to her mother."But what about the wedding?"

"What about it?" Greta asked Geir, shifting her gaze to him.

He exchanged a smile with Hedy. "Switzerland!" he shouted.

"Yes. Switzerland!" she exclaimed, sharing his excitement.

"Which means," said Margit, "we've got to get back to the boardinghouse and pack."

"I agree." Greta nodded. "But look—" She gestured at the crowd of more people heading toward the hotel's desk. "A herd. So Geir stay with your aunt while Hedy and I go up and get our things. And while I'm checking out, I'll make arrangements with the hotel to purchase tonight's train tickets." She glanced at the desk again, her tension appearing to increase. "If we do it that way, Hedy and I will be able to go to the boardinghouse with you and help you and Margit pack."

"And the Schroders and my friend Volker, who's apt to get drafted?" Geir asked. "What about them?'

"Give them a call and see if they want to go to Switzerland with us."

"Will do."

Though, with the tightly packed crowd at the hotel's desk, Geir had difficulty getting to the phone and call the boardinghouse.

"I'll try and get a hold of Volker," remarked Otto Schroder. "But I'll discuss our leaving when you return home."

His answer surprised Geir. Not to mention how taken aback he and Margit were that it took over an hour for Greta to check out, purchase the train tickets, and have a hotel attendant get them a cab. But once the attendant did, they were on their way.

"What time does our train leave for Zurich?" Geir asked Greta.

"Nine 'o clock. So you and Margit should have a couple of hours to pack."

"I'm coming back when this fury in Germany has passed," Margit informed everyone, as the cab picked up speed.

Geir tried not to act as excited as he felt, until they got to the boardinghouse. *Then*, he got out of the cab quickly and ushered Hedy inside.

She seemed pleased with the house. "A classic Edwardian style from a bygone era with vertical Dormer windows on your sloping roof."

And though the ceiling murals were faded, the gleam of the wooden floor no longer bright, and the furniture scratched, it didn't stop Greta from remarking, "It doesn't look as bad as I imagined. "Still—" She stepped over to one of the open windows and gazed at the noisy street outside, before adding, "Now that we're leaving, I doubt I'll buy it."

Pointing at the staircase, Hedy turned to Geir. "Is your room up there?'

"Yes—want to see it?"

"Of course. Especially since I'll be helping you pack."

They were heading toward it when the two elderly, but solid-looking Schroders walked in from street. The younger Schroder, holding a cane, walked behind them. "You've visitors," announced Otto, the oldest, who sported a well-trimmed, gray beard. "Your friends Volker and Charlotte Bandt." He gestured at them waiting in the living room.

Troubled, Geir stared at Volker. "What's going on?"

"This." He brushed back the strand of brownish-blond hair falling across his forehead, before shoving a draft notice in Geir's hand. "Have you got yours?"

"Mail's on the desk." Otto pointed, turning to Geir. "But since you and your aunt have been gone, I doubt you've checked it."

Hedy cut in front of Geir. "I'm getting it—" When suddenly, the shadowed expression on her face, made her look like she was about to crumble to the floor. "My God!" she exclaimed, holding the letter like it was burning her hand.

Geir quickly took it from her. "My draft notice too." His gaze drifted momentarily as he worked up the courage to ask her, "Are we still getting married?"

"As soon as we can get the license," she replied firmly.

Relived, he stared at the details on his draft notice: *Recruits will meet at the railroad station on Saturday, the second of September. And there they will board the train for Garmisch, Bavaria. Where upon arrival, buses will be waiting to take them to the barracks.*

It fluttered in his hand as Hedy reached for it "Not clear which bus to take."

"Guess they'll be marked." Even if he'd only known her for a few hours, it was excruciating to him to think about leaving her. "And I know we've talked, Hedy, but tell me, after I leave are you really planning on staying here in Berlin?"

"Of course. So if you come home, I'll be waiting for you."

This time he let it pass; though his logic continued to dictate that Switzerland was the safest place for her.

Greta rushed up and grabbed his arm. "If she's staying, then I'm buying the house and living here with Hedy and Margit. So don't worry."

Margit went rigid with apprehension. "And you and Volker are required to report in just five days!" She blinked hard. "Which is no time at all."

Geir stared at her, then at the letter. "You're right there."

"I'm so upset I'm going to the kitchen and get my medicine." And with a sudden, almost buoyant energy, she spun around and hurried through its door.

"Five days is much too soon," Otto told Geir as he watched Margit disappear. "But before we continue talking, don't you think some introductions need to be exchanged between Volker and Charlotte Bandt, and the *two* lovely ladies with you?"

"Indeed," said Geir. "And since *you*, Otto Schroder, are the oldest and maintain you three Schroders are my uncles. Then *you* should have the honor."

"Which will be my pleasure," he said, meeting Greta's gaze with a smile. "And standing next to Margit's dark, brown sofa behind me, is my brother Hugo and our younger cousin, Fritz. "

"I'm the one who hobbles around, because I got kicked by a horse when I was eight years old, "said Fritz. "But Otto and Hugo have always looked after me and even arranged for me to work with them. So it's never bothered me that much."

The two gentlemen extended their hands to greet the ladies.

"And I'm Greta Birnbaum, Daniel's wife," she said, her eyes meeting theirs. "And this is my daughter, Hedy Ritter, who's Geir's *fiancee*—"The sentence did not need completing as Hedy graciously reached out a hand to each of them.

"Certainly a surprise," remarked Charlotte, raising her hand in a greeting gesture.

"I agree," said Volker, looking a little dazed as he lifted his hand. "But when's the wedding?"

"Day after tomorrow," Greta answered. "Provided I can get my cousin, Dr. Frank Rath, to use his connections to get their marriage license."

"Dr. Rath's training me to be a nurse," said Charlotte, tugging at one of her blond braids.

"And he's highly respected here, so he'll get it."

"I'm in nursing school in Switzerland," Hedy told her. "However, now that I'll be living here, I'll probably be one of Dr. Rath's trainees."

"Then it'll be my pleasure to train with you. Since I used to tell Geir that he was so handsome, he needed a beautiful young woman like you."

Hedy's cheeks flushed. "I'm flattered you think that."

"So am I," Geir agreed, before turning and glancing at Greta. "We've train tickets to Switzerland, so what I don't understand is why we can't act like we never saw this draft notice and leave tonight—"

"Wouldn't be wise, "Otto broke in. "Orders are orders. And Since you're the right age for the draft, they'll be checking your papers at the border."

"And if they think you're trying to abscond, they're apt to summon the SS and have you shot," added Greta, peering anxiously at Geir.

Hedy looked at him, then her mother. "Something we clearly can't risk."

"Which is why I need to call Dr. Rath right now. And have him see about your marriage license."

"Then be my guest," Geir said, going over to the desk and handing her the phone.

She didn't talk long, but everyone in the living room waited in silence as she and the good doctor talked for several minutes. "All is well," she declared when she finished. "And the marriage license should be ready for Hedy and Geir to pick up tomorrow."

"Was Dr. Rath shocked I'm getting married this soon?" Hedy asked.

"Very. And when I joked about your being a mail-order bride, and that you were marrying Geir, Daniel's son, I think he nearly passed out. "

Geir and Hedy exchanged grins.

"What else was said?" she asked Greta.

"That Geir had been conscripted and had to report in five days. Words that appeared to galvanize Dr. Rath into action. Because he assured me the people he knew who handled marriage licenses, should have yours ready by tomorrow."

"Anything else?" Hedy asked, as if her mother was missing something blindingly obvious.

"Berlin's Philharmonic Orchestra. He's taking us there tonight, like he talked about doing before we arrived."

"With Geir and Margit?"

"Of course. And anyone else we want to bring along." Then as if needing a moment to reorient herself, she briefly looked away from the group. "And it's not only for the entertainment but dinner as well."

"Did you include us?" asked Otto.

"Naturally. Along with Volker and Charlotte Bandt."

Volker turned his eyes toward Greta. "I do hope Dr. Rath has a big car."

"He does. However, he's also sending another one."

"Then we should all be comfortable."

"I overheard the good doctor's treating us tonight," said Margit, returning to the living room.

"And I'm grateful." She blotted her eyes with a flowered handkerchief. "Even though I doubt I can relax."

"We'll make the best of things like we always do," Geir assured her, kissing her cheek.

"I think that's part of our problem."

"Could be? But it's too early to tell."

"Still, the idea of your fighting for those damned Nazis is more than I can take."

"It's more than I can take too," said Hedy, coming over and putting her arm around Geir.

He kissed her gently on the forehead, and she nuzzled her head against his chest.

"Two nights is not much of a honeymoon, "she whispered.

"I agree."

"Then what if we start early?"

"Like now?" She gave him a coy smile. "Why not?"

"No reason not too." He returned her smile. And his eyes clung to hers as he swept her up in his arms and headed toward the stairs.

Margit drew a startled breath. "Just where do you think you're going?" she asked, in a less-than-approving tone.

"Honeymooning," answered Geir.

"With someone you've only known a few hours?"

"The boundaries of a person's world change when their country's on the brink of war."

"Quite true, "Greta agreed, coming over and placing a hand on Margit's shoulder. "Hedy's father and I had known each other barely a week before the Great War came, and he got drafted. So he got it in his head to marry me, with our wedding happening the same day he left. Prompting us to honeymoon before we married. For which we had no regrets. Since it helped to give us some good years after the war."

Still holding Hedy like he was ready to carry her over the threshold, Geir paused halfway up the stairs and glanced sideways at Volker, Greta, and Margit. "This union between Hedy and **me** is meant to be," he informed them." So we'll see everyone later."

Volker stared wide-eyed at the couple. "Guess there's an upside, after all, to being drafted in the Wehrmacht."

Geir laughed. "Guess there is."

CHAPTER FOUR

Once they reached his room, Geir put Hedy down. "I don't have much furniture."

"Doesn't matter because you do have a writing desk."

"With the shelf above it holding my model planes, since I'm a kid at heart. Plus, some old school books and used philosophy books Otto bought me."

Looking at the model planes, then the philosophy books' titles, she nodded her approval.

"These books tell me you're on your way to becoming a scholar like Otto."

"Who knows?" He took a step toward her. "Considering I do have a question to ask you that isn't scholarly."

"Then ask me."

He grinned, holding her at arm's length. "Do you think two virgins will make it?"

"I don't see a problem." Then returning his grin, she reminded, "Especially since I've had some nurse's training."

"But do we have some kind of protection?"

"I was fitted for a diaphragm before I came. And I have it here in my purse."

"Good. Because I'd hate to make babies with a war coming."

"So would I. Since when we produce them, they'll be extraordinary human beings."

He smoothed his hands over her dark curls. "I agree."

She pushed herself against him and kissed him so fiercely, he felt an incredible sensation of wanting running through her.

He kissed her back, and she hugged him tightly. Inspiring him to lift her and carry her over to his bed. "I'm not believing this," he murmured as they helped each other undress.

"It is hard for me to imagine too," she said softly, wrapping her legs around his waist in what was obviously an expression of her joy

Their lovemaking was tender, passionate, and desperate. And even with her gasp from her brief split of virginal pain, she smiled through it. "We fit exquisitely," she acknowledged. "Like I knew we were meant to be."

"I'm certain we were," Geir said romantically. '*With death and the coming war fading into the background,*' he considered adding, '*As this union between us seals our commitment to each other and makes me wonder if such pleasure really exists? Or it simply my imagination?*'

As if further sealing their vows, he touched her lips with kiss after kiss as they lay in each other's arms until it seemed her urgency, like his, was building again.

Moving slowly at first, he waited until her feelings intensified, and she demanded more, before he thrust deeper inside her.

Quivers surged through them as their spirits joined in tempo. *She's as lost in me as I am in her.*

And her skin tingled as the sweet spasms shooting through her, scorched him with her flames of passion. And he moved faster and faster. *We've stumbled into a paradise where your nearness is blazing through me like a wildfire out of control*— "Unimaginable," he murmured, an instant before his primal groan of satisfaction, followed her moan of surrender.

Exhausted, they lay in each other's arms. "I love your muscles," she whispered, before she closed her eyes.

He looked at her and smiled. "I hope they don't make me look chunky."

"They don't."

He placed her hand against her silken belly. "Pleased you think so." He snuggled against her.

What will happen to us? He wondered. *Will this brief honeymoon be all we ever have...?*

Something so wonderful, it seemed for a moment almost more than what I could handle. Because down the road a voice in my head is whispering that Hedy and I will be parted by the heaviness of death A thought that cuts through me like a sharp, butcher knife.

⸻ ◆ ⸻

Later, after the dinner and the concert, Greta and Dr.Rath went in the kitchen so they could be alone at the boardinghouse. "Have you informed Daniel about your daughter's wedding?" the good doctor asked her.

But she shook her head. "I'm waiting."

"Waiting?" he questioned, removing the hat he wore to keep his white hair plastered down. "But doesn't he expect you to be on tonight's train for Switzerland?"

"He does. So I'll need to call him in the morning before we're supposed to arrive."

Appearing to mull it over, Dr. Rath curled his fingers around the brim of his hat. "And he'll say *what*—you think?"

"Not sure. Considering, he's mentioned the way Hedy won't let go of Geir's picture. So he might not be as surprised as we think."

Dr. Rath shot her a wry smile." We'll keep our fingers crossed, but where's the wedding going to take place?"

"Unless you know a better place, I'm considering the Adlon Hotel."

"Not good enough. So how about a small parish church attached to a monastery?"

"I'm for it unless—" She gave it some more thought. "It's not very far from the city."

He smiled. "It's just outside the city."

"And you can arrange it?"

"Won't be a problem."

"Then do it," she urged. "Because it'll make the occasion more memorable for them."

The next morning when Greta informed Hedy and Geir about the small, parish church Dr. Rath was suggesting, they were so excited it made their eyes water. "It isn't far, but with Dr. Rath arranging transportation, I'll need the guest list of those who those who'll be coming."

"That's easy," said Geir. "Everybody who went with us last night. As well as Volker and Charlotte's parents, and Hayim and his wife—"

"But, Mom, have you talked to Daniel yet?" asked Hedy, with a worried expression. "Surely he must be concerned we're not back."

"I'll call him now. So wait in the living room."

Greta went over to the desk and picking up the phone, asked the operator to connect her to long distance in Switzerland.

Almost immediately Daniel answered. "Where the devil are you? "he asked, his voice smacking of impatience.

Then she began going over the scenario of Hedy's attraction for Geir. "Your son," she reminded. "That Margit said you called' *your tarnished legacy'* as you walked out the door, leaving Geir in her arms."

"That I did," Daniel admitted in a perplexed tone. Then, as if he were at a loss, several awkward moments passed with his saying nothing. Until finally, Greta mentioned the draft notice Geir had received.

"For God's sake!" he thundered. "Hedy was supposed to bring Geir to Switzerland—so what in hell happened?"

"Then you knew?" she asked, completely baffled.

"I overheard her talking to his picture before she left. 'You'll be safer if you come *home* with us,' were her words.'"

"And you didn't tell me?"

"In view of the coming war, I wanted him to join us. But since Hedy was plotting what I should have been doing, I thought it best to let her handle the matter."

Greta considered his words carefully. "Why? Because after all these years something like that would have been difficult to explain to him?"

"Exactly. Which, to my great misfortune, is why I took my time about it." He paused, allowing some more awkward moments to pass before adding, "And all because I failed to take into consideration how unpredictable Hitler can be, with the Wehrmacht having more volunteers than draftees."

"True. But how could Margit just up and leave with three tenants?"

"She couldn't. Although, the Schroders have been with her for so long, they've like family. So, I feel certain they'd have come with her."

Then Daniel suddenly blurted," I came to love Geir from Margit's pictures and letters because she had a way of reminding me, that I'd loved him from the beginning. Though after my beloved Noelle's death, I had trouble admitting it."

Immediately, a tear rolled down Greta's cheeks. "You lost years you can't get back, you know."

"I know. And now our narrow window of time is closing...but how many days before Geir has to report?"

"Four — as of this morning. Which is why he and Hedy are getting married tomorrow."

"What can one expect? Since war can either bring people together or tear them apart."

"Do you want to come to the wedding?"

"Since I've missed all the major stages of Geir's life, I'd seem like a hypocrite. So it's probably better if I come day after tomorrow."

"But what about you? When are you coming back to Switzerland?"

"I'm not," she answered, trembling at the way the past and future were colliding. "Hedy and I are staying here with Margit. Since that way, Geir will have people to come home to when he gets leave."

"Dangerous, but makes sense. Especially with my being away on business so much of the time. Though rest assured, I'll visit at least once a month." He eased out a breath. "And you and Hedy?

Will she be doing her nurse's training at his hospital, while you'll be handing the good doctor's paperwork?"

"That's the plan."

"Then I'll see you day after tomorrow. " He remained quiet for a second before handing up the phone.

"Mom," Hedy called, holding Geir's hand as she stepped over to the desk with him. "What

did Daniel say?"

"That he's coming day after tomorrow."

⎯⎯⎯◆⎯⎯⎯

Immediately Geir's heart pounded with panic. There'd always been the dream that he and his father would come face to face. *But what will I say to him? 'That I'm not ready for this.'* There was *so* much that needed to be said between them it was like he didn't know where to start. Yet, now for some strange reason it felt like words weren't needed. *Obviously Daniel's trying to find a path back to me. Something that seems unreal. Considering I've read somewhere that young soldiers at twenty—my age—didn't have much of a previous life: just parents, work, school, and hobbies.*

Although older men had careers, wives, and children... But Volker—he doesn't even have a girlfriend.

While me— I have a soon-to-be wife. A root. Before the war takes me away which, in a manner of speaking, Daniel's given me.

And then it comes to mind how the years have passed with him never showing himself. Yet, believe it or no, he's somehow caused a miracle to happen. For my father, who's never come around, has managed to make up for the lost time between us by bringing Hedy into my life—who's everything I ever dreamed of.

"Geir," Hedy said, giving his forearm a meaningful squeeze. "You look sad, are you?"

"Not really." He searched her face." It's just that being loved by you is overwhelming." Her arms went around him as did his. And he hugged her possessively. "I thank you for coming to me."

"I hope to fill your life. So, those empty years without Daniel won't be so painful."

"And so far you're doing such an excellent job, that it inspires me every day to pray I can do the same in return."

"You *are*. With each minute that passes strengthening our bond. But before Daniel comes you must read this. "She handed him a battered-looking notebook. "It's Daniel's. And I'm giving it to you. Because there's so much unspoken in this gulf of silence between the two of you, that I'm thinking this will help."

"And I'm very much obliged." His fingers trembled as she handed it to him.

There were several ink smears at the top of the page. *Could they have been moistened by tears? Or perhaps a spill of some kind? And would Hedy know?*

He was thinking about asking her when she kissed his cheek affectionately. "Mom's taking Margit and me wedding shopping. So be sure and read it while we're gone." She hesitated, as if groping for the right words."A suit— do you have one?"

"An aqua-blue one I've never worn, that Hayim made me."

"Aqua-blue?" she questioned, surprised.

Geir chuckled nervously. "Hayim had so many orders he ran out of all his dark suiting material. And was practically in tears, that he couldn't make me a suit. So I handed him some aqua fabric. "Margit loves this color. So I think she'd be impressed if I had a suit made from it."

"I like it," said Hedy. "Knowing that it's a color said to reflect creativity and inspiration. As well as enhancing empathy and showing care." She kissed his cheek again. "But how about some thin, tuxedo socks that Daniel likes because they're comfortable? Do you have any?"

"I've seen them but don't have any."

"Then I'll definitely get you a pair."

⎯⎯⎯◆⎯⎯⎯

It was almost an hour after she left, before I found the courage to open Daniel's notebook and read it:

"When I first met my beloved, Noelle, she was quite sad. Moved to pity, I suspected, in these ruins of Berlin with all the dead surrounding her. For she was a delicate, young woman who needed food. With Margit and the wounded Wilhelm not having much for her or themselves. So, when I offered food for her and them, she paid me by spending the night with me.

The next morning I had no plans to see her again, but the way she looked at me— like she felt more sorrow for me than she did herself— made me not want to leave her.

She gave herself to me completely—anyway that she could. And I needed her, because even if she was a helpless person, her love made me believe in myself. So I came to look on the depth of my love for her as a magical happening.

And when she gave birth to you I was overjoyed... until her infection took us all by surprise.

Of course she could not breast feed, but no matter. Her doctor had developed a way for her to bottle feed you. And getting the bottles ready required time. But weak as she was, it didn't stop her from insisting on preparing them.

Margit would help her by changing your diapers. And I'd help her if she needed me. But if not, then afterwards, I'd curl you in my arms.

Unfortunately, the military made its demands. So I wasn't present when your mother died. However, I knew she was getting weaker and weaker. In fact, Margit said before she died, she reached out to you, her beloved son in your crib, before falling facedown on the floor.

'I don't know what to do,' I remember telling Margit. 'Because I can't accept her death.'

And to make matters worse, when you cried in Margit's arms, it was like you couldn't accept her death either...

O-oh how fatal my love for your mother had been! So I allowed a terrible numbness to overtake me, that drove me away from you. Even if Margit did keep pressing me, 'But the baby, what about the baby?' She asked me as I went out the door."

There were only these two pages in my father's notebook, but even so, I wrestled with the significance of what I'd read. Is the writing in this old notebook enough to settle things between me and my father after twenty years? If so, then why does his failure to show himself until now, continue to disturb me?

Margit has seen to it that I have a framed picture of my mother and him, enjoying the day at Lake Wannsee. Something as the years have passed I have became more and more hesitate to look at.

Because whenever I do I feel like I 'm reaching out to him, with the outstretched arms of someone drowning.

Still, he brought Hedy into my life. Wonderful Hedy. Sunlight flaming around her shoulders with a brilliance, like a heavenly shield casting its iridescence over her. Which clearly helps me to block the pain of Daniel's rejection. Even though, sadly, I still have an emotional need of him.

CHAPTER FIVE

Geir, in his aqua-blue suit, and Hedy were married the next morning in the small parish church outside the city. The guests thought Geir's aqua suit added to the wedding, with Hedy saying it gave it a unique appeal.

"As long as it doesn't detract from the bride," he said.

"Something I'm not worried about it." She smiled, holding his hand.

His smile reflected hers. "For which, my gorgeous lady, there's plainly no reason to be."

He made a furtive sweep at her wedding attire; a delicate, creamy-white veil crowned her head, haloing it. And though her pearl-seeded, lace dress was street-length, there were several moments when it seemed to him she was covered in a celestial mist, as she knelt and stood throughout the different phases of the ceremony... *My bride, I marveled! Never did I believe I'd have such an extraordinary wife. And lately, just before I fall asleep, there's a fleeting moment when my wild imagination takes over. And closing my eyes, I envision my* love *for Hedy being strong enough to stop this coming war.*

Margit had given me her gold wedding band to give to Hedy, which she'd admired. But to me it wasn't good enough. "If I had the money I'd have given you a diamond ring."

But she shook her head. *"I have two diamond rings already."*

Still, as we got in the car that would take us to the Adlon Hotel, I made her promise that she'd at least give me a picture of a diamond ring she 'd admired. So when the day came, and I had the money, I could have one made like it for her.

"I do carry a picture of one in my wallet. "She smiled in the bright light.

"Then give it to me, and I'll keep it with our marriage license until I can buy it for you."

Which she later did.

Geir was pleased with the luncheon and reception Greta had arranged at the hotel.

Food and wine flowed freely among the wedding guests. Although, after the four-tiered wedding cake had been cut, Geir and Hedy escaped. "We're being sneaky," they teased each other as they returned to the boardinghouse in a cab.

Had their situation been different, Geir knew he would have felt guilty for not restraining himself and allowing their honeymoon to start early. But considering his draft notice, what choice did he have?

"We did the right thing, adding the two early nights to our honeymoon," Hedy said, striping out of her wedding dress.

He reached out and pulled her toward him. "Which, with my going away, I'm certain we'd have lived to regret."

"I believe it." She put her lips against his neck, caressing it. "So let's stay ahead of our guests and consummate our marriage quickly."

"Yes indeed." He grinned.

"It'll be an extravagant indulgence to spend sometime alone in this big house," Hedy said with a smile. "Before Greta and Margit show up with the wedding guests."

"Hasn't been like this much in my life," Geir remarked.

She buried her face against his throat. "I'm sure it hasn't."

Several rounds of passionate and desperate lovemaking occurred between them, before she reached across the bed and turned on the radio for some Strauss music.

Though sadly, there was nothing on any station but shouts of "*Sieg Heil! Sieg Heil!*" Words which were followed by a speech from the *Fuhrer*.

Uncertain how to react, Hedy and Geir just stared at each other.

"They have the power," she finally said, tears in her eyes. "Which can't end well for Germany or *us*."

"No it can't," he agreed, turning off the radio. "Unless we can figure out something that will make it."

"Which I suspect won't be easy—"

"Not with my being forced into the Wehrmacht."

As they lay in each other's arms, Hedy soon fell asleep. But Geir was too troubled to sleep.

I have to think. Otto Schroder is good at solving problems. So maybe he might have some trick up his sleeve. It was certainly worth a try.

What was it about Otto and his brother Hugo and their cousin Fritz? They were certainly unique human beings. And growing up Volker and I used to have fun pretending they were from outer space.

But in reality they'd been meatpackers, who'd been given a deferment during the Great War.

And Daniel had known them and still corresponded with Otto; who like his brother and cousin was an uneducated man. *'None of us three had the opportunity for a university education,'* Otto had explained. *'But no matter.'* He believed reading would solve their problem so, reading they did.

'Practically living in the library,' Otto would say.*' With the result that I, like Hugo and Fritz, became so well-versed in business, history, and philosophy, people were in awe of our* knowledge.'

Eventually the three found employment in Berlin's large library. *'With the money we got from this work enabling us to pool our resources and retire after a time,'* Hugo and Fritz made no bones, about telling everyone.'

None of the Schroders had married since they believed it would require them having children.

'And male children,' so Otto said, *'would end up becoming cannon fodder for Germany in the coming war—which the secret, behind the scenes government was* preparing. '

'But what about the female ones?' Margit would ask him.

'Why they'll be forced to become whores for the Russians invading Germany.'

A prophecy that made Geir want to ask his father, *'I'm of the opinion Otto wrote you about this coming war. So why didn't you try to get me out of the country? Didn't you believe the Fuhrer was dangerous after what Otto wrote you?'*

He planned to ask Daniel about that tomorrow. And if he said 'yes,' then why had he left it up to Hedy? *Who gives me the impression she had to wait until she came of age, before Germany would allow her to get my Swiss or American citizenship. Was she told that, because Germany— even with all its volunteers— was preparing to draft its young men? She probably was knowing the shape the country was in.*

Daniel can't bring back what was lost between us in my childhood. Nor the grief I suffered over him. Yet, lying beside me now I'll never cease believing that you, my beautiful Hedy, is the greatest gift I've ever received from anyone.

Geir was asleep when Hedy gently shook his shoulder, waking him. *Early evening?* The soft glow coming through the window certainly looked like it. "Hurry and get dressed," she urged, swinging her legs off the bed. "Daniel's here."

"Now?" he questioned, blinking his eyes. "But he wasn't supposed to come until tomorrow."

"Apparently a change of plans."

Then he heard a loud male voice echoing throughout the house. "God in heaven!" Geir exclaimed, throwing back the covers. "You're right! We need to hurry and get dressed."

Hedy was already slipping into a powder-blue dress in the room' s extra *armoire*, Geir had robbed from the adjourning bedroom. But he was still groping for the shirt and some work slacks, he kept folded in a chest of drawers.

"Do I look all right?" he asked her, after he slipped them on.

"You look just fine," she said, flinging back the bedroom door.

It was time... All my life I've waited... And now here's Daniel. "I'm stiff with anxiety, Hedy."

"I know, but you have a quiet sort of strength. So if it helps, just remember I'm here because Daniel brought us together."

Geir laid his hand against her chest. "Your heart beats in time with mine. And if Daniel had given me citizenship, then I'd have never had such a wonderful wife. And like I've said, something in me loves him for that."

"Then just be sure to keep that in mind when you meet him. Because Daniel's really a good man. And since my father died before I got to know him, he's been like a father to me."

When they got to the landing, Geir could see the back of a large, dark-haired man in a brown suit standing at the foot of the stairs. One arm was wrapped around Margit as the wedding guests, having returned from the hotel with Greta, were thronged around him like they would have done a celebrity.

Their welcoming voices were quite loud, until Greta stepped up and announced the bride and groom were coming down.

Which prompted the guests to move toward the dining room, watching, as the couple approached Daniel. "Good to see you," he said, shifting abruptly toward the pair.

Then an extended silence followed, until choking back tears, he said, "Son—"

Different eyes in a different face from the one Geir had seen as a boy. *Letting me know he's here at last to mend our break.*

"What you must think of me," said Daniel, fumbling for what was obviously a non-existent handkerchief.

"Here," Geir said, handing one to him. Their fingers touched. "What I think is that you gave me my beloved Hedy." And gazing at her with great pride, he linked his arm through hers. "So, whatever opinion I had of you in the past is rapidly dissolving."

Daniel stared at him with a glint of wonder in his amber-colored eyes. "Something that gives me a measure of relief. But even so, you need to hear it from me, that after your mother's death there was such a great pain in my heart I didn't want to live. And I feared I'd kill myself. Which is one of the main reasons I left you with Margit." He stopped to blot his cloudy eyes as more tears fell. "Then as time passed, I'd often pack my bag, thinking I was coming to visit you. Until reality would strike, letting me know I couldn't. Because once I saw you, I knew I'd take you from Margit. Which knowing her as well as I did would have left her devastated. And since she was frail like your mother, it might possibly have caused her death —something that at the time seemed fair to me. Though not getting you the American citizenship was wrong. And my punishment for it is that the Wehrmacht is taking you from both of us."

The unbearable way he said it sounded like a man who was having difficulty masking his desperation.

"Daniel," Greta called, her voice cutting through the room. "Everyone's waiting for you to join them at the table. So they can enjoy the wine, sandwiches, and the rest of the wedding cake I brought from the hotel."

"Then by all means." He turned to the guests waiting at the dining room's open door. "Indulge yourselves, and I'll be with you shortly, while I finish talking with the bride and groom."

"We weren't expecting you today," said Hedy.

"I know. But I got to thinking with Greta buying this boardinghouse, I needed to be there for the paper signings later this evening. In addition, to getting your fraudulent German passports tomorrow." Then he said to Geir. "Even though your birth was a life time ago for me, my memories of you in my arms have not faded."

"Is there something we can do to help you with all your business here?" he asked.

"No." Daniel shook his head. "I came early to take care of all the business so, that way, we could have a fair amount of time together." He reached into his pocket and removed a wad of German marks. "But until then, take this."

He handed the money to Geir, who immediately refused it. "We've no need."

"But it's your wedding night. So go out to a fancy restaurant, cinema—or whatever?"

"We prefer to stay here with friends and family," said Hedy, kissing her step-father's cheek.

"Wasn't expecting to hear that. However, I do hope you started your honeymoon early."

"We did."

His lips curled in a smile as he met Geir's gray eyes. "Love at first sight— like your mother and I.

So if that's the case, do I have your permission to return the bride's kiss? And then, hug you?"

"Most definitely."

Gently he caressed Hedy, but when it came to Geir, he put his arms around him and held him so tightly it was like they'd become a tourniquet. "Son," he whispered as Geir hugged him back. "Part of your wonderful mother survives in you. Making me a truly fortunate man."

"Daniel," Greta called again. "Our guests refuse to touch the food and wine, because they're waiting for you to join them."

"Then since I have something of importance to say to each of them, I'd best get in there."

He took his seat quickly at the head of the table, indicating that Geir and Hedy sit on one side of him, and Greta and Margit on the other.

"Sorry to keep everyone waiting. But since you're such a mannerly group I'm hosting a dinner tomorrow night for all of you, at one of the city's most exclusive restaurants. And I'll be providing the transportation, so I hope everyone sitting here with do me the honor of coming."

Practically in unison, the guests said they would, as their hands reached for the wine bottles.

The hotel had provided a rich array of *canapes* to complement the sandwiches. But what Geir especially liked were the Edam cheese puffs.

"Mother thought those particular foods would be go well with our wedding cake." Hedy told him. "That's still only half eaten."

"Which I suspect after tonight, won't be —"

"I hate to be the host who rushes you along," Daniel broke in. "But since Greta and I are buying this place in an hour, and the owner's waiting. I can't afford the time to say to what I need to say to each of you." He turned Otto. "This man is like a seer. Which lets me know we all have much to discuss tomorrow morning about this coming *blitzkrieg,* he mentioned in a letter he sent me recently. Plus the way he feels the war will go for Germany. In addition, to the Italian surveying business I'm buying next week." He pointed at Hugo and Fritz. "And you two will also be expected to give your opinions for our guests here."

He then turned to Ernst and Alvina Bandt. "Volker and Charlotte's wonderful parents. I know we've corresponded ever since the Great War. And I know it's been a year since I met up with you again in Frankfurt. But I do recall your saying that if Margit wanted to quit running the boardinghouse, you'd be willing to take her place—"

"But I'm not ready to stop running it," Margit cut in sharply.

"Now don't get upset," Daniel said, gently squeezing her arm. "Greta will be doing paperwork for Dr. Rath, sitting here. Hedy will be in nurse's training. And Geir will be gone. So you'll need the extra help, I'm willing to pay for. And who could be better than the Bandts?"

"Not to mention it'll give you more time to do the sewing you love." Greta smiled, bringing a glass of the red wine to her lips.

The Bandts stared at each other, pleased, before thanking Daniel and accepting his offer.

Volker looked up from his plate at the good doctor. "Is there any way you could talk to that Wehrmacht general who's your patient, and see if he could arrange for Geir and me to stay together?"

"You mean like a buddy system?" Dr. Rath asked him.

"Yes. Because I'm hearing people say that in some cases brothers will be allowed to fight alongside each other. So would that be possible for Geir and me?"

He looked faintly surprised. "You mean for me to say Geir's your brother?"

"No. Just a friend who's like a brother."

"I'll mention it to the general. But with the war expected to erupt any minute, I have no idea what he's apt to say."

"Let's pray he agrees," said Charlotte, crossing her fingers." Or otherwise you'll have to appeal to one of those *other* powerful friends, with whom you have connections." Her gaze fell on Otto.

"Volker and I will be anxious to hear in the morning what you three Schroders have to say about this coming war."

"And I'll look forward to telling you, "said Otto, taking a gulp of wine.

Daniel gave Charlotte a knowing smile. "Given the circumstances you and your brother need to learn everything you can." His eyes then fell on the dark-haired Hayim and his wife, Judith, whose hair was so curly her nick-name was, *Bushy*. "We met here after the Great War. And several years ago you and your wife visited me in Switzerland. So with the *Jew* hatred surrounding you, it's imperative the two of you leave for Switzerland, where you'll find my home open to you." He paused. "That way you can resume your tailor business in a defunct shop I own not far from it, in a place that needs to be restored. Which I feel certain you'll be able to do."

"But we can's just up and leave," said Hayim, running a napkin over his mouth.

"You've no choice," insisted Daniel. "With the way the *Fuhrer* feels about Jews. So view the Aryan-Christian papers I'm getting for you tomorrow, to be a divine intervention. And start packing tonight!"

Hayim's wife looked a little frightened but said nothing as tears rolled down her cheeks.

A moment passed, then another, until finally Hayim said, "He's right, Judith. We have to leave for Switzerland."

His arms went around her, and she hugged him back. "Then I'll start packing."

Geir was pleased at what his father was doing for these two special people, and even more so, when Otto slipped him a note about it:

"They're lucky indeed to have him for a friend. And his generosity toward, not only them, but Margit, is like he's giving out pieces of his heart. For it appears he's come to sweeten the sorrows of your destiny, that life will force you to face in the coming days: a destiny that will undoubtedly take you to places you dare not imagine. And though, I still sense a certain sadness in you, I get the feeling you've forgiven Daniel. And hopefully, will now envision you, your mother, Margit, Wilhelm, Greta, and Hedy with your hands joined in a circle of love, that makes all of you one. Which in this fractured world, should be to you as glorious as the breaking light of dawn."

Words from a *true scholar.* Geir smiled, shoving the note inside his pocket.

Daniel ate his sandwich and slice of wedding cake quickly. "I'm finished and ready to go," he told Greta.

She rose, apologizing to everyone. But before he joined her, he waved his wine glass in the air, before finishing its remains in a single gulp.

The guests waited ten minutes, before they *too* got up. "We've left over food," Margit said. "So feel free take what you want." She laid a roll of wax paper down for them to wrap it in if they chose to do it, which most of them did.

They all wished Hedy and Geir well. "We look forward to dining with you again tomorrow," said Hayim as he ushered his wife through the door.

"Can we help you with anything?" Hedy asked Margit after they left. But before she could answer Otto announced that he and Hugo would be helping her tonight.

"Then we'd best turn in," Hedy told Geir.

He grinned. "And put our extra time to the best use possible."

CHAPTER SIX

Being newlyweds, Hedy and Geir resumed their lovemaking before they slept. And he surprised her, by turning her facedown and stroking her pleasure point from behind. *Certainly unexpected.* But what really caught her off guard was that when he turned her face up, he never left her body.

"How'd you do it?" she asked afterwards. "When you were a virgin like me."

"I've read books and asked Wilhelm questions before he died. So I thought it was time we should try another position on *this* our wedding night."

"There are so many. That we should try as many different ones as we can before you leave."

"I'm for it, *sweet Hedy,*" he said, covering her mouth with his.

The intensity with which he'd murmured, '*sweet Hedy*', several times during their lovemaking was something he hadn't done before. And her pulse leaped each time he said it, heightening her passion. "How I love the sound of my name rolling off your lips, "she whispered *Along with being loved by such a wonderful* man. *Whose picture I've held against my heart, more times than I could ever count. Something that would require a real stretch of my imagination to figure it out. But what about the times we've made love since that afternoon two days ago? Was it ten? Fifteen? Or Twenty?*

She guessed it was somewhere between ten and fifteen. "Need to keep a notepad with dates and put a star next to them each time," she said, thinking aloud.

"Each time *what?*" Geir asked her softly, the back of his hand stroking her cheek.

"Each time we make love."

"I'm for it." He kissed her hard." And I do believe there's an extra notepad with dates, in the desk downstairs."

"Then I'll get it in the morning."

His hands moved magically over her breasts, fueling her ardor. *Oh, Geir, my love. My first real love. How blessed I am to be lying here beside you.*

They made love twice more before drifting off in each other's arms. Yet, she knew there was a sacrifice to come. A conclusion the Wehrmacht would inflect on them that stood to challenge this glorious beginning they were sharing.

A pain that struck her like a prize fighter's fist, each time she thought about it. And later, when she awoke, there was a bone-shattering chill in the room.

"Geir," she cried, touching his shivering shoulder. He was thrashing back and forth, holding a pillow as if plagued with a night terror. "Wake up! You're having a bad dream."

"On my wedding night!" he gasped, opening his eyes. "Wouldn't you know—how bad is that for a man?"

"I was starting to have a bad dream too. But thank goodness, your cries of pain awakened me."

"What was your dream?"

"I can't remember exactly, but it had to do with the war."

"Mine definitely did."

"Did you get shot?"

◆

"No beaten to death." For an instant it seemed to Geir that a giant tentacle was sucking the very life from him.

"Who was beating you?"

"An SS man I think." He reached for a blanket. "And I was naked, being beaten with a cane in front of a group of half-starved looking men wearing striped pajamas. With this SS man saying that on the twenty-fifth stroke, I'd drop dead. And then be hauled out to some pyre where I'd become ash."

Hedy slipped on her pink peignoir. "Sounds like your old demon of a schoolmaster. But let's get some fresh air in here. So how about I open a window?"

"I'll do it." He put on his navy-blue robe and going over to his room's expansive window, drew back the curtains and wrenched it open.

"Isn't that better?" She smiled, her arms tightly encircling his waist.

"Much." The curtains fluttered as he took a quick breath of the night air.

"The air has a fresh smell."

"Which is great, considering it usually smells like exhaust fumes from the city's vehicles." Smiling, Geir held up his arms toward the sky. "And gives us another good reason to go back to bed." He yawned.

When he awoke the next morning the sunlight bursting through the window flooded him with a bubbling energy. *That frees me from this paralysis of anxiety caused by my nightmare.*

He stirred and stretched as he listened to what sounded like three people bustling around in the kitchen. "I think Alvina and Ernst are here," he said, going over and shutting the window.

"The Bandts?" Hedy asked, slipping her blue dress over her head. "Will they need our help?"

"We'll offer it, but more than likely they won't."

"They'll be living here now, won't they?"

He nodded. "Which is good. "Since the senior Bandt is a carpenter, and Volker worked with him—"

"—until he got drafted like you did," she finished, reaching for her sketch pad and pencil.

"Which if we're lucky," Geir said, "our good doctor will find a way to allow some *buddy system* between Volker and me, to come into play in the Wehrmacht."

"What I'm hoping." She waited a moment at the door." It's fortunate Daniel thought enough of Ernst Bandt to give him this job."

Geir shook his head. "Something I never expected," he said, still feeling a little confused as he tucked his shirt in his pants and headed toward the stairs.

They creaked under his boots. And looking over the railing, Hedy pointed at the kitchen. Its swinging door was propped open, filling the room with the smell of potato-cakes.

"Margit must be treating the Schroders to her potato-cakes," he told Hedy. "Who especially love them in the morning."

Alvina carried a large platter of eggs and bacon to the dining table where the Schroders, were seated across from Daniel and Greta.

Geir took special notice that Daniel —Hebrew or not— as he quickly devoured several slices of the bacon. *Even with his asthmatic condition, I also noticed he smoked a cigarette last night.*

"Butter and toasted salt risen bread is on the way," announced Alvina, immediately getting everyone's attention. "And soon the potato-cakes."

Charlotte and Volker circled the table, pouring hot tea in everyone's cup.

"How'd the paper signing for this house go?" Geir asked Greta.

"No problem. The owner was pleased to sell it to us at our price."

"Then congratulations are in order."

The food disappeared quickly with Alvina clearing the table, except for the cups and pots of hot tea.

"Potato-Cakes with whortleberries," Margit announced.

Charlotte was behind her with dessert plates and cutlery. And everyone but Greta remained seated as she served them. "If you'll excuse me, I volunteered to help with clean-up so Margit and Alvina could listen to what Otto has to say."

"Which was very thoughtful of you, "Daniel said, exchanging a smile with her.

He waited until she was in the kitchen before he stood up and announced, "I've brought us together so we can hear what Otto Schroder has to say on how this coming war will go. Since I consider him a scholar in history and philosophy."

Hedy ate her potato-cake quickly, before asking Daniel, "May I sketch this group?"

He waved a hand in the air. "Your sketching is our pleasure." Then, he turned to Otto, who opened a notebook.

"The truth is sad," he said, running his hand down the front page of it. "But time will prove I'm correct in what I'm about to read you." A lengthy moment followed as he looked around the table to see if anyone had a question, but no one did. In fact, their silence was as deafening as a radio turned on full blast. "Then I'll proceed:"

"On September the first, Germany will attack Poland —an in October, Germany and the USSR will partition off Northern Europe. The Lowlands and France will fall sometime in May, 1940. Followed by Africa in June of 1940. And then Italy and France will turn against Great Britain, and there will be a blitzkrieg. With Germany bombing Britain as a way of attacking the RAF. And Britain will retaliate. Especially when the Americans get in the war in December of 1941. But before that in June of '1941, the Germans will

make the mistake of attacking Russia...great pain will result for Wehrmacht soldiers fighting in the ice cold winter. Many will freeze, while others will be killed, starved, or tortured by the Russians. And the Jews in all these conquered countries will not fare well—"

"But when will this war end?" asked Volker, breaking his flow.

"Sometime around the middle of 1945. And Berlin will become a divided city between the allies and Soviets, with a wall of barbed wire."

"A dangerous but new reality," Daniel mused.

Suddenly unable to finish his potato-cake, Geir put his fork down. If anyone else were telling him this, he might have been able to dismiss it. But Otto Schroder was more than just well-read. He admitted having a very strong intuition, which as mentioned earlier, brought to mind a psychic or a seer. Still, he wasn't rich. Something Geir found peculiar with the man's extraordinary abilities.

Hedy laid her sketch pad aside and went back to the table, resuming her seat next to Geir.

Her hands were quivering, so Geir took both of them in his. *No wonder she'd stopped sketching.*

"If Berlin's going to be bombed, then are we all going to die?" she asked.

This time Hugo took the question. "It's not for me, my brother, or cousin to make that call.

Although, the cellar in this house *is* structurally sound."

"What we need to do is make a secret room in it, "Fritz added. "With plenty of food and water. And a toilet so we can hide from the Russians, until we can find a way to escape them."

"Your idea is excellent," said Daniel. He turned to Ernst Bandt. "I'll pay you extra to do it. And if you need to hire another carpenter just let me know."

"We three Schroders will help him for free," said Otto. "Since in our time we've done work like that."

"Damn!" Volker snapped. "Geir and I are in the Wehrmacht. Which means we'll be fighting for a cause in which we don't believe in. So just what in hell are we to do?"

"Be cannon fodder for Germany," remarked Hugo. "Which is all *you* can do."

"No!" Volker suspended his fork mid-air. "I refuse to be part of a herd of swine meant to be slaughtered. So there's got to be some other way."

A knot formed in Geir's stomach. "I know it's dangerous, but what if we became combat medics? At least we'd be helping people instead of hurting them."

"But you're not university men." Otto quickly pointed out. "Who'll take precedence over you for work like that."

Hearing that, Charlotte leaned over and whispered something to Volker.

"Well I'll be damned," he blurted after a moment had passed. "Takes a nurse to come up with that one."

"Come up with what?" Hedy asked.

"I told him a story, one of the older nurses at the hospital told me," said Charlotte. "Which was about a man in the Great War who got tired of serving and shot himself in his right hand, below his thumb."

Volker's tight expression relaxed. "And he got classified as being disabled, even if he did have to live with the injury for the rest of his life. Which is certainly something I'd be willing to do."

"He only got *by* with it because it was a different time," Otto reminded. "A deliberate action that could be easily covered back then. But nowadays, if the SS had any suspicion whatsoever, they wouldn't think twice about shooting such a man."

"Still, there's got to be a way we can do something like that and get by with it," Volker argued.

His forehead wrinkled in concentration as he appeared to give it some deep thought. Then suddenly as if he'd had an epiphany, he turned to Geir. "The foot. What if we get shot in the foot and couldn't march or run?"

Not terribly impressed with the idea, he considered it briefly before adding, "Plus, we'll have a limp for the rest of our lives."

Otto looked at Volker with a sullen expression. "Your idea sounds like something a soldier did in a cinema I once saw. And it didn't work in that film, and it won't work for you."

"I think I saw that movie," said Volker. "But the guy didn't shoot himself in the foot."

"It was the knee," Hugo put in. "And the guy didn't get away with it. And *two* buddy soldiers like you and Geir, won't get away with it either."

"But I have an idea," Volker was quick to say." We're in combat. And one of the soldiers with us gets shot and can't be saved. He's dying in pain and begs, 'Shoot *me*!' And Geir and I agree to do it, but only if he'll shoot us in the foot."

"And then what happens?" asked Otto, frowning at him.

"We'll tell our commanding officer that he asked us to shoot him, to keep his death from being so painful. But we refused until he shot both of us in the foot. 'Now you'll *feel* pain,' he said, before he died."

"It makes a good story," Daniel blurted suddenly. "But there's not a chance in hell you could pull it off."

Hedy tapped Geir's shoulder. "Would you do something like that?"

"No. Because Daniels' right. There's not a chance it could be pulled off."

Otto shuddered at the idea. "There are too many *ifs* in your plan, Volker."

"Maybe." He shrugged. "But do you have a better idea?"

"I don't. Because there isn't one, that's remotely feasible."

Charlotte, gripping the handle of her tea cup, shot Otto a disparaging look. "So what are Volker and Geir supposed to do?"

"Keep their fingers crossed and pray a lot—"

"Sorry to interrupt," said Daniel, "but since Greta and I have passport business to settle in less than an hour, we need to devise a code for the letters we'll be writing each other. Something Fritz has offered to help us with—so I'll turn it over to him."

Holding his cane, he stood up. "There'll be a censorship on all our letters. Which means if something in the war is bad, then we need to say it's good—and we'll understand. However, the trick will be to keep our code simple. Which we keep in mind as we to work together devising it-"

"But just remember," Otto broke in, "it's not wise to arouse the suspicions of German officers, because most are paranoid and looking for trouble. So be careful in your coding or otherwise, it'll give them an excuse to shoot you."

"Can't have that now," Volker replied.

Devising the coded words went quicker than Geir had expected. And when it was over, Alvina handed him a bulging envelope. "Daniel says to give you this."

"It looks like the money he tried to give you last night," Hedy remarked. "So keep it."

"Guess I'll have to." He opened it quickly and not only was the money in it, but a note:

"*Put some sandwiches in a basket, grab a bottle of wine, and head to Lake Wannsee for a picnic.*"

Geir shook his head. It was certainly more money than he'd ever had to spend. *Which* makes *me suspect he's giving it to me because he's at a loss as what to do for me. With the lost years between us something he can't bring back.*

He opened his wallet and put the money in it. "Would you like to picnic at Lake Wannsee, Hedy?"

"Sounds like fun."

"Then we'll do it. "

CHAPTER SEVEN

The few days before Geir and Volker had to report rushed by.

Most of the time Daniel was in the city on business. But when evening came he'd return, eager to wine and dine everyone at his expense. He had the fraudulent German passports made for Hedy and Greta, which meant they'd have to find a good place to hide their American ones.

Otto suggested hiding them—along with Hedy and Geir's marriage license— in a metal box that would he mortared, behind some bricks near the cellar's fireplace." Important papers that can't afford to be lost, stolen, or discovered."

"Good idea," Daniel praised him, the same as everyone in the household did.

Margit and Greta took the liberty of buying Geir new underwear, socks, and toiletries. "Volker maintained he'd checked with some soldiers, "Alvina remarked. "And they told him that was all they needed for their basic training."

"Take the rest of Daniel's money, "Geir told Hedy. But she refused. He then reminded her that the Wehrmacht would be sending her some of his pay check. "To use as you see fit— "

"But I don't need it."

"Then buy yourself some extraordinary *clothes*."

"No." She'd shaken her head. "I'll put it back. And should Margit need something, then I'll make sure she gets it. Since Mom and I plan on spoiling her."

"Something she needs after all her struggles."

"You know," Hedy said, looking suddenly troubled. "I keep thinking if I'd come here the minute I came of age and not waited a week or two, we'd be in Switzerland. And you wouldn't be in the Wehrmacht."

"Don't blame yourself for that."

"It was just that mother and I had such a great rapport I wanted her blessing. Because I knew that what I was about to do, could possibly take me away from nurse's school for several weeks."

"And that bothered her?"

"Until I convinced her otherwise, and she relented."

"I'm thinking Daniel feels the same way," Geir replied." Which is the reason that even if he declares he wants to develop a closeness between the two of us, he seems at a loss as how to do it. He didn't take me to America, or Switzerland. But the truth is that had he come to get me, I'd probably have refused to leave Margit and Wilhelm. So let's not waste these last hours before I leave, blaming ourselves. For if I'd been in America or Switzerland I'd have got some combat medic training and joined the allies...something I clearly wasn't meant to do."

A long silence followed before Hedy spoke, "I realize there are no records stating you're *half Jew* —"

"Who's fighting for the wrong side," he reminded, trying not to feel so helpless and distraught.

He hesitated a moment to recall Volker's epiphany earlier, when—to his astonishment— an epiphany hit him. *But yours, Geir Gallen, is not about being shot in the foot.* Then, overjoyed, he turned to Hedy and added, "Unless my fighting for the wrong side helps me to save lives that couldn't otherwise be saved."

Her troubled expression relaxed as realization dawned. "Why it might just *do* that."

"Which quite possibly could turn out to be my *destiny*."

"That it could," she agreed, clearly relieved.

• ⸺ ◆ ⸺ •

On Friday, September first, the day before Geir and Volker left, the radio spilled the news that Germany had invaded Poland. "The exact date Otto gave us," said Geir.

"Germany is now officially at war," Hugo remarked after a silence.

Everyone knew what that meant. And tears flowed from Margit, Greta, and Hedy like water from a damn breaking. "It means you won't get leave after your basic training," Hedy told Geir. "And you'll go straight into battle."

She buried her face on his shoulder as he held her tightly against him. "Who said I'd be returning after basic training? Otto never thought I would. Even if Dr. Rath said he wasn't sure if I would or wouldn't."

"In America," she said, I heard the soldiers got leave after their basic—"

"Not in war," Daniel broke in. "Or at least if they did, I didn't"

Despite the dreadful news of the German attack on Poland, the night sky was full of stars,

"With no cloud cover whatsoever," Geir remarked. And for a fleeting moment he imagined he and Hedy were on a tropical island—an island of peace— in this stillness of the night. He cupped her chin tenderly. "Have you ever been to Garmisch?"

"No, have you?"

"I've rarely been out of Berlin."

"What will your bed be like when you're on the front?"

"Probably some kind of a cot."

"Poland's winters are cold. So let me know if the clothing they give you isn't warm enough, and Dr. Rath and I will try and get you a fur-lined overcoat."

"Which I'm sure I'll need."

It was their last evening in bed like this...*until God knows when. Hedy was naked. Her firm breasts like crested peaks, above the flat depression of her stomach. And her legs. Such seductive legs, long and thin. Making my stab of desire for her so strong, I groaned aloud several times when my release came.*

They made love again before she decided he needed to get some sleep. "The train ride will be noisy. So rest while you can."

She was probably right, but he didn't feel sleepy.

"I 'm so very sad," she said. "With a great fear for you in my heart— "

"Why? Because you think those Polish soldiers will be the end of me?"

She made no response, but he saw the look in her eyes. *The same look in his Uncle Wilhelm's eyes as he lay dying. When life was leaving him but taking its time about it.*

"My love. My great love." He hugged her." You know I'll do my best to stay alive."

"Unless you're traveling on a path that doesn't give you that option."

That was all which needed to be said as his eyes like hers, overflowed with tears.

Being a man I've developed the habit of hiding my tears. But in war there are times tears, unexpected or otherwise, can't be hidden.

The train left at six o'clock the following morning. Geir and Volker were being escorted to the station by Ernst and Daniel in a cab. They didn't want the women coming. "It'll be easier that way, "Ernst had explained. "Since when I left for the Great War my mother couldn't stop crying. **W**hich was the memory of her I took to that war. A memory my mind refused to let me forget. So it's best to remember their female pleasantness in this home. Because no one is himself or herself when he or she is on a station platform weeping, as they watch a loved one go off to war."

Otto opened the boardinghouse's door for them. "Now don't look back."

Geir caught a whiff of Hedy's French perfume on his jacket. *When she'd leaned into me and kissed me good-bye*. And he wanted to rush back and kiss her again. *But knowing it'll just bring bring more pain, I won't.*

The train was waiting when Geir and Volker reached the station. And Ernst and Daniel went with them down the station platform where a guard was inspecting papers. "I'll be writing you," Daniel promised, giving Geir a hug. "So take care of yourself."

"I'll do my best."

Inside he found a seat next to the window. "Do you take it or me?" he asked Volker.

"You." He nodded. "Since from the looks of it, our fathers aren't leaving until this train departs."

"I think they should leave. Because the longer they stay, the harder it will be for them later."

"I agree."

Some more recruits stepped into the car, followed by two young women with a coffee urn from the field kitchen, they were rolling in a cart.

"At least we've got coffee," Volker said.

Although, it wasn't long before it came back empty.

On the station's platform some musicians began playing *"Deutschland uber alles."*

A song which appeared to motivate a couple of SS officers in their finely tailored clothing, to stare at the music players with a respectful silence.

A half-hour passed before the train began to move slowly. Daniel and Ernst waved and Geir and Volker waved back.

In no time the train was passing through the countryside, making Geir regret he'd come to the station without Hedy.

It had made perfect sense when Ernst had explained why she shouldn't. But now, it made no sense whatsoever. Because there were usually urgent feelings in a person's heart, when a leave taking such as this, became real. And words that hadn't been said, somehow got said.

Geir had branded the picture of Hedy in his mind when he'd left. She was wearing her purple, silk dress and silver high heels. Knowing how to dress was another one of her charms, and she'd looked like a Parisian model before he left. *So all I can think is about coming back to her. And if I survive, how lucky I am to have her waiting for me.*

Which, after having listened to the song *"Lili Marlene,"* he got the idea to carry a lock of Hedy's hair with him. Something, to his great joy, inspired her to do likewise.

Volker nudged him. "How about we try and get some sleep, Geir."

"I'm for it." He closed his eyes recalling how last night he'd been unable to sleep, even if Hedy had advised him to do so.

Hours passed with the train pulling into a good many stations before it finally reached Garmisch. And like their draft notices said, buses were waiting to take them to their barracks.

Garmisch-Partenkirshen was a tourist town with cafcs, hotels, and flashy shops with Bavarian outfits. The 1940 Winter Olympics were to be held here. However, with the country at war, Geir supposed they'd be cancelled... even if no one in his family had made mention of it.

He marveled at the buildings show windows with extravagant clothing. *It's a fashionable place Hedy would love.*

"Word has it that our training here is some kind of a trial-run experiment... which makes us Guinea pigs," said Volker, staring at the gaudy Bavarian outfits. "Since some elite mountain divisions are expected be training here—or possibly one or two are already training in a place not far from us."

"Which wouldn't surprise me—"

"Nor me. "Volker replied, his frown mirrored in the window of the bus. "Although I doubt history will record there were some early trainees here like us, who weren't in an elite mountain division."

"It probably won't," Geir agreed with disgust. "Considering we viewed as cannon fodder."

Contempt flashed in Volker's eyes. "And mark my words, if this elite group is already here, then there'll be a concentrated effort to keep cannon fodder like us, separated from them."

"Without a doubt." Geir shrugged to hide his exasperation.

The barracks buildings for the common soldiers were in the foothills of the Zugspitze:

Germany's tallest mountain, which was about thirty minutes away from the town.

Inside one of the buildings, a man who called himself, Siegfried Schmidt, informed them he was their sergeant. He ordered the recruits to take off their clothes and get fitted for a uniform.

Something that didn't take as long as Geir thought it might. Though, once every man had a green uniform and was now a number, he was expected to report in half an hour, to the courtyard for a meeting. "An unexpected twist," Volker remarked.

He and the other recruits were discussing it, when Sergeant Schmidt returned.

Immediately, they jumped to attention as he informed them they were not to speak unless spoken to. Then, when they were allowed to speak, they had to click their heels and say '*Yes, sir!*'—or otherwise they would be severely punished.

He told them they were all stupid, before adding— "No matter how good your report card grades or university educations were."

After this first meeting this angry, sadistic sergeant pulled Volker and Geir aside and asked them why they never joined Hitler Youth? The Nazi party? Nor worked in a coal mine or on a farm?

Their answer being they needed to support their families. But Volker whispered to Geir, "It's quite evident this sergeant senses our defiance. 'You're plainly not *Soldatenstole*—the soldier's pride and loyalty,' I can imagine him saying."

And was he right. Even if Volker did remind him, "I look like the perfect Aryan, with my blond hair and brows."

But it didn't matter. Because before he and Volker left the meeting, Sergeant Schmidt ordered them to clean the mule stables and horse stables, until they shone like a fine piece of Dresden.

"Clearly an impossibility," Geir and Volker grumbled beneath their breaths.

Although, they did try. And were pleased with their efforts, until this sergeant gave them a disgruntled look and ordered, "Your next assignment is kitchen duty. And your relief won't arrive till two in the morning—so get to work!"

CHAPTER EIGHT

Geir wrote in the small notepad he kept on his person:

"A punishment that gave us little time for sleep, since we had to get up at four-thirty, where we headed to the barber shop to get our hair cut quite short. If Hedy saw a picture of me like this, I bet she wouldn't be hugging it, was what came to my mind. Still, when I wrote her about it, she insisted I send her a picture in my uniform. Which I did. And surprise of surprises she quickly wrote back, "Geir, you're a very handsome man and couldn't be ugly no matter what."

There were other punishment drills like running, and making Sergeant Schmidt's bed twelve times. Although, we did learn between these drills a good deal about how to assemble and dismantle cannons. And following it, we received training on how to become expert sharp shooters.

But the worst punishment, I wrote to Hedy, was when Schmidt caught me looking at a photo of you. He asked who the, cinema star was and I said, 'My wife, who's a nurse.' He called me a liar because he maintained no woman who looked like that, would ever associate with the likes of me. So, I was given the job of clearing the snow in front of our barracks for the next four Sunday mornings. Something I reported to the master sergeant. Who simply frowned and ordered me to get back to work. Leaving me to feel the same way I had when that schoolmaster had used his cane, to give me what he called a good thrashing. My terrible memory.

"My poor Geir, "Hedy had written back. "Daniel's quite upset over what's happening to you and Volker. He's read his letters as well as yours—and Volker leaves nothing out in his. But in your letters, I get the feeling you're trying to spare me. So please don't. Tell me everything that's bad, because Daniel's asked Dr. Rath if he could approach one of his military friends to do something about your treatment. However, his friend said you and Volker would be staying together as buddies, which was the best he could do."

Otto has tried to comfort your father with these words he says he wrote to you: 'This too will pass, because it's only four months of training— 'But not quickly enough for me,' I said and shook my head."

"Unfortunately, we're just in our second month," Geir said, frowning at Volker.

"Which is something I'm trying not to think about."

But to their surprise, time flew faster than they'd expected, and soon it was Christmas.

Ordinarily, since it was his and Hedy's first Christmas together Geir would have been depressed. Something he fretted about until he learned that after the first of the year, he and Volker were being shipped off to Poland. "And we're getting a twenty-four hour layover in Berlin!" he'd written Hedy.

Who wrote back, "Then we'll be saving your Christmas until you make it back."

Geir wasn't worried about going into combat. Since word was being spread from the *higher-ups,* that the Wehrmacht had killed all the Polish officers, with only the disorganized partisans remaining.

Otto had written him almost the same thing.

What can you expect from the Wehrmacht. Geir frowned with disgust. And maybe it was selfish of him, but at least he and Volker hadn't been forced to shoot these Polish officers. *Although, there were probably others who feel the same as we do, who've been made to do it. But Polish officers or not, our time will come when we'll be forced to shoot some poor unfortunates —of that I'm certain.*

November and December passed quicker than he and Volker could have imagined. And before they knew it, they were on a train headed for their twenty-four hour leave in Berlin.

It got there quickly. And soon they were standing on the station platform with their families and friends. Geir hugged Hedy so tightly, he lifted her off the platform. She was wearing her fluffy fox coat.

"Which really does make you look like a cinema star," he said, setting her back on her feet.

He then exchanged hugs with Margit, Greta, Daniel, Dr. Rath, and the Schroders, before clasping hands with Ernst, Alvina, and Charlotte.

Geir was quite pleased the Brandts were living in the boardinghouse, since Margit had written him about the additional security they— along with the Schroders— had added to the place.

Although what really astounded him was that Margit and Greta, *who* were both wearing fur coats. "Is that a mink coat?" he asked Margit.

"It's mink, and I'm wearing sable," Greta quickly spoke up. "Daniel brought our sterling silver, my two fur coats, and Hedy's fox one from Switzerland. So now Margit has a fur coat to wear, which should keep her quite warm."

"She always needed a really warm coat," Geir said, admiring it. "And I'm certain we'll all appreciate dining with your sterling silver."

"But wait till you see what Daniel has given us." Hedy said, as they walked out of the station into the steadily falling snow.

Geir smiled. "Can't imagine—"

Something he had difficult doing when Hedy pointed at a Mercedes. A fresh snow carpeted the parking lot, but the powdered whiteness it left on the car had yet to erase its elegant, silver shine.

Geir marveled at it. "Why it's as bright as a glass Christmas ornament."

"I thought it was about time the boardinghouse had a car," Daniel said, lightly touching its hood.

"And I'm the chauffeur," Otto bragged, dangling the car's keys.

Geir was thrilled. "So we now have a chauffeur like Dr. Rath does."

"That you do." Otto beamed.

"Who'll be driving some of us, like Dr. Rath's chauffeur, to the Adlon Hotel for a dinner on me," Daniel announced. "So feel free to order what you want when we get there."

Which everyone did.

The waiter recommended lamb stew: a dish those in the party found to be a delightful.

And afterwards as the group sipped wine, Hugo and Fritz slipped out with Dr. Rath's chauffeur. "They're getting Christmas ready for us," Daniel explained. "So we'll remain here until the good doctor's car returns.

His car returned quickly, and even with the ice and snow, it also reached the boardinghouse quickly. Geir was surprised to see the Christmas tree was still standing.

"A tall fir one that we paid a man to cut the morning of Christmas Eve, "said Hedy. "And it's been kept fresh because it's standing in a bucket of water, covered by a tree skirt I had made." She smiled and kissed his cheek. "Waiting for your arrival."

Glistening Czech ornaments, chocolate wrapped in colorful foil, and gingerbread cookies, all dangled from this magnificent tree's limbs.

"The main reason Hugo and Fritz had left the dinner party early was to light the tree's candles," Margit informed Geir. "So they would shine with a magnificence."

Everyone was impressed when the lyrical music to *"Oh Tannenbaum"* began playing on the gramophone. "That beautiful tree has some entertainers in front of it," remarked Volker, smiling. He gestured at Hugo and Fritz whose voices were accompanying the music.

Geir quickly noticed that the presents for he and Volker were heaped under the tree. Bringing to mind what Margit had told them when they was younger: *'The Christ child has brought the tree and left the presents.'*

In times past the boardinghouse trees had been small, with only a few burning candles, glass, and straw ornaments—but no matter. The cookies and chocolate hanging beside them in colorful, small bags, had given the trees a pleasant appearance.

"Time to exchange gifts with our young men," said Greta, picking up a bell from the dining table and ringing it.

Volker moved forward with the suitcase Geir had bought, and opened it. Their gifts, were packed inside. "Which fortunately," Geir told Hedy, "I'd been able to purchase in a store on Garmisch's fashionable main street, before we boarded the train. And this store, to my delight, had wrapped each gift in brightly colored paper—"

"The moment we've been waiting for," Volker interrupted, passing out the gifts.

Each man received an Alpine hat with a feather. And all the ladies, with the exception of Hedy, received crystal and pearl brooches in hand carved wooden boxes.

Smiling, Geir savored every moment as he watched the men put on their hats, and the ladies their brooches.

But when he motioned Hedy to come forward, she gasped in awe as he handed her the largest of the packages in his bag. "For my very special lady."

She tore the wrapping off quickly, and to her delight, held up a leather handbag with a woven, mesh-like strap, embroidered with brightly colored Alpine flowers. "It's the loveliest bag I've ever had."

"Ever had?," Geir questioned, inclining his head. "But you have designer bags from France."

"Doesn't matter. These flowers on this bag make it more fashionable." She kissed him on each cheek.

"Good thing you insisted I take the money Daniel gave me. Or otherwise, Volker and I wouldn't have been able to buy Christmas presents for everyone."

"I'm glad you had it. Since I doubt the Wehrmacht's given you any pay."

"They haven't."

"Daniel's giving you some more money tonight. So hang onto it."

"Is that an order?" Geir asked, smiling wryly at her.

"From your wife. Who knows you need it more than *you* do."

"My gorgeous wife," he said, stroking a strand of her dark hair.

Her gift to him was French brilliantine and lederhosen. "Something I've not had since I was a boy." He smiled, holding them up with a gleam of pride.

"Charlotte gave me the same thing," Volker said. "So, not only will our clothes match, but our scents will too." He gave his sister a kiss on the cheek. "But we can't take that brilliantine to the barracks because it's in a glass bottle, and one of the officers will confiscate it. Since they fear a soldier might use it to commit suicide."

"Just one more reason to hate everything the Reich stands for," said Greta, handing the young men her gifts. "Fur-lined gloves."

Margit and Alvina stepped forward with several pairs of socks they'd knitted. Then Dr. Rath presented Geir and Volker with first aid kits, that he maintained were better than the Wehrmacht's.

But the biggest surprise was Daniel's gift to them: leather jackets with matching leather pants. "The only young men I ever knew who wore these had wealthy parents," Volker told Geir.

"So I'm certainly grateful Daniel's your father."

"One more gift," said Otto, handing Geir several books. "Now that your basic training's over, I thought you might want something to take along to read."

"Definitely." He glanced at their titles. "My life's been terrible without books."

"I can imagine."

After all the gifts were exchanged, Geir recalled when he was a boy, how he would go with Margit and Wilhelm to church to give thanks. *Of course Hedy was the most wonderful gift of all— always would be—and a reason for me to gave thanks everyday. But hell was coming, and when we'd be reunited again was no telling!*

Since the train left at six the following morning, Geir and Hedy hurried to their bedroom. And in nervous haste, they shed their clothes.

"Such abandonment," she whispered.

"An ecstasy of delight," he said, squeezing her tightly.

Their ardor reflected their desperation. So when she opened her legs to him, they quickly lost themselves in each other.

This time it was she who murmured his name, over and over.

Their bodies locked together in a burning fire that lifted them above Germany's madness, and into a storm of passion, warm and sensual. Rushes of pleasure followed, leaving them breathless. Until finally, they drifted into the deep slumber of satisfied lovers, with the war-troubled world that kept them apart disappearing.

A surprise came the next morning when they awoke and didn't see dawn's, mauve light trickling through their window. "Still a starred sky." Geir yawned. "So it's little early."

"I marvel you were able to be here," Hedy said, her hands on his chest. "Even if it was only for a few hours."

"The present is all we have," he murmured, his cheek against her hair." And when these special moments, like now, are thrown our way, we have to grab them as quickly as we can—"

"I agree. Because their beautiful memories will sustain us and give us the strength we need in these troubled times."

"How I wish *heaven above* would give me the sign that we'll share a ripe, old age together."

"I've asked Otto that same question, but he won't say."

CHAPTER NINE

"Which alarms me—" Geir said

"Don't let it." Hedy touched his arm. "Since I haven't given up trying to find a way to get you out of combat."

"Like Volker."

They lay cuddled against each other in tired silence, listening for the rustling noises in the kitchen that told them breakfast was being prepared. "Should we get dressed now?" Hedy asked.

"Not until we've made love one more time, "he replied, his fingers stroking the warmth between her legs. "Unless you're too tired."

"Never for you." She smiled, rolling on top of him. "Even if we've been terribly rushed since your arrival?"

"So rushed it's reminded me of water running through a sieve—"

"Or possibly the way everyone will rush to take cover, when the bombers begin dropping their bombs."

"Sounds like the hospital's briefed you about the coming *blitzkrieg*."

"In depth—even if I'm praying it won't happen."

"Same as I'm doing." He took a deep breath as he turned and eased into her body.

Passion pounded their blood which threatened to obliterate everything but their desire. Until replete with satisfaction, they sighed their release.

"Sorry it had to be so quick."

"Better *quick* than nothing at all."

Their plan was to be at the train station no later than five-thirty a.m. And this time everyone in the household—plus Dr. Rath —was going to see them off.

Hedy squeezed Geir's hand before getting on her feet. "They finally listened to me." she told him, reaching for her stockings and dress on the floor, where she'd tossed them in her haste.

"Especially when I showed them the letter you'd written saying that's the way you wanted it."

"Which I most assuredly did."

Coming down, Geir was pleased to note Alvina and Ernst were helping Margit serve breakfast. "With plenty of eggs, sausage, toast, and potato-cakes topped with whortleberries," Alvina informed him.

Greta was standing by a large coffee urn she'd purchased. "It will allow you to have as many cups as you want."

"Really adds to breakfast," Geir told her with a smile.

"Any idea how long it'll be before you two will be coming back here?" Daniel asked Volker.

"We're clueless." He shrugged, frowning. "Even if rumor has it that with the exception of the partisans, there's not much fighting going on in Poland right now."

Daniel met his gaze. "What I've heard. Though with Germany now occupying Poland, German soldiers must maintain vigilance in the towns and villages. And when they're not doing it, they're apt to be guarding German trains carrying aircraft parts and munitions—"

"Or," Otto broke in, "Germany could be testing some new theories on the use of armed forces, and air support for ground troops. Since our country will be attacking Russia in a year or two."

"Oh. Yes," Geir remembered, sunk in thought. "The upcoming Russian invasion."

After everyone finished eating, Daniel remarked bluntly, "I hate to be the teller of this tragic tale, but I heard it from my Catholic cousin, Dr. Filip Novak, who lives in Poland. He visited us several times when we lived in Switzerland. And recently visited here when he attended a medical conference." He stopped, as if bereft of speech for a moment. "He told me the SS, with their submachine guns, began attacking the Jews during the second day of Germany's invasion.

Going so far as to stop a train with some Jewish girls in their teens on a school excursion." The icy expression increased on Daniel's face. "The SS then ordered the girls, along with their teacher, to get off the train and lay facedown in a meadow next to the tracks, where they opened fire on them." "Good God!" Geir and Hedy exclaimed in unison.

Volker was beside himself. "What if we're asked to do something like that?"

"Why I mentioned it," said Daniel. "Because if you disobey an order, they'll kill you."

"Or send you on a suicide mission," Hugo added, shuddering as he set his coffee cup down.

Charlotte looked from her brother to Dr. Rath. "Our good doctor here is doing everything he can to get Volker and Geir assigned to a better situation. But so far— nothing."

Daniel exchanged a distressed look with her. "Of which I'm well aware. And if I could bribe the right people, I would." A heavy silence fell before he added, "Even though our good doctor, sitting here keeps insisting it wouldn't be wise. "

"Germany has to be losing the war before that can successfully be pulled off, "remarked Dr. Rath.

He turned to Geir and Volker. "And believe me when I say if there was anything I could do to get the Wehrmacht to train you as combat medics, I'd have already done it."

"Don't forget I can sketch a picture of a face I've seen only once," Hedy reminded. "Something I feel certain that would help the *higher-ups* in the military. With the only favor I'd ask of them is that Geir and Volker be allowed to train as combat medics—"

"Out of the question!" Geir exclaimed. "Because Berlin's authorities have devious minds.

Meaning that if you can do something like that, they'd keep you under their watch the same as they would a prisoner."

"Like they would Otto if they knew he was a psychic," Fritz quickly spoke up.

"Somehow we'll find a way to get Geir and Volker out of the Wehrmacht without having to be combat medics," Daniel assured everyone. "So let's keep them in our thoughts and prayers as we head to the train station. Where, sadly, we'll say our farewells"

❖

The train station was similar to the way it had been before. Musicians were playing *"Deutschland uber alles"* on the station's platform. Only this time the background noise of commanders shouting order sat the young recruits near the stairs below, made it difficult to hear.

Seventy recruits with whom they'd shared basic training were waiting to board. And Geir and Volker exchanged waves with them. "We'll have time to visit on the train," Volker shouted, tipping his hat.

A large crowd, surrounded by suitcases, baskets, and packages, waited on the platform.

"Looks like they're eager to get out of the city," Daniel observed. "With the SS standing over a guard as he inspects everyone's papers for the train that's due in half an hour. The same as that red capped station master standing behind him is doing."

Geir and Volker's train had a sign, *For Military Personnel Only.* Prompting them to exchange hugs one last time with each friend and family member, who'd come to see them off.

Since the station was crowded Daniel suggested that —with the exception of he, Ernst, and Hedy— those from the boardinghouse and Dr. Rath wait in their cars parked outside until the train left.

"He's right," said Otto. "Because those recruits at the bottom of the stairs are getting ready to board the next train. So let's evacuate."

"Then go, "urged Daniel dismissing him with a wave, before turning and shoving another wad of marks in Geir's tunic pocket. "I know I gave you some last night but don't argue. Because the way things are going in this war, you and Volker are apt to need more."

Hedy's arm was around Geir's waist. "I'll worry less about you if I know you have plenty of money." "Which is the reason I'm taking it."

Their moment of departure had come. *A gathering gloom.* And he kissed her. A final, passionate kiss with his arms wrapped around her so tightly in her fluffy fox coat, that he lifted her off the platform, like he'd done the night before.

"Be careful and take care of yourself," she urged, hugging him fiercely.

"Geir!" Volker called." Don't forget affection's forbidden in public. And one of those SS men is glaring at you. Which is a good reason to hurry and get on board—"

Hedy inhaled sharply. "Yes, Geir. Because I'm looking over your shoulder at that man, and he's taking a step in our direction."

Grabbing their packs, Volker hurried into the car. And grabbing a seat next to a window, immediately hung out his head. "I'm saving this seat for you," he hollared at Geir. "Cause most of that group from our detachment are finding seats in the empty car behind us. Which, unfortunately, isn't large enough to hold them all."

Geir kissed Hedy one last time. "I'll take care of myself as long as you do the same."

"You know I will," she whispered, returning his kiss. "Since I'll be waiting for you."

With a noisy clang, the train began rolling forward. So breaking free, Geir hurried to take his seat. Outside the window his sorrowing Hedy was waiting for him. And bracing an arm on its frame, he reached out and took her hand.

They held hands like that, with Hedy running beside the train until it picked up speed, and they were forced to let go.

She was still there, waving, as the train moved farther and farther away.

But when the train swung around a curve at the end of the station, adrenaline pounded his veins. "Hedy, oh Hedy—"He craned his neck to catch a final glimpse of her and might have succeeded, had two sheds not blocked his view.

Tears ran down his cheeks as his pain of a life without her returned. Making him fear that when she'd kissed him, she was she kissing him for the very last time. When suddenly, a whirlwind of images— her face in the center of them— gave him the feeling he was standing on the deck of a sinking ship. "Trying to salvage my most important memories of her," he murmured. "Before the water rises and washes me out to sea."

Hedy, oh Hedy... a gift from heaven... my hand in her very delicate one. With a great sadness in her eyes as she lets go of mine. Hedy hugging my picture against her heart. Hedy with sunlight flaming around her shoulders. Hedy— easing my sorrow— whispering,' I can give you the American citizenship you deserve.' And later, Hedy, as breathtaking as a rainbow's exquisite opulence, in her wedding dress... Her heart pounding against mine. Wiping out the pain of the past and the fearful future ahead. Wiping out all—except those few glorious moments that fulfill our promise of togetherness.

He wasn't about to die fighting for a cause in which he didn't believe in. *Volker and I are cynics who've yet to be in combat. And that story about those Jewish girls being shot by the SS in a meadow has done nothing, but increase our cynicism. So there has to be a way we can get out of the military or at least, combat duty.*

But so far— as risky as it sounds— Volker's idea of getting a dying soldier to shoot us in the foot or the knee, is the only one that had any validity. Possible— yes? But plausible—no!

They changed trains at the border.

Then hours passed, and when they arrived in Warsaw it was bitterly cold. "A mixture of snow and rain," Geir observed. "And since our detachment has a four hour layover, then we should have time to tour the city."

But did they dare? The reports of bombings in the Jewish parts of the city—plus small villages in other conquered parts of Poland—made Geir, like Volker, embarrassed to be in the Wehrmacht.

Nicholas Reicke, a lanky, blond fellow with piercing blue eyes, soon joined them. He was from their basic training and before boarding the train again, Geir purchased some dark bread and goat cheese for the three of them to share.

This time they were heading toward a small village. However, when they got within fifteen miles of it the train stopped, surprising them. *Was this in the outskirts of Warsaw?*

The sergeant then ordered everyone to get off. "And after roll call, fall in, and march. "

The weather was freezing with an overcast sky. But this time, in the event of an inspection or ceremony, they were ordered to show off the goose-step marching, taught them in their basic training.

They started out on a paved road, until it deteriorated into a dirt path. And then they went back to their regular marching. Something not easy to do with sticky snow and mud in a forest of large trees that had stacked icicles hanging from their limbs.

The soldiers sang German songs when they returned to their regular marching. "Singing while marching is considered an excellent, respiratory exercise," their sergeant pointed out.

When they finished three of their songs eight soldiers, two of which were officers, met them.

"Turn right and march again," one of the officers ordered the marching row.

Following his orders, their boots clicked in unison as they marched toward a stone wall.

Behind this wall was a courtyard, with another group of men larger than theirs, waiting inside it.

In the background was a huge, stone building. "Think that's our new home, Geir?" Volker whispered as they waited, once again for roll call.

"Appears to be," Geir said, frowning at it. "Even it does look like a prison."

"Gives me the creeps."

"Not exactly a Baroque chalet copied after a palace."

"Definitely not."

For a prison— so they learned later that day— it had been.

They went inside and put their packs down on the hard, wooden bed of their choosing.

It was mid-afternoon, and they'd missed lunch. Making Geir thankful Daniel had given him all that money, since they weren't hungry like some of the others in their detachment.

"Now to the rifle range," the sergeant ordered them. And once again they marched, singing, to the range. Which, unfortunately, was a good four miles away.

CHAPTER TEN

The shooting was non-stop. And the group of armed men who were leaving,handed them their guns.

Geir, Volker, and Nicholas were given thirty cartridges meant for them to fire, when their turn came.

It was getting later and later. And when they returned to their prison home, there was an early evening glow in the sky...though their guns had to be put back in the rack before they could retrieve their mess tins in their quarters.

When they finally got to line up in the darkening courtyard, Geir, the same as Volker, was worn out. But never mind they had to wait until their turn came.

The cook filled their tins with his ladle. "Hope you enjoy it," he told them.

The food was millet and ground meat covered in some kind of jam. It didn't taste bad, but Geir joked to Volker that he doubted it would be something the Adlon Hotel would serve. And laughing, Volker agreed.

They were thirsty, but the only water they could find was in something that looked like a rain barrel. So after cleaning their mess tins, Geir, Volker, and Nicholas filled them with the frosty water and took a drink, before hooking them to their belts.

A brief assembly and roll call took place inside the prison building that evening. They saluted the flag. Then stood at attention in front of it, until an officer wearing shiny epaulettes appeared.

"At ease, men." He then began talking about the greatness of the Third Reich; something all the world would soon recognize. "*Sieg Heil!*" everyone shouted their agreement.

It was eight-thirty when the bugle for lights-out sounded. And immediately everyone was dismissed to his room. "*Where we fell, exhausted, into a sound sleep,*" Geir later wrote to Hedy.

At five o'clock the next morning everyone was awakened for more intensive training.

So that day they fired at the shooting range, and afterwards, practiced hurling grenades.

As the weeks passed Geir noticed that he, along with Volker and Nicholas, were becoming expert marksmen.

The weather was freezing, but many of the days were still sunny and bright.

Letters begin arriving from Hedy and the others at the boardinghouse. She wrote Geir that she was finishing her nurse's training and was pleased she had chosen it for a career— *"But oh, do I ever miss you—"*

"No more than I miss you," he wrote back.

In her letters she was worried that he and Volker didn't have furlined greatcoats." Charlotte and I are eager to see you get them. But he and Volker wrote back that only officers appeared to be wearing them. So they had reservations about getting them, even if they did love the fur-lined gloves Greta had given them.

Margit and Daniel wrote they're doing fine, as were Hayim and his wife. "Who are now running a successful tailoring business in Geneva."

Otto wrote about France a lot. *A premonition?* Geir wondered. *Certainly seems like it*

He liked Otto's letters because at the bottom of all of them Hugo and Fritz sent their best wishes.

"You make me feel optimistic," Geir wrote back, wondering if he dared add that France would certainly be better than Poland?

When the weather got better they had additional training in driving jeeps and motorbikes, and also, maneuvering panzers or tanks up steep sloops. *"Something I especially like doing,"* Geir wrote Hedy. And she wrote back saying Daniel was going to buy him a motorbike with a side car after the war.

"Thoughtful of him, but he doesn't have to go and do that," was in his next letter to her.

A lieutenant and a *hauptman*, whose rank was the same as a British captain's, needed two jeep drivers in separate vehicles to drive them into a town thirty miles away. "We're more than impressed with your driving," they told Geir and Volker. "So get ready to go."

They were so excited they didn't mind driving down a narrow, graveled road through a heavily wooded area. They passed some Polish farmers with mules loaded with hay. And when the vehicles approached, they quickly moved to the side of the road.

The *Hauptman* Geir was driving, smiled at the way they seemed to cower in fear.

After that, Volker took the lead. And when they arrived at the town, the lieutenant he was driving ordered him to stop in front of a town-hall looking building flying a German flag.

"Return in two hours," said the lieutenant. "But until then, you and your friend will have some time to do some sightseeing."

There didn't appear to be much to see in this very small town, except a store with a counter where drinks were being served. Some German soldiers in their green greatcoats were laughing and drinking heavily. Something Geir like Volker shied away from, so they drank beer.

Two blond, Polish girls came over to them. "Well now, "Volker said, "Aren't they something." He then asked Geir if he would mind buying a beer for them. Which he didn't.

The girls spoke only Polish, making conversation impossible. But, nevertheless, Volker seemed to be getting along quite well with one of them. The other girl was attracted to Geir. But not wanting to hurt her feelings, he tried his best to explain he was married. She appeared to have no understanding of what he was telling her, so he reached into wallet and removed Hedy's picture. "*Wife*," he said several times. But she just smiled and finally said, "Cinema star."

Geir glanced at the town clock and seeing it was getting close to the time to return to their vehicles, he directed Volker to follow him. "So much for our adventure in this tiny hamlet," said Volker, smiling.

As spring approached the temperature was only thirty degrees, but still, the days were lovely. Eight of those in the unit had been assigned to guard a train with military equipment and weapons heading north to a supply center.

They were given tins of food to take with them, plus a first aid kit. But when Geir and Volker showed the first aid kit Dr. Rath had given them to a sergeant, they were allowed to take it.

They then took their place in front of the flag and shouted *"Sieg Heil,"* before being marched to the station.

Once they reached it they were warned about the partisans along the tracks, waiting to blow up the trains. It was cold this particular day. And shivering with their teeth chattering, they took their positions assigned them on the flat cars. "Where it seems even colder," Geir commented.

"This could be the day that could get us out of the Wehrmacht," Volker whispered to him

"By getting us killed?" Geir asked, frowning at the huge wing of a Luftwaffe plane on their flat car.

The train soon began rolling through a forest with snow still on tops of its trees. The air continued to get *colder*. But regardless, they maintained their patrol on the flat cars; the partisans could be hiding anywhere.

Something seemed to be bothering the sergeant as he made another check to see that all were in their assigned positions. And as the train slowed to go around a curve, he took his MP40 machine pistol and fired into the tree line. "Down!" he yelled as the train came to a stop.

Bullets whistled over Geir's head, getting closer and closer. "You're a bunch of savages!" shouted one of the partisans in German.

The sergeant then grabbed a rifle and motioned at Geir, Volker, and the other soldier on their flat car, to get down and follow him. More blasts were fired into the forest as they stepped into the brush. "Those rifles the damned partisans have are stolen German ones!" the sergeant informed them.

"Even so they managed to get away quickly," remarked Geir.

"They were too far back to do much good," the sergeant pointed out. "Which makes me suspect they were probably *new* partisan recruits—"

"Who were afraid and got away quickly, "Volker added, grinning smugly.

Geir looked up at one of the tall, pine trees in the forest. "Our first time under fire."

"And you got lucky," said the sergeant, motioning them to climb back up on their flat car.

The weeks passed quickly, and they convoyed some more trains and a good many trucks. But fortunately they didn't encounter any partisans.

Even though, they did deliver some supplies to parts of Poland close to where the Wehrmacht was in combat.

Sometimes, they passed bombed out villages, with children crying in their streets. A tragic situation, since Geir had overheard several soldiers say these were Jewish villages.

When the month of May finally came— like Otto had predicted— the Germans took the lowlands and France with very little fighting.

"Think we'll be going to Paris?" Volker asked Geir.

And he nodded. "They'll need plenty of soldiers in that beautiful city to reinforce their occupancy.

Because, after all, it's still just the beginning of the war."

Their transfer orders came at the end of June. "With the good news being we'll get another twenty-four hour layover in Berlin," Geir wrote Hedy. Nicholas was also being transferred, but since his family lived in Landsberg, there was no way he could see them with such a short layover. So, Geir and Volker invited him to be their house guest.

At the train station Hedy and Geir kissed and hugged like they'd been apart for years. And afterwards everyone hugged Geir, Volker, and even Nicholas. "I'm pleased he came with you," Daniel said, giving Geir another hug. Which he knew was clearly an excuse to stuff some more money in his pocket.

I know from experience, Son, that most of the soldiers I fought with had very little money."

"Very few I've met had any," said Geir.

"Like me?" Nicholas asked.

"Yes, like you," Geir teased.

Nevertheless, when Nicholas stepped up to Charlotte—whether he had money or didn't— the attraction between them was immediately evident.

"Would you believe it?" Hedy asked Geir, her eyes wide with surprise.

"Certainly unexpected from *those* two in these uncertain times."

"Definitely."

Geir was deeply touched by Daniel's thoughtfulness when he learned—despite rationing and shortages— he'd gone out of his way to treat everyone to dinner at a fine restaurant. "That still has an excellent quality of food."

"This time Daniels's taking us to the boardinghouse first," Hedy told Geir and Volker. "Since that way you'll be able to wash up, after that long train ride, before dining out."

"And we appreciate it." Volker acknowledged, smiling.

Geir loved the idea...especially since showers had been added to each upstairs bathroom. *It provides an excellent opportunity for Hedy and I to squeeze in some quick lovemaking before dinner.*

"I like the fact my father did this," said Geir, tipping a brow in his direction. "Since showers are usually quicker than tub baths."

Hedy offered him a sly smile. "Why I suggested it."

••••◆••••

Their dining experience later added to their excitement, the same as did the liqueur following it.

Geir skimmed over his one-time combat experience with Daniel and Margit, who wanted to hear more than what he told them.

"I'm so-o worried," Margit cried, obviously aware Geir was not telling her everything.

"Don't be," Greta soothed, gently squeezing her arm. "Geir and Volker will soon be in Paris. And something like that probably won't happen there."

The Bandts, Dr. Rath, and the Schroders agreed with her.

"We Schroders want to show how much we appreciate the bravery of the young men dining with us," said Otto, snatching the dinner bill from the waiter.

"Now, Otto," Daniel said, rising. "Give *me* that bill."

"No!" He was adamant about it. "You've treated us enough. So as of tonight we Schroders are treating you, your friends, and family with not only dinner, but a second bottle of the liqueur."

It was something everyone seemed to enjoy. "The exception being Ernst and Alvina, "Geir murmured, not taking his eyes off their disgruntled expressions.

"It' sad the Brandts aren't drinking because they're focused on the attraction between Charlotte and Nicholas," Hedy whispered to Geir.

"*Love* is out of the question for you until after the war." He overheard Alvina tell to Charlotte.

'Wrong.' He wished he had the nerve to tell her. *'What she needs to hear is that life is short. And she should take her happiness where she finds it.'*

Something it seemed she was beginning to believe when they returned to the boardinghouse.

"Nicholas and Charlotte make a good couple," Hedy said, her eyes flickering in their direction.

Nicholas was holding Charlotte's hand on the sofa in the living room. "It's like they've taken up residence in there," Geir observed.

A grin overtook Hedy's features." Yes indeed. And how late they stay up will be anybody's guess."

Nicholas's mother had grown up in Alsace-Lorraine, on the French-German border. And he spoke French as well as German. Something sure to aid him in France.

The military train they were taking to Paris was due to leave at five-thirty in the morning. *Much too early.* Geir sighed. But still, it didn't stop him from sharing some lovely moments with Hedy.

"Our parting won't be so painful this time," said Hedy. "Because Paris may be a war zone, but Daniel has business there with the communication equipment company he partners with another man. And he's going to be checking with the military to make sure everything is working as it should." She glanced at one of his papers on the table. "In addition to seeing if they're interested in purchasing some more equipment."

"I'm impressed, but what about you?"

"Since Greta will be going, the good doctor and I are working out a plan that will allow me to demonstrate, in the Paris hospitals, some advanced, medical techniques to aid the wounded. ""

"And Charlotte?"

"Now that Nicholas is in her life, I'll see she comes along and helps me with my demonstration."

"It all sounds good, but I'm still worried about this Berlin *blitzkrieg.* "

"That Otto keeps saying will happen in August," Hedy remarked. "But don't worry, Geir, we're prepared for it."

But who could really be prepared for something like that?

CHAPTER ELEVEN

When the time finally came, Geir was elated to be in Paris with Volker and Nicholas.

"I've always wanted to see Paris and sit in the sun in front of a cafe, sipping wine and dining on the city's legendary food," he told them.

Although, the really great news was that Dr. Rath had been able to use one of the connections he still had, to get Geir and Volker assigned as couriers for General Sauer and General Hirschland. "They live at the Ritz. Which means we'll each have a motorbike with aside car," Geir informed Volker.

"And we'll be going all over this beautiful city which—lucky for us—hasn't been destroyed."

But of course he and Volker would be delivering sensitive information, so Nicholas, carrying a submachine gun, had been assigned to ride beside Geir in the motorbike's side car. Another soldier, Rene Gonard, a Frenchman in the Wehrmacht, was assigned to ride with Volker.

July moved along quickly, and soon it was August. Geir looked forward to the end of the month because it meant he and Hedy would be celebrating their first anniversary. Daniel had made his business plans to visit the city with Greta and Hedy. And Geir could hardly wait when— to his delight— the unexpected happened.

General Sauer handed him a train ticket to Berlin with a dispatch to deliver to General Kruger in the city. "*For his eyes only,*" the order read.

Immediately Geir telegraphed Hedy and Daniel, informing them he would be arriving in the early morning of Friday, August twenty-third and returning to Paris on Monday, August the twenty-sixth.

"*Great news,*" Hedy telegraphed him back. "*And we'll all be there to meet you at the station.*"

"Everything couldn't have been better planned," Geir told Daniel, who put off his Paris business until next month.

"Something else to look forward to! " Hedy exclaimed. And Geir nodded his agreement.

He brought French perfume for Hedy, Greta, and Margit, who smiled and kissed him. "I've never had anything like this," Margit said. "But I heard soldiers had to stand in long lines in front of Chanel's fragrance shop to get it."

"Very long lines," he said, hugging her hard. "And some of the men were worried that the Free French might attack us with so many soldiers in one place —"

"Now, Geir, " she scolded, "don't risk yourself on my account."

"I'm not. Considering more and more French are joining our German troops. And besides, the Free French are mostly in the country."

Charlotte's gift from Nicholas was one bottle of French perfume for her, plus another for her mother. And he'd stuffed the two perfume bottles in a big envelope that contained a long letter. *"To my beloved Charlotte"* was written across the envelope. It also contained a picture of him in his uniform, standing in front of the Eiffel Tower.

"My Nick is wonderful," Charlotte said, handing Geir a small package to give him. "It has a picture of me in my nurse's uniform. Along with to some Swiss chocolates, and special cigarettes Daniel gave me to give him."

"I'm sure he'll appreciate his gift as much as you do yours," Geir assured her, shoving it in his bulging pack.

His gaze shifted to Hedy. "What strings have been pulled for you to visit Paris with Daniel and and your mother?"

"It took some doing, but Dr. Rath's finally made it possible for Charlotte and me to demonstrate some of our advanced medical techniques to the nurses and other care givers, working in the Paris hospitals."

Geir's grin was quick and warm, reflecting his elation. "So Charlotte's coming too. Now, that's certainly good news for Nicholas."

Hedy leaned over and whispered, "Don't tell anyone, but I think she and Nicholas are getting married."

"Then Charlotte must have listened to you."

"She did. When I told her that in war, you must take your happiness where you find it."

"Truer words were never spoken— as Otto would say."

Friday and Saturday went by with the two days filled with joy, since he and Hedy never left each other's side. Most of the time, except for Saturday, they had lunch and dinner at the boarding house.

On that day they returned to Lake Wannsee with a picnic basket and bottle of wine for lunch. Geir wore his lederhosen Hedy had given him for Christmas, and she remarked he looked dashing.

However, much later after they returned they learned— to their horror— that the Luftwaffe, attempting to bomb the RAF, had hit some buildings in London, where innocent people worked.

"Doesn't sound good," Geir said, shaking his head.

"Certainly doesn't," Hedy agreed, also shaking her head.

Still, since it was Geir's last night before returning to Paris, they decided to be brave and go to a movie in a theater two blocks away. "And afterwards, we can dine at a restaurant across the street from it," said Hedy. "A place I recently discovered, that still has some outstanding food."

On their way out Otto stopped the couple. "Be careful," he warned. "The RAF is apt to show up tonight." Then he explained, "On a summer night the days are longer, which makes the skies clearer."

"I appreciate the warning, but we're not going far," Geir said. "And besides, this part of the city is on the other side of those high priority places that are considered likely targets. So I don't think they're apt to bomb us."

"Though, even with the clearer night sky, the bombs dispersed can have difficulty hitting those desired targets."

"Hopefully, there won't be a bombing. "And that being said, Geir took Hedy's hand, and they walked off.

The movie they saw was about Mozart. And when it was over they went arm-in-arm to the the restaurant across the street. "They have excellent *Weiner schnitzel*, Geir" she informed him. "Which is the main reason this place is so popular."

"*Weiner schnitzel* is something I never seem to get enough of, "he remarked as a waiter ushered them inside.

"So Daniel told me." She brightened with pleasure. "Which is why I tried it out before you came."

Once inside another waiter came over and quickly took their orders for the *Wiener schnitzel*. "Be sure to include everything that goes with it," Geir told him.

"Which is a lovely tossed salad, *spaetzles*, and dark bread," Hedy quickly said.

"And the wine?" the waiter asked her.

She smiled at Geir again. "Whatever my husband wants is what I'll have."

"What about a young wine?" suggested the waiter. "Since with the war, we don't have as many selections as we've had in the past."

"Young wine and port was what Margit and Wilhelm always drank," Geir told her. "And when I came of age, they let me drink it too."

He was in his uniform, but Hedy was wearing her lovely red-print dress. Her dark hair was piled on top of her head and held in place by a shiny red ribbon. "You never fail to turn heads, my sweet Hedy," he remarked, noticing how the other customers in restaurant were staring at her with admiring eyes.

The waiter hurried back with the wine. "It's our best young wine," he said, opening it. "You'll see."

He had begun pouring it when all of a sudden, he stopped. "Do you hear that piercing sound?"

"Sirens! exclaimed Geir, springing to his feet. "So which way's your shelter—"

"Down those steps." The waiter pointed.

They led to a wine cellar, which was equipped with tables, chairs, and a radio.

"This is the air-raid shelter," said the head waiter, stepping aside for everyone.

Customers, many with their wine glasses, pushed their way toward the stairs.

As they descended the steps, a customer yelled, "Listen! It's the second warning—"

Geir's heart raced as terror seized him. "You're shaking and so am I," he told Hedy, putting his arm around her,

"What one can expect when planes are dropping bombs."

Several tremors rocked the cellar. Then came the sound of an explosion, like a distant blast of thunder. It was followed by another and two more that seemed quite close.

Geir and Hedy were squeezing each other tightly. "Easy, Hedy," he whispered," your breath is fast and uneven, so try and breathe deeply. Or otherwise you could pass out."

"What the nurses tell their patients."

But when the walls began shaking, and the lights went out, horrifying screams followed. A woman sitting across from them shouted at one of the waiters, "This restaurant's been hit, hasn't it?"

"No." He glanced at a box on the wall. "But apparently the wiring's been broken."

Suddenly people began striking matches. "Waiter— bring us some candles!" a man yelled.

Then came a roar—an unearthly sound— as loud as if the building was being struck by a flying object from outer space. *Like a meteor or comet.* Geir shuddered.

Everything appeared to be breaking up and flying in the air. Hedy's chest was now pounding. So Geir quickly pushed her against the floor and covered her body with his. The ceiling could fall any minute, hitting them with large pieces of debris. "Stay down, sweet Hedy, we'll get through this somehow."

More breaking and clattering followed. Then another roaring— and a sudden earth-shattering darkness. Both Geir and Hedy struggled for breath, in what seemed for several seconds to be an airless cavity.

Will this be our grave? He wondered, when a sudden light brightened one of the cellar's columns. A terrified woman screamed. "It's fire! We're burning up!"

Hedy and Geir scrambled to their feet, to see the waiters beating it out with tablecloths.

"Let us out!" shouted another woman. "We've got to get out of here!"

But the anti-aircraft guns outside were firing furiously at the RAF planes, making it dangerous to leave.

A Wehrmacht *hauptman's* hand shimmered under the light from the large candle he held.

Broken glass from bottles was strewn everywhere, with spilled wine pooling on the floor. "Be careful, Hedy," Geir cautioned, grabbing her arm. "It's slippery. And even with the candle's light it's hard to see."

Finally the guns stopped firing, prompting the headwaiter to appear at the door with everyone's checks. "This is a restaurant that needs money. So regardless of the attack, you're still expected to pay for your food and drinks." A good many of the customers grumbled, but no one failed to honor his request.

Geir stuffed a wad of marks in the man's hand, as he and Hedy hurried out the cellar.

The dining part of the restaurant looked like it had been turned upside down, but it wasn't damaged nearly as bad as he'd imagined.

"Feels good to take a deep breath," said Hedy, once they were standing outside in the gloomy, night air. "Even if my red-print dress is so streaked with ash, it reminds me of a dusty scar."

He stroked her cheek affectionately. "Doesn't matter as long as you're all right—but let's hurry home before the RAF decides to make another run at us."

Fires were burning in broken windows, the same as the heaps of rubble and debris now covering the streets. Yet Geir, holding Hedy tightly, managed to make it halfway to the boardinghouse before Daniel, rushing up, surprised them. "We've been extremely worried," he gasped. "And Otto's waiting at the gate should we need him. But are you two all right."

"W...we're fine." Geir coughed, still greatly shaken as dust seared his lungs. Then he took what seemed to him a clotted breath.

"But what about everyone at the house?"

"Sipping the cognac I poured them to calm their nerves," said Daniel. "Before I left to go see about you and Hedy."

A smile lit Geir's face. "Hugo and Fritz tell me they're planning on rebuilding what's left of the boardinghouse's old wine cellar."

"That they are. Because they maintain that if these air raids continue, then they're going to need plenty to drink."

"Makes sense.

When they reached the gate, Otto hugged them and said how happy he was to see no harm had come to them.

"Margit's still in our bomb shelter, "Daniel informed them. "And she's quite worried."

"Did she drink her cognac?" Hedy asked him, stepping into the house, which was now enveloped in a white, powdery-like haze from the bombing.

"In one gulp. And since apparently she's never had it before, she's quite drunk."

"Can't imagine that." Geir chuckled. "But it could be she's finding it difficult to breathe in all this dust. So we'd best see to her."

"Greta, Alvina, and Charlotte are trying to calm her," Daniel said, "but not having much luck."

"Then we'll see if we can't do something about that." Hedy remarked.

A crying Margit hugged and kissed them. And they assured her they were safe and urged her to get some sleep.

Hugo and Fritz were planning on staying in the cellar and sleeping on its cots. "Otto's probably right when he says there won't be another attack," Hugo remarked, reaching for the cognac. "Though even if this house did sail through with hardly a scratch, it's something I'm not willing to chance."

At the dining room table Geir and Hedy joined Otto and Daniel, who were sipping cognac and listening to the radio. "You two could use some cognac," said Daniel, pulling out chairs for them.

"I do think we need it," said Geir, helping Hedy into her chair.

Daniel glanced toward the kitchen. "Margit insisted on making some of her extraordinary, lentil soup, so if you're hungry there's some left."

Geir shifted to Hedy. "Want some?"

"My insides are still in turmoil."

"Same as mine."

The radio news maintained the city's damage wasn't that bad. Although, it did mention many Berliners registered shock, when they learned the only elephant in the Berlin zoo got killed.

Geir was dumbfounded. "The audacity of the RAF," he murmured, taking a sharp breath. "Why in hell did they bomb the zoo?"

"Because, like I implied," Otto remarked with a frown. "Bombing the desired targets is not an exact science. With mistakes often being made." He hesitated, then added, "Still, if the war goes the way I predict, this science will become so exact that the German people will find themselves in a circle of fire."

Geir poured himself another glass of cognac. "The insanity of the war. Which is the reason Hedy and I don't have a child on the way—"

"But you will later." Otto interjected. "Some wonderful children."

"Hopefully," Geir said, finishing his drink. It was ironic to him to think back to the time when he'd first met Hedy. He'd feared she was pregnant and was planning on using him to marry her—but two virgins they'd been. And now wanting a child, the war made them afraid to have one—"

"Geir," Otto said, interrupting his thoughts. "What about the train you'll be taking in the morning?"

"I don't know." He sighed. "Think it'll still be departing for Paris, like my ticket says?"

Daniel patted his arm. "Don't worry about it. Because I intend to have Dr. Rath get hold of his general friend, who'll telegraph your General Sauer in Paris. So he can issue you a new departure date."

"Sounds good. But shouldn't we try to get a message to Volker and Nicholas, to let them know we're all right?"

"Charlotte's taking care of that," Daniel assured him, before finishing the rest of his cognac. "And me— I know those people who own that restaurant where you were. So, I'm going there tomorrow and give them a financial gift for looking after you and Hedy. "He paused, cocking an eyebrow as if thinking. "Which I'm sure they'll repay— without my even asking—by sending this household some of their marvelous *Wiener schnitzel.*"

Geir's smiled his appreciation. "Considering the circumstances, they didn't fair too badly when the bombs fell. "

He was tired, the same as Hedy, who leaned over and whispered, "I think we'll calm down once we're in bed."

"It's worked in the past, so why not tonight?"

"Now if you'll excuse us," Geir said, "we'll turn in."

Daniel lifted his head and smiled. "Then we'll see you in the morning."

Geir put his arms around Hedy as they walked up the stairs. "I hope we're out of danger," she said as he held her close and tight.

"We should be."

When they reached their bedroom, it seemed the tumult of these times was swept away by the golden moon outside their window shinning down on them. 'It's always wonderful to be with you like this," she said, throwing back the covers.

He slid under them. "Especially with no bombs exploding."

"A beautiful silence. "

"But for how long is anybody's guess?" he remarked with a trace of unease.

PART 2

TRACKS

CHAPTER TWELVE

Three days later Geir was back in Paris, reporting to General Sauer. Eighty-one bombs had fallen that night in Berlin, but for time being all was well. *The exception being my concern for Hedy, and the others at the boardinghouse. More air raids were bound to occur. In fact, Otto predicated they'd be around five more bombings before the end of the year.*

Night was when the RAF was forced to navigate.

"A time that makes it difficult for them to disperse their bombs at their targets," a newspaper had written. "Creating a hit or miss—and more often a miss."

"Like that poor elephant in the zoo," Geir remarked.

The only time Paris had been bombed was in June; which fortunately had done little damage done to this beautiful city. Yet, obviously there was a Parisian neutrality toward the Germans. working out of the Ritz. Something that wasn't difficult for Geir and Volker to sense.

It was a palatial cultural legend, that had become the Nazi headquarters for its generals and other high-ranking officials who resided there. *Opulent splendor. Champagne cocktails. Food in restaurants, served on candle lit, white-linen dining tables.*

"With a war raging who would have thought such elegance existed?" Geir asked Nicholas as they stood marveling at the hotel.

In chauffeured cars, wealthy women wrapped in fur stoles and smoking cigarettes in long, ivory holders, made a point of mingling with the Nazi's living there. And quite often took them in to visit the jazz singers in the city's late -night cabarets.

Nicholas was planning to marry Charlotte in late October when she'd be coming with Daniel, Greta, and Hedy. "I'm making arrangements for the bride and groom to honeymoon at the Ritz," Daniel wrote Geir.

Nicholas's marriage was great news. "You're smart enough to recognize happiness. when you find it," Geir told him. "But Volker? Now that's another matter."

"How so?" Nicholas inquired with unconcealed curiosity.

"He's frequenting Francine's Hotel, a bordello, that's owned by a woman who speaks French with an American accent—"

"I heard all about it," Nicholas said.

"Then you're aware she has many exotic beauties from Morocco and other places, living and working there?" Geir asked him. "Which. sadly, in these dreadful times is just a superficial happiness."

"Agreed." Nicholas said. "But what can we do about it?"

"Not much."

Geir allowed another week to pass,before he worked up the courage to mention this French hotel to Volker.

"Ah, so you know," he said, checking a tire on his motorbike. "But the truth is you need to join me."

"What!" Geir exclaimed, dumbstruck. "When I have the most wonderful wife in the world?"

"You won't have her long if we get sent to Russia." His determination bordered on intimidation.

"Russia? When we're doing so well in Paris."

"Something that's bound to happen," Volker said, a wary look on his face. "Forcing me to take my chances since we didn't get sent to Africa."

"*Chances*?" The word jumped out at Geir. "Not if you get a venereal disease and end up being quarantined."

"Doesn't matter. I'll do it whatever the cost. "He sneered. "Even though I hear the military will eventually make a soldier do some jail time over it."

After a frozen silence, Geir gave his head several very firm shakes. "I can't believe you're talking yourself into such a dangerous escapade."

"Only because I'm caught up in a war I don't believe in!" Volker ranted, in a voice suddenly filled with rage. "And have no intention of winding up some poor, freezing prisoner the Russians beat and starve to death." He leaned against his motorbike with a look of detached inevitability. "Think about it, Geir, before it's too late."

"It's already too late. Since the day I met Hedy changed my life."

A long pause followed. "Then you have my sympathy," he replied in a headstrong, impulsive manner. "Because loving her like you do is not *worth* your life,"

"I disagree," Geir replied, infuriated. "Since there's got to be another way."

"None that I can see."

"I don't know who you've been talking to," Geir snapped. "But venereal diseases are self-induced diseases. And it's war time. So what's to stop the Germans from lining you up against a wall and shooting you?"

"Jail was all that was ever mentioned—"

"Which lets me know this person who's been telling you all this, doesn't know what in *hell* he's talking about! "

Volker shrugged. "Could be?" he replied in an abstracted tone.

Geir's pulse raced like it had when those Polish bullets had wheezed over his head. "It's a chance that's not worth gambling with your life. Because if you come down with syphilis, it'll eventually kill you."

"Of course." Volker remarked. "Although it'll get you out of the Wehrmacht. And besides, syphilis takes *years* to kill you, when in Russia, we could be killed our first day there."

"Maybe." Geir said, not surprised by the revelation. "Still, knowing the Wehrmacht, or rather our German military machine, what's to keep them from shooting their soldiers with syphilis, like I've heard?"

"In my case, Charlotte. Who will implore Dr. Rath to use his connections and not let that happen to me."

"God in heaven." Geir said, struggling to keep a hold on his temper. "You have more faith in Dr. Rath than I do. Since he couldn't even find a way for us to become combat medics—"

"Only because we don't have university backgrounds. Which in these desperate times makes them they look on us cannon fodder."

Geir gave a resigned shrug. "I know. But in the end contacting syphilis can be as dangerous, or more dangerous than being killed. on the Eastern Front. And if given a choice, I'd prefer to be shot by the Russians."

"Each to his own." Volker huffed.

Another week passed with Geir watching Volker leave the barracks every night and return half-drunk. Finally, unable to stand it, he confided his fear to Nicholas about Volker's deliberate attempts to get a venereal disease.

Nicholas didn't seem surprised. Since there was a distant relative of his, Louis Becker, who was a civilian with a venereal disease. "He'd grown up in Alsace-Lorraine, too." Nicholas explained. "And this fellow Becker had worked with Germany before the war, handling intelligence gathering equipment for General Hirshland and General Sauer—"

"For whom Volker delivers," Geir interjected.

"They were good friends until, to the general's great regret, Louis got diagnosed with syphilis."

Geir's brow raised in surprise. "Surely it was before Germany took France."

"Possibly two years before or longer," Nicholas clarified." For Louis, who'd spent much of his life on the German-French border, liked Paris and often visited the city. Where he became a favored patron of Francine's Hotel, since he always used condoms."

"So where is he now?" Geir asked, his curiosity piqued.

"In quarantine in a hospital in *Lille* near the Belgium border—"

"Which Daniel often visits in behalf of his Italian surveying company," Geir recalled. "But getting back to Louis— I'm surprised Germany hasn't shot him."

"I doubt they would. Since even if he's not in the military, I suspect he's a man the *higher-up* Germans could still find a way to use."

"Volker needs to see this man—"

"Definitely," Nicholas agreed. "Because from what I'm hearing, Louis really looks bad. "

They continued to talk at length, with Nicholas suggesting to Geir that he and Volker needed to go to *Rheims*—a place not far from *Lille*. Since it seemed the *Free French*—as these partisan attackers are being called—were creating a good deal of problems for the Germans stationed in *Rheims*.

"Problems?" Geir questioned. "What kind of problems?"

"There're sending our German-encrypted short wave messages to the British to break. Which obviously are connected to the two German field colonels in the area. Whose knowledge appears to be lacking in weather patterns, when they order them to be transmitted. And each of these colonels has his own classified operation with one reporting to your superior, and the other to Volker's."

Geir's curiosity increased. "Do they know Daniel's given a good many talks concerning weather patterns and short wave messages? And since he has an Italian surveying company, he's been asked to oversee some surveying in Belgium near *Lille*."

"Those generals don't know anything about Daniel. So don't blow your chance, Geir, by telling them about your father."

"But if I don't, then who will?"

"Your good Dr. Rath." A thoughtful smile curved Nichols's mouth. "Who'll have his general friend contact them. And, he'll suggest to this friend, that you'll introduce Daniel to General Sauer's field colonel, and Volker to General Hirshland's. Colonels working out of *Rheims,* who could possibly use some more information about climatic weather patterns."

Geir felt a little flustered by all this plotting. "I'm anxious for Volker to see how sickly this Louis Becker looks. Which, hopefully, will jar him to his senses about contacting syphilis."

"Hopefully." Nicholas sighed, like he wasn't sure about it."

"But getting back to this trip to *Rheims,* "said Geir. "It seems to me it's getting so complicated that I feel like we're going around the world just to get to this French place."

Nicholas's mouth tightened. "And it gets even more complicated when I ask you what excuse you and Volker are going to have to visit Louis Becker? A man you've never met. Who's quarantined in the hospital with syphilis."

"Well now—" Geir replied, his stomach roiling at the question. "That's a hard one to call."

"Then let me make it easy and suggest that you and I go to Francine's and inform her that my dear friend, Louis, in *Lille,* has a serious intestinal ailment. And that you're going to *Lille,* nearby, on Wehrmacht *business.*" Nicholas bit off the word. "And you've volunteered to visit him at the hospital on my behalf. Since Louis claimed to be as fond of you and your girls, as you were of him. So I believe he'd appreciate it if all of you sighed a get-well card." He hesitated for a long moment. "And that's when I produce it. A lovely card with pink flowers, blue birds, bees, and butterflies on it."

"Dear Lord," Geir said, staring at the floor like someone praying. "What 'd I ever do to end up getting myself committed to something like this?"

"Nothing," Nicholas replied. "Because it's not as bad as it sounds. Since Francine and her girls really loved Becker. So, I'm sure they'll be overjoyed to sign his card."

Geir looked at Nicholas quizzically. "I don't suppose *you* or Francine know someone here in Paris, who's had syphilis for awhile and looks awful."

"I don't. But going to *Lille* and getting Daniel involved with the Wehrmacht's short wave problems in *Rheims*, should put a feather —not only in your cap, but Volker's too. And if General Sauer and Hirshland are impressed, they liable to find a way to keep the two of you in Paris,when this projected war with Russia that's being talked about, breaks out."

Nicholas's words created a disturbing silence before Geir responded, "Certainly worth considering."

Since time was important, Nicholas suggested they get the card right away and have Francine and her girls sign it. "Like this afternoon. Before the good doctor contacts anyone. So that way we'll know for sure if they'll sign it or otherwise—"

"Is there a reason they wouldn't?" Geir interrupted, concerned.

"No. But a bird in the hand is always worth two in the bush."

"I've heard that before."

"Because it 's sound thinking."

Since it was still early afternoon, and time was of the essence, Geir went with Nicholas to buy a card to take to Francine.

When they arrived at her hotel, she was seated at her desk until Nicholas appeared. "My goodness," she said, rising and kissing him on the mouth. "Our client Volker was quite intoxicated one evening, so he asked me to call his friend Nicholas to come to his aid," she explained to Geir, gazing at him with a more-than-friendly expression.

Her hotel looked like it had been built in the last century, giving him the shivers. *My first time ever in a brothel. And wouldn't you know...its staircase looks exactly like the one at the boarding house. What* irony!

"And to whom do I have the pleasure of meeting?" she asked him.

"Geir Gallen. My transportation," Nicholas answered for him. "Plainly aware of his friend's tension."

"Well now, *Herr* Gallen." Francine smiled. "You're quite handsome."

"B...but I'm married," he stammered, opening his wallet with Hedy's picture."

But before he could produce it, eight gorgeous girls wearing shorts, heels, and shiny earrings that brushed their shoulders, came down the stairs. Each step they took was quite slow and quite seductive.

Some were black, some tan and others white. '*Quite a mixture.*' Geir was tempted to say. '*With grins that appear to be focused on me—of all people.*'

Quickly he handed Hedy's picture to Francine, who glanced at it and handed it back. "What is it about these Hollywood stars that gets young men like you, *Herr* Gallen, so stirred up? Their careers come first, and the men they marry are ones who can enhance them."

That said, the eight girls huddled around her to get a look at Hedy's picture. "*Cleopatra.*"

A pretty, blond girl smiled.

"Wasn't she in that movie?" inquired a girl with a gorgeous tan.

"My wife's a nurse. And hasn't been in any movies," he said, his uneasiness increasing.

But that didn't seem to register with any of them.

"Your face is paling, Geir," Nicholas whispered to him. "So I'll hurry and finish up here."

He then produced the card, explaining that his friend, Louis Becker, was quite ill with a stomach disorder in a hospital in *Lille*. And since he spoke so highly of everyone here, he thought they might like to sigh his get-well card.

"Poor, Louis," one of the girls sobbed. "He was always so-o good to us."

That sparked a chorus of sobs from the other girls. "We'll all be happy to sigh it," said Francine, swiping her eyes before taking the card.

The girls hovered around her desk... signing it with a get-well wish and then marking it, with a lipstick kiss.

When they finally finished, Nicholas quickly took the card. "Sorry we have to leave, but General Sauer is expecting, *Herr* Gallen, to deliver a message within the hour. So we need to hurry."

"We're just glad you came," said Francine, blowing a kiss at Geir.

It was an action that immediately prompted her eight lovely girls to do likewise.

⋯⋯◆⋯⋯

Within a week Geir and Volker were at the railroad station waiting for the train that would take them to *Lille*. It wasn't a main line train.

Something they found surprising, considering the ramp was crowded with a large number of people who seemed eager to go in the direction *Lille*. "I suspect this train hauls war supplies most of the time," Volker told Geir as they pushed forward, into the middle of people, when the train steamed in. "Since if I'm hearing correctly, the only main line ones run between *Lille* and *Rheims*."

"We'll find out when we take it."

They were fortunate enough to grab two seats. The only problem being there was nowhere to put their packs except under their feet. "With our rifles between our knees," Geir remarked, disgusted.

He looked at his first signed travel document which read, "Dispatched to *Lille*. And then his second document which read "Dispatched to *Rheims*. There was nothing else but a swastika emblem on each document.

Not being a main line train, the trip lasted over four hours with two stops along the way.

At each stop the more sophisticated passengers from Paris got off. However, the closer they got to *Lille* the men and women getting on, wore farm clothing and carried baskets of food. Their appearance confirming what I've read about the agriculture near the city," Geir remarked.

Smiling, Volker accepted a piece of cheese from one of the farm women. "I'm glad Daniel's meeting us," he told Geir.

"So am I," he said, also accepting some cheese from this woman.

He was pleased he'd written Daniel a letter, letting him know what was going on. "*Show it to Hedy and Dr. Rath, but no one else,*" he'd told him.

Volker knew all about the letter and understood it had to be that way. Because Geir had explained, "Daniel's an expertise at dealing with people. So, if someone has to talk the hospital workers into allowing us to personally deliver a get-well card to a quarantined patient there, then my father's the man who can do it."

Several more hours passed before they finally rolled into *Lille*; a city with Flemish roots, separated from Belgium by the *Deule* River.

The first thing they saw when the train pulled up to the ramp was Daniel waiting for them. "He looks distinguished in his gray fedora," Volker remarked.

"That's my father," Geir bragged.

"Everyone sends their best," Daniel said, giving them each a hug.

He'd booked a suite in one of the city's better hotels, which was much nicer than the German *Soldatenheim,* where food and lodging were offered for short term visitors.

Plus, Daniel took them to an Italian restaurant, Jollie's, that had some of the finest food they'd ever tasted. "Can't get Italian food in Germany or Paris like this," said Geir, savoring ever bite. "So I'm really surprised at finding such a place in a French town close to the Belgium border."

Daniel agreed. "When I'm not in Italy, I really miss good Italian food."

After dinner he ordered cognac, with Volker swallowing his in a single gulp. *Like Margit did during the August twenty-fifth Berlin bombing,* Geir recalled with a grin.

Volker brightened. "May I suggest we check out some of the city's bars, since some of our barrack's buddies are saying they're quite unique?"

' *As are the city's brothels,*' Geir wanted to add. Frowning, as he recalled what he'd overheard a sergeant tell Volker about them.

"We three need to get some sleep," Daniel reminded. "Because our schedule dictates we go to the hospital early." He held up their tickets. "The writing on them makes it clear that we're taking the noon train to *Rheims.*"

"Still, what can a few drinks in some of the bars hurt?" Volker asked.

"But Daniel like Geir, gave him a disapproving look. "Plenty," they responded.

"Too bad." Volker sighed, standing up and pushing back his chair. "But why visit this place unless you can do a little sightseeing?"

"Because I'm tired," Geir replied, frustrated with what Margit would call his friend's, *quicksilver* mood changes. *'He plans on doing one thing, then switches to another,'* she'd say.

"Then, *war buddy,* I guess I'm on my own, " Volker said with a light bitterness.

"Guess you are."

After he left Daniel shook his head in dismay. "Volker's really got it bad, doesn't he?"

"Fear's made him desperate."

"What it usually does to men in war," said Daniel, with a faraway look in his eyes, like a distant memory. "But as I've said, even though Margit and Wilhelm did a better job of raising you than I could have ever done, I'm here for you now... in this very crucial time." There was a moment when he looked as if he might cry. "I don't have any strong, German political connections. Because I fear that if one of Hitler's boys decides to dig deeper into my past, he'll discover that even with my Swiss passport, I'm really an American. Which unfortunately, means that all we have in the way of military or political connections is our good Dr. Rath."

"Better him than none at all. But tell me—" Geir said, bringing the conversation back to the reason they were there." What does Hedy have to say about all this concerning Volker?...Especially that part about Nicholas and I going to Francine's Hotel."

"Hedy says she hasn't got a better solution than what you and Nicholas are trying to do for Volker."

"I hope she knows I'd never look at another woman but her," Geir remarked with certainty.

"She does. Which is the way I felt about your mother. Who, by the way, had your gray eyes."

"So Margit told me."

"When I first met Greta, I couldn't believe what a remarkable daughter Hedy was. And I credited Greta with making her that way."

"Hedy loves her mother very much—"

"— and she was trying to convince her to come with her to Berlin to meet you, Geir." He held out his hand to him across the table. "But lost the *one* week, that wasn't in your favor." For a moment Daniel was silent, looking sad in the dim light before continuing, "Which as you know, so many of Germany's young men were volunteering, that it took us by surprise when the country conscripted you."

"I talked to Otto about that when I caught Hedy crying. Because she still grieves about losing that one week for me. 'If only I'd come sooner,' she keeps saying."

"Hedy did come close to getting you to Switzerland," Daniel reminded. "Though in the end it was all my fault for failing to get you that American citizenship."

"You're as hard on yourself as Hedy is herself. So like I tell her, 'don't be.' Because Otto maintains that what happened is all about *destiny*."

"Something I don't like to think about. "Daniel grimaced. "But anyway, as you know, my business demands I be away a lot. So in the interest of those we both care about, I'm trying to spend more time in

Berlin. Since I'm coming to love that boardinghouse, because you grew up there. In addition to the wonderful cooking Margit insists on doing, *that* keeps us at home and not out—"

"Otto writes you've put him in charge of the house when you're away."

"I have...considering his strong intuition usually tells him when the bombs are going to fall."

They had another glass of cognac before they decided to go back to the hotel and get some sleep.

"Think Volker will be back before morning?" Geir asked Daniel.

His mouth took an unpleasant twist. "Isn't there a curfew?"

"I think so."

"Then he'd better obey it. Or else, we'll spend the middle of the night hunting his ass."

But when it got later and later and Volker didn't show, Geir thrashed back and forth in his bed, the same as Daniel was doing in his. Only his was next to the window, where he occasionally got up and looked out.

'He's worried like me,' Geir was about to say, when suddenly Volker burst through the door.

"You missed out on some fun," he said, with one of his half-drunk smiles.

"I doubt it." Geir shrugged. He was grateful for the time alone he'd spent with Daniel.

'And I'm coming more and more to believe he did the right thing in allowing Margit and Wilhelm to raise me, he planned on telling Hedy when he returned to Paris. *'So I can't say he abandoned me, when he's here for me in this dreadful time.'*

"Although, I am curious about one thing. How was it Daniel had stayed in close contact with the Bandts and Hayim when they only seemed to know each other briefly, after the Great War?" he'd written in a recent letter to her. *"And the Schroders. How did he come to know them, when they showed up after he'd returned to America?"*

She'd quickly written him back, shocking him with what she wrote.

And now as Daniel and Volker lay sound asleep, Geir reached for his tunic in a chair next to his bed, and removed her letter from its pocket.

He'd read and re-read it many times, never ceasing to be amazed at her answers to his questions:

My Dearest Geir,

The Bandts and Hayim, so it seemed, needed food after the Great War, the same as did Margit, Wilhelm, and Noelle. And since they were all close friends, Daniel gave them anything he could. Even giving money to them, until times got better in Germany. But the Schroders —now that was a different story. Since Wilhelm and Margit were living in a shabby, two-room apartment, when this owner of the boardinghouse, Herr Behr, gave Wilhelm the opportunity to manage it. And although Hayim Glick advised him against it, Wilhelm didn't listen to him and immediately accepted the offer. Because after getting some pictures of the house, Margit was planning on sending them to Daniel and writing, that it was an ideal place to raise you— Geir.

Something that proved to be a great mistake with the way tenants came and went, due to the boardinghouse's strict rules. Because Herr Behr had inherited the place and was threatening to shut it down, when the Schroders showed up. They liked living there but weren't pleased, when their rent suddenly rose. Which Herr Behr maintained he needed to cover expenses. Margit said Herr Behr told the Schroders that he only got half the rent. Since the other half went to the Gallens'. Who made money on the side with their sewing and tutoring. Which, so this landlord believed, they stashed for a doctor in case they had need of one."

"But, Herr Behr," Margit had exclaimed, "by the time I feed these tenants, there's hardly anything left to eat for my husband, son, and myself."

But he'd turned a deaf ear to her pleas. Reminding her in these dreadful times that she had a nice place in which to live.

Margit had feared that if the Schroders didn't stay, Herr Behr would sell the place. And a worried Wilhelm confided to the Bandts, that even with the money Daniel was sending, they might be forced to move back into a two-room apartment.

So the Bandts then took the liberty of informing Daniel about the situation. Which unknown to Margit and Wilhelm, he made arrangements with the Schroders to send them rent money each month via the Bandts. That started a correspondence between Otto and Daniel, that led to the three Schroders meeting Daniel a number of times, in secret, outside Berlin. *"By paying our rent," Daniel said Otto told him, "we three Schroders were able to pool our earnings and retire early."*

Now, they refuse to accept any money from Daniel. Insisting it's their turn to do for the family. And there're doing it by paying for all the household's groceries. Which means nowadays they often have to stand in long lines, because of the many shortages the war is causing. But they never complain. And as you know, Otto's become our chauffeur and is enjoying the luxury of driving the Mercedes, Daniel bought for the boardinghouse.

Love to the most handsome and kindest husband in the world.

Your Hedy,

P.S. Daniel and Margit don't need to know what I wrote in this letter.

Geir had difficulty getting Volker up the next morning. So Daniel had room service bring breakfast and coffee."Drink it. And the light of day will look better," he assured him.

"So I know, "he said, with his half-smile... Although it took three cups of coffee before he began coming around and eating his Belgium waffle breakfast. "I could have slept all day."

"Of which Daniel and I are aware," said Geir in a not too friendly tone. "So get a move on—our time is running out."

A cab took them to the hospital where Becker was a patient.

"Which is just a simple, older-looking building on the edge of town, with a German flag flying over it." Geir observed.

"Those military flags are flying over every building in this town," Daniel remarked with an unpleasant expression.

At the desk a grim-looking, male receptionist asked him why he wanted to see Louis Becker.

"Because I'm Daniel Birnbaum and worked with him awhile back." he lied, adding, "Even if I fear he might not remember me, the same as these two gentlemen with me. Who met him briefly."

"And you're expecting *what* from him?" asked this grim-looking employee.

"Nothing other than getting him to accept a get-well card from some of his friends in Paris. "

"Paris!" this employee repeated, clearly shocked. "You mean you've come all the way from Paris?"

"No. I've come from Italy," said Daniel. "But the two gentlemen with me are from Paris."

"Then, if you don't mind seeing him for five minutes behind glass, in the waiting room, it'll be all right," the man said, pointing at a large room across the hall from his desk." So take a seat in front of the glass and wait."

And wait, they did.

It took forty minutes for Louis Becker to show up. And once he did, they immediately noticed he was wearing a black-and-white striped robe that resembled what prisoners wore. The only exception being were the blue slippers on his feet.

His pale face stared at Daniel. "Do I know you?" he asked through the glass.

"It's been awhile," he lied again. "But your friends at Francine's Hotel have sent you a get-well card."

"Do they know what's the matter with me?" he asked, raising his voice.

"No. Because I told them you were having severe stomach problems."

"Good." A faint smile crossed his face. "Then I thank you. So put the card on the table beside you and one of the employees will give it to me."

Daniel did as he was told, before exchanging farewells with him. "We have a train to catch in an hour, so forgive us if we seem to be in a hurry."

This time Louis smiled. "Forgiven."

Passing the reception desk on their way out, Geir mumbled not once, but twice, "I've never seen a human being look as bad as Louis Becker."

"Me either," said Volker, who's coloring was suddenly as pale as Louis's. "Our man, Becker, looks like he's been revived after having lain, prior to burial, in a mortuary for a week."

"What syphilis can do to a man," Daniel replied.

Volker turned to Geir. "If I visit Francine's again, I intend to use condoms."

"Good idea."

"Guess giving that get-well card to Louis paid off," Daniel whispered to Geir, as they exited the hospital.

"Certainly appears like it."

A cab took them back to the hotel, where they gathered up their things. Then, before they got to the train station, they stopped at a Flemish restaurant."They've got something for us," Daniel said, getting out of the cab and going inside.

When he reappeared he had a large sack in his arms. "I've bought us three cartons of Flemish stew for lunch," he informed them. "And I know we're running late." So he handed the cab driver some extra money, to get them to the train station quickly.

But they need not have rushed. Because even if the trains running between *Lille* and *Rheims* were supposedly the only main line ones in France, they weren't running on time. "So we eat our stew while we wait," said Daniel, handing Geir and Volker a carton and a spoon.

The stew was so marvelous they didn't object to the wait. Although, when the train finally arrived, they boarded it quickly. "Time is against us with this train running so late," Daniel said. "And I fear it'll be dark when we arrive." He shook his head like he wanted to get rid of the thought. "One good thing though, is I got permission for the two of you to stay with me at the hotel, rather than the barracks. Because that way, we can share a bottle of the famous *Rheims* champagne."

"Champagne and its Gothic cathedral, "Geir said, thumbing through a book about the city. "Two things *Rheims* is known for. In addition to being a badly war-torn city during the Great War, with its Gothic cathedral coming close to being destroyed."

"And we really appreciate the way you've arranged things," Volker told Daniel. "Since it'll be much easier for us to deliver you to the two colonels, you'll be discussing weather patterns with, why we wait for you nearby."

It was 8:30 a.m. the next morning, when Geir and Volker, in full uniform and regalia, stepped into the office where the two colonels waited. They gave their names, saluted, clicked their heels and introduced Daniel to these two colonels.

Immediately, the men rose, returned their salutes, and shook Daniel's hand. Then turning to Geir and Volker they dismissed them to wait outside the door in the hall until further notice. And as required, they saluted again before leaving.

Time passed as they waited expectantly. "It's half an hour past noon," Volker pointed out." So what do you suppose is keeping them?"

"Probably asking Daniel a lot of questions."

"Wouldn't doubt it." But another half-hour passed before the colonels, with Daniel, reappeared.

"These thoughtful colonels are treating the three of us to lunch in a restaurant nearby," he informed Geir and Volker. "And they've arranged for a canvas-military truck to take us there. Which afterwards, will deliver us back to our hotel, so we can retrieve our things."

"And you?" Geir asked him. "Will you be taking a cab to the train station?"

"I'll be going there in the truck. And once some soldiers are picked up, then you'll be going back to Paris in it."

The two colonels were very obliging, and as they entered the restaurant, they urged Daniel to visit them again. But since he'd be in Paris in late October, he wasn't sure he could work it into his schedule. "Let us know when, and we'll find a way to come to Paris," said one of the colonels.

Daniel promised to try as they sat down at the restaurant.

The food was divine: grilled chicken, potatoes, a tossed green salad, and a pastry for desert. But since Daniel's train was due to arrive in an hour, they ate quickly.

A grocery store was across the street, so Daniel hurried in and bought three loaves of French bread, three sausages, several large chunks of cheese, and three bottled fruit drinks.

The store's owner put everything in two sacks as Daniel had instructed.

The French bread was so tall it didn't fit very well in the sacks, but no one objected. "One sack is for me, and the other is for *you* fellows," he told Volker, handing him a sack. "Since we're apt to be hungry before nightfall." Volker thanked him as he helped him get back in the truck. "Let's just pray all goes well."

CHAPTER THIRTEEN

And later, on the ramp at the train station Geir like Volker, once again, thanked Daniel for his help.

"Which has kept me from the mistake I was about to make," Volker admitted. "Because now I know contacting a venereal disease is definitely not the answer to my getting out of the Wehrmacht. "

"No it isn't," Daniel agreed. "But somewhere, Volker, there's a way—"

"Which I've yet to find."

Geir hugged his father. "I appreciate everything you've done."

"Which, considering I never got your American citizenship for you, isn't that much."

"As Hedy's husband I have it unofficially. But like I keep saying, I'd still be in the war. Because if I'd been in Switzerland I'd have trained as a combat medic while waiting for the allies to get in the war."

"And like I keep thinking, if I hadn't had my head up my ass, I wouldn't have to worry about your ending up on that damned Eastern Front in Russia."

"Shush, Pa," said Geir, raising a hand to silence him. "You're being too hard on yourself—"

"No I'm not...think about it. After all these years I don't dare introduce you as my son, since I'm a Hebrew and fear one day the truth will surface. So where does that leave you? At the mercy of Russia when Germany attacks it." He stared at the soldiers on the station's ramp, waiting for the next train. "Which sadly means, I can't win for losing."

Bewildered, Geir took hold of his father's hand. "I disagree. So focus on Otto's word *destiny* that keeps popping up. And remember —that's what our getting together— at long last is all about."

Daniel embraced him. "Then take heart, Son. The end of October will be here before we know it."

"And I can hardly wait knowing Hedy, Greta, and Charlotte will be coming with you—"

The truck driver was getting impatient. "We have to leave *now*, Private!" he yelled at Volker, pointing at the train steaming in.

"Then *now* it is," Geir hollared at him, before giving Daniel a final hug.

"Who's meeting Daniel in *Lille?*" Volker asked as they hurried toward the truck driver's waving arm.

"Some German man in Belgium who's helping him with his Italian surveying company, will be on the train to Italy with him."

"After the Great War your father was always open to helping my family, whenever they needed money." Volker told Geir, as if suddenly light-headed. "Did anyone ever tell you?"

"They did. "

But I wasn't about to mention the person who did it was Hedy. Although I do wonder how much Volker knows about Otto's story? Since the Bandts were in on it too. And with Daniel paying the Schroders rent, I suspect Otto never used his psychic ability to make money, because he was aware of the devious minds of Berlin's authorities—and what they could do to him— if they learned of his ability. But now, thanks to Daniel, Otto's driving a Mercedes. Which I think is great! Considering my Uncle Otto is worth his weight in gold, with his ability to project what lies ahead. Plus, it goes without saying, he's helped me with my writing. And though we may not be blood kin, I'll always consider him to be family.

⸻ ◆ ⸻

Geir scowled at Volker as they bounced along the bumpy road in the back of the truck headed for Paris.

"At the last minute they've crowded so many soldiers in this truck with their rifles, that everyone's shoulders are touching," he remarked.

"Looks like they're over a hundred men in here," Geir replied, tensing visibly. "So just what the hell is going on?"

"We're going through some terrorist country," answered a burly, infantry sergeant overhearing him.

"Which is the reason you two men are riding in the back of the truck. Because we got word, you're working with our generals in Paris. And they gave orders for the two of you to ride in the back. So if the need arises, you can get out quickly."

"A most comforting thought," Volker mumbled sarcastically.

The military had given each soldier some tins of food but apparently had forgotten about

Geir and Volker. "Good thing Daniel was thoughtful enough to buy us something to eat," said Volker.

He'd devoured one of the loafs of French bread and had started on the second, putting the sausage and cheese between the slices he tore off, making sandwiches.

"Believe it or not I'm saving some for you," he told Geir.

But he wasn't hungry... *Because a shaft of fear spears through me at the strange, haunting silence on this open road.*

It gave the inside of the truck an eerie feeling. And he wanted to ask this infantry sergeant about these French terrorists, but didn't. *My throat's so dry I'm having difficulty swallowing. And the reason? We're about go to into battle!' a* voice inside him warned.

When suddenly, submachine guns opened fire at the truck, flipping it sideways on the road.

Explosion followed explosion. "Get out while you can!" ordered a screaming voice. "We've hit a mine!"

Blinded momentarily from all the smoke and dust, a frantic Geir and Volker struggled to crawl out of the vehicle and onto the road.

Dodging exploding grenades, they ran with a corporal and four soldiers to a line of trees bordering the road. "Where do we go now!" someone shouted at the corporal.

"That field!" He motioned at it.

"With no cover?"

"The road's their target—as is the truck."

More bullets whistled overhead, hitting not just the trees, but also the road and truck.

The front of the vehicle exploded from a fuel spill. "Damn!" Volker yelled. "Some of the men are still inside it—"

One way or another they'll get us all—fear made Geir think. *And no cover for us, except behind those trees.*

But luckily, squeezed between the corporal and four soldiers, who now surrounded them, he and Volker managed to make it to the trees.

Grenades continued to explode left and right in the field and on the road. The terrorist rifles were astoundingly accurate. Shooting, one by one, the few remaining soldiers in the truck as they crawled out.

Geir's heart beat wildly against his chest.

There're closing in, he thought desperately. *And if Volker and I step out from behind these trees, we'll be hit.*

"If we can make it through all this fire, that drainage creek in the field will act as cover!" Geir hollared at Volker.

"Then let's do it!" He sounded out of breath. "Since all this smoke and dust will also act as cover!"

Bullets exploded in front and back of them as they rushed toward the creek.

The enemy was now too close to shoot without attracting their attention. Although some infantry soldiers were firing their rifles from behind the overturned truck. "Where they'll soon be trapped. "Geir mumbled, panic-stricken, "due to all this small arms fire."

More shots hit the road, with someone yelling, "They're in this field moving upon us! So get back on the road and run to its opposite side— then follow the stream to the forest!"

The Free French in the field were now too close for comfort, filling Geir with anxiety.

He shouted at Volker, "Somehow we've got to get across that road!"

"With all those shots hitting it?" asked one of the soldiers with them.

"We take advantage of the next lull for reloading" said the corporal, counting the seconds until it got deathly quiet.

"Now!" he hollared.

A hailstorm of bullets whistled over their heads, as each man ran crouched over. *Hell had returned!* And Geir came within the snap of a finger getting hit full force, when a large piece of metal from the truck flew over his head. It was followed by a bullet ricocheting off it. "Am I still alive?" he gasped, his visions of fear threatening to overtake him.

A rapid succession of machine gunfire, explosions, shots, and grenades started up again.

Those French from the field moved forward until they were now less than twenty meters from the front of the overturned truck. And their rifles were trained on the soldiers, running alongside the stream toward the forest. "The only good cover out here," cried Volker. "And it's not that close—"

The smoke and dust had yet to lift, making it difficult to see the bodies scattered along of the road.

Geir's breathing slowed as a peculiar excitement pricked at his lungs, making it feel like they'd stopped working. '*Stumbling blocks* or *shields?* 'He mentally asked. *Shields.*

Since there's no way with all those damned explosions, Volker and I can make it across. So our only hope is to take cover beneath these dead men.

"Run!" Geir heard a voice. "The French are in front of the truck!"

Soldiers on the opposite side of the road who'd not made it to the stream, were firing their rifles steadily at these partisans.

"You men taking cover under those corpses—" yelled the infantry sergeant from the open back of the battered truck— "Get out and start shooting!"

Even if he hated to give up his cover Geir, Volker, and the four soldiers with them, began firing at the French.

"But the smoke in the air is still so thick, it's impossible to fire without any clear aim!" Geir yelled at the infantry sergeant.

"And we wasting our good bullets!" Volker bellowed.

Finally, the sergeant gestured at the stream across the road from the field. "Run, now!" he ordered his crouched over men.

It was an order to which they immediately responded.

Geir's legs tingled from the run, making him feel weightless. *Have I been shot?* he wondered, shaking them.

But when a comforting warmth quickly returned to them, he calmed down.

"Who the hell gave the French these weapons?" Volker yelled above the noise.

"The Brits—" Someone behind him answered.

"Damn them!" he cursed.

On the left side of the overturned truck, another canvas military truck heading toward *Rheims*, appeared. The *Strum Horst Wessel* was playing so loudly from it, that coupled with all the grenade explosions, it caused the French, firing their rifles from the road, to retreat into the field.

The soldiers inside the truck quickly jumped out. And pointing their rifles at the now greatly outnumbered partisans they opened fire, closing in on them,

Geir expelled a powerful breath of relief. *Thank God that truck filled with soldiers arrived. And we're safe—*

"Help me—can you help me? "came a fading voice less than a meter away.

The music was still blaring but, somehow, Volker managed to figure out the direction from which the voice came and darted over to a small bush. A man younger than he and Geir lay close to it, his chest opened by a grenade.

"It's the corporal!" Geir hollered, crashing to his senses when he saw the blood spurting from his chest.

Volker stared at the German luger still in the young man's hand. "And he's dying."

Geir uttered an oath "Those bastards got him—and he's in pain!"

Volker's eyes remained fixed on the dying man. "Too bad. But he's our chance. So shoot us in our shins before you leave this earth!" Volker implored him, seemingly unaware the luger had now slipped from the corporal's hand.

That sent Geir's temper soaring. "You're insane —and I can't understand why you're acting like this!" *Bile rose* in his *throat...any second and he'd vomit...* "Because the last words this man heard were you begging him to shoot you in your shin"

Geir's outburst garnered a string of expletives from Volker, before he added, "But he didn't. So now we'll probably end up like him."

"Like him?" Something snapped inside Geir. Volker was now someone he didn't know. So lifting his hand, he slapped him.

Looking stricken, Volker rubbed his cheek. "What in hell is this about?"

Geir slapped him again— only this time harder. "Don't you know?"

"Look at me, Geir!" Volker ordered, grabbing him by the shoulders and shaking him.

"No—let go of me!" Geir protested, attempting to free himself.

Volker's hands fell to his sides.

Suddenly Geir was more afraid than ever before of dying. "Poor fellow." He dropped on his knees beside the dead corporal. "This could have so easily been us." He gurgled the words as tears streamed down his face. It was the first time he'd even seen anyone die. Recalling when Wilhelm was dying, he'd taken his hand and told him to go with Otto to the Bandts' apartment, where he was to stay for a few days.

"So that's what this is all about?" Volker asked.

"No. "Geir wiped his eyes with the heel of his hand. "It's more. My father and I were concerned for you, so we brought you here to show you what a venereal disease can do to a man—"

"And you did the right thing."

"Even if you nearly got us killed?"

"Look, if this man would have lived long enough he'd have shot us at our request. And we'd have been out of the Wehrmacht."

"Asking a man who's dying to shoot us is a cruel and heartless thing to do," Geir accused him.

"Like being conscripted into the Wehrmacht isn't?" Volker asked. Which, to me, is just as cruel and heartless. So, consider this—you're right about the venereal disease. However, we almost made it out of the Wehrmacht with this man who just died. Which means this is a sign, Geir, don't you see it?"

"A sign of what?" He bristled. "When I'll always see that corporal's face."

"A sign of destiny," Volker said loudly "Something you're always talking about."

"That's because I interpret *destiny* one way, and you do another. So *no*, I don't see this as a sign of that."

"Then stand by and watch," he challenged him. "Since the lines between right and wrong are often blurred."

CHAPTER FOURTEEN

When Geir and Volker finally reached Paris, their generals insisted they go to the hospital because of the shrapnel cuts on their arms. They'd managed to patch them up, but still the generals were concerned. "You've experienced such an unexpected delirium of partisan terror, it's the right thing to do," they said. "And you may consider those shrapnel cuts minor, but an infection could set in."

"Quite true," Volker agreed." So off to the hospital we go."

Where to their good fortune, a doctor there ordered them three days of rest.

"It won't be long before Greta, Daniel, Hedy, and Charlotte arrive. And we'll tell them about our combat experience when they do," Geir told Volker.

"Hospital workers see a lot. So I doubt they'll be surprised when I tell them that arranging for me to meet Louis Becker, nearly got us killed."

"Something we should merely skim over in our letters," said Geir. "Saying that we got attacked

by some partisans on the way back, but the outstanding,German infantry soldiers in a truck, took care of them."

"But what about my mother and father?" Volker asked. "They'll want to know the attack details."

"They will," Geir assured him—"after we've talked to Daniel and Hedy.

"Think my parents will tell Margit about the partisan attack?"

"I'll let Daniel and Greta handle that." Geir paused and took a breath. *There was really no clear plan for discussing combat experiences with family. Who probably shouldn't be told anything."*

"Then if you want to handle things like this, I'll go along with it until Daniel arrives," Volker replied." Because under no circumstances, do I want anyone in the family —other than you, Daniel, and Hedy—to know why we visited Louis Becker."

"Otto will know."

"Yes. Your psychic, Uncle Otto."

The weeks rushed by with Geir soon receiving a telegram from Daniel that read: "We're on the way. "My father was certainly right when he said the end of October would be here before we knew it," he remarked to Volker.

And arriving on a Thursday afternoon, Daniel, Greta, Hedy, and Charlotte would be staying until Tuesday morning.

"I love you more than anything," Geir told Hedy upon her arrival. He put his arms around her at the station in an unstrained, welcoming hug.

"I've been terribly frightened ever since you and those men in that truck came under such a violent attack," she said, returning his hug." And feared we might never be together again."

"Who told you it was a violent attack?"

"Otto." A look of alarm passed over her face. "But as long as you're in Paris it's fine, still—"

"I'm not ready to die for a cause I don't believe in," Geir interjected. "So one way or another everything will turn out the way we want." He swallowed hard. "The war will end. The bombs will stop falling on Berlin. And we'll go back to living our lives the way they were meant to be." He refused to add that during the *Rheims* attack, their happiness had come within a hair of vanishing.

Geir and Volker hugged Daniel and Greta, but weren't able to hug Charlotte, since Nicholas had put his arms around her the minute she'd stepped from the train. "We'll meet up at the Ritz," she said, waving a cheerful good-bye at everyone.

Daniel had arranged for three suites at the Ritz. "That beautiful hotel that was once the swanky home of the *Lost Generation*—my generation, "he said, handing Geir their reservations.

"But now Nazi headquarters. With you and Volker working for some generals who encouraged us to stay there, since we're here on German business."

Geir glanced at the reservations. One of the suites was for his father and Greta, the other for Hedy, and the third for Charlotte and Nicholas.

"Great to be on German business in Paris," Charlotte had written in the letters she'd sent Volker and Geir.

Because Nicholas was getting married, he had been given permission to spend Saturday, Sunday, and Monday nights at the Ritz. "And not at the barracks!" he shouted, overjoyed.

Nevertheless, where Geir was concerned permission to spend his nights with Hedy at the Ritz had not been granted. "The circumstance of having a wife visiting in the city is a bit unusual," General Sauer had explained. "So given that, you'll be required to continue to spend your nights at the barracks."

Daniel had then written Geir:

"I realize you and Volker are working out of the Ritz for your generals. So why don't I treat General Sauer to dinner there? That way I just might be able to talk him into letting you spend some nights with Hedy at the hotel."

But since Geir knew that given the uniqueness of his situation, he 'd probably receive some unwelcome responses from the other soldiers in his barracks if he stayed there. So in a letter he wrote Daniel, he advised him not to say anything to General Sauer about it,

"Son, "Daniel said, once they were outside the train station." I still think you need to stay at the Ritz with Hedy in one of the hotel's palatial suites."

"There's nothing I'd like better—"

"Then I'll make it happen," Daniel promised. He went over to a cab parked at the curb, And told the driver, "Take us to the Ritz right away."

The man immediately smiled and stepping back, opened the door for Geir, Hedy, and Greta, who insisted Geir scoot in next to Hedy, since Daniel would be riding in the front with the driver.

The afternoon sky had an overcast with a slight drizzle, so the streets were vacant, allowing the cab to get to the hotel without any delays.

"Coco Chanel has a room at the Ritz," Greta remarked." That gossip maintains her Nazi lover, Baron Abwehr, made possible for her. And although her fashion boutique is closed, her fragrance shop on 31 Rue de Cambon is still open."

"And she still keeps an apartment above it?" Hedy asked.

"From what I hear."

"But didn't she write you she had some clothing from her boutique for sell in her room, at the hotel?" Daniel asked.

"Well," said Greta. "Since Coco and I get along quite well, she volunteered to help Charlotte put together the attire for her Saturday wedding. And also, she mentioned she'd stashed some pieces of clothing from her boutique that she thinks I'd like, as well as Hedy." She appeared to give it some thought, before adding, "And hopefully Margit. Since we're surprising her with a Chanel suit."

Geir thanked her effusively. "My aunt will be overwhelmed."

"She deserves it." Greta patted his hand. "For the way she raised my daughter's wonderful husband."

The sun was coming out by the time they reached the Ritz. "Wow!" Daniel said, an excited expression on his face. "How about after we get checked in, we sit outside on the terrace at one of the tables and sip some wine —with sunlight shinning on us?"

"Any other time," Greta replied, removing some notes from her handbag. "But since Charlotte wants me to help put her wedding attire together, Coco wrote she'll be expecting to see me as soon as I arrive."

"Then Hedy and I will sip some wine." Daniel grinned. "So what'd you say, Geir, can you join us?"

"Since I worked through my lunch break with deliveries, I'll have the time."

"Good. Then I'll tell the waiter to bring us a double order of *hors d'oeuvres*."

"The *hors d'oeuvres* here are excellent," said Hedy, squeezing his hand.

"I wouldn't know. But what do you like?"

"Their deviled eggs, turkey sandwiches with brie cheese, mini quiches, and the wonderful pastries that vary from day to day."

Everything sounded so good, Geir wondered if he'd heard her correctly. "All delicious I'm sure.

So order what you think we'd like."

He was grateful for this opportunity to go over the details of the *Rheims* attack with Hedy and his father. And he gave the waiter in coattails, a friendly smile as he ushered them to one of the larger tables. It was draped in white-linen, with the silverware on it shining in the bright sunlight.

Exactly like the silvery icing on the pastries in the rolling, tiered carts, the waiters are offering the guests. Geir noticed, his smile widening.

Daniel and Hedy were eager to learn what had happened during the attack, prompting Geir to begin talking the minute the wine and food arrived. When he finished the part about slapping Volker— because of the way he'd talked to the drying corporal —Hedy and Daniel shook their heads and each said, "Mother of God."

It was exactly the reaction Geir had expected from them. Yet, he had no suggestions as what to do if something like that happened again. Finally, Daniel, inhaling deeply on his cigarette, remarked, "All I've got to say, Son, is just be thankful you and Volker are alive."

"We are but—"

"I'm trying to see you and Hedy get to spend the night together" Daniel said, re-directing the conversation. "So we'll have dinner tonight around eight in one of my favorite dining rooms here. Which— as was told me by a bellhop earlier-is also one of your General Sauer's favored eating places. And he usually dines there around eight. So introduce me to him. Since like I've implied, if I can befriend him in some way then, hopefully, he'll also allow you and Volker to stay on here as couriers when Germany goes to war with Russia."

"You're doing all you can do," Geir remarked, checking his watch. "And though this is the best lunch I've ever had, it's time for me to finish my deliveries."

"We'll dine tonight," said Daniel, stabbing out his cigarette in an ash tray. "And we'll get up early and breakfast with you here. So feel to bring Volker, Nicholas, and that other fellow, Rene. who works with you."

Hedy took Geir's hand. "And I'll be there too."

"Absolutely. "Struck dumb with pleasure, he gave her a long, lingering kiss before pulling her towards him and wrapping his hands around her shoulders, squeezing them tightly. "Eating breakfast with you in this extraordinary place, certainly beats the *Kommando* mess hall."

⸻ ◆ ⸻

At eight that evening Geir, Daniel, Volker, Nicholas, and Rene Gonard stood outside one of the Ritz's most favored restaurants, waiting for Greta,

Hedy, and Charlotte to appear. It wasn't that late, and when they appeared, Greta was filled with apologies. She held up a folder, explaining it had the information Coco had given her concerning the wedding. And filled with delight, Charlotte said they were late because she'd read and re-read what this famous French designer had written and was so excited, it had taken her breath away. "Making me incapable of speech for a brief time," she explained, giving her future husband a hug.

"Then all's well." Daniel smiled, his excitement evident as he motioned the head waiter to show them to their table.

Hedy looked fantastic. "I see you're wearing one of Chanel's little black dresses, with some silver in it," said Geir, with an air of familiarity.

"So you know?"

"Hayim copied enough of them for his female clients." She was also wearing a white fox shrug, and emerald-drop necklace that matched her eyes. Geir touched it lightly. "You couldn't ask for a more flattering piece of jewelry."

As usual, she impacted the hotel's restaurant with her present. And the guests couldn't stop staring at her and Greta, who wore a mink stole with her a gold dress. Charlotte wasn't dressed as elegantly, but made an impressive appearance with her blond hair in a tight bun. *Like a golden halo.* Geir admired, pleased she was developing a sense of style.

The smoked lobster on the menu was everyone's choice. "By far the best," Volker remarked, handing the waiter his menu.

Daniel placed the orders. And at his request had the waiter bring out one of the hotel's finest wines. They raised their glasses, toasting Charlotte and Nicholas's wedding.

When, suddenly, escorted by a waiter, General Sauer appeared. Recognizing Geir he immediately headed straight to his table. "Well now," he said, stopping next to him. "I hadn't expected to see my courier dining here."

Geir stood up and did a small bow, acknowledging the man's superiority. An action that prompted Volker, Nicholas, and Rene to do likewise.

Daniel then stood up and extended his hand to the man. "Geir is my son-in-law. And he's had nothing but good things to say about you."

"Pleased to hear it."

"I'm co-owner of a communications equipment business the military is using," Daniel informed him. "And I'm meeting with some of your military officials, who are working with it tomorrow morning."

"Can't run the military without sound communication equipment," General Sauer remarked.

"And we feel ours is the best," Daniel bragged.

"At ease, soldiers." The general smiled indulgently. "I appreciate the respect, but you don't have to be so formal in this extraordinary eating place."

They took their seats, but Daniel remained standing as he proceeded to introduce Greta, Charlotte, and Hedy. "My pleasure," said the general with a slight bow. He then turned to Hedy. "Nicholas told me you looked like a cinema star, when he mentioned you and Charlotte would be doing a demonstration tomorrow at one or two of the hospitals here."

"I appreciate the compliment, General," said Hedy. "But I'm a nurse and love it."

"Even so, looking like a cinema star and being a nurse should bring joy to your patients."

"Anything to help them recover."

"We welcome your company, "Daniel told the general. "So feel free to join us."

But he shook his head. "I thank you. But tonight I'm meeting some people on business, in one of the private rooms here."

Daniel sat back down. "Then we mustn't keep you."

Sauer spun around to leave but stopped. "Private Gallen, I'm granting you permission to spend the next five nights here and not at the barracks."

"And I thank you, sir," he said, rising and bowing again.

"Think nothing of it." The general winked." Because I know from experience that a soldier takes his pleasures when they're present." He touched Geir's shoulder before departing.

"I'm bursting with impatience," Hedy whispered to Geir.

"I know the feeling," he remarked, grinning smugly.

The waiter began serving the food, with the smoked lobster bringing accolades from everyone at the table. "It's exploding in my mouth with a deliciousness that defies description," Geir marveled.

"Same as mine," Hedy said.

When they finished, desert arrived: a pear in caramel sauce topped with vanilla ice cream.

"An excellent compliment to our smoked lobster," said Nicholas, taking his fork and diving into it.

Like the others at the table, Geir and Hedy devoured it quickly. But unlike the others, they excused themselves the minute they finished and made a hasty departure to their suite.

"I thought this moment would never come," said Hedy, clearly aching with desire as she striped out of her black dress.

Geir struggled to get his tunic off. "Me either."

"Here let me help you." She unfastened his pants, and then put her mouth on him.

"My God, Hedy, I'm falling apart—"

"My intention."

"This is bliss beyond my wildest dreams."

"I'm so thankful General Sauer is letting you spend your nights here."

"Obviously a relief. Since I expected we'd have to be sneaking around when I slipped away from my deliveries, to enjoy each other like this."

"Sneaking around between deliveries sounds like fun."

"Mustn't lose our precious time together," he said, his fingers touching her breasts. "Because it's not right this *damn* war is keeping us from being together."

"It isn't. So whenever we're together, we'll have to make up for lost time."

"My thought exactly."

They made love several times before they fell asleep. And when morning came, he stopped and kissed her multiple times while putting on his uniform. "I have to get to the barracks and grab my pack. So I'll have a fresh change of clothes."

"Fine. Because Charlotte and I have to be at the hospital early for our demonstration."

"Which means we'll have breakfast as soon as I get back."

"I'll be waiting."

Surprising Geir and Hedy, Nicholas and Charlotte joined them for breakfast. Prompting Geir to whisper to Hedy, "I take it they started their honeymoon early?"

"They did."

"Good for them."

Charlotte's wedding was tomorrow afternoon in a small chapel nearby. "This afternoon Mom and I are taking Charlotte to have a look at the wedding suit Coco recommended," Hedy told Geir, "which Daniel is buying for her, since he's insisting her wedding is on him."

"He has such a good heart, but what about our lunch? Will we be meeting back here for it?"

"Yes," she said, followed by a shift in conversation. "Since I have a favor to ask of you."

"A favor?" He lifted his brows "Then by all means ask me."

Hedy blushed like someone embarrassed. "I want you to take me to Francine's Hotel."

"What?" he replied disbelievingly. *Was he blushing too?* "You've got to kidding."

"I'm not. We've been treating some prostitutes in the hospital, with whom I tend to be a bit standoffish. Which as a nurse— pledged to taking care of people— isn't good. So I talked to Dr. Rath about my visiting Francine's, and he thought it might give me some insight into these women."

Geir pulled her toward him. "Your dedication has never ceased to amaze me, when I think how you could have been a cinema star. Yet, chose to help humanity and become my beautiful wife. Which makes me question at times, if I'm worthy of you.

She kissed his cheek. "More than anyone else in the world."

"You're so very special. So *yes*, I'll take you to Francine's tomorrow."

CHAPTER FIFTEEN

When Geir entered Francine's Hotel with Hedy in her nurse's uniform, Francine was taken aback "My goodness, you're bringing a movie star to my place!" she exclaimed, her voice rising in surprise.

Geir's arms circled Hedy. "I told you she was my wife and a nurse, but you didn't believe me."

"Well I'll be darned," she said, gripping Hedy's hand and shaking it with enthusiasm.

The girls were watching from the second floor near the staircase. "Can we talk to her?" one of them asked.

Francine stared at Hedy with admiration. "If she doesn't have any objection."

"I don't."

Soon the eight girls were buzzing around her and asking her questions, exactly as they would have done a celebrity come to visit. Most of the questions were medical ones. However, if Hedy didn't know the answers, she had the girls write their questions on a piece of paper and give them to her. "Dr. Rath will know. So I'll send a letter to this hotel informing you what he says."

Francine urged her to visit again when she returned in three months, and Hedy assured her she would. "We'd stay longer, but we have a wedding to attend," she told Francine.

"Then we mustn't keep you," the older woman said.

"You handled everything quite well, " Geir complimented Hedy on their way out.

She took a deep breath and smiled. "Maybe now I won't be standoffish with some of the prostitutes who come to the hospital. "

"I can't imagine you ever being standoffish."

"I try not to be but despite my good intentions, I sometimes catch myself doing it."

Geir glanced at a large clock across the street. "We'll have to hurry if we're going to make that wedding at two o'clock.

"I agree."

They hurried back to the hotel and changed quickly.

"It's good this wedding's in this small chapel nearby." Geir remarked.

"Daniel made it possible." Hedy beamed.

"Sounds like my father."

Charlotte wore a beige suit with a pink rose on its collar, that matched the one on her hat with its veil And Nicholas wore his uniform. They made a lovely couple.

Afterwards, they went back to the Ritz Hotel where a large cake awaited them.

Hedy snapped pictures of the couple cutting it and then, smiling, as they fed each other small pieces of it.

Admiring it, Charlotte stepped back to get a better look. "The Ritz has certainly out done itself with this beautiful cake and—"

"I'd agree if it weren't so large," Volker butted in. "But who can eat all that?"

"The hotel is refrigerating it until we leave Tuesday morning," Charlotte told him. "Then they'll pack it in a large box. Which I'll take back to Berlin for everyone at the boardinghouse, and Dr. Rath at the hospital."

And surprise of surprises, Daniel sent round-trip train tickets to Berlin to Nicholas's parents. "With an invitation to stay at the boardinghouse," Charlotte said. "So, that way, we can get to know each other."

Nicholas put his arm around Charlotte. "I told them they'd love my wife so much, they'd accept Daniel's offer to spend Christmas with her in Berlin."

"Which reminds me," Geir whispered to Hedy. "What's the boardinghouse doing for Christmas?"

"Well." She sighed. "Due to shortages and long food lines, not as much as last year."

"And gifts? You're getting part of my pay—"

"Which I don't need to be getting."

"Neither do I, with Daniel stuffing money in my pocket every chance he gets."

"This Christmas we've agreed to give each other food gifts, Hedy informed him. And after Otto drives Mom, Charlotte, and me to the hospital, the Schroders are going out to grocery stores, buying stuff that won't be there when Christmas comes."

"Are there any other gifts besides food, you're giving each other?"

"Otto and I are sending you books. And Margit and Alvina, once again, are knitting socks for you and Volker. And of course, you and Volker will be getting some small cakes, cookies, chocolate, and other treats that we'll mail."

"Since you don't need my money like you keep saying, then how about taking some of it and buying gifts from Volker and me, to give to our boardinghouse residents?"

"If that's what you want but—"

"What? Since you're the most important person on my list, Hedy, what can I get you? And let me buy it here while you're in Paris —an early Christmas present."

She laid her hand on his arm." Geir, you don't need to—"

"Yes I do," he insisted. "So tell me something you've seen you like."

"A rose-colored scarf at the boutique where we bought Charlotte's wedding suit."

"Is it expensive?"

"It's not cheap."

"Good. Then we'll go there Monday during my lunch break, and I'll buy it for you.

But sadly, Monday came all too quickly. And Tuesday morning when Geir stood beside Hedy, who was waiting to board the train, she had it wrapped around her neck.

"Looks lovely on you, my beautiful Hedy," he told her— "Whom I loved from the moment I first met."

They kissed. And then the train's departure whistle blew. "Don't forget, "said Hedy, "we'll be back around the first of March."

"How could I ever forget?" He smiled, as Greta motioned her to hurry and get on board with Daniel and Charlotte."

<hr>

The months passed. March came with a visit and June another.

Then the big punch came. Germany declared war on Russia. Fortunately though, Geir, Volker, and Nicholas, now a corporal, were lucky enough to be allowed to stay in Paris.

"Dr. Rath's doing good work," Daniel bragged on him.

He continued to go to Paris several times a year, bringing Greta, Hedy, and Charlotte. And each time Hedy came, she and Geir would visit Francine.

Twice Geir, Volker, and Nicholas were ordered to Berlin to deliver sensitive information to three generals there.

"True to Otto's prediction, the Americans are now in the war," Volker remarked.

"And between the R.A.F. and the U.S.A.F. the bombardments falling on Berlin and other German cities, they're not safe places to be," Geir said, unpleasant images building in his mind.

Still, it delighted him to spend time with Margit, the Schroders, and the Bandts. And to meet Nicholas's parents. They were quick to visit whenever Daniel sent the round-trip train tickets and informed them of their son's intended visit. "We've got it better than most soldiers," Geir would remind Volker and Nicholas. Who would quickly agree.

Their last trip to Berlin was in June of 'forty-two, and Daniel took them to the train station, where he led them toward a concourse lined with box cars. Frightened looking men, women, and children with suitcases, were being prodded into the cars by soldiers with their rifle butts.

Geir was appalled. "Are they who we think they are?" he asked Daniel.

He nodded. "They're Jews— who're being taken away from here."

Volker shook his head. "But where on earth are they going? "Most likely to a work camp in Poland," said Daniel. "But as yet, nobody's doing much talking. The news we're getting from others appears to be scrambled. So, it's like we *know* but don't *know*."

Geir took his arm. "Those people being prodded into the car by the SS. They're going to be killed, aren't they? Like those school girls in Poland."

"What Otto thinks. Though later, Otto apologized to me. 'There's more negative energy in the world than positive energy,' he told me. 'But positive energy is stronger...something you need to keep in mind, since nothing is truly written in stone.'

"Nobody deserves to be treated like those Jews," Nicholas said angrily.

"Yet we're supporting this by being in the Wehrmacht. "Volker flared. "With no way to get out—" "And here I stand with no way I can help *you*, "said Daniel, a tear on his cheek. "Or help these people...*my* people."

Geir was alarmed. "There's got to be a way," he insisted. "Surely Otto has some ideas you've discussed with him."

Daniel wiped his eyes with his fingers. "Others in the household have tried but learned nothing. And as for me, all Otto told me was a story."

"A story?" Volker questioned, clearly intrigued. "Why didn't you tell us?"

"Because it deals with learning to survive, "Daniel said. "Or overcoming yourself. Which depends on finding and touching the strength in your soul. Something I've not been able to do." His amber-eyes widened."Even if I hope to do so before I die."

"Still," Volker persisted. "Otto must have given you some kind of instruction on how to find this strength in your soul."

"But he didn't," Daniel remarked, appearing to think about it carefully before continuing. "Just this true story he told me was about a middle-aged man from India who'd moved to London. And this man had brought a twenty-page horoscope with him, that he'd paid an Indian woman to make for him. Which was quite complete. Even mentioning his wife, three children and his move to London. But then it stopped. Making it obvious the woman had cheated him by taking his money for something she hadn't finished. And he needed this information about his future and his family's in this new country. So he showed the horoscope to several Indian people in London, who did horoscopes. And they agreed that he'd been cheated. Suggesting that when he went back to India, he should take it to the woman and demand she finish it. However, one British woman did look at it and say it had ended. What? His life? But she did not answer. Otto said that he must not have believed her, because the plane he was taking back to India for business reasons, crashed—killing everyone on board."

"But what has all that got to do with us?" Volker asked. "Or the poor souls in those boxcars being deported?"

"It's simple," Daniel said. "This Indian woman who did the horoscope left the man to finish it. In other words, so Otto believed, she left the door open. Which leads me to believe that it's what Otto would say about those unprepared people in the boxcars and *us*—"

"Which is, *Herr* Birnbaum?" Nicholas interrupted.

"That nothing can get to you if you don't let it. And if you're so inclined, then you have to learn to build, subconsciously, a shield of determination that you keep close. Like citizens in Hollywood's Westerns who lived in the townships and kept their weapons hidden in or under their clothing. A trick aiding them in surviving the terrible odds that often came their way."

Nicholas looked confused. "But don't you imagine there'll still be times, when a person will actually want to give up and die?"

"Oh yes," Daniel agreed.

"And *luck*?" questioned Volker. "You didn't mention it but don't underestimate it. Since regardless of a person's determination, it'll factor into whether he or she survives—"

"This is a lot to take in," Geir interjected, contemplating it.

"I disagree," said Volker." A dying soldier shoots us in the shins and we survive. And *that's* my shield of determination."

"Even if this dying soldier,like we found outside *Rheims*, dies before he can shoot us?" Geir asked.

A smile lit Volker's face as he bowed slightly. "That's where luck comes in. So, maybe next time this dying soldier will have enough life left in him to shoot us and then die."

"But what if this soldier doesn't die quickly and reports you to his superior? "Daniel asked, his sorrowful look appearing to draw Volker's attention.

"The soldier, who'll shoot us, will be begging us to shoot him. Since he'll be dying in great pain."

A thought that never failed to unnerve Geir, "Which seems so heartless," he remarked, losing count of the number of times he'd said it.

"Not when it's about survival, *war buddy*," said Volker. "So why do I have to keep reminding you that if we're going to live to be old men— then one way or another—we'll need to find a way that'll get us out of an Eastern Front death sentence?"

"I don't blame you, Volker, for not wanting to die for the Wehrmacht in Russia," Daniel spoke up. "But what about those people in the cattle or boxcars?" He gestured at them with a bewildered look.

"Would you die for them?"

"If I'm not in the Wehrmacht, then it's one less soldier fighting against them. And besides, war often robs a man of feelings."

CHAPTER SIXTEEN

Geir hated to admit it, but it appeared his friendship with Volker was losing ground with each passing day. *We're continuing to grow apart in our thinking. But war brothers we are, so what can I say? Especially on the fifth of December when new orders came.*

Volker and I are to go to Minsk—the dreaded Eastern Front on the twentieth of December. Where it's already unbearably cold. But Nicholas and Rene Gonard are to remain in Paris, since both men speak French and have studied at a university for two years.

Volker, Nicholas, and I have been given a fourteen-day leave. Where Nicholas will be spending his in Berlin with his parents, who'll be visiting at the boardinghouse.

Geir had ever intention of spending his days with Hedy. In fact, she'd even taken off from her nursing for fourteen days. "Don't worry. After you leave I'll work seven days a week to **makeup** the time."

"I find it amazing you have more money than any young woman I've ever met. Yet, you have a dedication to a career that doesn't pay half of what you're worth."

"If I can help people in small or large ways by taking care of them, then that's worth more to me than all the money in the world."

"I sometimes think you're an angel sent to us."

"No, if I were." Hedy sobbed. "Then you and Volker wouldn't be headed to the Eastern Front."

That brought tears, not only from her, but Daniel and Margit, who sat in the living room blaming themselves. "My entire fault—like I keep saying," Daniel would remark with tear-filled eyes.

"And as much as I hate the Wehrmacht— which is clearly the wrong army—I'd gladly go in your place, Geir, if they'd let me."

"If only I'd come to Berlin a week early," Hedy would say, misty-eyed.

"But you didn't know," said Margit, crying and squeezing her hand. "And me? I ached for a child—a gift from God. And even though I kept begging Daniel to take Geir, I knew that deep inside I'd never let him."

"Please!" Geir would urge them. "Stop blaming yourselves."

Then Otto would continue to add, that a great good would come from all this. However, he refused to elaborate, making Geir wonder if it didn't have something to do with saving Jewish lives.

But Volker didn't appear to be concerned about that. "We're headed to the *damned* Eastern Front to be killed. Where're we're hearing reports that Russians are target practicing, using German prisoners tied to a fence. And the Germans are tying Russian prisoners to trees and throwing grenades at them, so they'll die painful deaths. And sometimes. "He paused, as if making sure he had everyone's attention. "One German soldier is fighting twenty Russians."

"And that damned Eastern Front can get as low as twenty-five degrees below zero," Daniel would point out. "With many saying that hospitals on the front are often in trenches. Where the men just lay here and die. And there're long silences between soldiers and their families, because those on the front are so tired at night from shoveling snow and fighting the cold, they don't feel like writing home."

Such information brought an immediate onslaught of tears from Margit and Hedy. "Please," said Geir, pulling them aside. "We must try hard not to let this brief time we have together be spoiled with tears. So don't be sad."

"Can't be helped." Margit sniffed.

But Hedy promised she'd do her best not to let it. "Because I don't plan on leaving your side—And as for long silences, just write one letter to me that I can share with the household."

Geir kissed her. "You and I belong to each other— always and forever."

"And then we'd smile," he wrote later. *"Like we were happy, when we weren't. For my upcoming departure was stealing the sheer pleasure of the moment. And at night, in the morning, and sometimes in the middle of the day, we'd make love...wild emotions running through us. Making me fear we might never be like this again.*

So is this end for me, as it is for so many German soldiers? I wanted to ask Otto but knew better. Especially after that story he'd told Daniel about the man from India. "

Since the days were passing quickly Geir suggested to Hedy they picnic at Lake Wannsee before he left. "A wonderful idea," she agreed. "So let's do it tomorrow, when it's supposed to be sunny and fairly warm.

'Lake Wannsee makes me feel like the rest of the world has ceased to exist,' he was about to say, when he heard the ominous howling of the insistent sirens. *A grim chorus in the night's darkness, signaling many will die.* So quickly grabbing Hedy by the arm they raced with Daniel, and the rest of the household to the boardinghouse's shelter in its cellar.

Objects fell against the house, and the floor trembled each time a throbbing bomber from the enemy flew over. "My God!" Margit gasped, staring at the shaking walls, with a violence that threatened to shatter them.

The noises grew louder and louder— "I think our anti-aircraft guns are firing from balconies-like newspapers have mentioned!" Otto shouted above the noise.

The sky roared so loudly with German fighters from Tempelhof, that at times Geir could have sworn they were sweeping over the boardinghouse's roof.

The bombardment went on for an hour, until its brutal hurricane of fire and explosions, finally died. Then, a minute of heavy silence followed before everyone began making their way up the cellar's steps.

"I hope the Mercedes didn't get hit," Geir told Otto

"It shouldn't... considering Daniel and I hired people two weeks ago to do some more work on the garage. So that way, its structure should be even sounder—"

"Now comes being impressed into a cleanup squad," interrupted Volker, frowning. "But since we're soldiers on leave, we're really not expected to participate."

"Maybe not," said Daniel, mirroring his frown. "But I live here and am obligated to give people a hand in these terrible times. "He motioned at Ernst, Nicholas, and his father, Karl Reicke." So we need to see where they want us to work."

"On leave or not, we're needed," Geir told Volker. "So follow me."

Which reluctantly he did.

The Schroders were already outside waiting for their special team. "Since we have a reputation for locating the bombs dropped that are set to explode in the next twelve hours," Otto informed Nicholas's father. Fritz insisted on going with them, even if he couldn't do much. So the other two Schroders allowed their hobbling cousin to come, provided he stood a good distance back from where they were working. "That way, should we need some more help, you'll be in a position to motion at someone," Hugo told him.

"Some of the boardinghouse's front windows are shattered." Otto showed Daniel, pointing at them. "But I'll see they get fixed."

"No need. You do enough around here."

Otto shook his head, "Not really."

Expected to join the first-aid teams to help with the wounded, Charlotte and Hedy hurried in their direction, carrying their nurses' caps, jackets, and medical bags.

Geir still marveled that Daniel was living here in this war-torn city when he, Greta, and Hedy could be living in their Swiss chalet. And he often felt guilty they weren't. *Still, I'd have never believed Daniel would do such a thing for me. Which shows he's a courageous man who really loves me. Or why else would he be living here?*

———◆———

It was an exhausting night, and Geir and Hedy slept till noon. But when they awoke, a shaft of sunlight bled through the windows. And she smiled as she looked at it. "It's filled with a variety of possibilities. One of which is like trying to color the blood from last night, with a brightness that will lift the spirits of those injured. So let's go to Lake Wannsee as planned, where we can get away from all this destruction."

"We really should. And Otto will take us there and come back for us at the time we tell him."

Margit was pleased with their decision and insisted on putting together the covered basket with their picnic fare. And Daniel, coming from the cellar, handed them a bottle of burgundy, two small glasses, and a corkscrew.

Otto already had the Mercedes parked in front of the house. And dangling its keys, he urged Hedy and Geir to get in. The streets were still scattered with a good deal of debris and rubble. Although, much of it had been pushed aside so traffic could flow down the middle. "Berlin always tries to maintain something of its usual order after a bombardment," Otto remarked, driving around some wreckage yet to be cleared.

There was a lot of damage, and Geir saw numerous, ochre flames still flickering in a good many of the buildings they passed.

"There'll be funerals for the next two days," Hedy said. "If not longer."

Two days is all I have left. Geir sighed. *Which is not much time.*

Otto drove them to a sandy part of the lake that looked relatively unscathed. "Don't see any people," he said, glancing around. "Which from the looks of it means you and Hedy are going to have it all to yourselves."

Geir told him to be back at three o'clock in the same place. "Or otherwise,we'll have to take a motorbike taxi, "he teased.

"You know I'll be here." Otto chuckled." So, you and Hedy enjoy yourselves and take a nap if you feel like it." He tossed him the quilt on the front seat. "Since the chill in the air isn't too bad for this time of year, with the warm coats you have on."

Taking the picnic basket, Geir led the way to a place with tall trees, grass, and a single bench. Then covering it with the quilt, he and Hedy sat down.

The air had a dusty smell, but it wasn't nearly as bad as it had been last night.

"How about some wine?" he asked, lifting the basket's cover for the bottle of burgundy.

"After last night I think we could both use it."

"I agree."

She held the two small glasses as he skillfully uncorked the bottle with the corkscrew. "We need a proper toast." He grinned, filling the glasses. "Got any ideas?"

"So many I don't know where to begin. But since you're the one on leave, you make it."

His grin increased. "To the end of the war, and the start of our family."

Their glasses clinked and, smiling, she leaned over and kissed his cheek. "That's beautiful."

"As is this sudden, pleasant smell."

"From the wine or our surroundings?"

"Both."

A soft breeze stirred the air with an occasional hint of fragrance, he had difficulty placing.

Was it sunflowers? If it was, he didn't see any around.

Hedy removed the basket's cover. "Tell me, are you hungry?"

We didn't have breakfast so *yes*—very."

She rummaged through the basket. "We have dark bread, sausage rolls, Edam cheeses, ham, pickles, and gingerbread cookies."

"Margit's put together a feast."

"Like she always does when we come here."

They ate quickly, finishing everything in the basket. And afterwards, Geir took the quilt and spread it under a tree where, surprisingly, birds were singing. His grin returned as he lay down on it.

"They're happy because they've survived."

Hedy's eyes beamed with delight. "As did their peaceful song," she reminded, stretching out on the quilt beside him.

Their hands joined as they looked at the heavens. Happiness was flooding him like it was clearly flooding her. "We've yet to make love outside—"

"To my regret."

"Then there's no time like the present."

"Think anyone will see us?"

"Not with this lake void of people. But even so, we should probably just adjust our clothes."

"Definitely."

Her words spiked a strong desire in him. And unzipping his fly, he smiled as she slid out of panties, stuffed them in her coat pocket, and raised her skirt.

His skin flamed through hers as she opened her body to him. And looking into her eager face he realized that if he lived to be a hundred, he could never get enough of her...*Hedy. My love. My life.*

Tremors of excitement splashed across her face each time he kissed her passionately. And trembling from what was obviously pleasure rippling through her, she called his name several times as she melted in a long shudder of desire. Her gentle hands gripped his shoulders after her waves of her passion subsided, and with an urgency from this glorious sensual storm surging through him, his fulfillment came, and he collapsed against her.

"So beautiful to witness," she whispered, throwing her back her head.

Replete with satisfaction, a breathless silence followed as he tightened his arms around her. "Only two more nights with your charms," he reminded. "Then God knows what—"

"Shush...don't think about it. And try and get some sleep. We're both still tired."

Taking Hedy's hand he took her advice and closing his eyes, immediately fell asleep.

He had no idea how long he slept, but when sirens began howling, he sprang to his feet.

"Hedy! We've got to find shelter—"

"—but there isn't any!"

He was holding her hand tightly when the sky darkened with a midnight's blackness as hundreds of allied planes thundered over their heads. There were at least fifty German fighters already in the air, but the minute they began firing a window, like a giant's mouth, opened. *A Vortex!*

"Geir—we've got to get away!" Hedy cried. "They're coming for us!"

He tugged at her hand, as the steel from allied guns surrounded them. Then this giant's mouth opening wider, grabbed Hedy and began pulling her away from Geir.

"Hedy!" he yelled, running after her. But the closer he got the farther away she got...her image getting smaller and smaller until his arms and legs went limp, and he fell—

"Geir," said Hedy, shaking him awake." You're having a nightmare."

It was Hedy's voice above him. And when he opened his eyes, she was on the quilt beside him.

Otto had returned and was now standing over them, with a concerned look.

Geir's voice broke. "W...we got attacked, Hedy. And they took *you*— the love of my life."

"Nobody can take you from me—*remember* that. But Otto's here to drive us back to the boardinghouse, so let's go."

Throughout the rest of the day and into the night, Geir couldn't stop thinking about his strange nightmare. *Why had Otto looked so concerned?* But when he approached him about it, he'd merely said, "You're a soldier, Geir, and soldiers need to be light sleepers."

It was late that evening before he and Hedy went to bed. And after they'd made love, his thoughts returned to his peculiar dream. *What did it mean?* Obviously, he was afraid for himself as well as Hedy. *Nothing is uncertain in this kind of world where happiness is mixed with suffering. So is this* the *message my nightmare was sending me...? It certainly* appears *like it.*

When the day of departure finally came, Geir stood with Nicholas at the station, when he returned to Paris early that morning,

But Volker and I are not due at the train station until six in the evening... *almost another full day with Hedy.*

Margit, Greta, Alvina, Charlotte, and Hedy gave Geir and Volker some gifts: heavy pullovers, more knitted socks, fur-lined gloves, soap, a box of tinned food, and some cookies. "But it was these fellows who bought the items and put our names on them," said Greta, sweeping an arm in the direction of Daniel, Ernst, and the Schroders. "They made us promise not to tell, but here I am— unable to keep my mouth shut."

Otto, like Hedy, presented Geir with a book. "Be sure to use some of my money and buy yourself, along with everyone here, Christmas presents," Geir whispered to her.

"I will," she assured him, tears welling in her eyes.

This time, because of bomb damage, the only people coming with them to the station were Hedy, Daniel, and Ernst...with Otto driving, of course.

Earlier when Otto had taken Nicholas's parents to the station, he'd learned that Geir and Volker's Warsaw departure platform was now almost a mile away. So Daniel walked on one side of Geir, and Hedy on the other.

When they reached the platform, flags honoring the soldiers decorated its walls. Daniel hugged Geir, before stuffing some more money in his tunic pocket. "Write when you can. And know that I love you, Son. More than you can imagine. And if I could, I'd go in your place."

"I love you too, Papa," said Geir, returning his hug. "And even if you could go in my place, I wouldn't let you."

He handed Geir a letter. "Read it on the train. And hopefully you'll understand better why you don't have the citizenship you deserved." He heaved a heavy sigh. "Part of which was letting the riff I had with my mother get in the way...and though I never cared for babies, who but a *stupid lout* could deny not loving you, when I held you in my arms."

"Pa, we love each other now—that's the important thing."

Daniel hugged him again. "Then I'd best step back so you can spend these last few minutes with your beloved, Hedy. "

He went over and stood next Ernst and Otto. While Volker, his pack in his hand, was staring at the second carriage on the train. He was shifting back and forth, like he and Geir should hurry and board.

Geir and Hedy stood staring at each other, their hands joined. *She's as uncertain about what to say as I am.*

Soldiers wearing hob-nailed boots jostled them, as they pushed their way into the first carriage.

"Warsaw, Minsk, Russia," the red capped stationmaster called out, announcing the destinations.

"Better get on board," Volker shouted at Geir, a second after the departure whistle blew.

"I'll be back, Hedy— like I have before."

"And I'll be waiting," Tears choked her voice, the same as they were doing his.

So they kissed. "We'll start our family the minute this war is over."

"How I wish. "

The train started to move and Volker tossed his pack, along with Geir's, up the steep carriage steps.

The people on the platform next to Hedy were crying. And she grabbed Geir's hand.

Like me, she's clearly aware that the war, and the fear someone they love won't return, is giving this station a melancholy air.

They continued to hold hands like they'd done before, until the train, picking up speed, forced them to let go.

Leaving Hedy, and going to the Eastern Front is like the Russians are tearing my heart from my body.

And then for some strange, unknown reason it hit him: *something connected with the war will prevent Hedy and I from having the children we so badly want. Even though sex, in this terrible time, is the only thing life is not denying us.*

CHAPTER SEVENTEEN

Geir took the seat Volker had saved for him on the crowded train. "It's better than one of the straw-covered floors in back," he reminded. "Even if the back's supposed to be safer, should we encounter some artillery fire. Although a soldier did tell me earlier about a train in Poland where the coupling on the last car broke, and it slid into a marsh with Polish partisans surrounding it."

"Something certainly unexpected," Geir said, wishing it weren't so noisy in the car.

Most of the people on the train were in the military heading to the Eastern Front. *How many will make it back? Napoleon had failed to conquer Russia, so what made the Fuhrer think he could, he continued to question? A useless slaughter. That's what lies ahead for a good many of these men... like possibly Volker and myself.*

He reached in his pocket for Daniel's letter and began reading it:

Dear Son,

I know there are hard times ahead for you. Which doesn't make this letter any easier for me to write. I also know how I've told you that you were better off with Margit and Wilhelm. Which you were. Since I acted like an adolescent with a shell-shocked brain, when I didn't take you in my arms and head to America with you. It was a harsh thing to do with Margit holding you and begging me to take you. And what did I do? I slammed the door in her face. But it went deeper. I was an only child with a wealthy father, who had passed and left my mother an ample amount of money.

I really never had to work. But I wanted to show the world I could make more money than my father—which I eventually did. My mother was a bitter, unhappy woman whose father had died when she was only four years old.

Years later, I read in a book by a friend of Siegmund Freud's that children whose lose a parent when they're young and don't have counseling, will believe that if they were better, the parent wouldn't have died. So to my thinking my mother grew up disappointed in herself and took it out on me. She considered me a failure all my life. Comparing me to my cousins, who she thought to be much better and smarter than I was. She was eager for a grandchild. Which I came to believe, from the way she talked and acted, would end up being another person she could claim who was better and smarter than I was.

No way was I giving her a grandchild. Babies were a threat to me, so I didn't like them. Even if the love of my life was Noelle. And your face was her face. So yes, there was a time in your infancy I did love you—but after she died my old feelings returned. And I walked away, giving into this unlit part of my heart.

Margit and Wilhelm were extraordinary people. In fact, poor as they were, I wished they'd been my parents. Because eventually, I came to love you a great deal. And it was because of Margit's letters… with Wilhelm always writing a few lines at the bottom of them. You were such a good-looking child in the pictures she sent me. And later, such a handsome, young man.

You belonged to me. And by the time you were ten years old I would have taken you in a heartbeat from Margit and Wilhelm. For you were in the process of becoming a caring, extraordinary person. But if I'd taken you from them, then there's no telling the effect it would have had on you. Plus the effect on Margit and Wilhelm. Which taking you from them, would have been the same as shooting them and leaving them to die, wounded, in the desert.

You and Otto talk about destiny, but it's a small consolation. If I'd done the right thing, I'd have brought you, Margit, and Wilhelm to America. And made sure you three got citizenship. I can't imagine why I didn't, except for a selfishness in me. And now I'm paying the price as you go toward the meat-grinding Eastern Front: cannon fodder for Germans who are murdering Jews.

If you were in the American army I'd see you were in a much better position— an officer rising in the ranks. But I've kept you from this…and I accept my guilt. But if those damn Russians kill you, then I don't think I'll be able to survive.

I'll never forgive myself for being the stupid fool that I've been. You have forgiven me, but I don't deserve such forgiveness.

Thanks to Margit and Wilhelm you're not only the best husband Hedy could ever have, but a much better and stronger man than I ever was. And when my time comes, I'll go to my grave ashamed, for not being more like you.

You have a forgiving heart and goodness in you that transcends anything I've ever seen. So for whatever it's worth, know I'll love you to the end of time.

Your father,
Daniel

Geir read the letter several times. Then reaching into his pack he removed some paper and the book Hedy had given him. He put the paper on top of it and began composing a letter to Daniel.

Volker was complaining to a soldier across the aisle about their leave being so short. "Got a girlfriend here?" the soldier asked him.

"No, but he has a wife." He pointed at Geir.

"A wife. He's young to be married. Since I read somewhere a man's brain isn't fully developed until he's twenty-five.

"What I keep reminding him," said Volker.

"He's missin' out on a lot of girlie fun. But once on the front, shootin' Russians will prove to be fun too."

The talk angered Geir so much he caught his breath to ease his fury. "Damn!" He turned toward the window and quickly began writing:

My dearest father,

You've done for me what no one else could do. And had you taken me to America, even with Margit and Wilhelm, I doubt you would have ever met Greta and Hedy. Destiny was my meeting Hedy. And if my ending up going to the Eastern Front was the price I had to pay for meeting her, then I'll gladly pay it. I pray God will keep me safe while I'm there. But if I don't make it back, then all I ask is that you be there for Hedy. So stop blaming yourself, because I'm being forced to go to Russia. Things are playing out the way they were meant to do. Which is why you must take care of yourself.

Your loving son,
Geir

It was well passed midnight when they arrived in Warsaw. He and Volker's train passes had to be stamped by the military police before they could be given the number of the train they'd be taking to Minsk. *The reason being there were a lot of trains crowded with soldiers heading non-stop to the front: our dreaded journey eastward. Although fortunately for us, when we reached our numbered train, we were given some food and something to drink. Then, herded by the military police to one of the straw-covered floors in back. Where there were more green-uniformed men than had been on that canvas-truck, taking Volker and I from Rheims to Paris.*

It was a tight squeeze, and Geir was pleased Volker found a place, so he quickly jammed himself against the other soldiers.

He and Geir sat on their packs on the floor. And though it was difficult to sleep, from time to time they managed to doze.

They changed trains on the Polish Russian border and when midday came, they finally arrived at the Minsk station. The platform was as crowded as the train had been. And there was quite an assortment of people: civilians, soldiers with rifles, and Russian prisoners of war in brown uniforms.

Orders were given to the soldiers emerging from the train to help with the unloading of twenty-five trucks outside the station. It was cold, and the only food any of them had was what they'd brought in tins.

They worked well into the night. But after the trucks were unloaded, they were told they could sleep in them.

Then the next morning they were taken to what was said to be a military hospital in Minsk, where their shot records were checked. More shots were given as needed, before they were taken to their barracks near the edge of the city.

Minsk had been bombed heavily, with possibly only half of its houses standing.

Most of the city's streets were filled with extremely deep craters with boards laid over them, so people could cross.

The food the military gave them wasn't bad, but it never seemed to be enough with all the loading and unloading they were required to do. Checking the food prices in Russian stores, Geir was pleased to see that items were relatively inexpensive.

Minsk had some very nice Russian-run restaurants. However, none of the soldiers spoke Russian, and most didn't have the money to eat in places like that. So Geir was grateful for the wad of marks Daniel had given him. *Apparently he knows how hungry at times, we can be. And he's doing his best to take care of Volker and me with some fine meals. But he's also given me a wallet where I can hide my paper money behind a flap inside it, so it looks empty. And there's something else sewn inside—for emergencies only. Meaning bribery. It's a man's large, white-diamond ring, of which I have no intention of telling Volker about. Because it's a secret shared between Daniel and me.*

Geir felt fortunate that he and Volker could eat at the Russian restaurants. So he'd usually bring along one or two of the guys they'd made friends with in their unit: Rudi Herrenvolk, Walter Steinbrenner, and Klaus Warda. Who was their non-commissioned field officer or rather, *feldwebel*.

He had a gray streak in his hair which gleamed in the light. "Undoubtedly from the stress of his job," Volker remarked in a sour tone.

One of the restaurants had a nightclub in back where Russian singers and dancers performed. There were a few civilians in the audience, but mostly it consisted of military officers and the SS, **since** this nightclub was reported to be quite expensive.

Even in early December the temperature was below zero with snow falling continuously.

"It's five feet deep." A grim-faced Volker noted.

Supply movements were slowed, with soldiers on the front lines having little to eat.

"The reason our unit's been assigned as convoy troops, "Volker said in a resentful tone.

Later, an officer informed him, "Men, like you, will do some of the driving. But most of the time you'll be riding in the back of trucks."

On Christmas Eve Geir wrote in his notepad:

"Someone was singing "Oh Tannenbaum," when we were ordered by Klaus Warda to pack up. It was an order that *meant getting our uniforms in tip-top*

shape, with the brass on them as shiny as our polished boots. And then, we'll be traveling with supplies meant for our Stalingrad troops— that are in such dire need. The absolute sacrifice... but luckily our friendship with Warda grew. Which helped to ease things with this Sargent Kyer, who'd be traveling with us. A sergeant Volker and I found to be as sadistic and angry as Sargent Schmidt in Bavaria had been—if not worse. 'And to think his name means vulture,' Volker said, as we were issued military-blankets, sheepskin coats, and galoshes' with thick soles that went over our leather boots, gloves, and hoods of Melton or felted wool that were warm and soft

Blankets, food, heaters, medical supplies, and other essential items, were in huge boxes stacked in the backs of our trucks. Plus, there was an ample supply of munitions for the troops."

Another entry from Geir's notepad:

"Kiev, in the Ukraine, was two hundred and fifty miles away and would be the convoy's first major stop. Volker and I didn't mind helping the combat troops in such dire need in Stalingrad. But winter hit with such a fury of snow and ice, there hadn't been time to repair the damaged roads on which our convoy was traveling. And the cold—'So bad my brows have frost on them,' Volker said. 'Which wouldn't surprise me to learn the Artic was warmer than Russia. and when sleeping, no part of our body must be exposed for fear of freezing.

Our convoy had seven officers, five noncoms, two medics, but no doctor. And the strenuous work of shoveling snow— sometimes with our helmets, since we were short shovels— was continually required on our journey. And believe it or not, we found ourselves, sweating. But if this wasn't bad enough, getting forty trucks with their frozen engines rumbling and gassed up, took at least an hour every morning, in this deadly cold weather. Necessary work if the convoy was to make fifteen miles per day — and at best everyone tried. But icy weather like this, made the convoy's progress much slower than anticipated. 'This weather is attacking us with the vengeance of an SS man,' Volker commented.' And I agreed."

Still another entry from Geir's notepad:

"Potholes under the snow *make it really bad. Since they cause us to have to stop and shovel snow so much, that we fear coming under fire from the partisans. And when night falls we have a terrible time finding shelter. Forcing sixty or more*

of us to crowd into one of the A-frame log farmhouses, so we can get some sleep. Never mind, we're not well received by the Russians. And I felt bad the first time we stayed with them when I saw the man of the house and his wife, with their two frightened children, clinging to them. These Russians didn't speak German, so I placed a finger against my lips meaning 'shush.' And then pantomimed a handshake before taking the man's hand and slipping some German marks in it. He looked at me in surprise—especially when I smiled and nodded.

That was one of the few times Volker and I were in one of the log farmhouses. Since most of the time we ended up spilling over into barns, hay sheds, and other small storage places around these houses."

(This is where I stopped writing.)

* * *

"See, the officers have tents equipped for such appalling weather," Volker pointed out. "Which tells me, Geir, we need to find a way to get reassigned to a halfway decent place like Paris."

"And how do you suggest doing that?"

"Charlotte told me if we can get someone to nick our ankle bones, we can't march because we'll have to walk with a cane. "

Of course he was right. Even if getting wounded often meant going without morphine until a soldier could get to an infirmary or hospital. Or worse, getting frostbite so badly, that a waiting soldier had to have his leg or arm amputated. "Not worth getting wounded, Volker," Geir insisted. "Especially with the *ever* present threat of pneumonia. "

"I know." He frowned. "So I guess we'll just have to keep doing what we're doing."

A later entry from Geir's notepad:

"Hedy always complimented me on my cleanliness. But out here the cold made it impossible to keep clean. And were we ever filthy—with lice and other vermin. Something I'm sure would give Hedy cause for concern, as would our hands. Which are so blistered, cracked, and bleeding from all the snow shoveling we're being made to do, the work is quite painful. But thankfully our fur-lined gloves appear to be protecting us more than the woolen gloves most of the other soldiers are

wearing...which are fast becoming shreds. Something that makes me wonder how long before our fur-lined ones will do the same? Certainly not like Bavaria That's what shoveling snow in twenty-five degrees below zero weather, can do to a soldier."

From Minsk to Kiev, was their first important stop, Geir knew Stalingrad was still more than six hundred miles away. Where General von Paulus, in charge of the sixth **army,** was overseeing his men who continued to be fighting in terrible conditions.

The snow banks on the road the convoy was taking were often chest-high or higher. And God forbid the way necessity forced a soldier to shovel snow with the continuous heavy snowfalls— much less walking in it to do the shoveling. 'Almost more than a man could stand,' was a frequent complaint from Rudi Herrenvolk.

He was the dark-haired soldier who'd dined with Geir and Volker in Minsk, and hung with them whenever he could.

'Especially, Rudi, when the wind's so bad it's impossible to be outside and shovel, 'Volker would add, full of resentment.' Forcing us to take refuge in our trucks.'

And Rudi would nod. Cleary aware that shoveling snow in a freezing wind with its snow flurries, would have probably done them all in. But if the truth be known, Geir was more worried about Hedy and the Berlin bombings. *'Please, God,* keep *her safe.'*

That evening, despite his exhaustion, he wrote her a letter:

Dearest Hedy,

To say once again, that Volker and I have been shaking like fox-worn rabbits most of our time here in Russia, we give our thanks each day that we have hand-knitted socks from home and a pullover. I keep repeating this to show how much we appreciate these gifts from all of you at the boardinghouse.

Our kindly feldwebel, Klaus Warda, has made us aware that the convoy's road usually runs parallel to the railroad tracks. Which makes it easier for us to get an idea where the middle of the snow-covered road is. And it helps a little, but not much.

A lot of supply trains go through carrying war materials. But the trains usually have a fan blade in front of the locomotive. A giant snow chopper. Only if it hits a frozen cow or large animal on the tracks, it has to backtrack to a maintenance area to fix it. That's why at the risk of partisan attacks, most of the trains run slow.

However, even with the serious reduction of our convoy's speed, we finally managed to reach the Ukraine. 'Nothing but another blanket of white like the Russian plain,' Volker said, shaking his head with disgust.

And me? I recalled Wilhelm telling me that in 1930 a million people died from starvation in the Ukraine. Terrible!

Much love from your Geir

He read it and re-read it several times, before writing it again and coding some of the words.

◆

Their first night in the Ukraine, Geir and Volker were assigned guard duty.

The first patrol in the cold night. Whenever possible, avoid guard duty at night: the secret rule of the convoy troops. Something Volker and I —for some peculiar reason—were not able to do.

"Even the moon and stars look frozen," said Volker pointing at them. "And most likely our dreams tonight will be too. Since we're underfed with our rations getting scarcer and scarcer."

Five men developed pneumonia and had to be put in makeshift beds in one of the trucks.

"Alongside fifteen men, with cases of frostbite," Warda let it be known.

"With only two medical orderlies for the convoy," said Geir, exasperated. He was curious as to why there weren't more, but no one had an answer.

Four of the convoy's forty vehicles developed serious mechanical problems and had to be destroyed, along with their cargoes. "Can't let the partisans get them," Warda explained.

These problems occurred close to where a huge battle, not far from Kiev, had been. It was a place cited as having more Germans killed than Russians.

Something Warda told Geir about as the convoy passed a graveyard close to where the battle had been. But unlike the German graves that had a stick and helmet on top of them to identify it was an individual's, the Russian graves were *mass* ones. "But if Germany loses the war," said Warda, "these German graves will probably be plowed over."

"Buried by the war," Geir replied sadly.

• — ⋯◆⋯ — •

Kiev was a strong military center, where units from Rumania would soon be joining the Germans in an offensive expected to push them to the Caspian Sea.

"German soldiers with military vehicles are everywhere. "A surprised Geir remarked to Rudi. "Something I can mention in my next letter to Hedy."

Which he did, finding Kiev to be an attractive city that appeared to have not suffered as much war-torn damage as Minsk. And to the convoy's good fortune, there was a center where the troops could shower and rid themselves of their vermin.

Those with serious injuries were hospitalized in a small hospital. Which, to Geir's disdain, only had enough room for nine of the convoy's suffering men.

The food, however, *was* good, with a hot kitchen preparing it. And also, there was a small store nearby where Geir bought some extra tins of food for Volker and himself. Plus, there was mail.

He and Volker received letters from everyone at the boardinghouse. "With you, Geir, receiving a special package from Hedy and Otto containing books," remarked Volker, looking them over.

Just about everyone in the convoy complained about not getting to have more time in this city. But since motorized combat troops would now be accompanying them to protect the convoy from partisans, it was necessary to move on.

The commander, *Hauptman* Lang, of the combat troops accompanying the convoy, pointed out they would be able to attach four or five trucks to the back of one of their tanks. "It'll make it easier for you to keep from sliding in the snow," he informed the convoy troops.

Everyone in the convoy seemed pleased to have the combat troops with them. "And some are saying the cotton-like clouds from the powdered snow that are hanging above them, is a good sign," Geir told Volker.

"Not to me." Grimacing, he glanced upward. "I see it as a warning cloud of something bad to come."

And he was right. Because two hours after their departure from Kiev, explosions forced the convoy to stop briefly.

They didn't seem that close. But since it was better to be safe than sorry, the soldiers were ordered to grab their rifles.

Everyone kept moving, even when the explosions got closer. Some of the trucks began to hurry, and one fell in a rut because the driver slammed on his brakes. A problem that prompted ten daring men to leave their trucks and help him get his started.

The convoy was moving into a heavily forested, wooded countryside when gunfire, up ahead, brought it to a complete stop. Three of the trucks had fish-tailed on the ice, and the drivers were racing their engines. A *hauptman* was ordering, "Keep moving!"

Soldiers were being collected from the trucks to go to the head of the convoy, with Volker and Geir being two of them.

"Partisans up ahead," Warda warned. "So scatter and dig your one meter foxholes."

Doubled over, twenty soldiers ran. *With more Russians in the woods,* Geir suspected as he used his helmet to dig what Daniel would call, a three-foot foxhole.

This time, unlike the French partisans had done when he and Volker were leaving *Rheims*, the enemy managed to cross the road. The Russian guns in the east got louder. Although, there was strong, answering fire from a heavy, German machine-gun battery.

The noise was so loud it threatened to burst Geir's ear drums.

Explosions, machine-guns, then three Russian bullets landing close to my foxhole.

The sharp bursts of fire continued to get louder and louder. And Russians ran deeper into the forest as six tanks fired at them. Then a long, deep roar and— suddenly— all was quiet.

The road was now clear as soldiers began collecting the wounded.

Darkness fell quickly that afternoon, with orders to stop in a small town where the wounded could be cared for. It was a town that looked like it catered to the farmers in this area, because not far from it was a log farmhouse. "We're stopping here," said Warda, "and the floor in this house will be your beds."

A man and his wife, along with their two children, stared at them. There was another Russian man, who was apparently the brother of the man of the house, since they shared a strong, facial resemblance.

And to Geir's surprise, this man spoke German. So he slipped him some marks to give to the man of the house...which he immediately went over and did.

The next morning Geir had a queasy stomach. *Dysentery?* Something he'd been fighting, taking up all the pills for it in his first aid kit. Which meant that now, Volker had to supply him. *And I don't like taking them from him in case he needs them too.*

The convoy was making good time, when two of its trucks were suddenly hit by a Russian plane.

It appeared to be far away, but when two more planes flew closer to the trucks, all hell broke loose.

Immediately, the vehicles stopped.

Three turned over. Fifteen crashed into others. And four with explosives, caught fire.

"Run to the cover behind those snowy rocks in the woods!" ordered Warda, pointing. "The munitions cases are about to blow!"

Soldiers crouched as the three Russian planes roared overhead. The noise was as deafening as it had been the day before, with the machine-gun battery.

But when two trucks blew— even from a distance— the exposure to this tragedy was horrific.

The ground shook, and for a frantic moment Geir thought pieces of them had hit him. But then a sudden quietness followed. "Like being in the eye of a hurricane," he said on a breath. "Which means the Russians planes are regrouping for their return."

Only this time to his surprise as well as Volker's, two Luftwaffe planes roared over their heads. And—immediately—all was well. "Like a miracle," Geir murmured.

The exception being the smoke and debris in the road, and the five blackened bodies soldiers carried from the ruins of the trucks that had exploded. One Geir recognized as being all that was left of Walter Steinbrenner. *Who was of the fellows Volker and I dined with in Minsk and hung out with, whenever we could.*

"A great sorrow," Volker mumbled, as Warda motioned him back to his truck.

"This convoy is an endless journey eastward," remarked Geir to Warda, like he hadn't heard it before.

"With none of us really being prepared for what just happened."

"We came close to being wiped off the face of this Russian earth," Volker told Geir later. "Because a distance of four trucks from those that exploded, would have been the one you and I were in. So, considering we're not on the front yet, we'd better act fast and get out of this damned Wehrmacht— which means getting wounded! "

————◆————

Geir wrote:

"We're growing more fearful with each passing day *Lack of sleep, the bottoms of our feet aching from cold… our physical condition of filth is terrible. It's too cold to wash and almost impossible to find water. And what little water we can find comes from the peasants who don't understand a word of German. So at dark, from exhaustion, it's no wonder we sink into a deep sleep—*"

Geir laid his pen aside, wishing he could add: *"Being wounded means pain. Yet here was Volker continuing to say, that we had to be wounded in order to get out of the Wehrmacht."*

CHAPTER EIGHTEEN

As the dusk fell Geir and Volker's truck, like many of the others, slid in the snow.

It was getting colder and colder, and Geir was getting sicker and sicker. And of all times he got assigned first watch—*again*.

Damn! Night guard duty in this small hamlet on the German convoy route.

His stomach was gripped by an awful pain, followed by chills. *If I don't leave guard duty and take a crap, I'll dirty my pants.* So he hurried toward the closest latrine.

He had fever and his pain was getting worse. *Terrible to be a victim of uncontrollable diarrhea or dysentery.*

Suffering, he was halfway to the latrine when he looked up and saw Sergeant Kyer fuming with rage.

"Dissertation!" he roared. "I'll see you're assigned to a penal battalion for this. "Where you'll live the life of a prisoner— mine clearing, no leaves, burying the dead, and cancellation of mail." He whacked him across the mouth before adding, "So your family will think *your* dead."

Both fear and rage swamped Geir as he wiped his bloody mouth with the back of his hand. "B...but I've dysentery," he stuttered.

"Then dysentery be damned," said the angry Kyer, kicking him in the gut.

Immediately brown filth mingled with blood ran down Geir's legs, dirtying his pants. "Damn it!

I couldn't hold it back!"

Apparently Warda saw what was happening, because he and Volker hurried to Geir's side

"Can't you see he's ill and needs to be in the infirmary?" Warda shouted at Kyer. "So that's where he's headed—"

Geir's breathing faltered. "I...I have to clean up," he told Warda and Volker. "Because I'm filthy."

However, there were so many sick soldiers with wounds and fever, Geir has to wait in line at the infirmary for forty-five minutes.

Volker elected to stay with him in case he collapsed.

"You smell worse than some of dead under the snow in March… when it thaws," one of the *two* combat medics told Geir, taunting him. "And you have to shower before anyone here will put their hands on your filthy ass."

There was no hot water but a shower—nevertheless. *When was the last time?* Geir wondered. *Was it Kiev? He felt so terrible* he *found it difficult to remember.*

The cold water wasn't pleasant, but it didn't bother him nearly as his stomach. *Which feels like it's about to burst in flames…the way some of our convoy trucks did today.*

Finally, one of the medics came and gave him the luxury of a bed or rather a cardboard cot.

Volker took his dirty clothes, but left his greatcoat and tunic. "They somehow managed to escape all that brown drizzle," he said with a smug grin. "But Warda and I will personally clean your clothes.

And if they don't get dry, we'll wrap them in a towel in your pack and bring you some fresh ones in the morning."

Geir's stomach was now cramping as well as burning.

"What you'll be getting from us is one liter of this medicated enema," said this second combat medic, holding up a hot water bottle. "Plus two more such treatments during the night…making a total of three liters?"

His statement did not require a reply.

So with a pang of awe, Geir struggled with the unpleasantness of it. "Which means I'll have to tromp through snow in this freezing air, to the latrine… or rather that drainage ditch behind the infirmary," he said with a sudden bitterness. "So why in hell are the latrines outside?"

But this medic's answer was the same as the other one's "Because soldiers with dysentery smell worse than the snow-covered bodies thawing in March." Then he proceeded to add,

"And besides we have to sped things up since we've got wounded on the way, with no room for them. So where you're concerned we have to do in one night what's usually done in two, since you'll be expected to leave in the morning with your convoy but—" He grinned. "You'll have had one hell of a good gut cleaning, so turn over on your stomach."

"And I'm to obey without question?" Geir asked in a perplexed tone. He was hesitate to turn on his stomach until this medic, annoyed, whacked him across his backsides.

"I said *turnover*," the man ordered.

"Or what? You'll paddle me?"

"The thought has occurred to me," he remarked with complete indifference.

Aware his visual discomfort was showing, Geir bit his lips as this enema's burning, mediated liquid, increased the fire in his gut.

"Two more such treatments tonight like this, and you'll be fine," the medic informed him with an air of pride, when the first one was over.

Leaving Geir to question whether or not he'd be able to stand two more of these painful enemas? But given no other options he assumed a stoic acceptance that somehow, with the grace of God, managed to get him through this torture.

The next morning Geir was pleased Volker was waiting for him with the combat medic. "Geir's papers say he's on the way to being cured," said the medic. "Maybe he still a little fever but it's not bad. Which is proof that his treatment is beginning to take effect."

Geir wasn't in as much pain, but he was still going to the latrine with loose bowels and blood, so Volker had to help him climb into the truck. "It's got to be done right away, Geir," he whispered. "Make no mistake. We've got to get ourselves *shot*!"

"When someone has dysentery and his stomach is hurting badly, that's not something pleasant to think about, Volker."

"Probably not, after all those damned enemas... the way they'd treat cannon fodder. But remember, Otto says if a person's desperate enough, then that person can make things happen.

And this being forced into the Wehrmacht, in Russia in the middle of winter is horrible...! Sheer desperation, I'd call it."

Geir sighed deeply. "You won't get an argument for me about that."

They rolled along in the back of the truck. A Luftwaffe plane flew over, which they later learned had sent a message from its pilot to *Hauptman* Lang, and his combat troops. Some partisan movement was a mile up ahead. And even draped in white, sheet-looking clothing this pilot had glimpsed what appeared to be an anti-tank weapon.

So *Hauptman* Lang gave the order to have five from the convoy trucks, along with five in the combat troops, to go look over the area.

Warda came over to Geir and Volker's truck and asked for some volunteers. *Apparently Volker had told him I'd had to make frequent trips to the latrine or rather, the drainage ditch behind the behind the infirmary, until those medicated enemas—my outrageous treatment—became more effective. Even if the other convoy trucks stopped along the way, everyone was ordered to stay inside, and not allowed to get out and take a crap. So Volker volunteered, himself and me. Since the trip entailed a mile walk to check things out. And if I had to take a quick crap, I could. Our friend, Rudi Herrenvolk, also volunteered. "If you collapse or something, I'll be on hand with Volker to help you."*

We five soldiers from the truck convoy walked, with the five soldiers from the combat one.

Warda walked beside Hauptman Lang. His men had parked the combat truck at a fair distance. And taking our rifles, all of us headed eastward.

We continued to sink in the snow. But only up to our knees as we walked about forty minutes to the edge of a snow-covered forest. Breathing and sweating, we still found it a respite to get out. Even if walking in the snow continued to be difficult. I was sweating especially heavy, but I didn't mind. Hopeful, that some of the poisons would leave my system from all the perspiring I was doing.

Suddenly, a violent burst of sound struck us. 'Dig your foxholes!' shouted Warda as bullets buzzed over our heads. An exchange of grenades followed. Then noise from more explosions."

⸺⸺◆⸺⸺

"Couldn't be worse if we were walking though a mine field," Geir murmured.

He and Volker, now separated from Rudi, were huddled in their foxholes when a wounded, auburn-haired fellow from the combat truck reached out a hand to them. But before Geir could take it, the fellow fell facedown…his body motionless.

For several moments Geir couldn't stop staring. *'Life and death brushing shoulders,'* he felt like saying.*'Which makes them too close for comfort.'*

Guns were firing. And two other fellows from the combat truck aimed their rifles and shot at three figures in white sheets, running deeper into the forest... but nobody hit them.

Warda moved closer to Geir and Volker. "Bloody trail up ahead. So follow me."

They walked behind him until they came to a large, fallen tree. Where, covered with some snowy branches, a wounded partisan moved. He looked quite frightened.

"You kill him," Warda ordered Volker. "While I see to our wounded."

Volker took aim with his rifle preparing to fire, when Geir stopped him. "This partisan is the man who spoke German I met two nights ago."

The poor fellow was not only frightened but groaning in pain. "So, Volker, don't shoot him—" pleaded Geir. "He just might be able to help us."

"Do you think we can trust him?" Volker asked. "Since all I keep hearing is that Russians are great liars."

"I think we can trust him," Geir gasped. "But I'm feeling so terrible, you'll have to make that call."

Immediately a grin slid across Volker's face. "Then make that call *I* will." The partisan's hand was bloody with his gun still in it. "We can't stand the damned Wehrmacht. So if you want to live, then nick each of us in the left ankle with your gun."

Possibly because of the pain he was in, the Russian didn't look surprised. "Understand," he mumbled.

Overjoyed, Volker took it as his agreement. And before any more could be said, this Russian did exactly as asked.

"Now quick! Hide under those other snow -covered branches before someone comes! "Geir urged him. "Where it's more difficult to see."

The man's fear of death must have given him an adrenaline buzz, because he quickly managed to roll under them. Volker fired two rifle shots in the air. "We got him!" he yelled.

Geir stared at where the man had been. "I hope his friends come to his aid."

"Well, speaking German like he does, makes him a valuable asset. So why wouldn't they?"

There was now a trail of blood where this Russian had rolled. But there were some other snow-covered branches on the ground next to where Geir was standing, which enabled him to cover the trail quickly.

Volker, who always carried rubber tourniquets, put one on Geir's ankle and one on his. Then he tossed one at the Russian—who was heard to murmur, *'Danke.'*

Geir and Volker now moaned in pain and couldn't move unless they used their rifles as a canes.

Then, Warda returned. "What the hell?" he asked, staring at the pair.

"T...that wounded Russian shot us," Volker said brokenly. "But we shot him."

"And where is he now."

"He was dying. And making all kinds of painful sounds. Yet somehow he managed to crawl into those snow-covered branches."

"Then so be it. "Warda said, his gaze shifting to the tourniquets on Volker and Geir's legs.

"How'd you know to have those?"

"My sister," Volker answered, bending over in pain. "She's a nurse in Berlin— a smart woman— who insists we always carry them for emergencies."

"Good thinking on her part." Warda smiled. "But why were each of you shot in the same place?" "Because this Russian claimed he wanted to cripple us," Volker said, his breathing now quite heavy. "So we'd have a miserable rest of our lives."

Warda turned to Geir. "And he spoke German?"

He nodded.

"Unusual." Warda shrugged.

Hauptman Lang approached them, and Warda pointed at Geir and Volker. "Two more wounded."

Lang tossed them a glance. "Makes a total of five. Plus two dead. But one of my men is sending our two-flare signal to our truck driver to move forward. So help is on the way."

Rudi was also one of the wounded men. "It's a crease glancing off a rib in my left side," he told Geir.

"Then I'll patch it up temporarily," he volunteered, breathing lightly between parted lips. "O...once someone gives me the truck's first-aid kit."

"A...at least...we'll have some company," Volker gasped, the words broken by his pain.

Toward noon, when they rejoined their convoy in a small hamlet, they were put in a truck with three wounded men. One of whom insisted he was the verge of developing gangrene if they didn't get to a hospital.

But this hamlet, where the convoy had surprisingly stopped had no hospital. And there was only one main road leading out from it that joined the Soviet highway. "Which we'll be taking to Kharkov," Rudi remarked.

Warda was thoughtful enough to bring Geir, Volker, and Rudi their packs. And in a burst of appreciation Geir handed him some marks. "I saw a few stores in this small hamlet on the way in," he said. "So keep some of these marks for yourself. And if you wouldn't mind, see if they have something like a cane you can buy for Volker and I. And also, some more tins of food. "

"There'll be a lot left over," said Warda, staring at the German marks Geir had given him. "So surely it's not all for me?"

"Think again," Geir said.

A smile, in these uncertain, times found its way to Warda's face. "Then I thank you. The medic's bringing morphine for your pain, along with three more wounded. But even so, I'll go see what I can find."

It didn't take him long, and before the medic came Warda reappeared. "Two broomsticks minus the broom." he said, holding them up. "Not exactly Alpine walking sticks, but if you have to stumble a few steps, it's better than your rifles."

"It looks like from those stains on them— when they'd been brooms— they might have been used in slaughterhouses," said Volker, examining his.

"Quite possibly," Warda agreed. "Of course wheelchairs and hospital crutches are what you need. Which, if you're fortunate enough to get to Minsk, you should get them after your surgery...but here? "He reached for a sack on the ground. "There's plenty of tinned food in it for you."

"Did you buy yourself some food, too?" Geir asked him.

"A sack of food, like yours, with money left." He reached into his pocket. "But you need it more than I do."

"I don't." Geir shook his head. "You've been good to us. So I'd like to think I've been good to you."

Warda's eyes appeared to cloud. "More than you'll ever know. Since as is being said, our rations aren't as abundant as they've been—" Someone called his name and he turned. "The medic's coming with the wounded on stretchers. And two medical orderlies and two soldiers are carrying them."

"Emergency up ahead!" shouted the medic.

A hand in one of the trucks waved at Warda with a peculiar urgency. And grabbing his sack of tinned food, he hurried toward it.

Something about the anxious way he moved aroused a fear in Geir that he and this field usher— who'd been such a friend on this terrible journey— wouldn't cross paths again. *A friendship lost to the war.*

When the medic appeared, he quickly injected Geir, Volker, and the others in pain with some morphine. Then he tended to everyone's wounds as best he could, dressing Geir's and Volker's.

"It's bad when the hospital's in the next town," grumbled one of the orderlies.

"Then we need to get to it as quickly as possible," said Geir.

"We'll do what we can," snapped the medic, just as an ear-splitting explosion not too far away shook the ground and truck.

Immediately a feeling of foreboding gripped Geir. *Like an ominous chill that shakes the core of my being. Or— like being touched by death's hand.*

A cloud of black smoke rose as someone yelled, "Mines up ahead—one of our trucks blew!"

Everyone except the wounded was ordered to get out and help. "The road's heavily mined, and the mines are covered in powdered snow," the driver explained to his wounded men in back. "So you fellows will just have to make-do as best you can."

"With men in here dying if they can't get to a hospital!" Geir yelled.

"Either way they won't make it," the driver yelled back.

Geir was as desperate as a rat caught in a trap, until one of *Hauptman* Lang's combat troop men appeared."

"I'm Corporal Brenner," a very tall soldier introduced himself. And what I need to know is if any of wounded fellows back here are able to drive?"

Volker glanced at his left foot. "I could drive, but I can't use the clutch. Which clearly eliminates me and my friend, Geir, here."

"I can drive a little," said Rudi— "as long as it isn't far."

" It's about eighteen miles back to that Luftwaffe airfield." The corporal handed him a folded paper. "Captain Lang's put it in writing and radioed the airfield, urging someone there to fly this truckload of wounded men to Minsk. Which, being only two hundred and fifty miles away, is the fastest place you can get the help you need. So that way, you'll all be able to derive the benefits of the military hospital there."

"We're one lone truck with partisans out there," remarked Volker in a hard and resentful tone. "Got any ideas on how we're supposed to deal with that?"

"Put Volker in back and give him a rifle." Rudi answered before Corporal Brenner could. "And put his friend, Geir, in the cab with a rifle. But I doubt we'll meet up with any partisans, because after all they've done here, they're probably sound asleep. "

Volker's jaw clenched. "Still, Corporal, how many miles before we meet up with this convoy following us?"

About nine... and I'll radio them that you'll be coming."

"Have they been radioed about the mines?"

"Yes. And expect to meet up with us here, so they can double-check and see we got all of them."

Rudi gave a quick look in the direction they'd come. "And this truck?"

"When you meet up with the other convoy, one of their soldiers should take it and drive you to the airfield in it."

"And if the truck tracks we made in the snow earlier aren't visible now, what then?" asked Geir.

"They should be," the corporal remarked, in a reassuring tone meant to ease his apprehension. "But if they're not then stay in the middle of the road, and remember to use the railroad tracks running alongside it as a reference. And by the way, the other convoy has six wounded men in critical condition, who'll be joining your wounded ones on the plane. Because due to limited space, the Kiev hospital took only their most severe cases. The same as they did yours—"

"Whose wounded, like ours, are probably getting worse by the day." Rudi was quick to say.

"Indeed." The corporal shook his head before continuing, "But their truck with their wounded will be the last one. Which should make it easier for your soldier with his rifle— "he pointed at Geir," riding in the cab with the driver from the *other* convoy, to get their convoy truck to the airfield."

"I hope this Luftwaffe plane is a cargo Jonkers 52," said Volker. "So it'll be large enough to carry us, without making everyone uncomfortable."

"Don't count on anything," said the corporal." Since the Luftwaffe claims to always have operations pending. And even with the urgency of *Hauptman* Lang's orders, there's nothing to keep them from flying off and leaving everyone behind."

"I hear the Luftwaffe thinks it's better than the SS," said Volker. "And the SS thinks it's better than the Luftwaffe. So they're continually at odds."

The corporal's mouth took on an unpleasant twist. "That's what we're hearing too."

• ———— ◆ ———— •

"The SS shows no one mercy," Geir mumbled, his words a twisted mixture of hope and fear. *So, what if the Luftwaffe follows suit? Will it be the end for us? A thought that is quite painful. Which makes me question if I should be angry at Volker for what we did to become unfit for service?*

Which means exactly what? We can't go into battle, but we'd still be in the Wehrmacht with other tasks assigned us. Yet, Volker insisted that if we didn't do it, we'd either die on the Eastern Front, or end up in some agonizing Russian prisoner of war camp where we'd die from abuse. However, soldiers unfit for service but performing other Wehrmacht tasks, could still become Russian prisoners of war, couldn't they? So did Volker and I do the right thing, is the question I keep asking myself? Part of me keeps saying I encouraged Volker to do it because—due to pain from my dysentery— I was desperate.

Which I still am, after that insufferable medical treatment I received.

But despite his uncertainty Geir, like the other wounded in the back of the truck, was pleased when he saw the convoy following them.

Rudi drove to the back of it, where the truck exchanges were made. And soon, the two trucks were backtracking the eight miles to the airfield.

With the partisan threat still looming, the truck drivers were quite anxious to get back to their convoy, once they arrived at the airfield.

"But you can't leave these wounded men here," argued a man called, *Hauptmann* Helmer— who apparently was one of the Luftwaffe officers in charge of the place.

"Even if flying them to Minsk is their only hope?" asked one of the convoy drivers. "Or otherwise—"

"What?" interrupted Helmer.

"Most will die."

"Captain Lang has made it quite clear in these written orders," said the other convoy driver. "He shoved them in the Helmer's hand. "Didn't he radio you people here?"

"He tried. Mentioning something about mines, but there was a lot of static. So we weren't exactly sure what he was trying to tell us."

Geir immediately recognized this as an excuse to divest the airfield of all responsibility. "If you force these soldiers to return to the convoy, and they die," he spoke up, "it'll look bad... not just for you, but *this* war we're so desperately trying to win."

"And *we* here at the airfield are supposed to be concerned?" Helmer asked him in a sarcastic tone. "When the Russian Yaks are flying low and dropping their bombs on convoys? Why if it hadn't been for us the other day, I doubt you'd have a convoy."

That was true. Geir hated to admit. Even if his stomach roiled at the thought of the Luftwaffe refusing to help him, Volker, and the other wounded soldiers with them. *There's only one card left to play before our world stops.* And reaching for his wallet, Geir looked Helmer squarely in the eye as he asked him, "What if I paid you to fly us to Minsk?"

"*You?*" He seemed faintly surprised. "A common soldier? None of which I've ever met, had any money."

"There's always a first time— but what about this?" He handed him Daniel's ring with it's large, white diamond in the center.

Helmer's mouth dropped open. "Great God!" he exclaimed, mesmerized. 'It's magnificent."

His intensity caught Geir off guard. *He's obviously astonished by its enormous size.*

"But tell me," said Helmer. "How'd you get it? And don't say off a dead partisan."

"My father-in-law gave it to me, in case of an emergency."

Helmer slipped it on his finger. "The fortunes of war—eh? Then I'd say we have an emergency."

"Yes indeed," Geir agreed, relief sweeping through him.

A Jonkers 52 was positioned for take-off, with the smiling *Hauptmann* Helmer, motioning at the convoy drivers to begin loading the wounded. "I'll radio the Minsk hospital to send a truck to meet the plane."

"What if someone on the plane gets sick?" Geir asked him.

"There're some brown paper bags on it, stuffed with waded up newspaper sheets."

Geir made no attempt to hide his relief." For which I'm extremely grateful."

There was a gleam of excitement in Volker's blue eyes as he turned to Geir.

"Haven't you heard me say I always wanted to have a friend whose father was rich?"

"Father-in-law," Geir corrected. "Daniel told you to call him that until after the war...but before we take-off, I have to go to the latrine."

"Then allow me to help you stumble along," said one of the convoy drivers, overhearing him.

"I'm still having to crap more than necessary, "Geir told him. "But I'm better than I was."

"Good to know." The driver smiled. "And provided you're in good health, the hospital in Minsk should take care of it. Which—from the problem you're still having— doesn't appear you got the help you needed from the infirmary."

"Makes me wonder. But I'll find out once I get to Minsk." Geir glanced at the wounded men being carried on their stretchers. "Hopefully, the hospital's got a better treatment than what the infirmary gave me."

"It's an excellent hospital," said the driver. "So just hold on until you get there."

"Only thing I can do," Geir remarked, releasing a long, audible breath.

His stomach was clenched tight when he was put on the plane waiting for take-off.

"Aren't you afraid?" Volker asked him. "Since we've never flown before."

"I'm a little on edge. But let me put it like this, I'm more afraid of walking."

"Who wouldn't be."

Geir reached for his notepad. Certain words in it needed to be blotted out or coded, so he wouldn't lose the meaning of what he'd written. *I can't have someone reading about Volker and I getting shot by that Russian we failed to kill, while we're under anesthesia in surgery. So, they'll make no sense of the way I'm scribbling things. However, as long as I'm able to remember these events for later, it's fine.*

"Look, Geir," Volker nudged him. "We're lifting off. And hopefully it'll be like we're floating in outer space."

"I don't know about that. The sky has a sullen look. And from the heavy feeling in my stomach, it's already beginning to feel like we're heading into something unpleasant."

Once the plane was completely airborne, it dropped—jolting Geir as well as Volker. Then it dropped again— and once again, shaking the floor. *A vertical jarring... a new fear.* Geir wanted to throw-up.

"Where in hell is my brown paper bag?"

"Right here," said Volker, reaching for it on top of his pack." Are you dizzy too?"

"The motion's bothering me. Though, Daniel once told me, that if you fly enough, you'll get used to it."

Volker's head snapped up. "That is if you have the courage to fly again—"

"Who knows?" The flight got worse as they experienced the turbulence from a sleet storm. Only to Geir's surprise, he didn't get sick. *Am I getting used to flying? It seems like it. We're covering an amazing amount of distance in a short period of time. Which is good because we've escaped the Wehrmacht. And our lives are moving forward. Something that means Volker's plan has worked with this... anything but calm... plane ride proving it.*

And even if we walk with limps for the rest of our lives like Fritz does, there'll be no more getting up at dawn to start frozen engines. No more shoveling snow, until our hands are cracked and bleeding. And no more partisans, mines, or Russian Yaks diving down, dropping bombs. We're free at last, from fighting for a cause in which we don't believe. With Daniel Birnbaum being our salvation... Oh Daniel, blessed Daniel, you are the father I love so very much."

CHAPTER NINETEEN

Geir didn't like thinking about their rough landing when their plane arrived in Minsk. There was another turbulent sleet storm on the horizon with a blue-black sky, making him fear they wouldn't be able to touch down. And he'd gagged several times— *But luckily, to my great astonishment, we touched down before I could throw up.*

Along with the hospital workers, the covered truck requested by *Hauptman* Helmer was waiting.

They gave the wounded morphine shots, before quickly moving them and their packs into the truck.

Geir, Volker, and Rudi were the last to be moved. A Russian man, wearing what looked like a raw amber necklace, appeared to be giving orders. Because whenever one of the workers approached Volker and Rudi, he would shake his head. *'What in hell is* going *on?'* Geir wanted to ask him. And for a dizzying moment he imagined the plane had been captured by Russians, and they were now prisoners. *Going to where?* He shuddered to think.

The ride to the hospital was bumpy from all the pot holes in the roads. *'I'm growing weaker by the minute. Why?' he considered asking. 'Is it because the morphine's making me feel that way? Or is it because I haven't eaten in God knows when?'*

Minutes, hours passed. He wasn't sure. Someone was talking about Volker and him. having surgery scheduled for tomorrow morning. Going on to say that the most extreme cases of the wounded men who'd flown with them were being operated on immediately.

Was this just talk with the morphine confusing him? He was beginning to have difficulty believing he was really at the Minsk hospital and not in the back of a convoy truck, headed toward a road paved with mines. He wanted to ask Volker where they were, but he was no where to be seen.

The Russian man who'd been giving orders in the truck was speaking to him. "We've checked you for vermin, *Herr* Gallen, and since your papers say who had a shower day before yesterday at an infirmary, it doesn't appear you have any. So you're now in a ward. And hopefully your bed will not be uncomfortable."

He now remembered the medics had helped him off his stretcher and put him on a bed with a mattress, sheets, and a blanket. *A real bed.*

"I didn't think Russians treated their German prisoners this well," he said, relishing the beds comforting softness. "Is it because I'm in the Resistance?"

"I don't know about that, but you're a patient not a prisoner. And, by the way, I'm Dr. Alexi Zeroff. *An* in addition to Russian, I also speak German, English, and Polish."

A Russian doctor in a German hospital? Well now, I wonder how that happened? The man looked to be in his early forties and had brown-hair and green eyes like Hedy…who claimed her green eyes came from a distant Polish relative. So maybe Dr. Zeroff is Polish.

"We're giving you medication to help you sleep," the doctor explained. "And in the morning we'll prep you for surgery. But in the meantime, *Herr* Gallen, should you need something simply ring the bell, and one of the nurses will come."

"What I need, is for you to send a telegram to Dr. Frank Rath in the Berlin hospital and tell him Volker and I got wounded and have been hospitalized in Minsk. The name of his hospital is on a folded paper in my wallet, and if you'll give it to me, I'll also pay you for the telegram—"

"I'm pleased to do it. So keep your money."

He disappeared quickly, and Geir closed his eyes. He was so exhausted, he slept until early morning on this warm and very comfortable bed.

Two medical orderlies awakened him. "We're giving you a warm shower before your surgery," one of them informed him.

"That's wonderful. "He wished he could remember the last time he'd had a warm shower…*much too long.*

The two orderlies worked quickly with one of them holding him, while the other scrubbed him. *A blessed relief.*

"Your papers show you were treated for dysentery," said the orderly who was holding him up." And that you were supposed to be re-checked when your convoy arrived at Kharkov to see how well you were doing.

But since you never made it there, then tell us if you're still having some problems." "My fever's dropped slightly, but —"

"You'll need some more treatment."

"*Y...you mean like medicated enemas?*" he asked, stumbling over the words.

"No. Just some additional shots in your lower back—"

"Which means more pain in my poor butt, doesn't?" he grumbled as the medic dried him off.

"Afraid it does" said the other medic, turning him on his side with a needle in his hand and

giving him—*Was it two or three shots...? It felt more like four.*

Then these two orderlies hovered over him as they wheeled him away to surgery. *My drugged imagination in this desperate time is clearly saying, 'I'm done for.'*

Some time passed; how long he wasn't sure. It all seemed so unreal, he had difficulty swallowing the broth they brought him.

The only food left? No more tins? He and the few remaining men in his convoy were surrounded by Russians in this dreadful cold. With Volker saying he'd kill himself before he'd let the Russians take him prisoner.

And Hedy, his beloved wife. What about her? He'd have to forget about her once the Russians took him to a prisoner of war camp. The pain of his glorious memories with her would be too great My survival depends on forgetting everything I've lost as Fate swallows me, placing me in either another time or dimension. With this being as real to me as actors in a movie. A fantasy. A made-up story that people say is not real—like he'd once heard Alvina explain to her innocent, six-year old Charlotte.

'But it is real too,' the little girl had disagreed. 'It's happening as they act it out.' Someone's nightmare? Someone's dream? A story on celluloid. 'Is this the way people in another dimension are contacting us?'

Otto once raised that very question but then went onto add, 'If it is then in our world, it's what we'd call madness.'

<hr>

Geir wasn't sure how long it had been since he'd his surgery, but it seemed a full day and night had passed. A nurse was standing over his bed talking to Dr. Zeroff. "When he woke up his pillow was wet with tears "He's been through a lot so see that he gets another sedative."

More lapses of time followed. *Another day and night. Did it really matter?* But what happened next did. His forehead was being stroked by a nurse in a blue coat and hat. "I got here as quickly as I could," she whispered, in a voice that sounded like Hedy's.

Hedy here? Briefly, he clung to the fantasy before reality struck. *I'm dreaming—has to be. She's in Berlin, and this is Minsk. Where I'm a prisoner. So who is this woman? Just a ghostly figure?*

But when he felt her lips lightly brush his forehead with a sweet kiss, tears stung his eyes.

"Hedy! Is it really you?" he practically shouted.

"Of course. You asked Dr. Zeroff to telegraph Dr. Rath in Berlin. And when he got the telegram, he immediately made a long distance telephone call to Dr. Zeroff, here in this hospital."

"That must have cost a fortune," Geir remarked.

"We didn't care."

"Still, you got here quickly. So how long was your train ride?"

"A day and a night," she said, straightening the white, nightshirt-looking garb he was wearing. And now Charlotte and I are here. Mid-afternoon in Minsk."

He squeezed her hand like he was still unable to believe she was really here. "Did someone meet you at the station?"

"Dr. Rath telegraphed Dr. Zeroff, whom he knows from medical conferences. And he met us. Since this hospital's in need of more nurses for those wounded you brought in. So we're on loan here for about two weeks."

"How'd Dr. Zeroff recognize you?"

"We had on our nurses' coats and hats. And he said when he collected yours and Volker's things, he saw pictures of us in them."

"Good thinking on his part." Geir touched her hand. "But where are you and Charlotte staying?"

"Here. Sleeping on cots in the cellar."

"Sounds uncomfortable."

"It probably will be. But at least we won't be as uncomfortable as those heavily guarded, brown-uniformed, Russian prisoners we saw at the train station." She placed her hand against his head. "You feel like you're on fire with fever."

"I probably am—but what about Volker?"

"Charlotte's with him."

"And Rudi Herrenvolk? He was wounded too…but somehow managed to drive us to the convoy that got us to that Luftwaffe airfield."

"And he's in this hospital?"

Geir nodded. "Somewhere."

"I'll find out and thank him. "

"It was my first time to fly. And it was so bumpy I almost got sick."

"Just be thankful you weren't abandoned."

"We almost were. With *Herr Hauptmann* Helmer at the airfield not going to fly us-"

"But he did," Hedy cut in, "so how'd you manage it?"

"I produced the diamond ring Daniel gave me for emergencies. And then-he was more than willing."

"Daniel loves you so very much. And he wanted to come with us, but he's in the hospital with pneumonia. Which having an asthmatic condition, makes him prone to it. So believe it or not, we had to stop him from getting up and leaving with us—"

"Did you slip away?" Geir asked.

"No. I burst into tears and told him if he came with us, he'd die. And if he died, it would be like leaving you a second time."

"That it would—but how's he doing?"

"Better. Since he's anxiously anticipating your return." She reached for the medical papers which were attached to a metal clipboard hanging at the foot of the bed.

"And Otto?" Geir asked, looking at her uncertainly. "What's he got to say about all this?"

"He's keeping his mouth shut—even if Daniel has left him in charge."

"These papers say your surgery appeared to go well. And that you will attempt to walk on crutches tomorrow, with two medical orderlies assisting you."

Geir tensed. "Does it say I'll be like someone clubfooted?"

"Yes and no. Surgery has been known to help some clubfooted people. But your situation— though similar— is not exactly the same. So, we'll have to wait for some medical advances in the future."

"And you don't mind?"

"Not as long as it keeps you away from that Eastern Front slaughter ground."

"But I want to be able to drive a car and motorbike."

"You probably will." She glanced at his medical papers again." Although, you'll have to learn to use your footing a bit differently."

"Which I will."

He watched her as she read the top sheet of his papers. "You haven't eaten much, so how about some noodle soup and a roasted potato this evening? Two of your favorite foods."

"I'll try and keep them down."

She continued reading. "You still have some fever, like I suspected when I touched your forehead."

"I think they took my temperature this morning."

"It's written here." She pointed at it. "So they'll be taking it again this afternoon."

"Plus, I still have dysentery."

"What it says here." She paused to turn the page. "Though it's not as bad as it was with these shots they've been giving you."

"I've had so many shots that between the dysentery and my surgery, my ass feels like I've had another good thrashing with that schoolmaster's cane."

She put his medical records aside. "Mind if I have a look?"

"Hedy, you're my wife. So you can do to me whatever you want."

He turned on his side, and she looked at his backsides, then his stomach. "There's a bruise on your stomach that's turning green—"

"Where Sergeant Kyer kicked me when I left my post, sick, and trying to make it to the latrine."

"My God that's terrible! And the bruise beneath your eye?"

"Sergeant Kyer again...but that's not as bad as those three-liter, medicated enemas

the infirmary gave me. They forced me to go outside in the freezing cold to a drainage ditch behind the infirmary."

"Terrible." She continued to read his papers. "Those enemas helped some, but if they were going to cure dysentery that way, they should have given you more."

"Mercy!" he intervened. "Are they going to do that to me here?"

"No. Apparently the infirmary in that small hamlet didn't have the medicine to give you those shots."

"Those medicated enemas were awful."

"I can imagine. But if it's any consolation one of the first things we learned in nurse's training was how to give enemas. And guess what? We had to practice on each other."

"I don't know how you stood it."

"I had to if I wanted to help people. And when I told Mom about it, she just took me in her arms and—to use Daniels words—said, 'Sometimes that's how the mop flops.'"

"Hedy, you were born with money. And Greta told me when you and she were traveling with Daniel in Hollywood, a film producer saw you and offered you a part in his next film. So why didn't you take it—"

"Several reasons, besides wanting to help people."

"Which were?"

"We were leaving on a cruise to Honolulu, and I was looking at your picture frequently, letting me know that if I were ever going to meet you, I needed to return to Europe."

"Me again? I still have difficulty believing it."

"When we came together it was meant to be…but getting back to my nurse's training. The worst thing about it was the first time I had to witness an amputation, and I cried. Although, I knew if I were going to continue in nursing, I'd have to toughen up."

Hedy and Geir were so engrossed in conversation, that a moment passed before they realized Charlotte and Dr. Alexi Zeroff were standing at the foot of the bed listening to them.

Dr. Zeroff gazed at Hedy with admiration. "It's a good thing your gorgeous wife became a nurse, because she'll be assisting me with an amputation in the morning."

"On one of the men who came with us?" Geir asked him.

"The one on the verge of gangrene."

Hedy turned to Charlotte. "How's Volker doing? "

"He knows we're here, but they were giving him a sedative while I was standing over him. So right now, he's unconscious."

"Then I'll see him later," said Hedy.

"I have a break coming up," the doctor informed Geir. "And if I could borrow your wife, who told me how much she loves *you* on our way over, I'd be very much obliged. Since we have some hospital business to discuss."

"Be it in Germany or Russia," said Geir, holding Hedy's hand, "my wife's committed to nursing. And any help you can give her, I know she'd appreciate it."

"The doctor and I've already gone over what we need to know about this place," said Charlotte.

◆

"Which gives us time to check and see what we're supposed to be doing tomorrow," Hedy explained, before allowing the doctor to usher her toward the ward's door.

"We need to talk, *Frau* Gallen, about something other than hospital business," he remarked. a concerned expression in his green eyes as he opened the door for her. "I took *Herr* Gallen's wallet and other things and put them in his own locker for safe keeping. Since he's carrying an extraordinary amount of money concealed behind his wallet's flap. And one of the wounded men, who came with him, recalled seeing him bribe a Luftwaffe *Hauptman* with a diamond ring, to fly them here. So I'd say *Herr* Gallen has a rich father—"

"Who's quite well off. And is my step-father as well as my father-in-law."

"Now that's interesting." A faint smile touched the doctor's lips. "Which tells me you and your husband have some entertaining stories I'd like to hear."

"Before Geir and I go back, I imagine you'll know all about us," she commented with a sudden uneasiness.

She was not sure what Dr. Zeroff wanted with her, but she suspected he was mentioning Geir's money in an attempt to mask his concern. Because from the expression in his eyes, it was obvious something was disturbing him. So, the sooner she found out what it was, then the better. "There's a small room in this hospital where we can have some Russian tea and sit at a table where no one will overhear us."

That sparked a fear in her. Was something the matter with Geir that wasn't on his medical papers? *Guess I'll learn soon enough.*

When they got to this small room, Dr. Zeroff seated her at the table. A lovely dark-haired girl about sixteen, and dressed in a nurse-assistant's uniform brought them some tea. "*Frau* Gallen," said the doctor, "Meet Pauline Wagner, my very best friend."

Pauline pulled out the chair between Hedy and the doctor. "I'm pleased to meet you." Hedy smiled politely, before taking a sip of tea. "And I gather from your uniform that we'll be seeing a lot of each other." However, she did find it odd this fortyish-looking doctor, with silver-threaded temples, had a sixteen-year old girl for a best friend.

"My German father, Dr. Frederick Wagner, is head of this hospital," Pauline informed Hedy. "Someone I feel certain you met briefly when you arrived."

"Pauline calls me, *Alexi*, when we're not in a formal environment," the doctor told Hedy.

"And you may call me that too." He fingered his tea glass in its silver, filigreed coaster for a moment as if hesitate to add, "In the hopes if we called you *Hedy*, you wouldn't be offended."

"I wouldn't be—but what's wrong with Geir?"

"It's not a health problem."

"Then what on earth is it?" she asked, shifting nervously.

"I talked to Charlotte about Volker. And she agrees that it is peculiar two war buddies were shot in the exact same place by a wounded Russian who disappeared—"

"Alexi isn't questioning it," interrupted Pauline. "But my father thinks it was done deliberately, so Volker and Geir wouldn't have to be part of the dangerous convoys headed toward Stalingrad."

Hedy shuddered. *Of course it was done deliberately. Recalling how Volker was always talking about doing something like that.* "What's going to happen to them?" she finally worked up the courage to ask.

"Pauline's father insists that three doctors must sign a paper saying it wasn't deliberate—"

"And if they don't?" Hedy stopped the doctor mid-sentence.

"Since their physical condition prevents them from being assigned to a punishment battalion, it could mean a trip to the wall."

"A trip to the wall!" she exclaimed. A threat she found more terrifying than those bombs falling on Berlin. "Which we can't let happen—"

"And we won't." Alexi took a drink of his tea. "I'm signing Geir and Volker's papers. And I think your Dr. Rath will too, once they're his patients in his Berlin hospital, but...?" "My father's causing not just *you*, but Alexi and *me* a lot of problems," said Pauline, a deep frown creasing her brow. "And refuses to sign Geir's and Volker's papers. Which should help to release them from the suspicions concerning the way they were shot."

"Her father's a Nazi," Alexi explained. "And although I'm part Russian and part Polish, I'm only allowed to work here because of the great shortage of doctors." He fished inside the pocket of his surgical clothing, and removed a wallet-sized sketch. "At age ten I was orphaned and sent to live with my Russian uncle. Who was such an outstanding doctor here in Minsk, that his notoriety inspired me to go to medical school—"

"But Alexi returned to Poland," Pauline quickly interjected. "Where he met his wife of many years."

Hedy gazed at the sketch Alexi was holding that looked like one she'd done.

"But sadly last year," he said, "when my wife was returning from a visit to her mother's, the train she was on got derailed during an attack, and she was killed."

'Still, what does all this have to do with the threats against Geir and Volker?' Hedy was tempted to ask, when Alexi handed her the sketch of Geir's mother. "What's this got to do with anything?" she asked Alexi, starting to get a little angry at the way he'd riffled through Geir's wallet. He was supposed to be checking his money and keeping it safe, but while doing it, he'd gone and removed something that was none of his business.

Alexi made a gesture, indicating she turn the sketch over. "That pencil writing on the back, is it true? Can you really sketch a face after having glimpsed a person only one time?"

Hedy's voice hardened. "Not exactly how or why. But *yes*—I've always been able to it."

"Amazing." Alexi continued to marvel. "I've never known anyone who could do something like that."

"So people have told me."

"Then I think my problem and Pauline's is solved. As well as Geir's and Volker's—"

"Frau Gallen looks confused," Pauline interrupted again. "So let me explain our problem and how it connects with her husband's and Volker's."

By now Hedy was so uneasy, her hands were trembling. *Still, what harm can there be in listening to what this very attractive, young woman has to say?*

Pauline held up a photo of herself wearing a dance costume. "I'm a ballerina and have spent most of my life studying ballet and other dances. But recently at one of the night spots in this city, a good friend of mine became ill. She was in a troupe that entertained the nightclub's guests with Russian folk dances So, since she'd shown me how to do those dances, I volunteered to take her place at the nightclub with the group. I never expected to have any trouble at this night spot, but when we were taking our bows, a drunk SS man grabbed me and drug me down a flight of stairs in back. He tore at my costume with the intent to rape me. And I screamed for help. The nightclub was noisy, making me fearful that no one heard me. When suddenly I looked up and saw a young, German private. And before I knew it, he'd given this SS man a fierce blow in the mouth.

"Praised be," I gasped. Then, this young private grabbed me, and we hurried out of the club."

"My father spends most of the time in his small room here at the hospital, and not in the apartment he keeps nearby. So that's where this handsome, blond private or rather, Hans Fischer, took me. He was very comforting and asked if he might call on me the next day to see how I was doing. Naturally, I agreed. And over the next couple of days we were together every chance we got. I loved him, and he loved me so much he proposed. And if I'd been of age we'd have married immediately. But since I knew my father wouldn't give his consent, Hans and I became lovers. Then he got called to the front." She quivered as she glanced at Hedy with sad eyes. "Re-writing his *will*, Hans left everything to me and even introduced me to his friend. 'He's to inform you if I'm unlucky and something happens to me.'

'Which I pray every night it won't,' I told him.

When I learned I was pregnant I wrote to Hans. "One way or another I'll find a way to get back and marry you," he insisted in his letter. "But, sadly, before he could, his luck ran out, and he stepped on a mine."

Alexi took Pauline's hand. "Now let me finish up. So Hedy will see how this is connecting with her husband and his friend."

"Then proceed, " Pauline urged him.

"Well," Alexi began, "Pauline is three months pregnant, but not showing. And her father is threatening to force her to have an abortion." He paused, his frustration clearly taking over. "Even though she's vowed to him she'll commit suicide if he does."

"My father wants a daughter who's a dancer and not a mother," she explained.

"And he's right," said Alexi, "when he says Pauline is more talented than any dancer he's ever seen. Which is the main reason I've told him I'll marry her—a marriage of convenience. Because my wife was unable to have children" He stared at her, then at Hedy's sketch. "So this way I can help Pauline raise her child, while she continues her dancing career—"

"And my father will agree to it as long as we can get the name of this SS man who tried to rape me, she added."

Alexi released a deep sigh. "Someone who remembers the way this brutal man treated Pauline, told me he's a regular customer at the nightclub. However, if they knew his name, no one's talking—"

"And photos are forbidden?" Hedy asked.

"Yes...because they sell pictures of the Russian dancers—"

"So the next best thing is for me to identify that man and have you sketch him," Pauline broke in.

"And if her father has a picture of this man," Alexi said, "someone in the SS will recognize him. Since Dr. Wagner believes this man, who attacked Pauline, works in the Minsk ghetto."

"Jew killers," Hedy mumbled more or less to herself. "And her father is planning on doing *what* to this man?"

"Kill him after the war," Alexi informed her. "Because he believes Stalingrad will fall. Germany will lose this war. And this man will become fair game."

Hedy looked from Alexi to Pauline. "Certainly something I wasn't expecting to hear.

"If my father kills him before the war ends," said Pauline, "then he's apt to make a trip to the wall."

CHAPTER TWENTY

A trip to the wall...like Geir and Volker could possible be making. Hedy struggled to control the erratic thrashing of her heart. "You have my sympathy, Pauline."

"Which I appreciate," she said, holding out her hand to her. "Especially considering when my mother died, my father volunteered to travel with a convoy troop to the Ukraine. Knowing a good many of these troops didn't have doctors. And his troop came under some severe attacks. *I can do better in Minsk,'* he said. A remark that helped him earn the position he now holds in this hospital. And though I hate to be the one to say it—" She leaned over to refill Hedy's tea glass. "My father's senses seem to be disabled."

"So," said Hedy, still puzzled. "If you identify this man and I sketch him, then how does this help Geir and Volker?"

"It's simple," Alexi spoke up. "You're the only hope we have. Which means that if I can make a bargain with her father to get him a picture and name of this SS man, he'll not only agree to let me marry Pauline, but he'll sign the papers saying Geir and Volker didn't get someone to deliberately shoot them."

"And you think he'll do it?"

"As Pauline implied he's after revenge and not thinking rationally. So *yes*, I believe he will."

"Then when do we start?" Hedy asked, with a note of impatience.

"Tonight—if Dr. Wagner agrees." Alexi regarded her for a lengthy moment before he continued, "With the three of us dining in the restaurant that adjourns the nightclub. And then visiting it for drinks, entertainment, and dancing."

"Which is fine," Hedy declared, finishing her tea and setting down its empty glass. "As long as Geir is informed about it before we leave."

"Pauline's planning to tell both Charlotte and him, while you and I discuss the surgery you'll be assisting me with in the morning."

"Killing an unborn child is terrible." Hedy said, thinking about Pauline's dilemma. "And Geir and I don't want any children until after the war because with all the air raids, something might accidentally happen to them."

"Good thinking." Alexi commended her. "But one last thing. Geir's not in the Resistance is he?"

"Why do you ask?"

"Because for one thing this hospital is filled with war-time resisters—many from the Minsk ghetto, assigned to work here. And the other—" He glanced around the room. "When your husband was foggy-headed he told me he was in the Resistance. And that you were born in Germany, but later became an American citizen. Something that makes him an unofficial American, like an ally."

"I'm an American, but I keep a German passport—"

"Which you'd have to have to be here."

"But as far as Geir being in the Resistance, it sounds to me like he's wishing... so *no*— he's not."

"I'm a Polish-Russian, and the Germans have invaded both my countries. Which made me hope he was."

"The Nazis are cruel, "Hedy remarked after a silence. "And Geir and Volker got conscripted into the Wehrmacht...need I say more?"

"Absolutely not." Alexi smiled.

The sun was setting as they prepared to leave. With Hedy, not expecting to visit nightclubs, brought only one dress, other than her nurses' uniforms. It was an aqua-blue dress that went well with her blue coat. And she'd brought a scarf that matched her coat with touches of aqua-blue and brown in it, that went well with her umber colored, high-heeled shoes.

She was anxious to hear what Geir had to say about Pauline telling him they were going out tonight. So she hurried to his bed before leaving.

"You look gorgeous, my lovely lady," he said, taking her hand. "So be careful, even if Alexi is watching out for you."

"I'll do my best...but did Pauline describe this ill-tempered SS man to you?"

"She said he was over six feet tall, blue eyed, and blond haired. And when he was in his early teens could have been on a Hitler Youth poster."

"That figures."

"Pauline has a good heart," Geir said, obviously impressed. "And she kissed me on the brow and thanked me for being so loving to my beautiful wife. Who thought enough of me to make the dangerous train journey, so she could be here. 'Because if not for Hedy Gallen,' she went on to say. 'My baby wouldn't stand a chance.'"

"I'd better get a look at this man tonight," said Hedy, giving Geir a kiss. "Or otherwise you and Volker might not stand a chance either."

"Somehow we'll get through it, but Pauline—"

"Is a different story. "Hedy stoked Geir's cheek with the back of her hand. "Alexi's treating us to dinner tonight and every night, we have to go out. Because he says Pauline's worried and not eating well. So if there's anything I can bring you— like we're bringing Charlotte —just let me know."

"I'm trying the noodles and the roasted potato tonight. And maybe some crunchy toast."

"Once we get back, I'm checking on you and taking your temperature."

"Still, Hedy, you need to take care of yourself."

"The only way I can take care of myself is learning you're doing better."

"You're quite worried but don't be. Volker and I will be on our crutches in the morning, while you're in surgery."

"And once the surgery's over, I intend to check with you about that." She kissed him again before turning to leave.

"Do you recognize me?" came a voice from a young woman who had been standing behind her.

"Pauline?" she questioned.

"Alexi got me this wavy blond wig, so that SS man wouldn't recognize me. And it's so long it's halfway down my back."

Surprised, Hedy stared at it. "It's been awhile since I've seen anyone with hair that length."

"I didn't think I needed a wig since I was in costume and heavy make-up, when that wicked man grabbed me. But Alexi insisted we mustn't take any chances."

"He's right," Geir agreed. "Because I had no idea who you were."

"Has to be that way," said Alexi, appearing on the scene. "Which will make it easier for Pauline to identify him without being recognized."

"So don't worry about us," Hedy whispered to Geir. "Hopefully, we'll get through this as quickly as possible."

The freezing night air outside the hospital made Hedy regret she hadn't brought her fur coat. *I should have it to wear even if I wasn't expecting to go out at night.*

Minsk still had many of its potholes, craters, and broken windows in buildings and houses from the bombings a year of two before, that people were trying to keep heated. *Most likely because there's such a fuel shortage in the city.*

Dr. Wagner had given Alexi permission to drive one of the hospital's military cars. And Hedy was grateful he knew where those craters were, even though many of them had boards and planks laid across them. Particularly those near the restaurant, that he had to circle around to avoid.

Since most of the city's restaurants were reserved for Germans, the soldiers not officers, found them to be quite expensive. But fortunately, the restaurants had a high quality of food, prepared by Russian chefs.

Like Pauline, Hedy did not speak Russian and would have had no idea what to order, had Alexi not advised her.

"Your choices are excellent," she told him, especially enjoying the Borscht or beetroot soup. "And when I go back to Berlin, I'm going to miss these extraordinary culinary skills of your chefs."

The dishes served family style, were beef stroganoff, cabbage rolls, beef *shashlik* on skewers, and Olivier salad with potatoes, eggs, and vegetables. Dessert was a sweetened *Pierogi*, similar to a roll.

"Everything on the table tastes better with this restaurant's Russian tea," said Alexi, pouring more from the pot on the table into his glass. "And maybe I shouldn't say it, but even with this country's lack of freedom, I've always enjoy living here."

"And you're staying *where*, while you're here?" Hedy asked.

"Mostly at the hospital. But sometimes I stay with my uncle's daughter, or rather my cousin, who lives in a large, Edwardian style house, which I imagine is similar to your Berlin boardinghouse, Geir mentioned... My uncle once owned this place which is in the northwestern part of the city."

'*Not far from the terrible Minsk ghetto*,' Hedy started to say, but didn't. "And other people live in this house? "she asked.

It's communal housing. And we have three nurses and a woman with two children ages ten and twelve, that I pay to clean the place and do the cooking."

"And the common room isn't divided?"

"Not yet, nor the kitchen."

"Then your paying her must make living there much easier for everyone."

"I'm trying to make it more like a boardinghouse. Similar to what Volker said he lived in, with you, Geir, and Charlotte."

"Geir's father owns it," Hedy said. "So all goes well...but are you the only man in the house?"

"For now. My cousin's husband, along with the cleaning lady's husband, are both fighting for *Mother Russia*."

"And you, Pauline? Will you living there with your baby if you and Alexi are lucky enough to marry?"

She nodded. "Particularly since I want to study ballet here in Minsk— the capital of Belarus. Which performed the first Belarusian ballet, *The Nightingale*, in Moscow in June of 1940.

It received much acclaim. So it doesn't bother me when my father says if I'm dumb enough to marry a Russian, I deserve to live in this severely war-torn city."

"But I thought Russians weren't allowed to marry foreign citizens," Hedy remarked.

"Alexi is Polish-Russian. And I've seen his Polish passport, and if it's possible—" Pauline winked at Alexi. "I suspect he has a Russian one too."

'Like I have an American one and a fraudulent German one.' Hedy considered adding, but knew better. *Alexi can tell her when the time is right.*

"Hopefully, my father's attitude will change once he gets this SS man's name and picture," said Pauline." But even if it doesn't, I have no objection to raising my baby here."

Hedy grinned at Alexi briefly. "Then maybe, if we're lucky, I'll get to see your house before I leave."

"My instincts tell me we're going to be lucky," he spoke up, giving her arm a reassuring pat.

When they finally finished dinner, they made their way through the restaurant to the nightclub on the other side of it. The nightclub had a street entrance, but in the freezing cold it was easier for the restaurant patrons to remain indoors and go down a hall to its other entrance.

Same as the restaurants, the nightclubs were mostly reserved for Germans, with an admission fee of twelve marks.

"Close to the price of four packs of cigarettes," Hedy remarked. "Which is expensive for an ordinary soldier."

"Hans had a father who gave him some extra money, like Geir told me his father did," Pauline informed Hedy as the club's lights dimmed. "And of course with the German officers and the SS ones, they have many benefits. And it's not uncommon for many to stay here until two or three in the morning."

"Which I've no intention of doing, " said Alexi, as the head waiter escorted them to a table in a snug corner. "Since I have to be off to bed early with the surgery I'm performing tomorrow."

Near the center of the candle lit, table's white-linen cloth someone had placed a glass ashtray and a vase of small violets—obviously grown in a greenhouse.

Pauline told Hedy and Alexi that the musicians here tended to alternate between Russian folk music and German waltz music...since the *Fuhrer* had outlawed swing music. "Something I can certainly do without."

The head waiter asked Alexi what they wanted to drink, and he turned to Hedy. "I know Pauline's not a big drinker, and I'm not either, but what about you?"

"Excluding wine, I only drink during an air raid when my father-in-law fills our glasses with cognac. So I'll have what you and Pauline are having."

"Which is lemonade."

"Something I always enjoy."

Vibrant, Russian-folk music flooded the air. And soon dancers in brightly colored costumes, stepped up on the small stage and began twirling like they would never stop.

"Can you do that?" Hedy asked Pauline.

"Oh yes." Her face split into a wide grin. "Plus the leaps and jumps that follow the twirling."

"Amazing to be so young and talented."

When the folk dancing finally ended, and the dancers took their bows, the lights came back up.

And when they did, Pauline said, "Those SS men sitting across the room from us were with him that night—but look, there's a half-turned, vacant chair in front of their table like they're expecting someone."

"Which hopefully is our man," said Alexi.

When German waltz music began playing, Alexi asked Pauline and Hedy if either lady wanted to dance. "Not me," said Pauline with a long face. "Because I don't like the way that *Sehutzstaffel* or rather SS man seated next to the vacant chair, is staring at us with his steely eyes. And he even has the *Tofenkofp* on his cap, with its skull and crossbones."

"That means he must put his life at risk for the community," said Hedy, "though I'd be surprised if he did."

"I've seen that man at the hospital talking to several of the maids," Alexi recalled. "But not anyone in particular. And from they say, none of them admit to knowing anything about Pauline's attempted rape."

"I've also seen that man at the hospital," remarked Pauline." And I know this may sound crazy, but I suspect one of the maids is his lady friend. With my intuition telling me the maid who cleans my father's office is possibly the one."

"Who knows?" Alexi shrugged. "If he has a lady friend there, then he's covering it well."

"I'll dance with you," said Hedy, continuing to stare at the SS man. "Since if he tries to cut in, then maybe I can learn the name of his missing SS friend."

Alexi craned his neck in the man's direction. Certainly worth a try. "He took Hedy's hand as he rose from his chair." Just be careful.

CHAPTER TWENTY-ONE

"Which I will be. "Hedy assured him.

And though the lights were now brighter, shadows still flickered on the dance floor as Alexi spun her around. "You're quite skilled at waltzing," she complimented him.

"As are you."

They were in the middle of the dance floor when she noticed the SS man, sitting next to the vacant chair, began moving toward them. "May I cut in?" he asked Alexi, stepping up to him.

"Let him," Hedy whispered.

"Then be my guest."

"That's Dr, Zeroff, isn't it?" asked the man. "From what some are now calling the military hospital, since the other one closed."

"He's my cousin," Hedy lied. "And I'm on loan from the Berlin hospital to assist with so many of the wounded there."

"Then you're a nurse?"

"A surgical one."

"Impressive—"

"But who are you waiting for?" she asked him.

"Waiting for?"

"From the way the vacant chair at your table is positioned, it looks like you're expecting someone."

"Yes, *Christopher*, who's certainly not a beautiful nurse like you."

If that's the man's first name, then we're making progress, Hedy immediately prided herself in thinking.

"And you feel certain he'll be here?

"What he said."

"The lady and I need to finish our dance," said Alexi, coming over and putting his arm around her.

"Then by all means, Doctor," said the SS man, bowing slightly. "And by the way, I'm Johann Busch."

"Nice to meet you."

After the dance Hedy, Alexi, and Pauline stayed another two hours, sipping lemonade, waiting for this man, Christopher, to show. Which for some unknown reason, he didn't.

"I think we should go," Alexi finally said. "Since tomorrow is such a busy day."

They agreed and gathering their coats, left quickly.

Pauline had a cot in the cellar along with Hedy, Charlotte, and some other hospital workers. But before Hedy would go to bed, she insisted checking on Geir.

He was awake, waiting up for her. "Any luck?" he asked.

"Not exactly. However we did get a name, *Christopher.* Which could possibly be the man's first name."

"Better that than nothing."

She put her hand on Geir's forehead. "You still feel like you have a little fever, so I'll check." She reached for a thermometer.

"Those shots are really helping my dysentery."

"What they're supposed to do."

When she finished taking his temperature, she smiled, pleased. "You've very little fever."

"Good to know." He turned on his side. "But you'd better get to bed, because you're assisting Dr.Zeroff with his surgery in the morning."

"You're right. So sleep well." And leaning over she gently massaged his neck and shoulders before kissing him on his brow.

"My beautiful, wonderful wife," he murmured. "How I ache to hold you against me."

⸻ ⸱⸱⸱◆⸱⸱⸱ ⸻

To Hedy's relief the surgery went well the following morning, the same as Geir and Volker's experience with their crutches. And although not on crutches, Rudi was with them.

"You're doing so well with your rehab, that you might be able to trade your crutches for canes sooner than expected," Alexi informed them. "Which by the way, your friend,Rudi, will be going to Berlin with you and not returning to the front because of his injury."

"That's great news!" Rudi exclaimed, an expression of excitement in his dark eyes.

"It is," Hedy agreed, joining them from the door. "And you're welcome to stay at our boardinghouse there."

"I'd love to, but my parents, brother, and sister all live in Munich."

"Then my step-father will send them some train tickets to visit you."

"That's considerate of him."

Hedy smiled thoughtfully. "He does things like that."

"Which is good to know in these troubled times," said Alexi. He gestured at Geir, Volker, and Rudi. "You'll heal faster if the three of you are able to get out of bed and play some games like checkers and chess."

"We'd like to," remarked Geir. "But Rudi's the only one of us who plays chess."

"Then I'll teach the two of you," he volunteered.

The words were no sooner out of his mouth than Pauline appeared. Her hair was in a ponytail, and she was wearing a gold ballet costume with matching toe shoes.

In the background, music to *The Nightingale* was playing, and she twirled around several times, before doing some leaps and jumps.

"Pauline!" Alexi exclaimed. "You're three months pregnant, so you can't do this much longer."

"I know, but I'm being careful." She stopped and took a bow, prompting Geir, Volker, and Rudi to applaud loudly. "And besides the baby likes it when I dance."

"How do you know that?" asked Hedy.

"Because I dream about her every night, and she tells me."

Alexi's brows climbed. "*Her?*"

"I'm having a little girl, *Hansi*. And in my dreams Hans is holding her."

"You're a fantastic dancer," came a voice from the open door.

Hedy turned around to see a man with silvery hair and lined cheeks standing in it. "Why if it isn't Dr. Filip Novak!" she exclaimed, rushing over to him.

"My medical conference friend," said Alexi, shaking his hand. "What on earth brings you here from Warsaw?"

"I'm second cousin to *Herr* Gallen's father-in-law, Daniel."

Dr. Novak smiled at Hedy and gave her a hug. He was also wearing one of those amber necklaces like Dr. Zeroff. "I know this lovely wife of his and her mother, Greta, quite well. However, Daniel was so worried about *Herr* Gallen, that Dr. Rath talked his German general friend into sending me a round-trip train ticket from Warsaw to Minsk."

"Today was *Herr* Gallen's first day on crutches. And he's accepting the pain of walking on them," said Alexi.

"Shall we show him?" Volker asked, grinning.

"Not necessary," said Dr. Novak, as Alexi introduced him to the three young men.

"Do you have a place to stay?" Hedy inquired.

"No. Because I'm heading back to Warsaw this afternoon."

Another man now at the door wore a *Totenkopf* cap, with its death's-head insignia on it.

Immediately, Hedy's thoughts flashed back to the night before..*Johann Busch. The SS man with whom I danced.*

His unexpected visit made her hands tremble. "It's a big hospital, so how'd you find me?" she asked, tossing him a sullen glance, "when you didn't even know my name."

He took his time about answering, "Wasn't as hard as I thought. Even though due to the sexual diseases our unfortunate officers sometimes get, hospital walls aren't usually not tapped. However, I think it's to say that— be it as it may— hospital walls *do* have ears."

Across the room Geir was glaring at the man "Excuse me," Alexi told Dr. Novak, "but it seems we have a visitor."

Dr. Novak turned and gave the SS man a hard look.

"Can we help you, *Herr* Busch?" Alexi asked, stepping up to him.

"Just having my shot records checked."

"Did your friend ever arrive?" Hedy dared to ask him.

"Weber?"

Christopher Weber. Now she had the man's full name.

"He and the head waiter got in an argument the night before. So Weber told me he's not coming back."

'*Then where will he go?*' Hedy considered asking him, but hesitated.

Her hesitation was obvious; prompting Alexi to ask the question as Busch turned to leave.

"You want to know about Weber?" His gaze traveled to Alexi's eyes. "Why?"

"Because he was once a patient here, was he not?"

"Not that I'm aware of," replied Busch, giving a self-deprecating chuckle before stepping into the hall.

Quite concerned, Hedy stared after him.

"That man was our only hope," Alexi reminded, allowing an awkward silence to pass before adding," So, tell me, did I do right or wrong asking him about Weber?"

"It was a natural reaction. But what about the maid here, Pauline suspects Busch seeing?"

"Pure supposition. And besides, if he won't talk, I doubt she would."

Hedy paused, thinking about Otto's psychic ability. "If I make a long distance phone call, I might be able to learn where this Weber fellow is hanging out."

A grin traced Alexi's lips. "If you can do that, then you're wizard."

"Not really." Again she paused. "But I do know someone who is."

"Then use the office phone and make that long distance call."

"Where I'm headed."

Hedy got through to Otto, quicker than expected, and explained the situation to him.

He didn't seem surprised in the least, and quickly began describing the nightclub. "It's called *The Grotto* and has a medieval look. Stone walls. Stone floor. Wooden beams on the ceiling. Dark, wooded panels like the old aristocracy had in their homes. But once you identify this man hurry and get out**,** before something bad happens."

"Will do," she assured him. And returning the telephone to its rest she remarked beneath her breath, "*Otto's Grotto. How convenient.*"

When she told Alexi about *The Grotto*, he was flabbergasted. "You mean this man,Otto, who's like a seer, is a tenant in your boardinghouse?"

"He's more like a relative."

"I've met one seer in my time. So I believe you but still—"

"Have you been to *The Grotto*?"

"Yes—briefly."

Hedy felt a shiver crawl up her neck. "Since time is of the essence I think we should go there this evening."

"I agree."

The weather continued to get worse, giving Alexi cause to suggest they eat at the hospital. "I've given some money to one of our good cooks here. And he's making his special cabbage soup for the three of us and Charlotte. Plus Geir, Volker, and Rudi."

Charlotte was pleased to dine with them in the little room where they had the excellent Russian tea.

"I'll do my best to see our men and Rudi eat this excellent soup," she promised. "But the main thing is for the three of you to be careful—like Otto warned."

"We will," said Alexi. "However—" he stopped when a startling message came over the intercom.

Another shiver of anxiety ran through Hedy as a voice announced, "Stalingrad has fallen. In his last message from a short wave, Marshal von Paulus said that he and the Sixth Army have been forced to surrender. And he's awarding the Cross to all the brave soldiers fighting with him for their sacrifice." The announcer's voice sounded reluctant as he added, "Since they've been without food for four days and have only enough munitions for fifteen minutes before being overrun by the Bolsheviks. They have done their duty. Long live the Third Reich! Heil Hitler!"

"What my father predicted," Pauline reminded

"The same as Otto," Hedy added.

"Even if Geir and Volker realize it's the wrong army," said Charlotte, "it doesn't stop them from having kind hearts, where suffering people are concerned. And they're apt to be upset because the food and munitions their convoy was trying to deliver, didn't make it in time."

Pauline gave Hedy a small, relieved smile. "I know you're glad Geir and Volker weren't fighting at Stalingrad."

Hedy's eyes were suddenly misty. "Had Daniel not come to Geir's aid, they probably would have been"

"I have a feeling this announcement will cause many German soldiers in the area to slip off and join the partisans," said Alexi in an upbeat tone.

"If they have any sense they will," Charlotte agreed.

Before they left the hospital Pauline, Alexi, and Hedy stopped by Geir's bed. He let it be known that he was quite disturbed over the harsh treatment the soldiers, fighting at Stalingrad, had received. And he felt sorry for the young men who hadn't realized what they'd got themselves into, until it was too late. "Because many of them were too innocent to know they were fighting in the wrong army," he lamented."

"I'll say some prayers for them," Hedy promised. "And I'll also thank God you were saved."

Geir laced his fingers through hers. "Stalingrad disturbs me, but right now this trip you and Alexi are making to *The Grotto*, is disturbing me even more. So if the man's there, and you identify him, then get out quickly—like Otto says."

"Which I give my word we have every intention of doing, said Alexi, giving Geir reassuring pat on his arm. "

"Then go," he urged. "Since I'm anxious for you to get this over with."

"Like me." Alexi nodded, patting Geir's arm once again before heading out.

The Grotto was fairly close to the northwestern part of the city, not far from where Alexi lived.

"On the way back we'll stop at my house, and you can meet my cousin," he told Hedy.

"Something I'm looking forward too," she replied, even if she it seemed her reservations about tonight were growing.

CHAPTER TWENTY-TWO

The nightclub was a well-known place people visited for its medieval setting. It was a place described by some as a pub, since they were said to have some foods that complimented their excellent selections of vodka.

Turning her head toward a table off to the side, Hedy noticed, that even in the dim light, some German officers had their eyes glued on her.

It made her feel uncomfortable, and she would have loved to have walked out. *Though, nevertheless, the fear of what might happen to Pauline and Geir if I did, is much greater than my desire to leave.*

The head waiter ushered the three of them to a candle lit table near the back, with a whitelinen cloth covering it. Alexi nodded his approval and his time ordered vodka for them.

Several SS men were seated at a table across from them. And when a man with his back to them turned around, Pauline gasped like she'd been jolted from a dream. "That's our man!"

Hedy quickly lifted her gaze to him. "He'll be easy to sketch—so let's get out of here."

Alexi motioned at the head waiter. "Sorry, but we're going to have to leave. Since the young lady here—" He took Pauline by the hand. "Tells me she feels sick at her stomach from the drive over."

"Then by all means." The waiter bowed with Alexi, rising, shoving some marks in his hand.

Pauline and Hedy, also rising, hurried with him to the door. When taking them by surprise, a team of angry-acting SS men, threw it open and stomped in. *Danger—like Otto predicted*, Hedy mentally said. *Only I wasn't expecting it to come like this.*

"Stalingrad fell because of the spies among us," announced the commander of the group. "So we're here to check your papers."

Immediately, Alexi, Pauline, and Hedy produced the information he was after. "We're hospital workers," Alexi explained.

Glancing at their papers, the commander handed them back to him. "Then you're free to leave, Doctor."

"Not so fast," yelled a voice across the room.

Christopher Weber. Hedy was beside herself.

"How'd you know I'd be here?" he asked, his gaze penetrating through her.

"She didn't," Alexi answered for her. "Since none of us here know who you are."

"That's a lie, Doctor." Christopher flared. "My friend, Johann, tells me she's been asking him about my vacant chair at that other nightclub."

"Just making light conversation with your friend at the hospital," Hedy quickly said, braving her best smile. "Because I barely know him."

"More lies!" Christopher thundered. "You two danced together." And balling his hand in a tight fist, he struck Hedy hard in the mouth.

"How dare you strike my nurse!" Alexi shouted. He lifted his arm to strike Christopher and might have succeeded, had two of the SS men not grabbed him.

"I ordered the three of you to leave!" shouted the commander. "So get out of here before I arrest you."

Fragments of the icy sleet stung them as they hurried to the car. "You'll get to see my place like you wanted," Alexi told Hedy, handing her a handkerchief. "Since it's close. And I can patch you up there, until we can get back to the hospital."

"Never in my life have I been struck like that," said Hedy, fighting her tears.

"I believe it."

There was a gutted house next to the Edwardian-looking one where Alexi lived.

"And it's large like yours," Hedy muttered.

"Like so many of the houses built in the last century." Alexi remarked as he parked the car in front of it.

Only unlike Daniel's Berlin boardinghouse, this house where Alexi lived needed some repairs.

There was no longer any paint on the window sills, and its floors had darkened over the years.

The entryway had a large mosaic of a fish on its wooden floor. It had been copied from a piece of Roman art but now, Hedy noticed, the fish had part of it's tail missing.

"If this place survives after the war, we've been assured there'll be some remodeling," Alexi told her.

Hedy continued to gaze at the fish with its missing tail. "Who was the fan of Roman art?"

"My uncle. Who took it upon himself to have that fish put in."

"And there were no objections from the Party?"

"Why would there be? He was having something copied from a very long time ago."

A dark-haired woman in the common room went over to Alexi and gave him a hug. "We haven't seen you in a week."

"I know, but we've really been busy." He put his hand on Hedy's shoulder and introduced her to his cousin, Natasha Ulyanov. The lady Hedy recalled he'd told her was dying of lung cancer. "*Frau* Gallen's helping us with Dr. Wagner."

"So he won't force Pauline to abort her baby? "Natasha asked.

"Correct." Alexi nodded. "Nor keep *Frau* Gallen's husband and his friend, from taking a trip to the wall."

"The wall?" Natasha gazed at him with a somber curiosity. "Whatever did they do?"

"They were on a German truck convoy." Then after a pause, Alexi added, "But had a Russian shoot them, in order to keep from ending up in Stalingrad."

"Sounds like *Frau* Gallen's in the Resistance."

"Not exactly." Alexi bent his head as if thinking how best to explain it. "She's a nurse on loan for two weeks from the Berlin hospital. It's just that like us, she's not supporting the *Fuhrer*."

"And I commend such a lovely lady for being so wise," said a large man entering the room." "I'm Captain Joseph Ulyanov, Natasha's husband."

"But aren't you...? "Alexi asked.

"Supposed to be on the front." he finished. "I got nicked in the shoulder. So since my unit wasclose, they suggested I come home for several days to see if I could help Natasha."

Alexi stared at the bandage on his shoulder. "I'll have a look at it after we get *Frau* Gallen fixed up."

"What on earth happened to her?" asked Natasha, staring at her bloody mouth.

"The same son-of-a-bitch who tried to rape Pauline, struck her."

"And you two were hanging around that man?" Her dark eyes boldly met his green ones.

"I can see Pauline's wearing a long wig that disguises her but—" Natasha caught her breath.

"Whatever on earth were you thinking?"

"Pauline needed to identify the man for *Frau* Gallen."

"Identify?" Natasha questioned.

"Yes," Hedy answered. "Since I can do an exact sketch of a person if I only see them once."

"And since Pauline's baby could possibly be aborted," said Alexi, "and *Frau* Gallen's Wehrmacht husband making a trip to the wall for a self-inflicted wound, she definitely needed to see that evil SS man."

"So now, I can sketch a picture of him," Hedy spoke up. "For Dr. Wagner's desperate to see his face, since I'm told he plans of killing him after the war. And the doctor's promised Alexi that if he gets a picture of this SS man, Pauline can keep her baby, and my husband will get medical papers saying his wound was not self-inflicted."

Alexi looked at Natasha. "You know how Dr. Wagner's threatening his underage daughter with an abortion—"

"Because he hates the Nazis—" Joseph broke in.

"Hates Nazis?" Alexi questioned, his mouth dropping open in surprise. "Something I find difficult to believe."

"So did I," said Joseph." But look at the evidence. The father of Pauline's baby was a German soldier, as is *Frau* Gallen's husband. And even if her husband was attempting to keep from fighting on the Eastern Front, nevertheless, he's in the Wehrmacht." His voice rose abruptly as he asked,"Are you aware of the hospital talk saying they find it odd, that so many of the Minsk ghetto Jews working there, are ending up with death certificates issued by Dr. Wagner?"

Now curiosity was mingled with the surprise on Alexi's face. "And the German authorities haven't investigated these claims?"

"I suspect they're reluctant to do so with doctors in such high demand."

Alexi took a quick, sharp breath. "I've heard some rumors at the hospital but if they're true, then what happens to those Jews?"

"Why they're whisked off to the Russian partisans," Joseph informed him with a crafty expression. "By some of your Russian maintenance people who work there."

"All I've got to say is if they are, then it's quite an act Dr. Wagner's putting on with his professed adoration of Germany and the Wehrmacht," said Alexi, shaking his head with disbelief.

"Dr. Wagner's an excellent actor," Joseph remarked with a hint pride.

"Must be," Alexi replied. "And this knowledge is putting me in such shock, that I'm not taking care of *Frau* Gallen's mouth— or *your* shoulder."

"I'm going to get an antiseptic for Frau Gallen's mouth," said Natasha. "And as for Joseph, I think he just needs a fresh bandage on his wound."

Outside the wind was getting worse, but to Hedy's satisfaction, Alexi worked quickly, and soon they were safely back at the hospital. "Think your husband's going to blame me for not being able to keep that sorry SS man from slapping you?"

"You nearly got yourself arrested for not letting him do it again— so *hush*. Nobody's going to blame you for anything."

When Geir saw Hedy's mouth, he exploded. "What the hell happened that you didn't make it out of that nightclub it in time!"

"We were leaving when the SS barged in. And then this Christopher fellow stepped up and accused me of spying on him. So he slapped me."

"And I swung my arm back to hit him," said Alexi, "but the SS grabbed me and said if we didn't leave they were taking us in."

Geir, now sitting up, pulled Hedy down on his bed and locked his arms around her. "You're such a delicate, marvelous lady," he said thickly. "An if I'd known this was going to happen, I'd have remained on that damned convoy headed to Stalingrad."

"No! I'd have taken ten slaps or more like this, before I'd have allowed you to remain on that convoy. And I 've said it earlier, but I'll say it again— had Daniel not come to love you like a son should be loved— you could have easily been one of those soldiers at Stalingrad."

"Of that I'm certain." Geir lifted Hedy's hand and kissed it. "Even if I keep insisting that *destiny* is pulling Daniel and I toward something much bigger."

Charlotte, now joining them, touched Hedy's cheek with concern. "Let's pray this SS man doesn't pay us a visit here at the hospital."

"What I'm worried about," said Alexi. "So I think it would be best if we speed things up. And you and Hedy leave with your men at the end of the week on the hospital train, where you'll change trains at the Russian-Polish border."

"I'm for it," said Geir.

"If your appetite improves you can do your rehab in Berlin, the same as here," said Alexi.

"I ate all the cabbage soup," Geir bragged. "Like Charlotte said Volker and Rudi did."

"Then good for the three of you." Hedy smiled. "Though I need to hurry and get my sketch made, so Alexi can give it to Dr. Wagner in the morning."

"Oh yes," Alexi agreed. "Considering he'll then sign one set of papers for me to marry Pauline, and the other declaring Geir and Volker were victims of a Russian attack."

"Will you be marrying Pauline before we leave?" Charlotte asked.

"My intention."

"Good." Hedy said, a ripple of excitement in her voice. "So that way we can all be at the wedding."

———— ••••◆•••• ————

The next morning Geir was with Hedy when Alexi handed the sketch to Dr. Wagner. The name *Christopher Weber* was printed on the bottom of it.

Dr. Wagner didn't hesitate to sign the papers Alexi handed him. "Never expected to see anything like this. But you've kept *your* word, so I'm keeping mine."

Arrangements were immediately made for the marriage license. "That way plans for our civil marriage ceremony can occur in two days," said Pauline. "In the hospital's little room. "

"Where they have the excellent Russian tea you served us," Alexi reminded with a smile.

The two days passed quickly and Hedy, Geir, Charlotte, and Volker were present for the wedding, as was Alexi's cousin, Natasha. It was a simple ceremony, even if Alexi did bring a flash camera, and Natasha a two-layer cake.

"In addition to this small bouquet of flowers I managed to grow inside the house," she remarked with an air of pride.

Pauline wore a navy blue dress with a white lace collar. "No veiled hat for me. Just a faux flower headband from one of my ballet costumes," she informed her five guests, before the brief ceremony began.

Dr. Wagner had said earlier he would not attend, making the excuse of pressing hospital business.

No one had expected him to attend— nor wanted him. So, the wedding went smoothly.

Natasha took pictures. "I've seen many a hard-hearted man soften, once he glimpses the innocence of his new-born grandchild. So don't be surprised if your father becomes overly protective."

Even with morphine and in wheelchairs, Geir and Volker were doing their best to accept the pain required for them to attend the ceremony.

"It'll be awhile before we're walking with a cane successfully," Geir remarked. "And after we walk with one, I expect it'll hurt— like walking with the crutches hurts."

"Probably like trying to walk— or rather hobble —with that *damned* broomstick Warda got for us," Volker grumbled.

"All he could get us," Geir reminded. "And it did help us a little."

"Sorry about that," Alexi told Geir.

"When a person's injured, Doctor, there's pain."

"Then it's just something he or she often has to learn to live with."

He handed him a cup of the excellent tea. "Though there are times, Geir, when hopefully, you'll be able to walk without using your cane."

"Something Volker and I are certainly looking forward to."

After everyone had drunk their tea and eaten a piece of cake, Alexi told Hedy and Geir, "You've done a fine job of looking after Pauline and I—"

"Which we'll continue to do if the need arises," Geir quickly added.

"And in this terrible war," said Alexi, "Pauline and I will do the same for you and Hedy."

"We'll stay in contact with letters." Hedy smiled, closing her hand over Alexi's which was joined with Pauline's. "And please don't forget to send us a picture of the baby."

"With all the censorship nowadays," said Alexi— "And considering. I'm a Polish-Russian who's not in the military, it'll probably be better to send our letter to you and Hedy, in care of Dr. Rath at his Berlin hospital. Will that be all right?"

Hedy nodded the same as Geir.

"And we'll send our letters to you from the hospital," Geir said. "With Dr.Rath's hospital return address on them. "

"I sometimes write letters leaving wide spaces where I've written in invisible ink, that you can only see under heat," Alexi remarked with a grin." But even so, if we had time we could work out some letter coding—"

"My father and I worked out some letter coding," said Geir, "that I'll show you before I leave." "Absolutely." Alexi's grin widened. "Because considering what I call my *duel* citizenship, something's telling me it's better to exchange our letters using the Berlin hospital's address."

"Especially since I'm there almost every day," Hedy pointed out.

◆

The rest of the week passed quickly. "With Geir, Volker, Rudi, and four other wounded men, being assigned to a hospital-train car. "*Frau* Gallen and *Frau* Reicke will be caring for you," Dr. Wagner informed them. "So we'll begin preparations for your Berlin trip."

The seven men were striped of all their clothing and made to line up in front of Dr. Wagner for their final medical checkout. "Seven naked boys ages twenty-three to sixteen," he muttered at Alexi.

Geir, like Volker, was surprised they'd be standing naked with other men, in front of Hedy and Charlotte.

"Charlotte and I certainly aren't happy about it," Hedy told Geir. "But Alexi has said that if we're going to be your hospital-train nurses, then we're required to be there for this final medical checkout."

That made sense to Geir. *But standing naked in front of Hedy with everyone staring? When I'm naked with Hedy I'm either in the bed or the shower. And feeling like I do with this pain, it doesn't stop me from being eager to hold her... so eager I might get a hard-on while I'm standing there? Would that ever be embarrassing. But worse, Hedy's so gorgeous those men in line are apt to get a hard-on for her— a hard-on for my wife!*

When he'd mentioned it to Alexi, he informed him he'd already spoken with the men about it. "And I'm going to be there standing over them, watching. And if necessary, I'm taking them into the adjoining room."

"Can't thank you enough," Geir told him, filled with a great relief.

"You can always count on Alexi to help us," Hedy assured him.

That certainly appeared to be the case when the time came for the men to bare themselves.

Charlotte and Hedy flanked the doctor's table. Where, seated, he looked over each man's records.

Hedy's mouth was still badly bruised, with a black bruise now appearing under her eye.

Still, all seemed to be going well until a short, freckled-faced man lined-up behind Volker, stuck his head out and hollared at Geir, "I never suspected you to be a wife-beater!"

Immediately, Geir felt his face burn with rage. "If you plan on going back to Berlin with us, then you'd better keep your mouth shut!"

"Is that a threat?" the man shouted.

"You're *damn* right!"

Stepping out of line, the man lifted his fist at Geir, who with his crutch under one arm, punched him in the gut with the other.

"Boys—stop that!" ordered Alexi, stepping between them.

"Or otherwise you'll be hauled off to jail," yelled Dr. Wagner, rising.

Hedy started toward Geir, but Charlotte stopped her. "Let Alexi handle it."

"Get back in line, Schnell," Alexi told the freckle-faced man, giving him a shove. "Some medications can make our patients take it out on our nurses...so watch it when you call someone a wife-beater."

"Sounds like you're talking about the SS," Schnell pouted.

"What's Schnell's first name?" Geir asked Hedy later.

"Helmut."

"Well, I'm not going to forget him."

"Geir—let it go. He's not worth it."

"What kind or wound does he have?"

"Shrapnel...that's too close to the spine to operate. So the doctors are hoping it'll eventually work its way out."

"No wonder he's so mean."

"I'm told that, young as he is, he's an expert at handling explosives. And why he was in a convoy is unclear to me? But Alexi says he's being mustered out of the Wehrmacht. And that once he's released from the hospital, he'll be making bombs at an munitions factory in or near Berlin."

"Wouldn't you know he'd be living in our city," Geir remarked with contempt.

CHAPTER TWENTY-THREE

On a snowy, February morning, the hospital-train from Minsk pulled into the Berlin station. There where several trucks waiting to take the wounded on stretchers to the hospital.

Geir and Volker were overjoyed when Dr. Rath lined up with Greta, Margit, the Brants, and the Schroders to welcome them.

"Home at last." Geir said, attempting to exchange hugs and kisses with Margit, Greta, and Alvina on his stretcher. "Hard to believe, but somehow we managed to make it back alive."

"And I commend you," said Dr. Rath, "or we wouldn't be here right now."

"But where's Daniel?" Geir asked.

"Still recovering in the hospital," answered Greta. "And he's in the best room, with an extra bed in it, waiting for you."

"And Rudi and I?" Volker asked.

"Daniel got the two of you a large room across the hall from his."

"And we appreciate it," Volker acknowledged. "Since we three wounded fellows have been through a lot together."

Dr. Rath went over to Hedy. "Dr. Zeroff telephoned me the minute you left Minsk. And he asked me to tell the family about that SS man striking you, because of the sketch you made for Dr. Wagner—"

"So he'd sign Geir and Volker's papers," Hedy completed. "Which, by the way, here are the papers he gave *me* to give to *you*." She handed them to the good doctor. Then she began telling him about Alexi's wedding to Pauline, and the wounded soldier Rudi. "He helped get Geir, and the others like himself, to the Luftwaffe airfield."

Clearly concerned, Greta touched her daughter's face. "Are you feeling better now? From the way it looks, that SS man hit you really hard."

"Doesn't matter since we got Dr. Wagner's papers, stating Geir and Volker didn't get shot deliberately," Hedy spoke with a slight boastfulness. "And in so doing, we were able to save Pauline's unborn child."

"Daniel's been really upset about that SS man striking you," Greta let it be known.

"Especially since it was over Volker and me," Geir snapped.

Hedy took his hand. "It's all right. But Daniel's quite anxious to see you. So the attendants are coming to take you, Volker, and Rudi in wheelchairs to your rooms."

Geir put her hand against his cheek. "Will you be coming with us?"

"Otto's coming in a few minutes. But I'll drop in later. Since Charlotte and I have to help the the other four soldiers who came with us, get situated in the ward." She planted a kiss on Geir's cheek. "So go see Daniel before he leaves his bed and comes down here."

"Then we'd best take the next elevator, *Herr* Gallen," said the medical attendant pushing a wheelchair in his direction.

When this attendant rolled Geir into Daniel's room, he got out of his bed and rushed over to him.

"Son-in-law you're home! Which is all that matters."

"Volker and I aren't doing very well on our crutches. Yet, we're to get canes in the very near future."

Daniel hugged him, "Just give your injuries time to heal."

The attendant removed Geir's shoes, as he requested, and rolled his wheelchair over to his bed.

"Can I do anything more, *Herr* Gallen?"

"Not right now."

"Then I'd best tend to *Herr* Brandt and his friend."

Daniel waited until he left before he turned to Geir. "Hedy says you and Volker are going to be similar to someone clubfooted. But don't worry, because after the war I'm taking everybody at the boardinghouse to America."

"Including Nicholas in Paris?"

"Absolutely." Daniel nodded emphatically. "And your new friend Rudi, that Dr Rath said helped save you. So if he wants to come too, I'll see he does. But getting back to you, Geir, and Volker. There're some excellent doctors in America. And if I have to move heaven and earth, I'm going to find one who'll put the two of you back the way you were."

"Hedy wants our children born in America," said Geir.

"So do I —especially after this war. Because Germany's going to be overrun with allies who'll be treating those here, like they're villains. Which I'm one, for not helping the Jews like I should have done."

"You say that but given the circumstances, what could you do?"

"Well." He sighed. "My cousin you met, Filip Novak, and I have several ideas. Nevertheless, at best they seem impossible—"

"Is it all right to come in?" Otto called from door."

"Please do," said Daniel.

Otto turned to Geir. "I just talked to Volker, and he reminded me, that despite the odds, his plan to get shot by a Russian *did* work."

"Certainly appears like it. "Geir reached for a bottle of pain pills. "So what did you tell him?"

"That he was desperate. And desperation often has its own repercussions."

Geir could feel his eyes clouding with anguish. "One of which was Hedy getting socked in the face by that SS man."

"When it's safe to talk about it," said Otto. "I want to hear all the details."

"You will. Because either she or I will tell you once we're back at the boardinghouse."

"We should buy her something expensive for having to go through that," said Daniel.

"I've offered. But all she wants is for the war to end, so it'll be safe to have children."

"How many grandchildren are the two of you planning to give me?"

"At least two—and maybe three. She says it's always nice to have a boy and a girl."

"I agree. And I'm anxious to be a grandfather."

With his socked feet now on the floor, Geir looked at Otto. "But tell, what you've done to the house?"

"Arranged for two bedrooms to be created on each side of the staircase, with a shower and a bath added to each one. Since that way, you won't have to climb those damned stairs—"

"Which would really be difficult for me right now."

"I told Volker on the way up, and he asked me to have an extra bed put in his room for Rudi."

"And of course, it'll be done by the time you leave the hospital," Daniel added. "And don't worry about moving your things. Since Hedy and Charlotte have already done it for the two of you,"

"That was thoughtful of them."

"They wanted to make convalescing at home as pleasant as possible."

A tear rolled down Geir's cheek as he stared at Daniel. "Just being home and getting away from that damned Eastern Front is pleasant enough—" He stopped, reflecting on the enormity of his father's sacrifice. "And at times, it still overwhelms me when I think you could be living in Switzerland away from this bombed— soon to crumple— city of ours."

"Wrong, Geir," he said firmly. "If you're *here,* I'm *here*! Considering how I've neglected you enough in my life."

"You saved my life and others with that ring you gave me. Which is something we can never repay." "Yet, you're still in the Wehrmacht," Daniel commiserated.

A sudden silence descended as he stared out the room's curtained window, like a bomb had suddenly shattered it.

"Now, Daniel," Otto responded. "You know what Dr. Rath's getting his general friend to arrange."

"Pencil-pushing for the Wehrmacht. Which will include Geir, Volker and possibly this Rudi fellow—

"And they'll be living here in Berlin with permission to live at home and not in the barracks,"

Daniel said, looking directly at him. "But still, I just don't like their having to remain in the Wehrmacht."

"I don't like it either," Geir spoke up. "Although, even with the air raids, it's better than the front."

"Provided the air raids don't get so bad we have to move to the country, leaving you and Volker here," Daniel said, his expression somber. "But what's really getting me is this general, who's Dr. Rath's patient, keeps saying that you and Volker got shot deliberately to get off the convoy—"

"Which is odd," said Geir. "Considering our medical papers are signed by three doctors who disagree."

"Well, Son, or rather son-in-law, all I can say is it's never good to have a Wehrmacht general thinking things like that."

"So what does your intuition say we're supposed to do for the Wehrmacht? "he asked Otto.

"We're permanently disabled—"

"—with your loyalty to the Reich still being questioned," he remarked.

Daniel looked at Otto like he was being pushed to the breaking point. "But what if this general decides to make trouble for Geir and Volker?"

"Well—" said Otto, a sadness passing over his face. "They'll have to show their loyalty by joining the SS."

"The SS!" exclaimed Daniel, flabbergasted. "Doing what? Killing Jews like we suspect?"

"No," Otto replied sharply. "Because they too, have pencil-pushing jobs for people who're disabled."

"Where?" Geir frowned. "At the camps?"

"This is madness." Daniel flared. "How could you even suggest it, Otto?"

He took a step toward Geir. "Think back to what I said about desperation."

"How can I forget?" he asked, cringing. "Since it often has its own repercussions." Now—overcome with a sudden, silent anxiety—he thought about adding, *'Something guaranteed not to give me a good night's sleep tonight.'*

"Give it some thought," Otto suggested. "And we'll talk more about it later."

He was turning to leave, when Hedy dropped in. "Be back at five, Otto, to drive Charlotte, Mom, and me to the boardinghouse," she told him.

"I'll be waiting. Even though Hugo, Fritz and I maintain it won't feel like it's home, until Geir and Volker are back."

Daniel motioned Hedy to step closer. "Let me see your face."

"It still has a little swelling, but it's not as bad as it was," she said, touching it briefly.

"I punched that guy, Schnell, in the gut for calling me a wife-beater," Geir informed Daniel. "And I was about to do it again when Dr. Zeroff stepped between us.

"Was this fellow you punched standing in line with you?"

"He's one of the four guys that came back with Volker, Rudi, and myself on the hospital train."

Daniel looked alarmed. "And he's *here* in this hospital?"

"In one of the wards."

"And he's going back to the front?"

"He's got shrapnel close to his spine," Hedy answered for Geir. "So he's being mustered out of the Wehrmacht and assigned to a munitions factory here in the city."

"And they're not doing surgery?" Daniel asked.

"They're hoping this piece of shrapnel will manage to work its way from his spine before they do." She shrugged and sighed. "I know, because Dr. Rath's waiting to get my opinion and Charlotte's, concerning the rehabilitation treatments done on these men—"

"Then don't keep our good doctor waiting," said Daniel, rising.

"I'll be back as soon as I can," she told Geir, giving him a quick kiss before hurrying out the door.

Watching her leave, Daniel pursed his lips as if in thought. "Bomb making requires a considerably skill at handling explosives."

"Which this fellow's supposed to have." Geir remarked, scowling. "Having got his expertise from his uncle, who worked with explosives during the Great War."

"And this fellow, Schnell. Is he a Nazi?"

"Probably not. Since I heard him grumble about the SS."

Daniel sat back down. "Don't take this the wrong way, but I need to get acquainted with him."

"Acquainted with him?" Geir questioned." Why on earth would you want to do that?

"It's a secret but my cousin Filip Novak, whom you met, is working with the Polish partisans— "

"The partisans!" Immediately, Geir felt a tremor pass through him. "While the SS continues to murder Jews?"

"Yes— *my* people again," reminded Daniel, his eyes filled with fear. "That Otto feels will be murdered by numbers you can't imagine at Auschwitz and other camps."

"Terrible. Since your people are *my* people," said Geir, extending his hand to him. "So what can any of us here do?"

"Nothing at this point since we need explosives and someone who can make bombs. Because the plan is that Polish partisans,disguised as SS, will go into Auschwitz and learn where the SS keeps their weapons. And then they'll give these weapons and explosives to the camps inmates, to insure a strong resistance."

"And this man, Helmut Schnell, who works with explosives, could possibly be the fellow you need?" Geir asked, jarred by the thought.

"Who knows? But it's worth a try. Which is why I'd like to get to know him—to see if I can trust him."

"You've always got Otto's intuition."

Daniel's hand reached to cover Geir's. "Whom I suspect, like me, will want Schnell to move into the boardinghouse with us."

"It's a start...considering Schnell's being mustered out of the Wehrmacht."

"And our place would be a good place for him to stay."

Geir shot his father a dubious look. "Even if he and I are at odds?"

"Well now... "Daniel released a pent-up breath. "That's where Dr. Rath comes. I'll see he advises him to stay with us, because he'll have some nurses close."

"Which, needless to say, Schnell and I will have to patch up things between us," Geir said, forcing a smile."

"He'll be more than willing, I suspect. Once he learns I won't be charging him rent, but paying him, for the fine work he'll be doing for the Resistance."

A terrible foreboding pierced Geir each time he thought about the Auschwitz Jews. "When it comes to saying lives, I'll do whatever needs to be done...so proceed."

Dr. Rath brought Schnell to Daniel and Geir's hospital room that very day.

"Free living at the boardinghouse!" Schnell exclaimed. "With nurses living there. Who could ask for a better deal?"

"Just one thing." Dr. Rath pointed at Geir. "Even with the hard feelings between you and him, the two of you must get along."

"Oh we will," Schnell assured him. He turned toward Geir. "And I apologize to you. And when your lovely wife comes in, I'll apologize to her."

Which pleasing them both, he did.

"War with its passion for survival, often generates a sudden brutality in people," Otto later explained. "That quickly becomes like a tool, enabling a front-line man to survive in his warring world."

But I'm no longer in a convoy traveling to the front, Geir reflected. *It's a different kind world now. Or is it? With all these air raids, and the Russians in a year invading us like Otto says.*

Then there's Auschwitz—now that's a whole different story. Bringing to mind what Klaus Warda told me, as we struggled on the convoy. 'The darkness of the night is often like death to a soldier.

Whereas when dawn breaks it reminds him he's survived.' The way I suspect those poor souls in Auschwitz also feel.

Geir, Volker, Rudi, and Helmut Schnell were released from the hospital sooner than anticipated. "Tell me what you think of your downstairs rooms and bath?" Daniel asked Volker and Geir.

"That you went to a lot of trouble," they both answered.

"Never mind as long as you don't have to climb those stairs."

Geir gazed at the staircase. "Which would be impossible right now. But fortunately,you bought us crutches, brass-topped canes, and wheelchairs, so we can at least get around on this lower floor."

Rudi took it upon himself to help Volker any way he could. Particularly in the shower, where he washed him, the same as the medics had done.

Helmut took Geir's old room upstairs.

It was on the opposite side of the hall from Margit's, the Schroders,' the Brants,' and Charlotte's.

Downstairs, Daniel and Greta retained their room so if their crippled soldiers needed help, they could quickly get to them.

Geir loved the new room Hedy had fixed for them; especially the leather journal she'd bought him and put on his desk. *With my books and model planes on the shelves above it,* Only this room was larger so Hedy could also have a desk, her extra *armoire*, and the gramophone they loved, with everyone's favorite foxtrot record. "Dardanella," along with the other records were hidden in the room.

Geir guessed she'd hidden them because the *Fuhrer* didn't allow swing music, which he viewed as including jazz and foxtrot.

"Feel like taking a nap?" Hedy asked Geir as he got up from his wheelchair.

She handled him his cane, and he hobbled the two steps to his bed. "I'd rather make love. But I feel so clumsy that uh "

"I've figured it all out." She smiled, taking his cane and putting it next to the bed. "I'm getting on top and doing all the work—"

"But, Hedy, that's not right."

"Yes it is. And besides, you're making such great progress with your therapy that if making love like that bothers you, then it won't be for long."

"Nothing you do bothers me," he murmured, a second before her mouth covered his.

Caught in the memories of their passion, his life returned. *Giving rise to my excitement along with hers.*

His organ throbbed through her, with the tempo flowing between like a beautiful Strauss waltz.

Her heart beat steadily against his as he squeezed her tightly. "How I've wanted this," she whispered, joyful tears rolling down her cheeks.

"No more than I have."

He loved Hedy so much he knew for a fact, there could never be another woman he could ever love like he did her.

"I've missed this more than you could ever imagine," she murmured.

"Like me." Geir breathed, his body vibrating with a sudden, yet awesome fulfillment.

"Only in my dreams were you with me these past few months," she whispered. "But now—" She grinned as her body lurched against his with a wave of pleasure. "They've become a reality."

Sometime later she informed him, "I'm washing you in the shower in the morning, like Rudi's doing Volker—"

"Don't put yourself out."

"I'm not in the least."

Poor Volker. Geir sighed. *He doesn't have a wife like me. Which still amazes me that I have one— when I didn't even have the money to court a woman... Regretfully, a lot of young fellows on the convoy didn't have money to court a girlfriend either. So as many of them said, 'We ended up marrying the army.'*

And then there was Daniel. Who came back in my life when I needed him the most.

Geir, Volker, and Rudi were expected to return to the Wehrmacht with pencil-pushing duties in June.

Dr. Rath was pleased that Geir and Volker were doing much better, after the daily therapy they received. "There's still some pain, but otherwise, we're doing quite well," Geir informed Margit. "Even if the threat of daytime air raids is ever present, with more and more expected to come. So we need to work on moving faster with our canes."

"That's true," Dr. Rath told him. "One of the main reasons I want you to walk by next year without needing yours so much."

It was what Geir wanted too.

In the bedroom things were returning to normal between Hedy and him. "No more having to do all the work," he'd remind her, smiling.

But later, in his new journal, Geir wrote:

"If war weren't raging in Europe, my story and Hedy's might have ended here...but the war has not forgotten us. With one of those voices inside me warning, that a terrible darkness, involving Hedy and me, has yet to come."

CHAPTER TWENTY-FOUR

Geir noticed that Helmut Schnell, Rudi, and Nicholas— whenever he returned from Paris to Berlin — spent a lot of time talking to Otto.

"None are Nazis. And they hate to hear what Otto maintains he believes is happening to the Jews in those work camps, "Daniel told Geir one evening. "So things are looking up. And plans are forming for the time we deem right when Helmut, without arousing suspicions from his German employers at the factory, will request a medical furlough."

"Because of his condition is not improving?"

"Exactly. Since it's written in his medical records he'll need surgery when this shrapnel moves further away from his spine... which only then, will allow him to get the furlough Dr. Rath will claim, he needs."

"And Herman will actually have this surgery?" Geir asked.

"He'll supposedly go to Warsaw for it," Daniel said. "Where he'll be under the excellent guidance of Dr. Novak. And a week or so after it, he'll be instructing some of my cousin's partisans on how to make grenades and bombs, in the hopes they'll either attack Auschwitz or slip these weapons to the prisoners to do it quickly... "

He did not finish, but Geir knew what he meant.

"I hope there're successful."

"So do I." Then, Daniel added with a tinge of despair, "Even if Poland seems to be more interested in the war on the Eastern Front, than attacking the Germans in that Jew-killing camp."

"Do you think conditions in the camp are as terrible as Otto seems to think?" Geir asked, struggling to keep fearful images from building in his mind.

"The word of a psychic." Daniel frowned, appearing to contemplate it for a moment. "But he says, like me, that without actually being in the camp or getting movies of it, how can anyone really know what's happening there. Since no one in their right mind would volunteer to be a prisoner. Even if Dr.Novak claims there was a Polish man who supposedly did."

Dumbstruck, Geir gazed at his father. "A horrifying thought I have difficulty believing."

"So do I." Daniel's eyes flashed with frustration "If only I could find a man, who could make some movies of what'd happening in that camp without getting himself killed."

"But hasn't a rumor been circulating that some Poles have escaped the camp?"

"If they have, nobody's listening to them."

"They're probably hiding."

Geir's head jerked up. "I know I'd be. But you mentioned something earlier about Dr. Novak hearing that German Red Cross ambulances— if they're not doing it already —will be delivering Zyklon B gas canisters to the camp."

That's probably just a tale, Son."

"But what about this expensive equipment Helmut will need to make these grenades and bombs?" Geir asked. "Will you be providing it?"

"Dr. Novak will be helping me."

"And Otto?" Geir's eyes narrowed. "What does he have to say about you two doing this?"

Daniel gazed at him with a concerned expression. "Not much. Which I've learned is his way of saying it's a gamble."

"It does seem to be one," said Geir. "With Otto urging, 'Think like a partisan, because the more SS you can mow down, the better for everyone.'"

"If only we had photographic proof," Daniel insisted. "The world would have to listen. But since we don't, I suspect the partisans will mainly use the explosives Helmut trains them to make, to stop trains and rob them of their munitions."

"Something of which I'm well aware," Geir said, remembering the bullets wheezing over his head in Poland. "And I'm pleased Volker and I have also become such good friends with Helmut."

Daniel cocked his head. "So am I. And he jokes with me that he's now your freckled-faced buddy."

"He had a lot of anger before he moved in here with us."

"Yes he did," Daniel agreed. "And he confided to me that his anger came from being orphaned and raised by a cranky but moneyed aunt, who continually brow-beat her war-injured brother. Who was so skilled at making bombs, he earned a Grand Cross from the Great War, that he bequeathed to Helmut."

"If this uncle had a Grand Cross, then it's a wonder he didn't blow his cranky sister up."

"I think this uncle died sooner than expected. So anxious to get away from his aunt, Helmut seized the opportunity to join the Wehrmacht but—" Daniel paused. "Shifting our conversation, I know Rudi will be working in the same building with you. Yet, have you and Volker heard anything about the work you'll be expected to do, besides the pencil-pushing you've been assigned?"

"Menial work like filing," Geir grumbled. "And finish filling out the paperwork the senior officers who are too lazy to complete. And of course, making coffee and cleaning the latrine—when there's no one else to do it. Which, I suspect, there won't be."

"They're putting shit on you, Son," said Daniel, banging a hand on the table in front of him. "And doing it every chance they can get. And I don't mean, cleaning the latrine."

"Making things unpleasant appears to be their intention," Geir remarked with disgust. "But at least it beats the convoy and the front."

"That it does," Daniel agreed.

The following day a letter came addressed to Dr. Rath at the hospital, from Alexi Zeroff.

"Look at this." The doctor smiled, holding it up for Hedy and Geir to see. "I suspect this is the letter you've been waiting for."

Hedy took it and quickly opening it, nodded it was. "We've exchanged only a few letters since leaving Minsk. Because Geir and I urged Alexi and Pauline not to write unless they had the time."

Dr. Rath's smile widened. "Which was smart thinking, since in that particular hospital I'd say the Zeroffs are a very busy couple—"

"That hospital's always needing help," Hedy interjected.

"But hurry and read us the letter," Geir urged.

"I'll do better than that." She held up a picture of Pauline holding the baby, with Alexi standing next to her. "It's a girl like Pauline predicted," Hedy read. "And her name is Hansi, and all is well. Which means that after the war we'll get together, so you can meet her. Much love, from the three of us."

"Why she's beautiful!" Geir and Dr. Rath exclaimed.

"I'm getting a small frame and hanging this wonderful picture in our room. "Hedy smiled, admiring it.

Breathless with emotion, Geir put his arm around Hedy. "And to think, little Hansi wouldn't be alive if it weren't for you and your unique sketching ability."

"It'll be easy for me to do a sketch of the baby from this picture. So I think I'll do it tonight and mail it to Pauline and Alexi."

"Something I feel certain they'll always treasure," Dr. Rath replied.

Which they did, with only a week following before they sent a thank you card. "We love it so much we've framed it," Alexi wrote. "And we can't thank you enough. The only problem is Dr. Wagner's come around, like Natasha predicted, and he wants a picture of little Hansi too."

"Then I'll do a sketch for him." Hedy wrote back.

The summer moved along smoothly, until August. *A terrible time, when bad news came at us with a ferocity resembling a swarm of allied plane, dropping their bombs.*

First was the encoded letter from Alexi, parts of which on its skipped lines, were written in invisible ink. It was obviously a coded message addressed to Dr. Rath at the hospital, which under Alexi's Russian name was written, *Medical Business.*

"So naturally I opened it," said Dr. Rath, blotting his eyes before he handed it to Hedy and Geir. "And I learned with great pain, how hard it would be for me to deliver to you such news."

Tears were immediately in their eyes too. So the good doctor, taking back the letter, began reading it to them in his soft voice:

Dear Special Friends,

I hate to be the barer of such terrible news, but Pauline and Dr. Wagner have been murdered! That SS man, Christopher Weber, went to the hospital with severe stomach pains. And before the night was over was pronounced dead from a heart attack. His friend, Johann Busch, accused the doctor of killing him. (Which, of course, Dr. Wagner had wanted to do, but I doubt he did.) Wagner and I shied away from treating him, since Pauline was now quite happy. So another doctor, who had no knowledge of Dr. Wagner's threat, was assigned to treat Weber.

Johann Busch, like Pauline suspected, was having an affair with the hospital maid who cleaned Dr. Wagner's office. And it came to be known that Busch gave her the materials and instructed her on how to wire the doctor's desk, so a bomb would explode and kill him. This evil man was hiding not far from Dr. Wagner's office door. But since only the maid was allowed to be in it without the doctor present, he used her to plant the bomb. Unfortunately, Pauline was with her father at his desk when the bomb went off. He'd called her in to give her some money for little Hansi. (Not that we needed it.) However, as her grandfather, he wanted to participate and have Pauline buy the baby some expensive items from him.

I wasn't far away, treating a patient, when the bomb went off. It sounded like it came from Dr. Wagner's office. So I went there as fast as I could. The three Russian maintenance men, who'd helped the doctor save so many of the Minsk, ghetto Jews, rushed in with me. The maid was crying and hollering at Busch, 'We've also killed Pauline, the ballerina!' Busch was trying to shut her up and get her out of the building when I arrived. And seeing Pauline on the floor, I ran over to her and threw my arms around her as she took her last breath.

Before I knew it, the maintenance men had grabbed Busch and the maid and taken them off to God knows where? I suspect they either murdered them or handed them over to the Russian partisans. Who probably ended up having them shipped off to Siberia, where they'd be forced to work in the salt mines for the rest of their lives.

Knowing the Gestapo would question me, I didn't ask these maintenance men anything.

Pauline and her father were Germans. With people in the hospital gossiping that an SS man and a maid had killed them and disappeared...so the Gestapo really didn't want to delve too deeply.

Now comes the big question, 'What about little Hansi?' My cousin loved her, but since she was dying of lung cancer, she knew she couldn't take care of her for very long. Also, with the Russians on the verge of re-taking Minsk, the city would become quite dangerous, with many more of its houses expected to be blown up. Certainly not safe for my baby—nor was the hospital, with all our sick patients.

Natasha had friends who lived in the country. The family loved children and had two of their own. Their ages were around fifteen and eighteen. And they were more than anxious to take little Hansi. Who, due to Pauline's lack of milk, was on bottles. And when I offered them money, because they were collective farming people, they refused to take it. Until Natasha explained they were talented people who were doing quite well farming. 'We'll keep little Hansi until after the war,' they promised me.' But if you don't make it back, she'll just remain our daughter, where she'll be safe.'

Under the circumstances, sad as it was to me, I had no choice but to leave her in the country where she'd be safe with these fine people.

So my heart is breaking but don't be sad for me. Just be thankful in these dreadful times, I've found a way to keep little Hansi safe. And, God willing, I'll get back to her.

Yours,
Alexi

Geir and Hedy were now weeping loudly. "Little Hansi's safe," said Dr. Rath after a silence. "And as bad as things are just remember that she's all right."

'But without Pauline and Alexi, could things ever be all right for Alexi's tiny daughter?' Geir considered asking him.

In 1943 daytime air raids near Berlin were rare. So Geir and Hedy were not particularly concerned when Otto, looking somewhat uneasy, announced, "These days the rationing is getting worse and worse. And I'm having an extra hard time getting supplies for the household. So Hugo, Fritz, and I will need to try to do some more marketing today."

The heavy rationing meant that sometimes,they had to go to eight stores in order to acquire the household's needs. "Even with my strong intuition concerning diminishing supplies, I'm not always able to locate food and other items, such as toilet tissue, in the various grocery stores and other shops."

"And believe me I've tipped the store owners generously to call us when they get what we want," Daniel would add. "But even that's not helping much. Which is the reason I'm accompanying the Schroders today." He then he turned to Margit, Alvina, and Ernst. "So I'll be calling in from time to time if something unforeseen comes up, and you need to be driven somewhere. "But they all said getting food and other supplies was more important. And advised me not to worry—they would be fine.

Since Greta was going to the hospital early, to finish last night's paperwork, she hitched a ride with Daniel and the Schroders. However, Otto before leaving stopped at the door, turned around, and regarded Margit and the Brants with a hesitant expression. "Remember—get in the shelter if there's an air raid. And don't worry about us."

In view of the need to give the grocery shoppers an early start, Dr. Rath sent his car with his excellent driver, to pick up Geir, Hedy, Charlotte, Volker, and Rudi to drive them to work. "It'll be a narrow squeeze, but you'll make it," the doctor joked on the phone.

These days people lived in constant fear of daytime air raids on the city. And Geir was particularly worried about Margit, as was Dr. Rath who came to the house three evenings a week to check on her.

"She hasn't seemed the same since I returned from Russia," Geir informed the doctor.

"I know. And I'm doing all I can for her."

That was the way it had been for several months.

"You're not nearly as talkative as you used to be, " Geir reminded Margit, before he left for work that morning. "And as of last week, you announced you weren't going to do the sewing and cooking you love to do. So what's the *matter*? Is it the air raids?"

"That's part of it," said Margit. "But then again, everything has come to pass that I wanted for you." She reached out and took his hand. "You're happily married. Daniel loves you. And you're not returning to the convoy or the front. So it's like my work is finished."

Geir kissed her forehead. "You've done so much for me I don't even know to thank you."

"Just remember I love you."

"As I do *you*."

Two weeks ago Daniel had suggested to Margit that she and Alvina go to a village not too far from the city and spend time at a lovely country inn there. "It'll get you away from these damned air raids," he'd pointed out. "And besides the Schroders love to cook and don't mind helping Ernst do some of the cleaning."

"I know," said Margit. "And Dr. Rath keeps reminding me he has a doctor friend living nearby, who'll check on us."

"Then go," Geir urged her. "There's nothing to keep you here."

But she shook her head. "If I'm to go down, it'll be here."

"And Alvina feels this way?" he asked.

"She's willing to go but, like me, doesn't want to leave her family with all these air raids."

That being said, there was nothing more anyone could do.

CHAPTER TWENTY-FIVE

Alvina noted the sun had a pleasant light that morning when the Daniel and the Schroders went shopping. "With its golden shine offering a world of possibilities," she remarked, smiling.

But when an hour passed after they'd left, and Margit complained of a sharp pain in her right side, Alvina quickly put down her ironing and called the hospital. "Dr. Rath was in surgery," said the male voice on the other end of the phone. "But if *Frau* Margit Gallen could come to the hospital, he'll probably be finished by the time she arrives.

"Should we take a cab or the trolley bus?" Alvina asked him.

"These days it seems the cabs are slow. So take the trolley bus. And you'll probably arrive when the doctor's finished and has a little time before his next surgery."

Margit had asked Alvina not to bother Hedy and Charlotte, who were also in surgery with the doctors, *nor* Greta. "Who's usually quiet busy with paperwork at this time of day."

The trolley bus was just down the street, loading up passengers, so Margit, Alvina, and Ernst didn't have to wait. It revved its engine and proceeding in the direction of the hospital, it made only two more stops.

People going to work crowded in it at each stop and found seats. Margit and Alvina were seated together, with Ernst directly behind them.

He was the first to hear it and nudged them. "Listen." It was a soft hum that sounded like it came from a musical instrument. And then it suddenly got louder. *A siren—but from what direction was it coming?* Alvina, like Margit, tilted her head as if in question.

"It sounds like it's coming from a different part of the city," said Ernst, rising with a worried look. "Those planes? Are they twelve minutes out or six?"

"Six!" someone hollared as three allied planes suddenly came into view. They circled and dove down like a hawk about to pounce on a rabbit. But, surprisingly, to everyone's relief, they passed over the trolley bus and headed in another direction.

Then the wail of the sirens increased, with cars slamming on their brakes, and several passengers screaming at the trolley driver, *" Get us to a shelter!"*

"I'm headed to the big one at the hospital three blocks away!" he hollared back— a second before the shadow of a fourth allied plane appeared.

Time was rushing, rushing, rushing— toward something that wasn't that far away.

"Where's the Luftwaffe?" shouted an voice in the back.

Alvina had her arms wrapped around the terrified Margit. "I knew it would end like this!" she cried as this allied plane came at them.

"A missed target!" someone yelled.

The bombs were close.

Explosions from a blackened sky. Flipped vehicles. Burnt buildings. And large chunks of glass, dust, and debris began lining the street.

The trolley bus was turned upside down.

Helpers were waiting to aide the victims once the *all-clear* siren blew. But sadly, the only person still breathing in the trolley bus was Alvina— who wouldn't be for long.

"We've lost two friends and now three family members in one month," Geir remarked to Hedy, Charlotte, and Volker at Alvina's bedside.

Tears were on all their faces, even Alvina's.

"It's so awful, Geir." Hedy sobbed. "That my handkerchief is absorbing my tears like the desert would do a rain falling on its dry sand.

"With the bad news *this* time being an allied air attack, " Volker replied, wiping his eyes. "Instead of the murders of Pauline and Dr. Wagner."

Charlotte held Alvina's hand as she uttered her last words, *'W...we'd almost made it here.'*

"It's terrible they didn't make it, " Geir told Hedy, his arms around her.

"The trolley was close us," she informed him. "But there was such a great deal of fire it made it difficult for us to get to the people."

"Sounds like the allies must have dropped some incendiary bombs like we dropped on London."

"I'm sure they did."

When Otto learned of Margit and the Brants' deaths, he was quick to blame himself. "I can't see everything. But why couldn't I at least see this? "

"There are some things we're not meant to see," Daniel pointed out, tears in his eyes.

"Even so I turned back to look at Margit as I left." He hesitated, allowing a moment to pass before continuing, "Because there was something about the pale color of her complexion. Was she ill? And I thought about mentioning it to her, but whenever Dr. Rath would remark, 'you look pale.' She'd just brush him off. 'I haven't been in the sun very much, since I saw you last.' Which she hadn't."

Rudi and Helmut made no bones about how deeply grieved they were for the loss of these fine people. But regardless, they tried to hold themselves together for their friends.

Rudi helped Charlotte make a telephone call to Nicholas in Paris. And he promised he'd get to her in Berlin, the same as his parents, whom he'd be calling right away.

"He's certain the general he works for will give him a brief furlough," Charlotte said, putting the phone back on its rest.

Everyone was beside themselves, with Dr. Rath stepping in to help Daniel, Volker, and Charlotte with the funeral arrangements.

Rudi and Herman also helped him with them.

At first Geir and Volker were inconsolable, but gradually came to understand that had they not been wounded, they'd have made it to the front with their convoy troop. "And we wouldn't have had these special months we got to spend with our loved ones," Geir said.

"That's for sure," said Volker, tears in his eyes.

Margit was buried in a space between Wilhelm and Noelle, with the Brants buried only a few feet away. Geir along with Volker, Nicholas, Rudi, and Helmut saluted them and clicked their heels together.

Daniel insisted on paying for all three of the funerals. "It's the least I can do for these fine people," he said through his tears. "And Margit. I owe her a lot for the way she raised my wonderful son, who's such a great human being."

When Nicholas and his parents arrived, they did everything they could to comfort Charlotte and the others who were in such dire grief.

Particularly the Schroders, who were so grieved that for several days they neither ate nor slept.

Due to the night's air raids they went with Daniel and Geir, the day after the funeral to the cemetery. It was early dawn, but it didn't stop each man from lighting candle at the graves.

Geir also lit a candle at his mother's grave.

Back at the boardinghouse, Greta would burst into tears whenever she'd pick up an unfinished piece of sewing Margit had put aside.

Naturally, everyone did all they could to comfort her. "She's upset too. Over our concern for the Jews in Auschwitz and other camps," Daniel replied." And I've caught her crying about it several times."

"Which the allies aren't doing anything about." She'd sob. "With it being rumored that Roosevelt won't allow the camps to be bombed."

Daniel took her hand. "Doesn't make any sense to me. Unless Roosevelt hates Jews too. Because bombing them would create the panic that would allow many prisoners to escape. And if some died, then it would just be a release from their torture."

"Well at least it might alert the world to the camps," said Helmut. He produced a report from an underground Warsaw newspaper, that described the horrors of Auschwitz. And he went on to say Dr. Novak had read in an underground paper, that sometime back, a Polish princess had slipped out of the country with a request to the British to bomb the camp."

"But the other story," said Dr. Rath, listening to the talk, "is that several years ago, exiled Polish agents, were to be parachuted into Poland with eight hundred pounds of equipment. Which included dynamite and radio transmitters. But there was a thick cloud cover, causing their pilot to overshoot. ' Damn! The Tatra Mountains are coming into view,' he was said to have informed the Polish agents. So if they'd actually planned on bombing, their accuracy would not have been guaranteed. Plus, the eight hundred pounds of equipment was weighting the plane down, so there was no time to adjust the fuel. An irony, that forced these Poles to bail out directly over Auschwitz. With each man having been given a cyanide tablet—in case he got captured."

"Which unfortunately some Polish newspapers said was just propaganda," Daniel added with a sigh. "Something that does raise questions," remarked Dr. Rath, giving his head a shake. "But in the meantime your life here must go on. Which brings me to a couple I know, who'd be willing to do the housework that Ernst and Alvina did."

Daniel smiled briefly. "Then send them over, and I'll hire them."

The phone rang,and he turned to Geir and Hedy who were standing beside him. "It's the operator. So the call Dr. Rath and I have been trying to get through to Dr. Alexi Zeroff at the Minsk hospital, must have gone through."

Geir took the phone Daniel handed him and informed Alexi what had happened.

Immediately he was filled of sorrow, offering to do whatever he could. Then Hedy took he phone and asked him about little Hansi. "She's doing fine with the farming family she's staying with. But if some really bad things happen, I'm pledged to look after you and Geir in this terrible war, the same as you're pledged to look after me and little Hansi."

"We'll always do what we can for you and your daughter," Hedy assured him, before hanging up.

The following day Helmut told Otto. "The next air raid will probably be at night. So if I'm with you Schroders, while you're searching for the additional bombs dropped apt to go off twelve hours later, then I'll be able to disarm them."

"You're a valuable man," said Otto. "Just make sure you take care of yourself, since you're doing deadly work. Not just with explosives, but your willingness to share your knowledge of them with the Polish partisans."

"Which is the reason I'm heading back after the funeral to the factory. So that way, I'll be able to make more explosives for the German military machine."

"Has to be like that," Daniel explained to Geir and Volker. "Since as you know, the way the war is turning out to be, the munitions factory is not allowing him to have his surgery. And he's working some long hours, in order to get plenty of three-day weekends. That way he'll be able to meet up with Dr. Novak, who has a house in Poland just over the German border. And this house has a secret room for the grenade and bomb-making equipment we've purchased."

"And Helmut will be training Dr. Novak's partisans?" Volker asked.

"Yes indeed," said Daniel. "With these partisans also providing some gun powder and othersupplies from the smaller convoys they're holding up that are moving through Poland."

"Dangerous work."

"Very." Daniel nodded. "And Helmut's telling me that Dr. Novak is saying many of the partisans keep reminding him that it would be impossible to liberate Auschwitz, unless seventy-five per cent of the prisoners had guns."

"Of course it would," Geir agreed.

Volker glared at Daniel with a suspicious look. "But what's really blown me away is that Helmut says Dr. Novak's hearing from the partisans, that there's a resistance cell in Auschwitz." "Resistance cell?" Geir gave his head a doubtful shake. "Impossible. With people being beaten and starved to death there—like the rumors say."

"Apparently the partisans are claiming it's not rumors," Daniel countered icily. "With the Polish prisoners being able to escape the camp better than the Jews. And these Poles maintain that SS officers are being attacked, radios stolen, messages broadcast, and some facilities sabotaged. With these prisoners maintaining there's been some record copying with names, which have been smuggled out of the camp, to the free world."

"If Volker and I joined the SS," said Geir, we could copy the records in the camp, like we're doing records here in Berlin. And then smuggle them out. And if Rudi and Nicholas were in the SS with us, then think how we could help those starving prisoners." He threw back his head. "Why we could slip food to some of them."

"That's enough, Son!" said Daniel, staying him with a gentle hand. "The idea of the four of you being in the SS terrifies me. And even though you and Volker are doing well with your canes, you're still having some difficulty. And, Rudi, with his medical problem, is having some difficulty too." His breath froze for an instant. "Why if the SS ever got wind of what you were doing, they'll torture you, before killing you. Which could mean such terrible things as those *kapos*—male and female German prisoners from prisons and mental institutions, beating you until your genitals bleed. Or taking you to the hospitals and other parts of the camp, where you become infected with lice carrying typhus. Something that makes a person suffer terribly before he or she dies. "He frowned with obvious concern. "And what about that Dr. Josef Mengele? Who's rumored to be doing horrible medical experiments on many of the prisoners."

A chill swept through Geir each time he recalled his nightmare on his wedding night, about being naked and beaten to death by the SS. "Even so, as SS men we'd have guns and would be able to fight back. And besides, a good many of those in the SS are aware that once the Russians arrive, they're doomed. So maybe they could be bribed?"

"With what?" Daniel asked. "A diamond ring like you gave that Luftwaffe pilot? "Then he stopped suddenly, as if a new idea was forming. "Being a Jew, I know Jews. And a good many will have diamonds and other precious gems sewn in their clothing. Clothing that's being ripped apart by Jewish workers in the camp for some kind of German industrial use. Which makes me suspect the workers are finding and hiding these gems."

"Or giving some to this to this resistance group, so they can bribe the SS—"

"Which would be the smart thing to do," Daniel acknowledged. "And with these gems, these Jewish workers are possibly getting some extra food for themselves and their friends." He was obviously so intrigued by the idea, he even tipped back his chair. But after several moments passed, he added with a sudden, downcast expression, "Though from the rumors I hear, many in the camp are dying from starvation."

"The Wehrmacht is tolerating us because we can't be on the front," said Geir, rising. "But the truth is they want only able-bodied men. So if a man's disabled but still wants to serve Germany, the SS is the only place he can go. And Dr. Rath could get his general friend to assign us to Auschwitz. And since we're coming in late, we won't have to have that terrible SS tattoo, like those who trained earlier have on their arms"

Daniel vaulted from his chair. "My God!" His gasp for breath made such a desperate sound, it reminded Geir of a fish trying to breath on dry land.

"Take it easy," Geir urged him.

"I won't! When I think that you, Volker, Rudi, and Nicholas would actually consider asking the doctor to *do* that for you?"

Frustration hammered Geir. "If it meant saving lives we would." He closed his eyes trying to imagine the pain of those in Auschwitz... *with the sickly, sweet smell of its crematoriums, that Helmut told me Dr. Novak had learned about from the underground.* "Which mean somebody's got to help those people! "Geir shouted. "Because it's a fact that Auschwitz is the heart of the Nazi's great domination."

"You're a terrific person, Son. But being crippled limits you. So leave it for someone else to do it."

"If there was someone, I would. But there isn't. The allies and the partisans aren't doing much. And the Russians, when they arrive, what'll they do? Oh something, but by that time many of the prisoners will either be dead from starvation or having been gassed to death. And those surviving, will have disappeared with the Germans to other camps."

"Geir." Daniel reached out a hand to him. "You mustn't do anything right now. Just wait. The allies will do something—"

"Even if Roosevelt's forbidden it?"

"He's not speaking for the French, British, or Russians. And we don't have any pictures or movies of the camp. So we can't prove the rumors are true that we're hearing. Which is why you have to wait until we know for sure."

"And when will that be?"

"Hopefully, in the near future."

⸻ ◆ ⸻

Geir wrote in his journal:

"The near future. Will it ever come? The year has passed from forty-three to forty-four. Otto managed to get us a roast goose, so we had a fine Christmas meal. But what we really liked was the Christmas card from Alexi with a recent picture of little Hansi. The toddler certainly looked to be growing. And appeared to love her farming family. We weren't surprised by the card, even if the Russians weren't supposed to be talking about Christmas and religion. Alexi was Polish and raised in the church like Hedy and I, but still?

We sent him a card too, but in a package with two gifts: silky-tuxedo socks for him and a teddy bear for little Hansi. He thanked us in a note and apologized for not getting us anything. His cousin, Natasha, with the lung cancer had passed away, despite the experimental treatment she was receiving.

We wrote back expressing our sorrows. Becoming friends with you has been a gift in itself."

⸻ ◆ ⸻

As events proceeded, Geir asked Helmut about the Polish partisans. "They have a great appreciation for the way I'm helping them," he told him. "Yet, they're still not able to do much about Auschwitz. The Russians will handle it when they come,' they say. However, most partisans feel as threatened by the Russians as they do the Germans."

Something that became quite evident in June of 1944, when the Russians began heavy combat against the Germans as they fought to retake Minsk.

Alexi wrote in one of his encrypted letter that Captain Joseph Ulyanov, Natasha's former husband, insisted he take a job in Poland in the hospital where Dr. Novak worked...which was once a Baroque chalet. "Sounds interesting," said Hedy, looking at the letter over Geir's shoulder:

"According to Captain Ulyanov, it'll be awhile before the Russians re-take Poland," Geir read aloud. *With the house where Natasha had lived now gutted out. So Ulyanov has urged me, to get out of Minsk, because little Hansi will need me— her foster father— after the war."*

CHAPTER TWENTY-SIX

Geir also wrote:

"With the war winding down, Alexi's letter makes me wonder how long it will be before the Russians invade Berlin? At least the boardinghouse has a secret shelter. But if it got bombed, then what? I was worried about everyone living with us—especially Charlotte, Greta, and Hedy. Since the Russians are greatly feared by many of the women in Berlin. Though I need not have worried about Greta. Because in July she was walking to one of the still halfway decent bakeries a few blocks from the hospital, when a siren sounded. Everyone in the area panicked, and a cab, driven by a drunk driver, ran over her. She died instantly...

If losing Alvina, Ernst, and Margit wasn't bad enough, we've now lost Greta. I blame myself, saying over and over if she and Hedy had stayed in Switzerland— and not Berlin because of me— this never would have happened. Still, Hedy and Daniel had to remind me countless times there were good German people and bad German people. And the good ones— especially— needed our help. 'Mom and I were meant to help people,' Hedy would say. 'And with the world being at war, people need us. With Daniel having moved here to see after you. And although you'd come of age, he was worried about you. And when you got drafted. So regardless, it wasn't in our hearts to be in a place like Switzerland. Where we couldn't help the people, struggling to survive, in this terrible war.'

I wanted to believe her, and at times I tried hard to do so. 'Son', Daniel said. 'Remember I tried to get the women here to move to a country place, I was ready to buy for them. But they wouldn't hear of it. So we have to be prepared for whatever Fate throws our way.'

A thought that grazes my heart with a dreadful uncertainness."

Events turned swiftly.

Due to the air-raids, Geir learned Daniel's newly hired couple had some relatives in the country and decided to go and live with them.

"You should do like them." Geir joined Daniel, in urging the Schroders, Hedy, and Charlotte to get out of the city "And move to the country house my father's picked out to buy for you."

But none of them would hear of it.

These days Nicholas came to Berlin frequently with his general's deliveries.

Rudi and Helmut enjoyed talking with him and soon came to appreciate his friendship, the same as Geir and Volker did.

Nicholas's parents attended Greta's funeral to be with their son, whose general gave him a short leave.

Dr. Rath was deeply grieved and wanted to take off work for a week, but with a doctor shortage it wasn't possible. Fortunately though, he was able to get a call through to Dr. Novak and Alexi who were quick to express their sympathy to Daniel, Hedy, and Geir.

"These are terrible times," Daniel murmured, tears pooling in his eyes.

The boardinghouse with Greta gone was now quite empty. So arrangements were made for a cleaning woman to come once a week with her sister, who though a chain-smoker, still managed to do most of the washing and ironing.

The Schroders continued to do the marketing, cooking, and dishwashing. "With Daniel always giving them a hand, like he's hired help," Geir remarked to Hedy.

"To be so wealthy, Daniel never ceases to amaze me," she said, with a look of admiration.

"Who's providing the inspiration for the rest of us living here, to pitch in anyway we can."

"You're a lot like him, working so hard at the hospital when you don't have to."

"Growing up I may not have realized it but looking back, I can now see how Daniel's work ethic rubbed off on Mom and me."

"He's a great man," said Geir, stroking Hedy's cheek affectionately. "But don't let his work ethic keep you in this dangerous city."

"I'm not," she assured him. "And I realize Daniel's influence has made a strong impression on me, but people here are in need of help. So regardless, I'm following my heart."

There was a lingering silence as years ago, Geir recalled reading an article that said, *"People who love a lot, don't mind taking risks for those in dire need—"*

"And I know I haven't mentioned it," said Hedy intruding on his thoughts, "but one of our medics has such a great fear of being trapped in a shelter that whenever the sirens go off, he hurries to sit in the courtyard at the hospital. Or if he's home, the courtyard at his apartment."

Geir was more than a little amazed. "Now that's enough to make a person's stomach fall at their feet."

"That it is," she agreed with a worried look. "And he's tempting fate. But so far, he's made it."

Which amazingly as the months rocked along, he continued to do.

"It's now October," Geir remarked Otto. "With Germany losing the war like you predicted." "Which certainly won't be pleasant for Berliners when the Russians come," he replied, shaking his head.

Otto was holding an encrypted letter from Dr. Novak that Daniel had let him read. "The partisans are claiming there'd been an uprising at Auschwitz," he read aloud. With explosions at Crematorium 4, which the Sonderkomed *men*— builders of the crematoriums— were attempting to blow up.

They were using bits of gunpowder that female prisoners, working in an ammunition factory, were bringing to them. And these builders were using it to make grenades out of tin cans, having stockpiled some knives and axes...none of which stood a chance against the SS machine guns."

Sad as it was this failed uprising did have an interesting flashback on Helmut.

As it turned out his boss at the munitions factory, where he worked, had a cousin who was an SS officer at Auschwitz. "With the Russians on their way, *Herr* Himmler wants the crematoriums destroyed to hide evidence," this cousin had informed him. "But the *Fuhrer* doesn't. With it being rumored *Herr* Himmler intends to go against the *Fuhrer* and destroy them any way." "So why do you suppose he told me that?" Helmut asked Geir and Daniel.

Daniel appeared to give it some thought. "Did he mention anything about cameras?" "Cameras," Helmut repeated, looking surprised. "He asked if anyone had camera experience." "And your answer?"

"Photography was one of the few pleasure my uncle had—"

"And he taught you?" Daniel asked.

"When we had film. And when we didn't, we'd scout out places to photograph later, discussing angles."

"Then it appears you're our man."

"To do what, *Herr* Birnbaum?"

"Photograph Auschwitz."

"Isn't that what your boss is getting at?"

"Possibly."

Helmut then explained what his boss's cousin had told him. "He wants to show the *Fuhrer*, that all these Jews and other undesirables, can't be successfully destroyed without the crematoriums. Since it's estimated that six thousand people a day are being gassed and burned—"

"Help us, God!" exclaimed Daniel.

"When I heard that I went to the latrine and threw-up," Helmut told him.

Daniel rose. "Something I'm about to do."

"Don't you dare, "warned Geir. "Helmut's news means we'll get the proof we need—

"Yes indeed," Daniel said, after releasing a pent-up breath. "Especially since I'm buying him the finest motion picture equipment I can find."

That said— preparations moved forward. Plans were discussed with Dr.Novak, and he promised to have development equipment in his house. "Easy to keep in my place where the partisans make their munitions. And also get the medicines to smuggle to the Auschwitz prisoners. The partisans are paid with jewels that female prisoners, working in the *Kanada* warehouse, find hidden in the clothing there. And then they're given to the women, who work outside the camp during the day, to give to the partisans in exchange for food and medicines."

Luckily, one of these partisans knew how to develop movies and make copies of them.

Helmut's boss was soon discussing the movie making with his SS cousin, Gunther Haar, who in turn talked with one of the senior officers in the camp.

With the proviso Helmut wore the SS uniform, this SS cousin provided the papers for him to *come* and *go* at Auschwitz with a camera.

———◆———

When Helmut returned to Berlin, he wrote this document to be read after his movie was shown:

"And I, Helmut Schnell, saw it all. On this day October, twenty-eighth, which I was told was the date the last transport of Jews had arrived. They were coming from Theresienstadt—1,589 Jews—and were gassed immediately.

'Threats from the Russians,' Kommandant Richard Baer, the head of Auschwitz One, informed me. 'And those crematoriums at Auschwitz-Birkenau are necessary for those sorry, sub-human pieces of humanity who destroyed Germany. And without those crematoriums, it would be a difficult thing to do in these perilous times.'

'Beside the twenty minute walk between Auschwitz and Birkenau, what's the difference between the camps?' I asked the kommandant.

'Birkenau, often called Auschwitz Two, was made mostly for Jews. Where our Auschwitz One here, has political prisoners as well.'

We were now at the camp's administration block, with its many offices. Kommandant Baer insisted I film it first. Which, after that, I was free to film whatever I wanted... And as I filmed I saw things, I wish I'd never seen. Beginning with what appeared to be the sign over the Auschwitz gates—Albeit Macht Frei. What the prisoners arriving saw. My boss's SS cousin, Gunther Haar, *who prided himself in his uniform, was more than willing to talk. And he encouraged me to ask him questions. Laughing and saying, Herr Schnell, 'That sign, Albeit* Macht Frei, *means if you die working here your soul is free.'*

The rail -sharp, barbed wire fences were electrified, with razor wire above them. And guards with rifles were posted in watchtowers, ever so many meters, waiting to shoot any prisoner who tried to escape.

Floodlights and searchlights were also across the perimeters.

Most of the prisoners, so it seemed, had arrived by train in cattle cars. 'Stragglers,' the blond, Aryan-looking Gunther called them. 'And they have to be beaten with sticks and snapped at by guard dogs to get a move on. Fortunately, the kapos all have sticks. Considering these transports come day and night to Auschwitz and Birkenau.'

'How long does a person live in this camp?' I asked him

Gunther shrugged. 'Some only six weeks. However, others have been here a good while. And have no intention of riding in the Black Mary death cart— as we call it.' I took particular care to photograph the prisoners with their shaved heads and striped clothing. The women had covered their heads with scarves, and some were allowed to wear clothing from the Kanada warehouse. It was named after the wealthy, allied country where the items, taken from the prisoners, were stored.

The barracks in most of the blocks consisted of a single floor. 'And often a hundred prisoners are in each room,' remarked Gunther. 'Which is approximately twenty-eight square meters. With the mattresses on the floor usually shared with one or two other prisoners.'

In the back was a latrine with an open trench. 'Were there some other type facilities?' I asked.

Gunther nodded, adding, 'But most have long lines.'

There was only one cistern in the yard for washing. Although Gunther did mention a shower block. But was it safe place or a way of gassing prisoners, as had been rumored? Perhaps both.

Roll call was usually every morning. Which didn't mean there weren't other times too. Those kapos, taken from German prisons, were murderous people who were expected to prove their ruthlessness to the SS. Particularly, when overseeing the work at the gravel pit, where a man could die quickly if he wasn't careful.

There were two meals a day. Morning and evening. In the evening it was usually a thin potato or barley soup... And there was always the sound of floggings and random shots in the camp.

The hospital housed prisoners who were too sick to work. 'Have to make a good impression on the Red Cross,' said Gunther, excusing himself for a minute as an SS man outside summoned him.

It gave me time to ask Dr. Novak's friend, Dr. Jules Bach, some questions. He was another Jew who'd become a Catholic. And he'd worked in a Warsaw hospital until his niece, Yelda Yashi, got bombed out of her hiding place with her toddling, baby daughter, Yelena. The Gestapo took them, with Dr. Bach speaking on their behalf— since Yelda's husband had been killed. Yet, the doctor's pleas angered the Gestapo so much, that he ended up getting thrown in Auschwitz with them. 'You might be a Catholic, but we suspect you're still a Jew—like your niece,' he told me the SS had yelled at him.

The baby would have been killed instantly had the coppery-haired, Yelda's, great beauty not attracted one of Auschwitz's senior officers. Hauptman Rudolph Bischoff. Who just happened to be Gunther's best friend. And soon Yelda became his mistress. 'Love at first sight,' Hauptman Bischoff had told her. So he kept her daughter hidden in the hospital, to be looked after by Dr.Bach. Who from my observation in the time I was there was treated more like a paramedic or nurse, than a doctor.

It was good Dr. Bach, and I got to talk.And my last words to him were, 'Help is coming.'

Dr. Novak said Dr. Bach was well-connected with some the men who were still in the Auschwitz Resistance. But nothing was happening now. Since shots, presumed Russian, were said to be heard in the distance. Which, sadly, were too far away to liberate the camp. In fact, I could have sworn I heard some of those shots later that day.

As I continued filming, a large amount of prisoners—as was rumored—looked to be on the edge of starvation...with bones sticking out all over. I was shocked to see human beings in such a state. And Gunther let it be known that if they begged for scraps from the kitchen, the kapos made a point of stepping up and abusing them. Unless, they could get a bribe from a prisoner, who was slightly better off than those they were abusing.

And finally, there were the gas chambers and crematoriums. Red bricked buildings at Auschwitz-Birkenau having large windows and huge chimneys. And the horrifying smell of roasting flesh was coming from them, as were charred flakes...falling like snow on us and our surroundings. 'How long does it take to die in a gas chamber with that Zyklon B gas?' I asked Gunther.

'Maybe three to five minutes. And this gas is delivered in a Red Cross ambulance to Auschwitz about five minutes before a transport of prisoners have arrived for extermination, at one of the Auschwitz-Birkenau crematoriums.'

One horror on top of another— all I needed to hear. 'I think I'm filmed enough for your cousin, Herr Haar to make a good case with the Fuhrer about keeping the crematoriums.'

' Herr Himmler is determined to destroy the crematoriums and the gas chambers attached to them. So that way, there'll be no evidence of them when the Russians arrive.' Gunther pointed at the gaschambers Crematoriums 3 and 4, which were near the woods. And then remarked there was an ash pond between Crematoriums 4 and 5.

'Your cousin mentioned what Herr Himmler had said. But the prisoners here— what will happen to them if they're not gassed and burned?' I asked Gunther.

'There's talk of marching them back to Germany to some camps there. Which many won't be able to make. Since we can't stop long enough to give them food and water. So, this possible evacuation, is being called a death march by some. But those that make it, will continue to labor for the Reich. And should the need arise, we'll ransom them off to the allies.'

I flinched. 'Parts of Germany are three thousand two hundred and twenty kilometers away from this camp.' (Or two thousand miles away, I remember Daniel remarking.)

'I realize the distance,' Gunther said. 'And at some point in this death march, most of the prisoners will be put on trains.'

I stared at some of the pathetic-looking prisoners. 'And this is just for the prisoners here?' I questioned.

But Gunther shook his head. 'There are also the sub-camps at Wodzislaw, Slaski, and Gliwince?'

Sub-camps hadn't been mentioned, and it made me curious. 'What are those camps for?' 'For?' Gunther repeated, looking surprised I didn't know. 'To provide labor for our German industrialists. And we've just sent some prisoners to a new sub-camp that's opened up.'

'Even with this threat of invasion?'

'Which could or could not happen. 'Gunther turned toward the east. 'Did my cousin not tell you?'

'No.' My curiosity increased as I stared at the railroad tracks outside the camp. 'If these transports do occur, then which route will most of the prisoners be taking to Germany?'

Gunther jerked around. 'Probably the one running through East Upper Silesia and Lower Silesia. Although, there is some talk that a few of the men will be marched to the Baltic. Where they'll board a freighter under guard... but one more thing... you should at least film a little of the life we in the SS have here—especially since you're in an SS uniform. And if my cousin decides to edit it out, I won't mind.'

I gazed at him with a guarded expression, but agreed to film it. With once again, my eyes stretching wide as I pointed the camera at what amounted to a vegetable market, theater, cinema, and a place where dances were held. And *for food, they had excellent sausages, cheese, breads, and whortleberries with whipped cream. Plus, a hot kitchen that served excellent German meals to those dining in the small area next door to it.*

'We even have schnapps and vodka,' Gunther added, jabbing the air with his thumb.' And sometimes we get drunk...but only when we have some entertainment.'

'You have entertainment here?' I asked him, finding it difficult to believe.

'We did,' Gunther said, after taking a deep breath.' And from one of our senior officers— of all people.'

'Who was a singer?'

'No." Gunther shook his head. Ventriloquist. He found a strange red-headed dummy in one of our Kanada warehouses. Which made us suspect, it had belonged to one of the gypsies who'd performed in a nightclub. And this man— along with his people— went up the chimney. But to everyone's surprise, this dummy began talking to this senior officer. He couldn't imagine how, unless there was a battery-powered record player inside it. In fact, he claimed this dummy told him, 'I'll do all the talking, so people will think you're a ventriloquist. And such entertainment will bring you lots of money.'

I was shocked.

'It was a joke that always brought laughs from us,' Gunther informed me.

'And where is this dummy now?' I asked

But Gunther merely shrugged. 'This officer got called to entertain some troops. But there was an explosion on the way, and he got killed—along with some of his men.'

Disgusting. As was everything about Auschwitz. Particularly, watching SS officers gamble for the gold teeth taken from murdered Jews. So, at the first opportunity I thanked Gunther and excused myself... praying I'd get out of the camp before I passed out cold."

◆

Geir took the two rolls of film that Dr. Novak's partisans had helped develop for Helmut. "One is for my boss in the morning, and the other for your father,"

"We've waited a long time for this, Son," said Daniel, grabbing the roll Geir handed him. "We've heard so many different stories." He sighed with a troubled look. "But now we should know for certain what's true and not true. And I'm a little frightened."

Dr. Rath had come for the viewing, as had Nicholas...who luckily was here with a delivery from his general in Paris, to give to Dr. Rath's military friend.

Hedy, Charlotte, Volker, Rudi, Dr. Rath, and the Schroders were also present. And they stared at the screen with fearful eyes once Helmut switched on the projector, and the film began rolling.

A violent cold seemed to strike the room as the horror of what they saw mortified them. Geir came close to collapsing— *Starved faces of prisoners, with disease and exposure to the cold, threatening to snatch the life from them.*

"A...are any of us strong enough to face this?" Daniel stuttered.

Fearful of passing out, Geir—the same as everyone present— could hardly look at the screen.

And Charlotte, poor Charlotte, stared at it with a stricken face, "I feel like I'm going to faint—" she told Nicholas, who took her in his arms.

Hedy's trembling hands grabbed Geir's. "It's like the Devil's taken over heaven!" she cried.

"Deep inside I knew this," admitted a stone-faced Otto. "But we Germans were supposed to be civilized. So I couldn't face the fact that we were the careless ones who allowed the Nazis to come to power."

"Indeed we were," Hugo agreed, with Fritz also nodding.

Volker covered his eyes with his hands. "The truth we've been searching for is now before us."

"How could Germany do this?" asked Rudi, when the film was over. "And why did those of us here in this room, sit on the sidelines and allow something like this to happen?"

Daniel swiped his tear stained face with a damp cloth. "One room in the prisoners' block or barracks looks to be three hundred square feet for over one hundred prisoners. How dreadful! "He bowed his head. "This movie should surely get the word out—"

"But only after the war," Otto pointed out. "So keep this film in the metal box behind the bricks in the cellar, until the war's over."

"If Nicholas and I have children," Charlotte sobbed. "then they'll ask us, when they come of age, why we didn't do something to help these people." She gulped hard before adding with a sense of conviction,

"That they are the Devil's tools being used to expose humanity's wickedness."

"Which is one of the many reasons why Volker, Nicholas, Rudi, and I need to join the SS," Geir remarked.

"I refuse to have children unless I can find a way to help these people," said Hedy, tears streaming down her cheeks.

Daniel swallowed like he had a knot in his throat. "Geir, what have I said about you and Volker being crippled and in the SS at Auschwitz?"

"That it limits us. Although, we've had excellent therapy, so we're not using our canes as much. And at times can even walk fairly fast—"

"No one in this room may not have said it, but I'm saying," Nicholas cut in. "That I feel certain that the number of people who've been in Auschwitz is so great, we can't count that high. And there's probably paperwork on each person who's been there. And if Himmler's so hell-bent on destroying the crematoriums before the Russians arrive, then you know he's just as hell-bent on getting that paperwork destroyed."

"And more help will be needed," Rudi pointed out. "Which means there'll be jobs for me and my friends." He gestured at Geir, Volker, and Nicholas."

"Oh, God! My son in Auschwitz, "Daniel cried, a *great* fear in his eyes. "And if he's there, then it means I'd be a fool not to come and check on him."

"I feel it to be the *destiny* I was called for," said Geir, squeezing Daniel's arm. "So don't risk yourself."

"I won't be. Since after all, you're my son-in-law, which should give me a good reason to visit. And besides, if I do get a good look at that camp, then when my time comes, and I approach the throne, I have every intention of asking God, 'Why did you this do this to your chosen people?' And became our destroyer."

Dr. Rath, in the corner of the room, suddenly surprised everyone with his loud sobbing.

"I've never seen him like this before," said Hedy, getting up with Charlotte and going over to him.

He blotted his eyes. "Like Otto says, we Germans are supposed to be civilized people. But knowing I'm a citizen in a country who's doing something like this to innocent people, makes me want to die."

"Don't we all," said Otto.

"Don't *we*," Helmut repeated, preparing to read his notes to the group. He held up the paper he'd written. "This is what Gunther told me. Which I'm hoping will give you some kind of idea on what we can do to help these people."

"Then proceed," Daniel urged. "Because we need all the information we can get."

Helmut read the document he'd written, and when he finished Dr. Rath ran some ideas past everyone.

"I feel certain my general friend, or rather patient, can get the paper-pushing jobs in the camp for Geir, Volker, Nicholas, and Rudi. Resistance workers. With something telling me that Hedy, Charlotte, and I, need to be working in a hospital not far from Auschwitz. That way should our men here need us, we'll be close enough to help them."

"Judging from the map the doctor sent you that chalet-hospital where Dr. Novak and Alexi are working appears to be only about—"

"Twenty miles. Or thirty-two Kilometers from Auschwitz," Daniel put in.

"Exactly. And Dr. Novak is in need of help with the way they're taking the overflow of the wounded from other hospitals. Who, warmly wrapped, often arrive at this chalet-hospital in horse-drawn carts. from these other hospitals. So he's been begging me to work there. With the pictures he's been sending of the hospital, reminding me of a castle."

"If you, Hedy, and Charlotte work at that hospital," said Daniel. "Then I'm going to be there doing volunteer work. And if our men here need us, then I'll be able to help *you* with them."

"So you hospital workers are going to be in the Resistance with us?" Volker asked the doctor.

"Yes." He smiled faintly. "In what I'm calling the *Stand-by* Resistance."

"In Minsk Captain Ulyanov declared me a resistance fighter," said Hedy.

"I remember hearing you say that," Geir replied.

"If these people are going to be death marched without food or water through upper and lower Silesia," said Dr. Rath, his brows coming together as if giving it some serious thought." Then, we're probably going to need a truckload full of extra food standing by for them. Since knowing the kind-hearted Silesian people like I do, they'll want to help those poor death marchers. So we need to give them some extra food, in case they come their way."

"And get it where in these dreadful times?" Daniel asked.

"If we pay for it, I suspect the Red Cross will deliver it to the Silesian people—"

"Which I'll gladly help you do," Daniel assured him, cutting in on his words. "But let's get it ahead of time, so we'll be prepared."

"The Red Cross will alert the people of Silesia," said Dr. Rath. "And once we know for sure about these marchers, they'll deliver it in one of their trucks."

Holding the roll of film that Helmut had handed him, Daniel turned to the good doctor. "And if the prisoners are *not* marched through upper and lower Silesia, then what about the food?"

"Then the Red Cross will deliver it to Auschwitz, in the hopes some of the prisoners have been left behind."

Daniel turned to Helmut. "But this talk about some prisoners being marched to the Baltic—"

"What about it?"

"Dr. Novak has an interest in a freighter at a port there, which goes up and down the coast delivering supplies for the SS and Wehrmacht. So what if you talk to Gunther's cousin and see when I visit Auschwitz, if I might suggest to *Kommandant* Baer to allow the SS guards to travel on Dr. Novak's freighter with the prisoners. That way they'll be able to deliver them to one of the German camps not far from the ocean."

"A freighter." Helmut repeated a bit warily. "Why would you do that, *Herr* Birnbaum?"

"Because it'll give the partisans an excellent opportunity to kill some SS guards."

"Then by all means do it," Helmut urged, a sardonic smile on his lips. "War is war. And my movie should make it clear how inhumane these SS people are."

"Do you think this *Kommandant Baer* will agree to it?" Daniel asked him.

"If he doesn't then Birkenau's *commandant* will —especially since Gunther implied the Germans were not as brutal as the Soviets."

"Well now—" Daniel's gaze shifted from Helmut to his document. "I suspect there's still some uncertainty with these transport marches and the Russian invasion."

"There is. But SS plans are generally made ahead of time just in case—"

"—they have to evacuate the camp," Daniel finished.

"Then it all seems to be settled," said Volker with a sage nod.

"Maybe from your point of view," Dr. Rath responded crisply. "But what can four SS men in the Resistance do?" He hesitated before adding a moment later, "Other than help the prisoners working in the office pretend to sabotage records— but in reality, help to conceal them."

"We can hide prisoners, when necessary." Geir spoke up. "Slip food and medicine to those most in need. Help the medical staff. Bribe a kapo to stop abusing a prisoner. And shoot all in the SS we can, without getting caught."

Dr. Rath sighed. "It sounds like you've got your resistance work cut out for you—"

"*Damn* dangerous," Daniel muttered uneasily. "Is what it sounds like to me."

"It is," Nicholas agreed. "But being in Berlin with bombs falling on the city is dangerous too."

"War is war— like Helmut said." Geir reminded.

A silence followed before Otto remarked, "If my calculations are right, the Russians will be in the camp around late January. Which is a little less than two months."

Daniel threw up his hands, "But, Otto, will the Russians believe our SS men are in the Resistance?"

"Hopefully. Because some of the prisoners, who've managed to hide from the evacuation, will be able to vouch for them. But one more thing. This talking dummy or puppet, believed to be owned by one of the dead gypsies, has a demon inside it. A gypsy or Romani curse on the camp. And this senior office who died was a good friend *of Kommantant Baer.* Whom I feel certain ordered those gypsies' deaths—"

"But that dummy got blown up, didn't it?" Volker cut in.

"A complex question," said Otto, darting an uneasy glance at him. "If it had a demon inside it, then it's still out there. And means it could reappear at Auschwitz any time."

Volker chuckled. "So this time it's the dummy's curse instead of the *mummy's*."

Rudi pantomimed a shudder. "Gives me chills as icy as Russia's winter, thinking about it."

"Is it likely to appear at one of the *Kanada* warehouses again?" Geir asked Otto.

"Yes." He closed his eyes as if pondering it. "Which will be the one at Auschwitz, because I'm seeing fire over the one at Birkenau."

Nicholas looked ready to jump out of his skin. "Sounds to me like we need to change the subject."

Dr. Rath nodded his agreement. "Absolutely."

"Dr.Bach and Dr. Novak are good friends," said Daniel, he pointed at Helmut's document. "And in it you wrote that you told Dr. Bach help was coming."

"I did. So our SS resistance fighters, sitting here, will need to allow Dr. Bach to direct them on what they, should or should not do. When it comes to helping the people there."

"My thinking exactly," said Daniel. "And this SS man, Gunther, what about him?"

"He's a Nazi, so beware," Helmut warned. "But having met me and knowing from my boss that I'm living in the boardinghouse with you, then you'll probably need to make friends with him. So, that way, you can get information from him." He gave Geir a censured glance. "Just remember that until the camp is liberated, you must act like a die-hard Nazi."

"You make it sound like I'm soft."

Helmut's features brightened slightly. "You had me fooled when I first met you. But now, I realize you, like your wife, have the biggest hearts I've ever seen... I mean I could never find a woman like Hedy—"

"Yes you can," Geir replied. "Because after the war, Hedy and I will help you."

"Words from a big-hearted man," remarked Helmut, offering him a sudden, arresting smile. "Which is the reason I'm warning you not to let your big heart be your downfall at Auschwitz."

CHAPTER TWENTY-SEVEN

Another week passed as arrangements were made for Geir, Volker, Rudi, and Nicholas to leave the Wehrmacht, join the SS, and head to Auschwitz.

Dr. Rath talked his general friend into making the transfers. And afterwards with a bright expression, the good doctor made arrangements with Dr. Novak to join him and Dr. Zeroff in their chalet or palace-looking hospital.

"It'll be interesting working in such a unique hospital," Charlotte told Hedy and Daniel, the night before they left.

"I agree," he said, moving his packed bags next to the front door. "But what I really like about it is that should our men need us, we'll be close to them."

"Which should be a little less than two months before the Russians move in," Otto pointed out again.

"Almost the same length of time Geir and I were apart when we he was on that convoy," remarked Hedy, clearly disturbed.

He was waiting for her at their bedroom door, and when she joined him, he quickly ushered her inside. "Remembering that terrible nightmare I had on our wedding night about being beaten to death by an SS man? So am I doing wrong going to Auschwitz?"

"It was just a nightmare. But still— you must do what you can without getting caught. Think you can?"

He released a long breath. "Nobody can be certain of anything in these unstable times."

"True. But next question. Am I doing wrong, saying I won't bring a child into the world if I can't do something for those poor souls imprisoned in that terrible camp?"

He turned toward the half-open window with its gold, fluttering curtains. "People marvel at the way we love each other."

"I know. And it gives us the strength to—"

"Rise above our own interests," he completed. "And help those most in need."

"Which appears to be this *destiny* you're always talking about. With me standing by your side and helping you anyway I can."

"God's love gave us vision as well as strength. And I feel this great love between us has become a blessing meant to be shared, as we struggle to rise above our own interests."

Hedy sucked in a breath. "But what if one of us dies? Or worse, both of us? We could get killed at the hospital or Auschwitz, since it's the same as being in the middle of a war. Are we prepared for that?"

"Who could ever be prepared for something like that?"

"Then what do we do? Continue in the direction we're headed or back off?"

"We should back off. But after that horrible film we just saw—" He stopped as the warning sound they all greatly feared blasted the room.

"A siren!" Hedy shrieked. "God help us!"

"Reminding us we're under bombardment in the middle of a war!" he shouted, grabbing her trembling hand and heading in the direction of the cellar.

"And like we just said—" Her voice rang out. "We could be killed."

She paused a second before reminding, "The same as Margit, Alvina, Ernst, and my mother."

"Then I guess we have our answer," Geir remarked, once they were in the cellar. "We're risking ourselves staying here. The same as I'll be risking myself at Auschwitz and *you,* at the hospital."

He held her tightly as they endured the terrible sounds of bricks fracturing, windows shattering, and Charlotte screaming each time a the loud boom from an exploding bomb shook the house.

When it finally ended the Schroders, along with Helmut, left the cellar to wait in front of the house for to be picked up to locate the bombs that would explode in twelve hours.

Fortunately, those who questioned Otto about how he could locate them so easily were satisfied with his answer of, '*Simple intuition.*'

Due to their disabilities Geir, Volker, and Rudi were not able to offer much help. But since Rudi had the lesser of the disabilities, he usually tagged along with Hedy and Charlotte to assist them any way he could.

Daniel would have helped the clean-up crews had his health not forbidden him. "This cold weather could lead you to another bout of pneumonia," Hedy told him. "So you need to remain at the boardinghouse."

Which he did…unaware of the lethal blow falling on Helmut and the Schroders.

"I left them standing in the middle of a pile of debris on the main floor of a bombed-out building," explained the driver who'd taken them to the building. "And then, I waited in my car across a wide street." He stopped to catch his breath. "Their cousin Fritz was standing at the open door of the building, when Otto suddenly shouted, "Run! The bomb in here's about to explode!"

"From what I could make-out," the driver continued, "Otto, Hugo, and Helmut were racing toward the door…and Fritz, who was in the street not far from the curb, appeared to be waiting for them. Although, when the building blew it was with such force, that even the one next to it was instantly reduced to a pile rubble. Which went without saying that Otto, Hugo, and Helmut were immediately killed. And Fritz, though still breathing, was in such terrible shape that I doubted he would make it…"

The next day on the phone Helmut's boss explained to Gunther at Auschwitz, about the deaths of the boardinghouse residents. And he informed him that everyone would be arriving later than expected.

Likewise, Dr. Rath contacted Dr. Novak. "All of us will report to their new assignments the following week," the doctor informed him.

"Danger's everywhere we turn," Hedy told Geir. "So this air raid just reaffirms what you said about the risks we're taking with our new job assignments."

"Something I'm not about to deny."

Later that evening Daniel informed everyone that Otto had recently purchased three cemetery lots close to where the others in the boardinghouse were buried. "Do you think he knew?" Geir asked him.

"I think he, Hugo, and Helmut were so ashamed of the German people that they didn't care one way of the other. Which greatly saddens me. So I'm paying for Helmut's funeral and making sure that his mangled body, like Otto's and Hugo's, is buried next to them.

Geir felt a lump rise in his throat as he watched his father stroke the Grand Cross that had belonged to Helmut's uncle. So looking away, he quickly changed the subject. "And Fritz? What's the latest on him?"

"He's still alive. But in such a great deal of pain it's doubtful he'll be around much longer."

◆

That evening Geir wrote in his journal:

"I grieve for Fritz, the same as I grieve for those in some of the earlier failed uprisings at Auschwitz, that Dr.Novak wrote about in his encrypted letters. He'd mentioned in one of the letters, that he'd received some reports from the partisans about the Auschwitz Resistance, before their attempt to blow up Crematorium 4 had failed. And the reports were as followed: In April or May of '44 the partisans were told some Jews had escaped Auschwitz, with the help of the camp's resistance movement. Immediately, they reported to a secret Jewish council in Warsaw, who got word to the West...but,unfortunately, nothing was done.

A cause for more grief. Then, on the upbeat side some Jews and Poles, working outside the camp, managed to escape. And two people wearing SS uniforms had freed two prisoners from the camp. Though, when another man disguised in an SS uniform attempted to free a prisoner, he got caught, the same as did some of the people in the active resistance movement inside the camp. It was said they bribed an SS man to sneak them out in a truck...only to end up being betrayed by this SS man.

"According to the partisans, the goal of the resistance movement in the camp is to survive," Dr. Novak wrote in another letter:" So they can tell the world about the Nazi cruelties... help prisoners escape... and co-ordinate an overall resistance movement with a military connection... Something that has yet to happen.

◆

"How well I know," said Geir, closing his journal. Next week he'd be living at Auschwitz. A frightful place to be, as he continued to wonder if he was truly prepared for what he'd be forced to witness? *Which I'm not. So how am I going to hold up? A question for which I have no answer.*

The following week came sooner than he expected, with everyone packed and ready to depart in a truck the doctors has provided for the chalet-hospital. Word had been sent there were only two trucks at the hospital and a third one, would be greatly appreciated.

Geir and Hedy made love the night before their departure. *A desperate kind of lovemaking. The same as I imagined a Viking's might be… with the years passing without his wife as he sails across the ocean, to explore the new world.*

Another encrypted letter from Dr. Novak had arrived the day before, reminding them that upon our arrival at the camp, they should contact Dr. Bach at the hospital. "He knows the prisoners you can trust," it read. Then he went on to say, that partisans had reports from prisoners working outside the camp that the records of all who'd been in Auschwitz, were being destroyed.

An order from *Kommandant* Baer—'*Get rid of all the evidence!*' Which some of the prisoners, working in the administration block, were being required to do.

A huge task. Since the great number of prisoners who'd been in Auschwitz over the years was, like Nicholas said, 'Too high to count.'

The office-working prisoners in the administration believed these records should be salvaged, and did what they could to save them. Film negatives ordered to be burned had been retrieved from the flames at the last minute by these prisoners. But later, a Nazi official sent a list from Himmler, specifying that certain records were not to be destroyed but taken to Germany instead. And the list was long. So the records, salvaged by the prisoners trying to save them, ended -up getting scrambled, since they first had to be reorganized in order for those in charge to make sense out of what needed to be destroyed, and what needed to be kept.

"Then I know what my job will probably be," Geir remarked to Hedy.

"And mine," Nicholas added.

"But what about Rudi and me?" Volker asked.

"This letter goes on to state that these partisans are hearing that many in the SS are getting quite lazy," Daniel answered. "So I suspect you and Rudi will be assigned to unscramble records too. And not just watching over female prisoners working in the offices— like these lazy SS bastards are suppose to be doing. And, whenever possible, those bastards are making themselves unavailable."

"Obviously the reason we got transferred from the Wehrmacht to the SS so easily," Rudi remarked.

"There's no doubt in mind," said Nicholas.

"If later, prisoners are ordered to destroy records, then I'm helping hide them," Geir told Hedy. "A situation that might not allow me to see you again until the end of January—"

"Which could make you similar to the character of the banker who never took a vacation," Daniel broke in lightly. "This man was stealing money and knew if he ever took a vacation or didn't show for work due to illness, he'd get caught."

"Just so long as you get out of that camp before the Russians come," said Hedy "The only problem being that if the SS leaves before the Russians come, then where will you go? It may be thirty-two kilometers between the hospital and the camp, but it's a distance that could be difficult to cover if the SS, remaining in the camp after the transport marches, have to hurry and evacuate."

"We've worked that out," Dr. Rath spoke up." Dr. Novak's given photos of Geir, Volker, Rudi, and Nicholas to his partisan friends so they'll recognize them. When from to time, different ones of you will be meeting with them at a small train station not far from the camp. Where they'll slip you the medicines from Dr. Novak for the prisoners. And if in the final days, the remaining SS have to hurry and evacuate to a place like Warsaw, then these partisans will be waiting at this train station for the four of you. So that way, they can get you to one of their hiding places."

"And those of you at the hospital?" Geir asked Dr. Rath. "If you have to evacuate where will you go?" "Arrangements have been made with the partisans to help Dr.Novak 's Polish workers return to their homes. However, since the hospital's small, we Germans will take the wounded in the hospital's three trucks and head back to Berlin with them."

Geir reached for his pack and cane. "All that needs to be said."

So those heading for the chalet-hospital and Auschwitz reached for their luggage and packs, before walking out the door toward the waiting truck. They were not overnighting anywhere, with Rudi and Nicholas doing most of the driving. Geir and Volker did a little of it, but Nicholas felt uneasy at the way they accelerated and braked with their injured feet.

Although, their SS uniforms with the lightning bolts on them did make them good guards.

Volker usually sat with his rifle next to the driver while Geir, sitting in the back of the truck, sat with his. "Just in case we come upon some partisans who don't recognize us and realize we're working with them," Nicholas remarked.

Daniel, Dr. Rath, Hedy, and Charlotte were in the back of the truck, watching over the food and water they'd packed for everyone.

"So do we all have our keys in case we have to come back to the boardinghouse?" Daniel asked, holding his up.

"We do," Charlotte replied. "But what about Fritz, should he make it back to the house?" "Unlikely," said Dr. Rath. "But the hospital has his personal effects, which include a house key." "God, *please* help Fritz, "Geir prayed in a whisper. "And see he recovers."

CHAPTER TWENTY-EIGHT

It was a lengthy trip traveling by truck in Poland's bitterly cold autumn weather. But once they reached the hospital, Geir, like the others, marveled at its beauty. "Which even without a walled fortress is to me, more like a storybook castle rather than a chalet," he told Hedy.

A forest with fir trees was close by. And a moat with a covered, stone bridge connected to a walkway that led all the way to the large, stone porch with a huge, wrought-iron door and balcony overlooking it.

"Oh my!" exclaimed Charlotte, stepping into the chalet's main room. She pointed at the room's twisted columns and vaulted ceiling with angels painted on it.

A large sweeping staircase led to the second floor; however, an elevator had been installed so it was easier to move patients.

Dr. Novak and Dr. Zeroff were delighted to see everyone.

"Do we have any new pictures of little Hansi?" Dr. Rath asked.

Alexi nodded and immediately headed to his locker to get them.

Anxious to see them, Geir and Hedy could hardly wait until he returned.

"She loves the family keeping her, and they love her," Alexi let it be known. "So when this war's over I do hope there'll be room for me in her life."

"There will be," Hedy assured him, admiring the little girl's pictures.

"Sorry to interrupt," said Nicholas, "but Gunther's expecting us to call him the minute we arrive."

"At Auschwitz." Volker shuddered, like the thought was cutting through him.

"Well, he's coming to get us," Rudi reminded, preparing to make the call. "I just hope the phone here is working."

"It works some of the time," said Dr. Novak.

Making a sound of frustration, Geir moved closer to Hedy. "So, that being the case, you and I probably won't get to talk much."

"Don't worry." Her lips brushed his cheek as she squeezed down on his hand. "I'll be busy. You'll busy. And as far as visitation, who knows?" She shook her head, adding, "But the good thing is the way this war is going, we won't be apart very long."

He returned her kiss, sparking a grin from Alexi.

"And I'll not only be looking after Hedy," he reminded him, "but Charlotte and Daniel as well."

Geir, Volker, and Nicholas hugged him. Just as Rudi, putting the phone back on its rest, announced, "Gunther says he has chains on his car and even in this cold and ice, he figures he'll be here in less than an hour. "

Which he was.

And he was ushering the men in the car when Daniel, grabbling hold of the porch railing fiercely, rushed down its icy steps and informed him about Dr. Novak's part ownership of a freighter on the Baltic. "And should these death marches occur, Dr. Novak would like me to visit and talk with *Kommandant* Baer about using the freighter."

"Don't see it as a problem with your son-in-law now working at Auschwitz," Gunther answered, before starting the car.

"Good." Daniel smiled. He waved at him as he slowly drove off.

• ——— ••◆•••• ——— •

Geir wrote this in his new notepad he carried in his pocket:

"What do I remember about my first day at Auschwitz? What Helmut told me: crematorium fire, burning day and night, that even in cold weather seared a person's lungs. Then, gunshots from the guard towers that made me jump, as I suspected they were shooting innocent people.

And I remember how Helmut mentioned Gunther had said that until recently, trains arrived filled with people in cattle or boxcars, who are forced to abandon their belongings to those in charge... Albeit Macht Frei! Albeit Macht Frei! Albeit Macht Frei! 'Work makes you free,' as Daniel would say.

This is the place where starving people are made to work day and night. Beginning at 4:30 in the summer mornings and 5:30 in the winter ones. Eleven hour shifts. With Sunday being their only day off.

'Welcome to Auschwitz,' said Kommandant Baer, interrupting my thoughts. He startled the four of us new arrivals with his greeting. 'We are pleased—disabled or not—to have you working here with us.'

We smile and click our jackboots. Then lying, express our pleasure at being able to work for him.

And I close my eyes as memories return of what Helmut said Gunther told him about this Kommandant and the ones before him. 'Work hard,' they would tell the prisoners. 'And if you disobey there will be consequences.'

Later, these prisoners were given striped pajamas to wear and tattooed—since survival depends on numbers. And then they were sent to the barber to have their heads shaved.

Frosty tears roll down my cheeks as my memories return to the present. And I suddenly look up to see a kapo beating a prisoner. At times I know we have to pretend to be ruthless to impress the SS, but this

'Watch it!' Volker warns me. 'Or you'll get us caught. And even with the money Daniel's given us for bribes, we four won't be able to do any good here.'

Definitely true.

But still, I can't stop remembering everything Helmut told me: 'Keep your heads down at all times and do not raise your eyes,' he said the Germans shouted at these new prisoners. And then a whistle would blow, and they would be taken to a shower block, before being shown their living quarters. However, many were gassed and never saw any living quarters.

Another frosty tear rolls down my cheek, which makes it obvious to Volker, Nicholas, and Rudi that I've seen enough here for one day. So, Nicholas asks Gunther about the administration block— where our work will begin. And, smiling, he motions us to follow him.

As speculated, we soon learn that we four are given the assignment of guiding and overseeing many of the office-working prisoners. These people are to help us re-organize camp records for each of our six departments…logs of records from 1941 to present day. With lists of names, record books for the daily prisoner count, construction in Auschwitz, work done in the nearby sub-camps, and logs of records by duty officers. With almost all the record revealing information about the many prisoners who have been here—records that include photos, names, and numbers about each prisoner. And what the SS wants us to do is to put them back like they were. So that way, it will be easy for them to locate what needs to be taken and what needs to be destroyed.

It's a tremendous task that makes me question where we're to hide these records after the SS has found what they're looking for? We can't allow them to be destroyed. But will we be able to trust these prisoners working for us…?At least we won't be like the banker who never took a vacation. Because records will have to be sorted first, then viewed by the Germans before being destroyed.

Gunther laughs after we learn about the huge amount of records we'll be sorting, even with the help of prisoners working in the offices. 'One interesting thing that you'll learn about the camp is that we have a room here that's approximately four meters high. Or as Americans would say, twelve to fifteen feet high. And it's filled with so much toilet paper for us, that it touches the ceiling.

'Certainly surprising,' Nicholas remarks.

'We need to get to the hospital and meet this Dr. Bach,' Volker says, turning to me. But before he could suggest it, Gunther told us to grab our packs and follow him to the officers' quarters. Certainly something unexpected, since Nicholas was a non-commissioned officer, but we certainly weren't.

'We're putting you there because three of you are disabled with canes,' he explained, reading my thoughts. 'Especially since our officers' quarters are the main ones. With Birkenau's quarters only a small building. Plus, we have some extra space in ours, due to the fact, that a few of our officers got transferred—' Making me wonder where and why?"

———◆———

After having been shown their quarters, Geir asked Gunther to let them have a look at the hospital. "Not the place you'd want to be if you get sick." He chuckled. "Since it smells like vomit, urine, feces, and blood."

"Doesn't matter," Volker spoke up. "We four have been in the Wehrmacht and seen plenty."

"Then, hopefully, you won't be shocked."

But they were.

Geir doubted anyone got out of the hospital alive until Dr. Jules Bach, coming over, assured him there were patients who did. The doctor had close-trimmed, silver hair. *And was a good-looking man for the likes of this place, with light blue eyes that watered when I whispered, "We're here because we're working with Dr. Novak."*

Gunther ordered a nurse to show them around. So Geir stayed with Dr. Bach while Volker, Nicholas, and Rudi followed the nurse.

As Dr. Bach talked with Geir, it quickly became apparent to him, that he'd earned the trust of the SS doctor who oversaw the hospital.

And as they moved through the wards with their three-tiered bunks, Bach told him in a low voice that when he'd first come here, he'd been a stretcher barer. "Who was to make the decision whether a sick prisoner lived or died. And when a person died, they were put in a wheelbarrow and taken off."

Many of the patients were skeletal, like in the film Helmut had made. "Lice are still a problem, but not as bad as I hear it was several years ago," Dr. Bach informed Geir. "Nurses now wake the patients at dawn. Scrub them down. And give each one a fresh hospital gown and a change of underpants. Also these nurses scrub the floors with chlorine, empty mess buckets, and leave the windows open in this icy weather to clear the air."

"We've brought money, so we can slip more food to he prisoners," said Geir, trying to sound upbeat in all this gloom.

"Everything helps. But there'll never be enough to keep some of the prisoners from starving." The doctor stared at him with a long, unblinking gaze. "Sadly, there're just too many people here. Because even with the jewels, Yankee dollars, and South African pounds some of our female prisoners find hidden in clothing at the *Kanada* warehouse where they work, it's not enough. Although, was certainly a bounty that came as a surprise to us."

Geir agreed, nodding solemnly. "I want to meet some of the prisoners we can trust in the both the male and female blocks. Who in a manner of speaking, are overseeing the other prisoners with extra food and possible medicines."

"Some of our resistance fighters—eh?" He flashed a crafty smile at him. "Or former ones. Since with the Russians coming, we don't have much resistance going on right now."

"I can imagine," Geir said, nodding again. "But how did these resistance people, get these other prisoners to trust them and not turn them in?"

"Food bribes helped. Along with the continued reminder that we were all in this together. Then, there's the radio here." He pointed at some floorboards near the sink. "It's under those boards. And there was a time one of us could listen briefly to the BBC news and afterwards, spread around what we heard."

"And now?" Geir asked.

"Like I said, we're hanging on." He glanced away, staring at one of the open windows. "Waiting... so if you and your friends will bring us some news—"

"Which we'll be more than happy to do."

"Which will greatly help us—but follow me. There's something I want to show you."

Geir had no idea what it might be, until Bach shoved a metal stove to one side and lightly put his fingers on the wall behind it. "There's a cavity here, *Herr* Gallen."

"A cavity?" He craned his neck to get better look. And what he saw made his smile. A baby girl, no more than a toddler, with beautiful coppery hair. She was wearing an amber-teething necklace **and** was seated on a tiny, extremely-clean mattress and blanket holding a coppery-haired rag doll.

"Meet my niece, Yelena." Bach said.

"Helmut mentioned her when he was here filming here."

"Did he tell you about my gorgeous, younger sister who was her mother?"

"Only that she was *Hauptman* Bischoff's mistress."

"Who out of love—so he claimed—forced her to take cyanide. Since he had no place for her. And he feared the Russians who were coming would take her prisoner to Siberia for consorting with the enemy."

Anxiety darted up and down Geir's spine. "But how would they know?"

"Because she didn't have her head shaved. like the other women. And was nicely dressed. However, the most telling thing about her was that she looked to be well fed."

Geir was silent for a moment before asking hoarsely, "So she *just* took the cyanide he gave her without question?"

"As long as he gave his word that Yelena would remain safe with me, and receive a daily ration of milk."

"And she believed him?"

"Of course not. In fact, lately, his good friend, Gunther Haar, has been over here every day asking about Yelena."

"And that means *what*?"

Bach immediately tensed. "It's rumored that a last gassing will be taking place sometime in December. And that the *Sonderkomed* units, who staffed the gas chambers, will be gassed to keep them from telling the world what they were forced to do." He pointed at Yelena. "And since the Germans claim that we Jews have the enemy's blood, then my sweet little angel is apt to be thrown in with them."

"Good God!" Geir gasped. "Just thinking about a baby like Yelena being gassed is enough to shatter me. So let me try to get her to Dr. Novak—"

"No!" Bach held up his hand to stop him. "Yelena's considered a prisoner. And if you did that it would be looked on as helping a prisoner escape. So we have to come up with something else."

"Like what?"

"Like possibly bribing Gunther Haar." Bach reached in his pocket and handed Geir a small bag.

"What's this?"

"Diamonds from the Jewish clothing the girls working in the *Kanada* warehouse found."

"Amazing," Geir said, looking inside the small bag.

"Surprising the stuff they find in there that the Nazis don't know about. And it's helped a lot with our prisoners working outside the camp. Because they've been able to bribe those, who aren't prisoners with whom they're working, to slip the warehouse girls extra food to pass around."

"Should these transport marches occur, my father-in-law, Daniel Birnbaum, is planning to come here to talk to *Kommandant* Baer, about getting some of the prisoners moved to a freighter on the Baltic, that Dr. Novak and another man own. So, if we can get information about the date these gassings are going to happen, then I'll make sure Daniel's here. That way I can figure something out. With possibly this bribe, helping to get Yelena to the hospital with Daniel."

"And you'll be driving him?"

"Rudi probably will since Daniel plans to stay overnight."

"Terrible place to stay," said Bach, returning the metal stove to its position to hide Yelena.

"Not if you're like Daniel and later planning to tell the world what you saw...but moving on. Since most prisoners are off on Sundays, is there a chance you can take us to some of the male and female blocks? That way we can meet those prisoners who've aided the Resistance."

"You'll have to get permission from someone. And then they'll ask why you need *me*?"

"And my answer will be because you work in the hospital, it makes you familiar with a good many of the prisoners."

"Still, won't Gunther Haar question why you're going to these blocks?"

"Considering we're sorting a huge amount of Auschwitz's scrambled papers, we need to learn more about the camp. So, hopefully, the more we can learn about it, the faster our work will go."

Bach removed a small, folded paper from his pocket. "As good excuse as any, I suppose. Just keep one of these dried, four-leaf clovers in your pocket." He handed the paper to him.

"Four-leaf clovers?" Geir questioned.

"They're all over this place in the spring and summer. And if a prisoner finds one and gives it to the SS, he usually gets an extra piece of bread. Or sometimes, maybe even part of a sausage. So we keep a stash of dried ones in a jar for the winter."

"I didn't know about lucky, four-leafed clovers here, and will definitely be dipping into your stash."

"It'll be an excuse the SS won't think twice about, should they see you giving a prisoner a little extra food. "

Noisy footsteps in the next ward let Geir know that his friends were returning with Gunther and the nurse. "Well," Volker remarked, scowling as he joined them. "I think we've seen enough of this ghastly place."

Geir asked Gunther about the good doctor showing them around Sunday. And he said he'd check with *Hauptman* Bischoff, but he didn't see a problem. "In fact, considering all the paperwork you'll be unscrambling, I'm sure he'll agree with you, about getting to know more about how things are run here."

Which the *hauptman* did.

⸻ ◆ ⸻

Geir enjoyed being with Dr. Bach.

"My four resistance fighters," he replied when Sunday came. "That pleases me to spend time with. "

"As we're pleased to be with you," Nicholas said.

Bach took them to the various male blocks and introduced then the block's appointed leaders, who had been working secretly in the Resistance. And the doctor would whisper to them the word *Help*, and they would catch on.

In one of the female blocks, Geir gave a sausage to the kapo, and she smiled. *Bribery of course.*

When they were alone, Geir informed Volker, Nicholas, and Rudi about Yelena. And they were horrified.

"I'm trying to come up with a plan," Geir told them. "And it centers around Daniel being here when this last gassing takes place."

It's a good idea," said Rudi, "but how is Daniel going to help us to pull it off?"

"I'll talk to Gunther and let him know about my father-in-law's forthcoming visit," Geir told him. "And he can talk to *Hauptman* Bischoff about getting some prisoners with guards on Dr. Novak's Baltic freighter. Who in turn, will ask *Kommandant* Baer about it. Reminding him that the Russians are getting closer and closer—"

"And if Baer doesn't agree to it?" Nicholas interrupted.

"Then even with Dr. Novak's shortage at the hospital and Daniel's volunteer status, he's allowed to come whenever he wants. "

"Dr. Novak wrote me an encrypted letter that says I need to meet with the partisans at the train station next week," said Rudi. "And afterwards, I'll make a detour to the hospital in order to explain all this to Daniel."

"Sounds good," Geir said. "But one last thing—don't tell Hedy about Yelena. Because if this little toddler dies, it will be a great pain to me. And although Hedy's never seen her, it would hurt her." Rudi pantomimed one of his shudders. "It's something I don't think any of us here could stand to think about."

The week that followed was time consuming. More papers arrived each day as they strove to help the prisoner office workers, unscramble them. Geir sent a request to *Kommandant* Baer to list the papers he wanted taken to Germany.

"A very long list," Volker said angrily, flipping through it when it arrived.

"But where do they want us to put these papers they're not taking to Germany?" Nicholas asked.

"The *Kanada* warehouse," Geir quickly informed him. "Since we've been told we can stash them inside the warehouse's empty trunks and suitcases."

"And then?" asked Rudi "Will they be destroyed?"

"No." Geir remarked, smiling. "Remember what Otto said? According to him the Birkenau warehouse gets blown up, but the Auschwitz one doesn't."

"Otto did say he saw fire over the Birkenau one," Nicholas recalled. "Which, I suspect,was his way of telling us that so the world will know later."

"Exactly."

CHAPTER TWENTY-NINE

December came and Geir, along with Volker, Nichols, Rudi, and Dr. Bach were keeping their ears to the ground as to when the gassing of the poor *Sonderkomed* men was due to occur. And sure enough— it happened sooner than expected.

Geir had only talked to Hedy a couple of times on the phone. "Like I've talked to Charlotte," said Nicholas.

The connections were frequently bad,and when they weren't, the women were often in surgery.

Other times Geir and Nicholas were so tied -up with the unscrambling of Auschwitz's papers, they couldn't take a break.

'Otto said the Russians would come near the end of January,' Hedy would remind Geir whenever they were able to talk. 'And we'll be together.' Then she'd hesitate before saying, 'Just be sure to get out before they do.'

'Which I have every intention of doing,' he would assure her.

When word of the last gassing was finalized, Geir informed Gunther that Daniel needed to visit. "So that way he can talk to *Hauptman* Bischoff or *Kommandant* Baer about Dr. Novak's offer to use his Baltic freighter to haul some of the prisoners. However, as a volunteer working at an understaffed hospital, Daniel has to pick his time to come and go." So now was the best time for him?"

Geir requested that Daniel stay in the officers' quarters with them for the one night he would be here.

And since it had two vacant beds, permission was granted.

Daniel would be driven there and back by Rudi. Who asked permission of *Hauptman* Bischoff to use the car, which had once been attached to a gassing trailer. And Bischoff was quick to grant his request, as long he put chains on it."

"Probably because it has a small Red Cross on its door," Geir whispered to Rudi.

"Probably so."

There were two sets of keys, but Rudi informed Geir he was keeping one set. "In case we have to make a quick getaway out of here."

"Good idea."

The gassing was scheduled for day after tomorrow, so Rudi picked up Daniel the day before. He exchanged hugs with Geir, Volker, and Nicholas. Then he went with them to the hospital to meet Dr. Bach.

"I'm certainly thankful you've come," was the good doctor's response.

"As you probably already know," said Daniel. "I've come to help Geir save your niece."

"I do know and words cannot express my gratitude."

"But this afternoon I intend to look around. Or otherwise, I can't tell the world about this place—

"First though he's meeting *Kommandant* Baer," Geir interjected.

"The doctor smiled slightly. "Then the sooner, the better."

"We need Gunther to help us with that," Nicholas reminded. "Has anybody seen him?"

"He's overseeing something about some mistakes somebody in one of the offices made," Volker answered. "So let's get a move on."

Near the office building, Gunther introduced Daniel to *Kommandant* Baer, who advised him to discuss the using of Dr. Novak's Baltic-freighter with *Hauptman* Bischoff."You can meet him in the SS dining area, not far from the cinema."

'Awful to show anybody this terrible place and then see the comforts the SS enjoy,' Geir felt like saying. *But Daniel's right. The world had to know.*

First he first took him to the back door of the kitchen, where a kapo was beating prisoner. "He's begging someone in the kitchen to give him some food," the kapo said.

"Here, "Geir said, removing a sausage for his greatcoat's pocket and giving it to the kapo. "Maybe you're hungry too."

Nodding, the kapo grinned before hurrying off.

"But what about that poor, half-starved man?" Daniel asked Geir.

"Just waiting until that kapo's out of sight." And when he was, Geir reached into his other pocket and handed this poor, beaten man two sausages."

The man couldn't believe it and bowed several times to Geir. "Bribery's a necessary evil in this place," Geir informed Daniel. "Though if you want to see something really bad, then I'll show you what came in a paper across my desk two days ago. "He released a ragged breath. "It concerned gassed bodies being crammed in a building here."

"And you've seen them?"

"No. But that paper I got could possibly provide us with a good excuse to do so."

"Then let's go. Since you have your destiny, and I have mine. Which, like I've said, is to tell the allies what Germany's done to Europe's Jews and others."

A tear leaked from Geir's eye. "If you can stand it, then follow me."

He motioned Daniel toward a large steel door nearby, with an SS guard in front of it. *Bodies from a gas chamber.* "I suspect this gassing happened in November," Geir told Daniel. "However, some peculiar paperwork came across my desk about a young man who was supposed to die, but didn't—"

"Didn't?" the guard questioned, overhearing him. "Why?"

"Because it's believed he managed to get a tattoo number changed on his arm." He shook his head in feigned disgust before plunging on, "It was a number that matched a prisoner's who wasn't supposed to die. And then this young man took off for parts unknown—"

"—with one of the prisoners reporting it," the guard added. "And since this other prisoner had disappeared, they gassed the prisoner who wasn't meant to die."

Geir was shocked. "How'd you know?"

"It's a story being passed around," the guard informed him. "Which doesn't surprise me you got some paperwork about it."

"But I'd still like to have a look."

"Then be my guest," said the guard, before opening the heavy door.

It was a huge room, and when Geir and Daniel stepped into it, the cloying stench of death was so strong they had to hold their breaths.

The guard made a slight sound of frustration as he pointed at the hundreds of naked bodies of men, women, and children stacked on top of each other. "If you feel the need to dig through these bodies, you're welcome to do so."

"Afraid not," said Geir, stepping back.

"Like everyone else who comes here." The guard frowned. "Which— if you ask me— is just a *lie* to keep us in the SS on our toes." He stopped talking to cover his nose with handkerchief." The Russians are at our doorstep, and we're experiencing some delays in cremating these people. Because as I'm sure you know, *Herr* Himmler has ordered the crematoriums to be destroyed."

His mouth agape, Daniel stared, horrified, at the piles of bodies. "This defies a person's reason and imagination. So how will you *dispose* of all these bodies without a crematorium?"

"Probably through some of our pits here that have underground pyres."

"Let's get out of here," said Geir. He struggled to keep his bottled -up emotions at bay as he gripped his cane and headed toward the door.

Daniel followed closely behind him. "I refuse to accept the idea, Son, that holocaust Jews are standing for humanity's wickedness."

"So do I."

"But you look like you've lost weight—have you?"

Geir tilted his head back to look into Daniel's eyes. "I'd be doing better if I could save more people.

And *yes*— I have lost weight."

"This place we're dining at tonight. Do you eat there?"

"Mostly officers eat there. But there're places not far from the officers' quarters, in both Auschwitz and Birkenau, where we enlisted men usually eat."

"Is that where we'll be eating breakfast?"

Geir was sweating, despite the ice and snow. "You can, but I won't be."

"O-oh but you will— since I'm bound and determined to get some food down you." His father gave his bony shoulder a nudge for emphasis. "So remember, you can't help others if you get sick."

"What Dr. Bach says."

"And he's right."

Geir glanced away so Daniel wouldn't see how disturbed he was. "Even with all the help, nothing takes my mind off this place but sorting through all its paperwork."

"And you eat then?"

"No. These dozens, thousands, and millions of numbers we come across daily gets my attention For only a brief period of time. Until one of the voices in my head whispers, 'Survival for these prisoners is all about numbers.'"

"Knowledge that keeps you from eating," said Daniel with a stricken expression. "Which is not good enough, because you *need* to fatten up!"

The rest of the day passed quickly, with Geir pleased that his and Daniel's dinner with *Hauptman* Bischoff went smoothly.

"And these male prisoners will be marched under guard to the Baltic?" Bischoff asked Daniel. "To be put on Dr. Novak's freighter?"

"Correct."

Then Bischoff handed Daniel a pad and pencil. "Write down some information about the freighter's exact location. Since these days we're hearing that due to some severe Baltic bombings by the Russians, many freighters are holed up and not carrying any cargo."

Daniel wrote down the information. And after dinner Geir, accompanied by Dr. Bach, took him to meet some of Bach's block companions. "Your son wants you to see the way the prisoners are forced to live," the doctor told him." And also, meet some members in the Resistance living here." "Awful to live like that," Daniel later whispered to Geir and Nicholas in the officers' quarters. They couldn't talk much with the officers coming and going, but they at least got to rest up for their big day tomorrow.

"Are we still bribing Gunther with that bag of diamonds?" Daniel asked Geir.

"You bet—but why are you asking?"

"Because I've brought another large, diamond ring. So do I need to put it in the bribe?"

"No!" Geir shook his head emphatically. "This bagful of diamonds is more than enough. Since Gunther strikes me as a man who's never had much."

◆

When morning came they ate breakfast in the place Geir had mentioned. He didn't eat much, just a slice of the black army bread, that he drank with the standard *ersatz* coffee made from roasted barley. Then, as planned, he complained of having a painful stomach ache and wanted to go to the hospital.

"So I'll need to escort you there," Daniel told him.

"Where we'll wait," Geir murmured, leaning against his cane. "Until Gunther shows up to get Yelena."

At the hospital Bach handed Daniel a picture of Yelena's parents. "Which you need to give to Geir's wife, who'll kept it safe for her."

Daniel put it inside his coat pocket. " Rest assured my daughter-in-law will."

Rudi pulled the car around in an out-of-sight place not far from the hospital.

Then joining them, he pointed out several times that he needed to get Daniel back to the chalethospital. "But I'm not leaving until Geir gets better," Daniel would insist.

All part of our ploy, Geir reflected with pride. *So we'll be ready when Gunther shows up to take Yelena to the Birkenau gassing.*

Which he did....*And on a motorbike-of all things —in this icy weather.*

"The Red Cross ambulance has just pulled into Auschwitz, and once the Zyklon B is delivered, the gassing at Birkenau will take place. So hand Yelena over—"

"Not on your life!" Geir exploded. "She'll either freeze to death on that motorbike or be thrown out without any way to secure her."

Disgusted, Gunther shook his head. "We either kill her or the Russians will. So what does it matter?"

"And you know that about the Russians *how?*" Geir asked him.

"Because that's the way those uncivilized people are."

Dr. Bach now had Yelena in his arms. "She's frightened! Can't you see she's crying?"

"Then I'll give her a chocolate," said Gunther." Like we do all the children who're going to die to ease them."

"Chocolate before you die?" Geir questioned, taking Yelena from Dr.Bach. "Now that's a hell of a trade-off. "

"Makes you wonder who thought that up," Daniel mumbled beneath his breath.

"Geir will follow behind on the motorbike. And I'll drive *you*, Gunther, to Birkenau," said Rudi." Along with Daniel and Yelena." Focusing on his clothing, he looked him up and down before adding, "Since you're not dressed warmly like Geir, for this icy weather—"

"Doesn't matter," Gunther quickly cut him off. "I'm use to is."

"Don't take chances," Daniel warned, gesturing at Geir, who was now wearing his ear muffs." He'll follow behind us on the motorbike."

"And I'll put another blanket around Yelena," said Dr. Bach, taking her from Geir.

The women from the *Kanada* warehouse had slipped her some warm clothes. So after wrapping the blanket around her, Dr. Bach wiped her tears and kissed her on the cheek before handing her to Daniel.

Outside, Geir put his cane in the motorbike's sidecar as Rudi prepared to drive off with Gunther, Daniel, and Yelena.

The gas-chambered crematorium was in Birkenau's forest, not far from the railroad tracks. *A good many fir trees in this silent forest,* Geir remembered, thinking about the first time he'd seen it.

The birch trees were quite close together. And in addition, there were some sycamore and maple trees mingled with some strange-looking crooked trees.

'The closeness of the trees before their leaves have dropped, makes me feel like I'm looking down at the camp from them,' Gunther had told him, when he'd shown him around. *'And there's* an escape *tunnel here that was dug by hand by one of the prisoners—'*

'I can't imagine,' Geir recalled telling him.

When they got closer to the crematorium, he gunned the engine on his motorbike and swung around in front of the car. It was an action that forced Rudi to stop a slight distance from Crematorium 5.

"Why are we not driving up to it, *Herr* Gallen?" Gunther leaned out the car's window and yelled.

"Because we can see what we need to see from here," Geir answered, coming over to car with his cane.

Yelena was crying loudly. "Hush, sweet little one, hush," said Daniel in an attempt to sooth her.

Up ahead were the *Sonderkomed,* who were obviously numbed by the cold as they waited.

"Those poor men are as naked as the bare-limbed trees surrounding us," Geir murmured, gooseflesh sprouting on his arms. But when he saw three warmly clothed violinists playing Strauss music in front of the crematorium, it paralyzed his senses.

Daniel's face registered disbelief. "What the hell!"

"Music helps to ease them before they die," Gunther replied. "Like the chocolate we give the children. So hand over the toddler now!"

Adrenaline rushed through Geir's veins. "Not on your life," he snapped. "She's going back with Daniel and Rudi."

"Going back?" Gunther questioned in an angry tone. "Are you out of your mind! If you don't hand her over, I'll make certain you, Daniel, and Rudi are all gassed—" He flung back the passenger door and stepped out.

Geir's heart took a leap as he struggled to maintain his balance. "Not if you want this." He opened the small bag of diamonds. "There's a fortune in here."

Immediately Gunther's mouth flew open "A...are they—"

"—diamonds," Geir completed, watching him stare at them with disbelief.

"How'd you get them?"

"From some Jews in Berlin who were being deported," he lied. "And they're all yours if you let Yelena go."

A long pause followed, with Gunther touching several. "But still—"

"Are you fearful of the consequences if you accept my offer?" Geir asked, sensing his concern.

"Yes." He drew back from him. "The toddler has the enemies' blood and if she doesn't die—"

"The Russians say *we* Germans have the enemies' blood," Geir reminded, "And don't think for a minute they won't treat us like we're treating the Jews."

"But what can I do?" Gunther asked. "It's not like I can desert the SS."

"As you know Rudi's driving Daniel back to the hospital," Geir said. "So get sick and go back with them and Yelena."

Gunther focused his attention on the naked men waiting outside the crematorium. "You're talking crazy."

"Not if you do what I tell you to do," said Geir, leaning against his cane to steady himself. "You and Yelena shared chocolate you bought from some store in Warsaw. And now it's like both of you have been poisoned. You're desperate. And don't want to be in that filthy Auschwitz hospital. So you're demanding that Rudi take you to the one were Daniel works... even if it's thirty-two kilometers away."

"And then what?" Gunther asked, a slight tremor in his voice.

"The hospital doctors think it might be poison. But, also, could be a contagious disease. So they'll put you in isolation. And Dr. Novak will phone *Hauptman* Bischoff and explain the situation—"

"Which is?"

"You die that night. Yelena dies. And Dr.Novak issues death certificates and sends them to *Hauptman* Bischoff."

Gunther stood transfixed. "And I leave the hospital as a free man?"

"Exactly. In one of the hospital's trucks. Where you'll be driven to a fairly isolated train station and put on a train."

"And no one will recognize me?"

"You'll have facial bandages resembling a mask and false papers."

"Sounds like you've worked it all out, *Herr* Gallen," said Gunther with a smirk."

"I've had to. Because if you don't accept my offer, I have no choice but to follow those into the gas chamber and die with Yelena."

Shock pervaded Gunther's features. "You'd really do that?"

"I won't stand by and watch a toddler killed."

"Then get me to the hospital before I change my mind," said Gunther, just as the SS guards were moving the freezing, naked prisoners into the gas-chambered crematorium.

Damned Nazis! Geir mentally cursed. *Sadly, in three to five minutes, those poor men will all be dead.*

He was on the verge of tears when Daniel shouted at Rudi,"Wait! I need to talk to Geir." And leaving Yelena in the car, he got out and hurried over to him. "Son," he whispered. "I won't get any sleep until I hear from you So call me the minute you've talked to *Hauptman* Bischoff... and if the phone connections are bad—"

"I'll try and send a Morse. Since lately its connection has been good."

"Thankfully." Daniel smiled, giving him a hug. Then taking Geir's hand, he stepped back as if to admire him. "My *son* at Auschwitz. My *son* saying, he'd die in a gas chamber with a toddler. M...my *son*—" His voice trembled. "Who like his beautiful mother is too good for this world."

Geir returned his hug. "Tell Hedy to talk to me about Yelena."

"I know she'll love her—"

"But she'll have to word things like, 'she's *sad* the baby's dying'."

Rudi honked the horn, and Daniel turned. "Time for us to go, Son."

"You'd better, before Gunther changes his mind."

"*Damn him* if he does!" Daniel was quick to exclaim.

"Still," Geir replied, his gaze focused on the crematorium. "You can never tell about the SS."

"You're got that right." He gave his son's arm a reassuring squeeze before hurrying to the car.

Another hour passed before Geir went to *Hauptman* Bischoff and told what had happened to Gunther and Yelena. He deliberately waited until they had plenty of time to get to the hospital.

"I can't believe this!" exclaimed Bischoff. He was shocked, but sympathetic. And agreed they did right taking Yelena to the hospital, instead of killing her. "Have to find our what's happening to Gunther and that toddler before anyone else dies."

"Once Dr. Rath's examined them, he'll be calling you," Geir told Bischoff. "So we'll just have to wait."

The wait wasn't long.

Later, Geir learned from Rudi that when Dr. Rath called, he'd informed Bischoff he suspected food poisoning. "From the chocolate Gunther bought at a store in Warsaw and shared with the baby. However, stomach pumping hasn't seemed to do much good."

"Even if I did drive, lightning fast, on icy roads getting to the hospital,"Rudi remarked, grinning at Geir. Then he proceeded to tell him more about what Dr. Rath had told *Hauptman* Bischoff. 'A contagious disease was unlikely but couldn't ruled out. So both Gunther and the baby are in isolation.'

And also, Dr. Rath requested that I wear protective gloves and pack Gunther Haar's things—plus anything the baby had. And then bring the items to the hospital because there might be something among them, that would give him some more insight into what had happened to Gunther. 'Was it possible *Herr* Haar had been in contact with something other than the chocolate?' Dr. Rath had asked Bischoff.

He didn't know but had asked the hospital to telephone him the minute someone knew something."

◆

When Rudi returned from his second trip to the hospital, he'd told Geir to let Daniel know all was well—at least so far.

Then, Geir called his father as promised, who put Hedy on the phone. She'd feigned sadness, even if she seemed to have difficulty hiding the excitement in her voice over Yelena.

Geir was excited too.

"Now Hedy and I are no longer childless," he wrote: *"How fortunate... though it doesn't stop me from I'm praying to God that everything continues to go as smoothly for us as it has for us."*

The hours drug on. Only this time it was Dr. Novak who talked to *Hauptman* Bischoff. The baby had died, and it was feared Gunther Haar would follow suit. Which another hour later, he did.

A mortician was coming in the morning to take the bodies and do an autopsy, Dr. Novak informed *Hauptman* Bischoff. "And you will learn the cause of death the minute I get the report."

However, the report that came was vague. It seemed a type of poisoning, but nothing anyone could identify. "Death certificates are being issued and sent to you," Dr. Novak later told Bischoff. "And since we know so very little about what happened, the mortician has made arrangements for a quick burial in a country cemetery."

Bischoff offered to pay for it, but Dr.Novak refused. "It's not that much and given the unusual circumstances of their deaths, the hospital is willing to foot the bill."

Dr. Novak went on to say that he was telegraphing some hospitals in Poland and Germany. "Maybe they've encountered something like Private Haar's *so-called* poisoning. And whatever information I come by, I will share."

Oddly, some telegrams came later that afternoon that reported some strange poisonings. However, nothing quite like Gunther's.

"Now am I free to leave for this out-of-the way train station?" Gunther asked Dr.Novak. "At Auschwitz, the sound of Russian gunfire in the distance, seems to be getting closer each day."

"And you're anxious to get away?"

"Yes.

"I can't blame you." Dr.Novak reached across his desk for a large envelope. "These false identification papers just came for you. And there's also a train ticket, and some currency. So you should be on your way."

"Where am I going."

"It's a long trip, but your ticket says Madrid."

"In Spain!" Gunther exclaimed, aghast.

"It's a safe place. No one will recognize you. And your money will go far in that country."

"Then Spain it is."

"I packed some extra facial bandages in you bag," Dr.Novak said. "Which you'll need to change on a daily basis to keep up appearances."

"But once in Spain I can get rid of them, can't I?"

"Correct."

Dr. Novak was now standing in the doorway next to Daniel, who was waiting to go with Gunther in the truck to the train station. "I appreciate all you did for me," Gunther said, reaching for his pack.

Daniel gave his shoulder a pat. "And we appreciate what you did for Yelena."

"I didn't want her to die. And you may find it strange to hear me say it, but I never liked seeing all those people in the camp die. But what could I do?"

"At this late date probably nothing," Daniel countered with a sad smile. "But in the beginning, you should have sided with the allies."

"I know."

"But more one thing, Private Haar. When you see someone who's down and needs help, give them a hand in memory of those you couldn't save."

"Definitely." He gave Daniel's shoulder a squeeze. "Because you people could have killed me and taken back the diamonds, but I gambled you wouldn't—"

"—and won."

⋆◆⋆

Christmas was approaching, but Geir couldn't have been more depressed. "The camp had a large Christmas tree several years ago," remarked a fattened-up kapo. "And the bodies of Jews were put under it like they were Christmas presents."

"But not this year," Geir insisted, on the verge of throwing up. "With the Russians headed our way we're as short on ammunition as the

Wehrmacht. "He turned toward one of the watchtowers. "Even if there're still a lot of shots being fired in this camp."

The kapo agreed. "Ammunition is being wasted."

"Geir," said Rudi, practically brushing shoulders with the kapo as he was leaving. "You're not eating right, and Hedy's worried."

"I guess Daniel told her."

"He did. Because you're not numbing yourself to what you see. Which you'll have to do in order to survive."

Rudi had just returned from the hospital, after getting some medicines for the prisoners.

"What are they doing at the hospital for Christmas?" Geir asked him.

"They're having a luncheon Christmas day and expect you, Volker, and Nicholas to join them."

"And not you?"

"I told them I'd be the one to stay at the camp. Since the three of you probably wouldn't go because it was a holiday for everyone, including the prisoners. And you three, like me, would fear something terrible might happen to some of them."

"Like killing some and putting their bodies under the Christmas tree?"

"Sadly." he replied in bewilderment. "Which is why I agreed to stay with Dr. Bach. Since he's apt to get word from his resistance team if something brutal is about to happen to some of the prisoners."

"And then you'll do *what*?"

"Use some bribery on those doing the brutalizing. Which most likely will be the kapos."

Geir nodded his understanding. "Still if we go, we're bringing you and Dr. Bach something good to eat from the luncheon."

"I'll like that, and so will he," said Rudi. "But what I'd like most, Geir, is for you to give that small notepad, with your writing, you promised Daniel you were going to give him. Because, like I've said, he wants it and if someone finds it, we'd in a lot of trouble."

"I know I've been holding off. But I've coded the names and blotted out some things, so I will see Daniel gets it for safe keeping. Since he maintains with the Russians at our door, the German world is being turned upside down, with those in the SS getting careless—"

"Let's hope so," Rudi cut him off.

"But tell me, how Hedy and Yelena are doing?" Geir asked, turning the conversation. "And everyone else working at the hospital."

"Hedy adores Yelena— like the others there. And Christmas may be close, but that little one's having Christmas everyday."

"What's she getting?"

"Hedy wanted to pay for everything. But Daniel, along with Charlotte, Alexi, Dr. Rath, and Dr. Novak wouldn't let her."

"And there were able to do some shopping?"

"No. But a lady, who loves children, and works in the kitchen volunteered to do it. And soon there were gifts for Yelena everywhere."

Geir's interest was immediately piqued. "Like what? Toys?"

Rudi shook his head. "Yelena only likes her rag doll. So they bought her a high-chair, bed, clothes, and a brush and comb. With Hedy insisting she have a pair of red shoes—which the little one loves. Plus, a music box that plays a lullaby. Prompting Daniel —not to be outdone— to buy her a silver spoon. Since she's trying to learn to hold one, so she can eat with it instead of her hands."

"I'll get her a toy," said Geir. "That she loves as much as her doll— but what about the others? What are they doing for us? And what are we doing for them?"

"Well, since they're in Poland and hardly have any time to shop, the lady from the kitchen suggests making it an *amber* Christmas. Because she has relatives who're in the Baltic amber business. And now, they have a tiny shop in the hospital, where everyone can purchase inexpensive gifts."

"But will this shop be open Christmas day?"

"That's what's good about." Rudi grinned. "With outsiders coming daily, to buy Baltic amber teething necklaces for their babies."

"And the grown-ups?"

"They buy these raw-healing amber necklaces for their headaches and joint pain."

"Sounds like magic."

"It is. As long as its skin on skin contact," Rudi replied. "Because raw amber has something called *succinate* in it."

"*Succinate*," Geir repeated. "I'll have to ask Dr. Rath about that."

"And he'll tell you that like Dr. Novak and Dr. Zeroff, he too is now wearing a raw amber necklace."

"Still, why not before?"

"Because in the past a good many Germans have frowned on it. Deeming it as a Polish, cultural thing. Though now, with the Russians at our door, they've got more important things to be concerned about than their disdain of the Slavic, Polish culture. So you, Volker, and, Nicholas enjoy this Christmas while you can."

Geir flashed a leisurely smile at him. "We intend to."

———◆———

Geir wrote:

"A beautiful Christmas. Which had begun with my kissing Hedy and our daughter. Then exchanging bear hugs—if you can believe it— with Daniel, Dr, Rath, Dr.Novak and Dr. Zeroff. And I tried to hug and kiss Charlotte— but she couldn't get her away from Nicholas."

CHAPTER THIRTY

"It's been almost a month since we've seen each other, Geir!" Hedy exclaimed. "And I couldn't ask for a better present than having you here, with this wonderful daughter you gave me. But still, like Daniel says, you're getting too thin. So what are you doing with your food? Giving it to the prisoners?"

"Most of it." He looked at the floor. "Since I feel I'm not doing nearly enough for the prisoners."

"You saved Yelena." She kissed her on the cheek." And *that's* really something."

"I'd have given my life for hers."

"So Gunther said."

Yelena touched Hedy's face several times. "She does that often."

"Because you're so beautiful she has to touch you— her wonderful mother— to see if you're real." Geir said, handing the toddler a the blue-eyed, brown teddy bear, a woman from the *Kanada* house had given him.

"She's the beautiful one," said Hedy, helping her hold the bear.

And she certainly was... with a bow in her hair that matched her red dress and shoes. "Do you think she remembers me?" Geir asked.

"Absolutely," said Hedy, returning the bright smile lighting Yelena's face as she clutched the bear.

"She loves her grandfather too, "Daniel reminded, touching her tiny arm.

"And us," said Alexi, gesturing at Dr. Novak and Dr. Rath.

"Alexi's made a Christmas wish," said Dr.Novak. "Which is for Yelena to meet little Hansi and the two become best friends."

"A beautiful wish." Geir smiled.

The owner of the amber shop rang a bell, and Dr. Rath announced it was the signal it go pick out what they wanted for Christmas. The three doctors and Daniel had given Hedy, Charlotte, and their husbands, along with Rudi and Volker, the raw-healing amber necklaces... as well as all the hospital workers.

In return, Hedy and Charlotte gave their husbands, Volker, Rudi, the doctors, and Daniel cuff links.

They were set in silver with cognac polished amber. "And here's an amber necklace to give Rudi," Hedy said, handing it to Geir.

Which he was pleased to do. "But now, I must get you a present. So let's head to this amber room and shop."

Nicholas and Charlotte were already there, and she showed off the large, cognac-colored amber ring Nicky had purchased for her.

"Would you like a ring like that?" Geir asked Hedy. And she nodded.

A key chain with a carved, amber fish and insect inclusion-fossil in it caught his eye.

"How about if I also buy this for you?"

"No." She gave her head a vigorous shake. "Let me buy it for you."

"But you've already given me a gift."

"Doesn't matter, it's yours. "And she promptly paid for it.

Lunch followed with Yelena sitting in her high-chair between Hedy and Geir. "She's learning to hold a spoon, "Hedy said proudly. "And I know there are some children her age who can do it but given her situation, she didn't have the opportunities they had."

"Still, she's a fast learner," Daniel remarked, closely watching her.

They were eating chicken stroganoff which everyone, including the patients, seemed to enjoyed.

Though it was the cake with its fluffy, whipped topping that brought the most praise.

Yelena held her spoon. But since she was not able to use it well, she allowed Geir to feed her mouthfuls of the delicious dessert.

Volker, seated at the other end of the table, checked his watch. "We promised we'd head back after lunch."

"The kitchen folk are preparing the food to take back to Rudi and Dr. Bach," said Dr. Novak, rising.

"I agree we should go," said Nicholas, also rising. "And I know it's rude to eat and leave. However, there's no telling what could be happening Christmas day at the camp, with a good many of the SS getting drunk."

Alexi, Dr. Rath, and Daniel pushed their chairs back and joined Geir as he prepared to leave. "Hate to leave the two of you," he told Hedy, as she walked alongside him with Yelena in her arms.

"And we hate for you to go."

When they got to the doorway Geir, once again, exchanged bear hugs with the doctors and Daniel.

"You have my blessing, Son," his father whispered, taking the small notepad he handed him with his notes about the camp. He then turned and took Yelena from Hedy's arms.

Geir kissed the baby, then Hedy.

"I'm convinced God called us to do what we're doing," she said.

"So am I," he agreed, kissing her again. "Because if we hadn't, little Yelena wouldn't be alive. It's just that—" He paused to draw a shaky breath. "I don't know if I can ever be he same after seeing what I've seen."

"How could anyone? Since what you see at Auschwitz wounds a person's spirit." A tear trickled down her cheek. "But no matter the outcome, we'll never truly part—"

"—until we meet again."

"Whenever that may be," Hedy murmured.

All the way back to Auschwitz, Geir kept thinking about how his spirit was wounded. *Hedy's certainly right about that. So, in the end, what will be the outcome for us?*

An unanswered question that was still in his thoughts, when he arrived at the hospital and gave Rudi and Dr. Bach their food.

All appeared to be well. "Probably because the Russian shots are now *quite* close," Geir remarked to Volker and Nicholas.

The hospital office was vacant, so Bach and Rudi gobbled their food in it. Geir gave Rudi his cuff links and amber necklace "If I could I would have brought you some gifts." Geir told the good doctor.

"Oh, but you did," he assured him. "You saved Yelena. And Rudi's telling me how great she's doing in your wife's hands."

"That she is. And she looked especially wonderful in the red bow, dress, and shoes Hedy had her wearing today."

'But how long will the hospital last with the Russians coming?' Geir hadn't dared to ask anyone. *It has three trucks. And I just pray they have enough time to get the hospital staff and patients in the trucks, before they head back to Germany. Because I feel certain, the Russians will descend on the hospital, along with Auschwitz... Daniel told me it was rumored the Russians soldiers*

knew nothing about Auschwitz. However, Stalin did. Something that makes me wonder what exactly these soldiers will do when they show up there?

The first two weeks in January seemed to Geir to pass slowly. He got to talk to Hedy a couple of times on the phone, but the ice and snow were getting worse making the connections bad. *Hauptman* Bischoff contacted Dr. Novak on the Morse for the exact location of his freighter. And since the phone lines were down, the doctor returned the information on the Morse.

"Next to go will be the Morse," said Bischoff, on his way out of his office. "But luckily, these transports will be taking most of us out of this damned place."

Later in the officers' quarters, Geir reminded Volker, Rudi, and Nicholas, "These death marches Otto predicted, will be coming near the end of January."

And sure enough on a bitterly cold morning with ankle-deep snow, preparation for these transport marches began.

"At least Dr. Bach won't be going on the marches," said Rudi. "Like I hear they're making those other doctors. "

"Dr. Bach would be going if he didn't typhus and is dying," Volker reminded. "Which is a sorry trade-off."

"He doesn't have to die," Geir interjected. "If only we could lay our hands on the Russian version of that new drug, the Americans are calling penicillin. Hedy talked about it being hard to get these days."

Wiping his runny nose, Nicholas turned to Geir. "You told us to keep a lookout for it—"

"—which you're doing."

"But sadly no luck."

"As I've said," remarked Rudi." I've heard the SS whispering about the drug. Saying they heard one of their officers got it off a Russian prisoner. But like us, couldn't put their finger on who this officer was."

"With this camp evacuation getting underway, the SS here are going crazy," said Volker. "Which, hopefully, with all the confusion, might enable us to learn who this officer is, and take this drug from him before Dr. Bach dies."

Geir frowned at the despair of the situation. "I know one thing. We can't let this officer leave on one of these transports."

"What about the three hundred Russian prisoners of war at Birkenau?" "Nicholas asked him." "I've just heard a rumor one of the prisoners possibly knows this officer."

"It's worth a try to find out. Even though word has it these prisoners were shot yesterday."

"Certainly a waste of ammunition," Volker piped up." Which keeps getting scarcer each day in this place."

Rudi's eyes rounded like he had a sudden thought. "Still, if there're a medic or medics among those Russians who's still alive, then we might learn something."

"A medic would be the logical person," Geir said, putting on his gloves as he prepared to leave his quarters. "And maybe a man the SS would kept alive, while they decide whether to take him on this transport march or shoot him."

"Didn't Dr. Bach mention a Russian medic prisoner who spoke German?" Rudi asked Geir."

"If memory serves me right."

"But before you go hunting this medic," said Volker, following Geir to the doorway. "Let's grab breakfast first, since we have to report to the administration building."

Which they quickly did.

Inside, the working female civilians and female prisoners cowered at the shouting SS men. "Grab the record books and papers!" they ordered.

An SS man, whose hands were filled with papers and log books, yelled at Geir, "Where are you keeping the records to be destroyed?"

"Crematorium 5—that *Kommandant* Baer has ordered blown up," Geir lied. He wasn't about to tell him it was the *Auschwitz* Kanada warehouse. *Where all the papers we've sorted and filed are in suitcases and trunks.*

"The *Kommandant* didn't tell us, *Herr* Gallen," the man retorted hotly.

"Probably because we're not finished."

"Then we're taking what we can," said another SS man, as he and his team grabbed at cards and sifted through papers.

"All you can do," Geir murmured. "So this evacuation is happening tomorrow?"

"Tomorrow morning." The man nodded, his arms filled with papers. "The Russians are coming, and we can't leave evidence. So you and your men need to help us gather up all these papers you didn't have time to sort," he directed. "And do your best to finish the job."

A direct order. Possibly forcing Geir, Volker, Nicholas, and Rudi to work through most of the day and into the night. "Gathering up the papers, we're attempting to put them in order for these damned SS men," Volker remarked with contempt.

Nicholas's face lit up. "They won't get them all, because I've discovered several wall cavities in this building where we can manage to hide some more."

"Just what we need to hear on this terrible day," said Volker. "With a good many of these pending death marches tomorrow morning. Plus— the others occurring the day or days after."

"I'm glad we're not going on those marches," said Rudi. "Since it would mean seeing a lot of innocent, starving people either shot— if they're stragglers —or torn apart by dogs."

"Daniel's made sure the people in upper and lower Silesia will be waiting for these prisoners with food and water," Geir reminded. "Which should help them get to the trains, that eventually most will be taking... but what about Birkenau's Russian prisoners?"

"We've heard too many shots for them not to have been killed by now," Volker spoke up.

"So it seems we're a little late."

"Maybe we are," said Geir. "And I know the four of us have closed our ears to the information about these helpless Russians being shot, but I can't let Dr. Bach die until I've exhausted all possibilities."

"I've got an idea," said Rudi. "Since I have the second set of keys to the car. And it's well-fueled and still has its chains on, let's drive over there and see what we can find out."

"Won't the SS think that strange?" asked Nicholas.

"We have so many stacks of papers, cards, and books, we'll lie and say we can't work effectively, until there're out of our way in Birkenau's Crematorium 5. So Geir will need to help me."

"That's a great idea," Nicholas commended him. "Considering it's more than a twenty minute walk.

And because a walking person sinks in the snow, then no man using a cane should attempt it."

"Then hurry and go," Volker urged.

So out they went in the thick snow toward the car, Rudi sometimes joked was his own.

In minutes they were at Birkenau. And recognizing a kapo that was one of the nicer ones, Geir asked Rudi stop the car. "Do you know of a Russian medic here who speaks German?" Geir asked.

The kapo nodded. "Then get in and show us where he is," said Rudi.

It was a tight squeeze with all the papers in the back, but the kapo directed them to the men's block or barracks. "He's in there with the tattooist."

Rudi opened the car door. "Then go inside with us and point him out."

Geir reached into one if his greatcoat's pockets and handed the kapo a fat, wrapped sausage

"Be glad to," said the kapo, smiling at the treat.

The medic was talking to the tattooist in this strangely deserted men's blocks, where the smell of death and ruin was stronger here than any other place in the camp. And there was blood on the snow.

Where is everyone? Geir wondered. *Dead? transported? When the weather's this bleak and icy they're usually not made to work outdoors. Since nothing much can get done.*

Both men quickly stepped back when they saw Rudi and Geir. "You're needed at the hospital," he informed the medic. "One of the doctors is sick. So get in the car with us and shove some of those papers in the back seat, out of the way."

The Russian looked surprised but did as was requested, staring at the tattooist with a helpless expression as the car pulled away.

"Do you have a name?" Geir asked.

"Maxim Semenov," he answered, his voice trembling.

His hair was blond stubble, and he was thin and slightly built, reminding Geir for some peculiar reason, of a starved wolf. *I'll try to save this poor man,* he vowed. *Who's not dressed for this terrible weather. And even if he doesn't know anything about this medicine we're seeking, I won't let it stop me from trying to keep him alive.*

"First we go to the *Kanada* warehouse at Auschwitz," said Rudi, interrupting Geir's thinking. "Which— as we know —is the better one for our purpose when it comes to getting rid of these papers. And while we're there, we'll ask the women to help Maxim pick out some warm clothing."

It didn't take long, and the hospital wasn't that far. "We need to get some food down you," Geir told Maxim, handing him a wrapped sausage from another pocket of his greatcoat, "And while we're at the hospital we'll have someone make us some tea."

"Who are you?" he asked. "You're not—" He gestured at Geir's uniform."

"One of them," he completed. "Yes and no. We're in the *Allgemeine* SS that enforces racial policy.

Since the *Waffen* SS is combat. But we don't think or feel like the rest of them here do. Because we're on a mission to help people like you. Who're in such dire need."

"Are you working with the Red Cross?"

"Unfortunately, *no*. Because they might have what we're looking for."

"Which is?"

"A small vial of what some call the Russian version of American penicillin. Which an SS officer took from one of the prisoners." He hesitated before asking, "Do you know anything about it?"

"I do...since it was mine."

"*Yours?*" Geir questioned, now beside himself. *Who else would have it but a medic?* "Words to brighten this very dark and bone chilling day."

"Probably the reason, that so far, I've been spared," Maxim remarked.

"Do you remember the name of the officer who took it?"

He nodded. "*Hauptman* Bischoff."

"Did he say why?"

"Not really. He just implied to another officer that it was something of value."

"Great value." Geir asserted with a smile. "The difference between life and death."

They took Maxim into the hospital and introduced him to a dark-haired nurse, Ana. She was a Polish political prisoner who was one of Dr. Bach's closest friends. "How's the doctor?" Geir asked her, pointing at his sick bed.

"We're giving him water, but he's getting worse. Since the Russian version of penicillin we had, has long been gone. And we have no other medicine that works, with which to treat his typhus."

"I feel certain I can get the medicine. However, I'll have to bargain for it. So I'll need some gems." He went over to the doctor, who was unconscious. "Can you get the women at the *Kanada* house to help me?" Geir asked Ana.

But she just shrugged. "Doesn't appear to be anything there any more."

Geir's heart leaped. "Please—hear me out!" He grabbed both her hands. "They're emptying the camp tomorrow. And if I don't get that medicine in the next few hours, Dr. Bach will die—"

"Then don't bargain with gems," Rudi cut in. "We've marks and a stash of Yankee dollars Daniel's given us. So that should work, shouldn't it?"

"It should," Geir agreed. "It's just that you can't tell about some of these SS officers, who think currency is not as good as precious jewels."

"That's their stupidity." Rudi grimaced, shaking his head.

"*Hauptman* Bischoff will probably accept your offer," said Ana." Just don't mention the doctor because he's a Jew."

"We'll tell him it's for Nicholas," Geir put in. "Who has a slight cold. And since we're not going on the transports we need all the help we can get." He paused, once again running an appraising eye over the doctor before adding, "Considering we're expected to finish gathering up these records to be destroyed as well as locating some more papers, which at the last minute *Kommandant*

Baer has decided he needs to take with him too."

"Telling him about Nicholas is a good idea," said Ana. "It's just that we'll have to hide the doctor some place."

Geir stiffened. "Why?"

"They're only talking the prisoners who can walk. And shooting the others."

"Who told you that?" asked Rudi.

"The female kapo in my block," Ana answered. "And they're planning on evacuating the medical people here."

Maxim's blue eyes darkened. "The SS won't hesitate to shoot anybody who falls down or can't make it. Trust me, I know."

"My God, that's a crazy waste ammunition with the Russians nearly here." said Rudi, his brow dipping into a deep frown. "But don't any of you hospital workers go on this transport." He pointed at the ceiling. "Stay in the wards at the back and hide in the rafters. Since it's been my experience most shooters don't look up."

"If they come in this hospital to shoot the sick prisoners, we'll take care of them," Geir remarked, nodding at Rudi. "And with the confusion of emptying thousands of prisoners out of this camp, it'll probably go unnoticed."

"We certainly hope so."

"But what about the musicians?" Ana asked Rudi. "We've heard they're going to be killed."

"I'll see they also get word to hide in the rafters."

"Don't be surprised if they start evacuating the blocks tonight," she said. "Because the women in mine are frightened and huddled together."

"If that's the case," said Geir, "then Rudi and I had better get busy and strike up our deal with *Hauptman* Bischoff."

"And you should hurry," she urged. "Because Dr. Bach won't last much longer."

Knowing she was right, Geir and Rudi rushed out the door to the administration building, where they collected Volker and Nicholas's Yankee dollars and put them with theirs. Then, after quickly counting them, they headed to *Hauptman* Bischoff's office.

His office was as chaotic as the rest of the offices in the building, with the SS and frightened workers, continuing to grab at books, cards, and papers.

"Have you found the other papers *Kommandant* Baer is looking for?" Bischoff asked Geir.

"Not yet."

"Time's running out."

"So Rudi and I know, but I need a favor, "he reached for the dollars in his pocket. "Nicholas has a bad cold and is working non-stop. And if you leave and there's no medical here, then should he get worse, he might die."

"And I'm supposed to do *what* about it?" asked Bischoff in a disgusted tone.

"One of the officers in our quarters mentioned that you had the Russian version of penicillin in a small vial," said Geir. "And if you do, I'd like to buy it from you."

"An officer in your quarters," he repeated, surprised. "How the hell did he know?"

"He said he saw you take if from a Russian," answered Rudi.

Geir laid the Yankee dollars across Bischoff's desk. "Will this be enough?"

He looked at the money, then at Geir. "I wasn't aware I was selling my vial."

"I know."

Bischoff began counting the dollars. "There's a lot of money here. So, tell me how 'd you get it?"

"My father-in-law, Daniel, with whom you dined. He did business in many countries before the war, and he gave it to us in case of an emergency— like now."

"Well." Bischoff sighed. "I'll guess I'll have to sell you the vial, since you'll be left here with the Russians, who're only a few days away. So it's not like Nicholas can afford the luxury of getting sick and not being able to help you locate those papers *Kommandant* Baer is looking for. Which means you'll have to work *faster*, with destroying what's left over, continuing to be a problem in itself."

Geir didn't need to be reminded about that, but he did have one final question. "If we can't find some of these papers *Kommandant* Baer is seeking, what do we do if we find them after he's gone?"

"Those officials here, who're not going on the transport, will be in Warsaw for a few days, "said Bischoff, handing Geir the penicillin. "And after that, Berlin—" He quickly grabbed a card and scribbled an address on it. "So, if you're able to make it to Berlin, then deliver the papers at this address. But if you can't, you'll have no choice but to destroy them. "

'*Hell— under no circumstances,*' Geir had to bite his lip to keep from saying. But with the penicillin deal now being sealed, it was time to go.

Though on the way out, Rudi did bump into one of the SS women, with the papers and account books she was holding, spilling on the floor. "Let me give you a hand." he offered, but she shook her head.

Once they were in the hall, Rudi whispered to Geir, "I'm pulling the car close the hospital. Which means I'll be collecting our packs and putting them on the floorboard. So that way, if we have to shoot some SS and make a quick getaway, we can do it."

"And if anyone asks about me, tell them I'm staying at the hospital because I think I'm catching a cold."

Rudi grinned slightly. "You're lying."

"Of course. But the keychain Hedy gave me with the amber nugget is in my pack. So be sure to collect my things too."

"I'll put your pack on the car's floorboard with ours, while you and Maxim are giving the medicine to Dr. Bach. Because he's the only doctor here, with the German doctors leaving the hospital well in advance of this coming evacuation."

"That seems to be the plan," Geir said, stepping inside the hospital. *And these doctors are probably on their way to Berlin,* he suspected. *But hopefully most of the hospital workers here are in hiding. Since a few have been put on the transport, making the others fearful they'll be too.*

In the hospital's first ward, Maxim was sitting beside the unconscious Dr. Bach. "Did you get the penicillin?"

"Right here." Geir handed him the vial. "Do I need to help you?"

"Just hold his mouth open while I put some drops in it."

Despair threatened to shatter Geir as he glanced at the trembling doctor. "I hope we're not too late."

Maxim frowned. "So do I."

For the next several hours, he and Maxim sat by the doctor, watching, with Ana coming in periodically to see how things were going. But it was hard to tell at this point with the pull of the typhus still appearing to be quite strong.

Night approached, and it wasn't long before Rudi, Volker, and Nicholas burst into the hospital. "SS officers are going in every female block and painting a red slash down the back of each woman's coat."

"What was expected," said Ana, tears in her eyes.

As the night progressed, so did the commotion. Rifle shots were fired repeatedly, and Rudi and Volker rushed out in the heavily falling snow to see what was happening.

Then some more time passed. And when they returned, they described the rows thousands of women were being put in. "A great confusion between the SS and prisoners who are not exactly sure what to do," said Rudi, in a desperate tone. "And they're being put on the march without food or water—with the women who fall, being shot! But, fortunately like we know, our blessed Daniel did make arrangements for a good many of those being evacuated to receive food and water, while on this terrible march."

"Yes. Our blessed Daniel," Geir murmured— "but look, Dr. Bach's trying to hold his head up." "Praise the Lord," replied the voices of Ana and Rudi.

More time passed, and when morning came the hospital appeared to shake from cannon fire and explosions. "The Russians have come!" Ana shouted, overjoyed.

"Unlikely," Volker contradicted her. "It's too soon. "Still, he and Rudi went outside.

Time continued to pass. But when they returned, they reported things were

chaotic between the fearful SS and the frightened male prisoners they were putting on the move.

The gates were wide open as thousands of prisoners walked through them, toward a train with a blast of white exhaust, which was waiting outside. And the guards, with their dogs, were ordering the prisoners to hurry and get on it.

A good many of the frightened prisoners headed back to their blocks; while others stared helplessly as every inch of room on the train was quickly taken up.

And then as it pulled away, the SS opened fire on those who weren't on the train...with the snow falling so heavily it would soon cover their bodies.

"Damn!" Geir shouted. "We're sure not able to help the people like we wanted."

"God!" said Rudi, staring out the window. "In the middle if all this outside upheaval, *Hauptman* Bischoff's heading toward this hospital."

"What do you suppose he wants?" asked Nicholas.

"I don't know, but I thought he'd be gone by now," said Volker.

"Let's hide in that vacant doctor's office over there," Rudi directed, pointing at it. "And we're staying there until we can learn what he wants." He turned to Ana and Maxim. "So you need to join us."

"I'm staying here," said Geir. "Since he probably wants to talk to me about the penicillin I bought from him."

"It's all right," said Volker. "Rudi, Nicholas, and I have got you covered—should he try to pull something."

They watched as Bischoff flung back the door and burst into the ward.

"He's angry," Geir mumbled, standing up.

"I came to see if Dr. Bach's still alive," Bischoff ground out, his hand on his holstered pistol. "Which apparently he is. And he's even trying to hold his head up." His eyes blazed with the fury flaring inside him. "Appears the penicillin worked."

"What makes you think I gave him the penicillin?" asked Geir with a sudden tenseness.

Bischoff pinned him with his gaze. "That large sum of money you gave me. Penicillin is costly and hard to come by these days. However, I could have bought at least three vials with that amount of money you gave me. And then, I got to thinking how Dr. Bach and Dr. Novak were once in practice together. And that Dr. Novak was a relative of Daniel Birnbaum, your father-in-law. So it made sense you were using the money he gave you to get the medicine for Dr. Bach—a Jew of all people. Who doesn't deserve to live."

"But didn't you care for Dr. Bach's niece?" Geir asked, gazing at him quizzically.

"Merely a respite from the war," Bischoff scoffed. And removing his holstered pistol, he fired two shots at Bach. However, Geir— throwing himself in front of the doctor on a sudden, lightning-fast impulse— caught both bullets.

━━━━◆━━━━

A startled Volker yelled, "Geir!" as Rudi and Nicholas gripping their pistols fired two rounds into Bischoff's back.

His body jerked around and then dropping to the floor, rolled like someone in an unfamiliar place.

"He's dead!" Nicholas gasped.

"My God!" Ana screamed, rushing over to Geir with Maxim.

"W...we didn't expect Bischoff to do that!" exclaimed Volker, gasping in dismay at Geir, who also lay unmoving.

Blood covered his chest. "I...is Geir alive?" Rudi asked brokenly, shooting Ana a glance.

"I'll find out," Maxim said, reaching for his pulse.

CHAPTER-THIRTY-ONE

Geir's vision dimmed. *I'm looking down from above in this hospital ward. And I can see myself clearly. But am I dead or alive? I can't leave now with so much still to be done.*

But he couldn't draw a breath. Violent shudders shot through his body, rattling his bones, making him wish he could say, *'It's cold here, so very cold.'*

"He's dead!" Maxim declared. "He's no breath and no pulse."

"No breath—no pulse," Ana repeated, sobbing. 'Which means he's gone to be with God."

Dr. Bach tried to lift his head as her words, like tears, seemed to fall on him. Though he was still not strong enough to sit up.

Then to everyone's surprise, two SS soldiers with pistols suddenly burst into the ward. "*Hauptman* Bischoff's sent us here to kill the weak," barked one of them. But he stopped when he saw Bischoff's body in the middle of the ward's floor.

Immediately, an exchange of rapid gunfire tore through the air as Volker, Rudi,and Nicholas, now at the other end of the ward, took aim and fired. Though before another round of bullets could follow, the SS let loose with more gunfire.

The whine of their bullets exploded in front of the three resistance fighters, requiring them to return fire. Until the two astonished-looking SS soldiers, taking a step forward, stumbled, before toppling in a heap on the floor.

Fear and desperation ensued. "The gunfire inside this ward is echoing the gunfire outside it!" Ana exclaimed, blinking back tears.

"Your jacket fronts are covered in blood!" Maxim shouted, hurrying over to Rudi, Nicholas, and Volker.

Recovering from their shock of the firefight, they glanced at their jackets in agony.

"We've got to get to the other hospital!" Rudi pressed. "They're the only ones who can help us at this point."

"Ana and I will compress your wounds to try and stop the bleeding, "said Maxim, reaching for bandages and disinfectant. "But get to the hospital as soon as possible, so hopefully you won't risk—"

He stopped like he hated to say it. "Internal bleeding."

"I've driven those thirty-two kilometers on the ice with an incredible speed, "said Rudi in an anguished voice, as Ana cleaned his wound. "But before we go, dress Bischoff and those soldiers in the prisoner's striped pajamas and put their bodies outside—" He struggled for breath. "The snow will quickly cover them—"

"But their uniforms," Maxim broke in as he bandaged Nicholas "What about them?"

"Put them in the wall cavity behind the stove," he added before Rudi could. "Then take their weapons and bullets. And should the few SS men being left here, show up to kill the weak and sickly, then don't hesitate to shoot them."

"And Geir—what about him?'" asked Volker, his breathing ragged as Ana tightened his bandages.

"We'll dress him like one of the prisoners," answered Maxim. "However, we'll leave him in his bed for time being." He reached for some more tape. "The stench of sweat and blood is strong in here. Because I suspect, many dead prisoners in the wards weren't able to get the medical attention they needed.

So I imagine that when the Russians come, they'll probably bury everyone in a mass grave."

Tears flooded Volker's eyes. "How very sad."

"It is," Rudi agreed. "But if we want to stay alive, we've got to hurry and get out of here!"

"Then you three take advantage of those wide open gates—and *go*,"Maxim urged, rushing to open the door for them.

⸻ ◆ ⸻

The weather was getting worse by the minute, so Rudi motioned at Volker and Nicholas to follow him to his car in back. "We'll make it," said Nicholas, his breathing labored like Volker's.

The ice was bad, and the car zigzagged before shooting forward. But Rudi, even with the terrible pain now slicing through his lungs, and his breathing growing shallower, pressed down on the accelerator.

"No matter what, I'll get you there quickly," he assured Volker and Nicholas.

When they finally arrived at the hospital, the workers descended on them with stretchers. They were followed by the three doctors and Daniel, with Yelena in his arms, Charlotte and Hedy burst into tears as Volker cried over and over, "They've killed Geir! And Dr. Bach is dying!"

"I fear Volker, Rudi, and Nicholas are bleeding internally!" exclaimed Dr. Novak.

"Which means we'll have to act fast!" shouted Dr. Rath.

The story of all that has happened to Geir, the dying Dr. Bach, and *Hauptman* Bischoff came from the lips of Rudi and Nicholas... with Volker having suddenly collapsed.

Alexi, who was crying too, had his arms around Hedy and Daniel. "What happened to Geir's body?" a sobbing Hedy asked Rudi.

"Most likely it'll be buried in a mass grave with all prisoners' bodies who weren't able to make the evacuation," Rudi answered, in a strained tone as Dr. Novak prepped him for surgery. "And it'll probably happen when the Russians arrive."

"Buried by the war." Daniel sniffed, trying to console Yelena who was crying loudly.

Hedy swallowed the sobs that rose in her throat. "My baby's crying because we are—"

"Here, let me take her," interrupted the lady from the kitchen, whose relatives owned the amber shop. "And we'll go see if we can find a cookie."

Large beads of sweat broke out across Rudi's forehead. "I...I don't think I'm going to make it, "he said, his voice growing frailer by the minute.

"It's a miracle the three of you got here as quickly as you did," remarked Dr.Novak.

"My God Volker's dead!" Dr. Rath suddenly blurted.

He was preparing him for surgery, the same as Charlotte was preparing Nicholas.

"A...and me," Rudi struggled to say, before closing his eyes.

Immediately a dead silence fell over the hospital's ward.

In the Auschwitz hospital, Geir sees a haze of glory surrounding Dr.Bach. *Is the good doctor dead? Must be. And me? What about me? Am I dead too?*

He now had the distinct feeling that he was in a tree in the snow-covered forest near the Ash Pond.

But he really wasn't in a tree, nor was Gunther when he'd said, 'The closeness of these trees, when their leaves haven't dropped, makes me feel like I'm looking down at the camp from them.'

And then Gunther had gone on to point out there was an escape tunnel not far away that had been dug by one of the prisoners with his bare hands. So if I could find this tunnel, could I escape this death I feel that's on me?

Suddenly, a voice is calling me. And I lift my eyes in surprise...it's my mother. The beautiful Noelle.

And she's standing in front of a circle of angels, singing their angelic songs. "My son, welcome." And her hand reaches out to me, letting me know I've risen heavenward.

I take her hand and say in an urgent voice, "I have to go back, Mother. My work's not finished—" "Shush." Her hand presses against my lips for silence.*"I know. And your mission or destiny, as you call it, will do much to give the world a lift in this terribly dark time...a lift that will enable it to keep going. So that much of what has been lost can be returned."*

Then it's like a screen comes down, and I'm suddenly seeing the death marching prisoners as they move into Upper and Lower Silesia. She points at them *"They have no food nor water—but look."*

And I see the long line of people, reaching out to them with food and water. "Has that happened yet?" I ask her?"

But she shakes her head. *"Time is different here. And I show this to you so you'll know that it was your goodness, that made Daniel love you so much. And made him reach out to these people with the food and water he helped bring to them."*

"Still, I have to go back," I remind her. *"There's something for me to do. It's just that—"*

"You don't know what it is. "She finishes. "But you will. Because when you return, you'll be in a coma for a time. However, you'll be able to hear everything going on. "She plants a kiss on my cheek. *"But once you open your eyes, you'll know your destiny."*

And immediately, like the phoenix from the Greek myth, I feel I'm being returned to life. "But one last question before I re-enter my body... Is Hedy an angel?"

"Could be. The Lord's been known to move in mysterious ways. "

And then— I'm back. In my own body on my bed in the Auschwitz hospital, with my eyes shut tight. Voices surround me but what are they saying? I need to know—when suddenly, everything comes crashing down around me.

✦

The Russians have now taken Warsaw! Evacuation. The chalet-hospital—a mass exodus. All the Polish hospital workers have left. And the German ones are busy loading the three trucks with the chalet's sick and dying patients. "*The Russians are at our door!*" German voices ring out.

Hedy was overcome at times. *Losing my beloved Geir is like I'm exploding with pain.*

And then wiping the tears from her eyes, she'd sink down in a chair and remind herself. *But I've no choice but to keep going. Daniel and Yelena need me. Which gives me the reason to rise in the morning.*

She feared Daniel, in the basement, was the verge of pneumonia. He had a terrible cold and fever. And Yelena, also in the basement, had developed the same thing.

Then there was Nicholas, who also had pneumonia making him too sick to leave his bed in the ward.

"Just let me die here," he told Charlotte, "as long a you're safe in the basement."

In addition to his pneumonia, he was still suffering from his wounds.

Bringing to Hedy's mind the recent note the partisans had sent the hospital:

"*Even if the war is winding down, with many of the wounded developing bronchial infections, we're unable to supply the Russian penicillin, like we've done in the past.*"

"Terrible to be without medicine like that," she'd piped up bitterly. And she'd fretted about not having it until a few hours ago, when word came they were getting it.

Dr.Rath said it was perfect timing and remarked it was what many would call an *amazing coincidence.*

"I just got a note from my cousin, Captain Ulyanov, that penicillin is on the way," said Alexi. "Which means there's no need to risk taking Daniel, Yelena, and Nicholas in the trucks heading to Berlin in this terrible weather. Because I'll soon have the medication they'll need. And once I get this it, then those of us who are left here, will be driven to the Warsaw train station in one of my cousin's military trucks, where we'll board a train to MInsk."

Relief overrode Hedy. "The graveness of our situation is clearly eased. Since if we stay here much longer, I fear this building—chalet-hospital or not— will become a target for the Russian Yaks."

"There's no doubt in my mind," said Alexi, looking at the sky. "Which is why I urged Dr. Novak to evacuate the hospital two days ago."

"I know," admitted Hedy. "However, there were so many problems he simply couldn't do it."

She and Alexi were standing on the chalet's front porch, watching, as Dr.Novak and Dr. Rath climbed into the hospital trucks.

"I hope they make it," Charlotte remarked from the doorway.

"So do I," said Alexi, staring at the German driven trucks as their drivers turned on their headlights, before heading into the icy rain.

Then, all was quite for about ninety seconds until the sudden thundering of the Russian Yaks in the sky, shattered the silence. Blotting her tear-filled eyes with an embroidered handkerchief, Charlotte glanced up at them. "I guess we'll soon be in the hands of the Russians."

Alexi tipped his face toward the Yaks. "Meaning me? You know I've given my word I'd do whatever I could for all of you remaining here."

Hedy opened the folded note Alexi had shown them earlier. "It's quite clear in this note the Polish messenger boy delivered several hours, that our safety will soon depend on Alexi—"

Charlotte gave him a pensive look. "But *you're* leaving this evening."

"Just for *one* night... like the note says." He took hold of her arm in an obvious attempt to quell her anxiety. "And when I return in the morning, I'll have the Russian penicillin Nicholas, Yelena, and Daniel so desperately need."

Once again, Hedy glanced at the note that had come from Captain Ulyanov:

"My commander, General Davitovich, has been severely wounded and needs surgery. And he needs a good doctor like my cousin Alexi. So, since we're in the area, I promised the general I'd enlist Alexi's help for the coming night and return him to the hospital the following morning."

"And I sent a message back," Alexi reiterated, "that said our hospital was being evacuated and had exhausted its supply of penicillin. And we needed it for some for the few remaining patients here. Who were too sick to be evacuated—like my cousin's General Davitovich."

"And Captain Ulyanov, who's in his truck in a forest clearing close by, radioed this General Davitovich," Hedy reminded Charlotte. "And he assured him he had an adequate supply of penicillin for himself and *us* as well."

"Something we weren't expecting to hear," said Alexi, turning to Charlotte and gazing at her with a look of surprise. "Nor the fact that there'll be a German-speaking, Soviet soldier with a submachine gun, who's been assigned to watch after you—who are *our* resistance friends— while I'm gone. So dry your tears and pack your things" He handed her another handkerchief. "And if I'm not back in the morning, it'll be because we've encountered some enemy gunfire. But one way or another—I will return."

A few hours passed before the darkness of the night fell. And soon, the Polish messenger boy appeared with the Russian soldier assigned to guard the hospital. "His name's Mikhail," Alexi said. "And he'll help you with anything you need."

He was a bright -eyed soldier with reddish-blond hair, and he looked to be no older than seventeen.

"Remember Mikhail speaks flawless German." Alexi smiled, before giving Charlotte and Hedy a goodbye kiss on the cheek. "So enjoy his company while I'm gone."

The rain was now coming down in sheets, with each icy drop quite painful... *Like being shot with* a *hypodermic needle.* Hedy shuddered, feeling sorry for Alexi and his people. She waited on the porch until he and the Polish messenger boy were out of sight in the forest. Then, she went back in the hospital to check on Daniel and Yelena... but they were still the same.

The hours passed. However, no one was hungry. "Not good," Charlotte declared, putting together some cheese sandwiches.

Daniel managed to get his down, but Yelena refused the milk and cookies her lady friend from the kitchen had left her.

Cannon fire and gunfire echoed and re-echoed throughout the night. "It's less than ten miles away," remarked Mikhail.

"Which means the Russians are nearly here," said Charlotte.

"No." Mikhail grinned. "Counting me, they're already here."

He was from Moscow and talked about his mother and father, who were both teachers. "Did you know the Germans got within sixty miles of Moscow? Which made me determined to fight for our *Mother Russia*."

"So I heard," said Hedy,

No one slept that night. Nicholas continued to get worse. And Hedy packed two small bags to take to Minsk. One had Geir's notepads he'd given Daniel, and the amber keychain she'd given him, along with several other sentimental things. She asked Daniel what he wanted her to pack, but all he wanted was an extra change of socks, underwear, and clothes. "Along with my amber cuff links and Helmut's Grand Cross."

Of course, he still had the large diamond ring he carried sewn in his wallet's pocket. A safe place, that had prompted him to slide the photo of Yelena's parents beneath it.

Hedy didn't ask Yelena what she wanted, because she knew all the little girl would want, would be her doll, teddy bear, music box, silver spoon, and red shoes. A full bag. But at least, with the exception of her earmuffs on top of the bag, she was already dressed in her winter clothing.

"This fuel shortage here has made us all dress warmly," Hedy told Mikhail.

"No heat anywhere," he said. "But what about your passports?"

"Dr. Rath took them to Berlin," she said, with a shaky sigh of relief." Because he said resistancesupporters or not, they were German passports. And it wouldn't be wise to take them to Minsk."

Mikhail offered to help Charlotte pack, but she refused. "Nicholas is dying," was all she said.

When morning came she was still sitting by his bed, so Hedy fixed some cheese sandwiches and offered one to her, but she shook her head. "Too bad," said Mikhail. He then helped Hedy pack what was left of the cheese, bread, cookies, and several sealed bottles of Yelena's milk.

Alexi had said he'd come in the morning. Although, when noon came and he hadn't returned, Hedy grew anxious. *Geir's death continues to weigh so heavily on me that if Alexi gets killed... and Daniel and Yelena die...then I don't think I can keep going.*

So back and forth she paced.

"Russian Yaks!" shouted Mikhail suddenly. "You can't mistake their sound. So get to the basement! The nightmare 's beginning!"

But Charlotte, still at Nicholas's bedside, refused to leave. So Hedy hurried with Mikhail to the basement as the noise got louder and louder.

"Explosions —getting closer and closer!" he shouted, listening.

Yelena was screaming. And in an attempt to block the sound, Mikhail grabbed the earmuffs on top of the bag and put them on her.

But the sound of explosions got worse as their bomb droppings struck the ground outside with a fury that shook Hedy and the floor.

"This is hell!" Daniel shouted. And began swearing under his breath like someone performing an incantation. When, surprisingly, it got quiet.

"They're regrouping for another attack!" Mikhail said, just as a voice at the basement door yelled, "*Hedy! Hedy! Are you in there—?*"

"Alexi!" she cried.

"You've got to get out of here! This place is a target!"

She flung back the door and within seconds, the sound of steel-shod Russian boots thundered down the steps. Two of the soldiers helped Daniel, while Mikhail holding Yelena, indicated another soldier grab the two bags Hedy had packed earlier.

Alexi had his arms around her as he helped her up the stairs. But when Charlotte refused to follow them, he and Hedy grabbed her arms and pulled her away from the dead Nicholas's bedside.

They aimed her toward the walkway with its covered bridge. "The Russians think the Wehrmacht's in here! "Alexi yelled. "So run, Charlotte— the Yaks are back!"

"Doesn't matter! Nicholas is dead and I'm going too—" she hollared, abruptly swerving away from Alexi's grip.

"This place will soon be nothing but a heap of remains! "Hedy cried, trembling as their explosions struck the earth around it.

Thankfully, Mikhail, holding the crying Yelena, was near the edge of the forest. *Same as the two soldiers carrying Daniel—* "But my God! Charlotte's turning back! "Hedy yelled, filled with panic at her friend's exposure.

The Yaks were shooting rockets into the hospital. And it was now on fire— "But exposure or not, I have to stop her!" Hedy shouted. And she took a step toward her, with Alexi only a few footsteps away, yelling, "No, Hedy— another attack!"

The Yaks made a swoop at the hospital again, filling her with more fear as flames from its rockets swallowed Charlotte.

"God in heaven help us!" Hedy pleaded.

When, suddenly, it was like the blood in her legs froze, and she couldn't move. *'Glued to the spot.*

Exposed.' She was about to cry, when something like a pistol butt struck the back of her head.

"W...what's happening?" she asked brokenly. The pain slicing through her was so terrible it made her wonder if her bones, like the hospital, were in the process of becoming ash. Especially when her legs gave way. But instead of crashing to the ground, Alexi caught her. And she collapsed in his arms. "D...did I hit?"

A large rock on the ground flew up and struck the back of you head."

"Better than shrapnel."

"I think so."

"And the Yaks?"

"Their engines sound like they're fading into the distance—but even so, we need to hurry and get out of here."

'But I can't walk.' She was about to say, when darkness seized her, and she passed out.

⸻ ◆ ⸻

Later, when she opened her eyes a ray of moonlight flooded the window she was propped against. And steel-shod boots, shuffling up and down an aisle, made it feel like the floor was rocking. *Am I on a train...? Yes. And soldiers are here.*

But other people were also here, with each seat taken. Which explains the musty stench in these surroundings. And Daniel, sitting beside me, is holding Yelena, but the two are sound sleep.

"I don't remember anything about getting on the train," Hedy told Alexi, who was mopping her brow with a damp cloth.

"That's because I gave you and Daniel medicine to ease you. And even a tiny bit to Yelena, who was quite upset over the bombings.

"How'd we get to the train?"

"We changed trains at the Polish-Russian border, with the Russian soldiers putting us up in a hotel next to the train station, where we spent the night. And the next day the hotel staff helped get us to this train, that will get us to Minsk later tonight."

"I'm not hungry, but did any of you get anything to eat, Alexi?"

"I had some of your cheese and bread, and Yelena a little of her milk. Though, Daniel didn't want anything. Which makes me suspect he'll be hungry later tonight..." Alexi suddenly brightened. "But important thing is we've made it, Hedy. And our train is headed to Minsk."

"I presume they got the penicillin," she said, aware the pounding in her head wasn't nearly as bad as it had been earlier.

"They did. And luckily, since Daniel and Yelena hadn't developed pneumonia from their infections, the penicillin is working much faster."

"You got to them in time, Alexi," Hedy praised him— "even if Charlotte killed herself when pneumonia took Nicholas from her."

"Unfortunately."

"She was the closest I had to a sister."

Alexi's green eyes darkened with pain at the loss. "I know. And you risked yourself trying to save her which is the reason you got hit in the head with a rock."

"At least you kept me from being caught in that explosion."

"Indeed I did. And hopefully after the morphine I also got from General Davitovich, your pain is not as bad as it was."

"It's not. But what about your cousin and Mikhail?"

"They're heading east toward Berlin—" Then he stopped and turned away, like he had some bad news. "The three hospital trucks with Dr. Novak and Dr. Rath, and all their patients, were said to be bombed to ash—"

"My God!" Hedy cried. "Was it the Russians?"

"Since the trucks didn't have a Red Cross on them, they claimed they thought they were military."

Tears blinded her. "Are we going to lose everyone we love?" she sobbed, fearful something could still happen to Daniel and Yelena.

Alexi's arms encircled her. "Not as long as I'm around. Since I'm here to do whatever it takes to keep the four of us alive."

"Which means we'll probably end up living in Russia," Hedy remarked, not particularly happy about it.

"Could be. Because if I don't get you and Daniel Russian passports, you could possibly end up becoming prisoners." He paused before adding, "Which doesn't give us much choice with the Russians heading to Berlin."

Living with the Soviets. So *little freedom.* And though feeling better, the thought made her nervous.

"P...please, Hedy, try not to worry," Alexi said brokenly, his eyes suddenly misty.

"I'll do my best," she promised. "Because no matter the consequences, I can't lose you."

So, taking his hand, she kissed it and placed it against her cheek.

PART 3

REVELATIONS

CHAPTER THIRTY-TWO

"When you return you'll be in a coma for a time. But you'll be able to hear everything going on." My mother's words— Geir remembered.

"A miracle!" Ana was exclaiming to a man who had introduced himself as a lieutenant in the retreating Wehrmacht. And he'd come with his men to the Auschwitz *Kanada* warehouse to see what they could find.

"We thought Geir was dead—no breath, no pulse, then— he was back," Ana explained to the lieutenant.

"I gather this man in the coma is in the SS," remarked the lieutenant. "Since you've got a uniform folded and stacked on a bench next to his bed." Standing with his feet apart this lieutenant looked concerned.

"What happened?" Did the Russians shoot him? Does anyone know?"

"All we know is that he got shot during the evacuation," Maxim answered. "And someone brought him to us in a wheelbarrow."

"Good thing they did. Still, has anyone in the SS been around to check on him?"

This time Ana spoke. "Only two men. Because since the evacuation, they've been short-handed.

An example being we no longer have sentries, only patrols."

The lieutenant coughed several times. "The SS blew up that warehouse in Birkenau, didn't they?

"They did. "

"Getting rid of stuff. Which I presume since the Russians are so close, those in the SS that are still here will soon be leaving for Warsaw."

"Appears to be their plan."

"With the Russians now in Warsaw, they'd better be disguised, because—" He hesitated. "I suspect some of the merchants and shopkeepers they've done business with, will identify them."

"Probably will... but what brings you to this hospital?"

"I sliced my hand on something that felt like a knife in the warehouse. And my first aid kit hasn't seemed to do much good. So, I think a doctor should look at it."

"I'm right here," said Dr. Bach. "Show me, and I'll put something on it before I re-bandage it."

"It's good you're here. Because at that other hospital, thirty-two kilometers away, I heardn an English speaking person say it got bombed to rubble by the Russians. As did the three trucks, evacuating from it, with its personnel and patients."

"What!" Ana's voice shot up. "Our communications have been down for quite sometime, so we didn't know."

Sobs from Dr. Bach immediately followed with Geir listening: *Hedy was dead—like being swept into that horrible vortex I'd once dreamed about. Daniel was also dead. And Yelena, poor Yelena, they'd failed to save her. Darkness on my heart now— and forever.*

More names followed: Dr.Rath, Dr.Novak, Dr. Zeroff. Charlotte and Nicholas. All dead, along with Volker and Rudi. Each a name of someone so very dear to me... yet I'm still here. Why? Oh yes— I have a destiny to fulfill. And I should be crying, but I can't open my eyes. 'When the time is right, you'll open your eyes and learn your destiny,' my mother said. But how long before that time comes? Soon— I suspect. So I'll need to keep listening in order to know what to do.

Did you get the figure of how many prisoners were left here, Doctor?" Maxim asked him after the lieutenant left.

"My resistance-block companions —who managed to hide— estimated there are nine thousand."

"Without food, water, and fuel," remarked Maxim, straightening Geir's bed cover. "And I know snow can be water, but food and fuel?"

"Geir had two fat sausages in his greatcoat's pockets," Ana reminded. "Which isn't much, but with the little food we have, it's better than nothing. Besides, some of our hospital workers in the back wards have been known to make a little food go a long way for their patients."

"Even so," said Bach," my block companions have heard rumors that before the SS departs, they were to kill the sickly here—along with most of the other prisoners.

"Yes, indeed", Maxim retorted hotly. "Since those damned Germans are crazy enough to waste their ammunition."

"There're other ways," said Bach. "My block companions are also telling me that it's being rumored the SS is supposed to blow up the

Auschwitz *Kanada* warehouse —like they did the one at Birkenau. Plus— Crematorium 5."

"To hide evidence from the Russians before they arrive," Ana added. "And the crematorium will probably go before the warehouse."

"They may not be able to squeeze all nine thousand prisoners in those places," Dr. Bach pointed out. "But they can squeeze a surprising amount in them."

"Which won't hide evidence," Maxim reminded.

"No," said Ana. "But later in Germany, the SS can claim those people were hiding from the Russians. And when the soldiers entered the camp, they believed the people to be the enemy. So, they blew up the buildings, killing them, in order to save ammunition."

"Exactly," Maxim agreed. "Since very few Russian soldiers know about Auschwitz, the way Stalin does."

A fair amount of time passed. *A day. Maybe two?* Listening one afternoon, Geir heard a man say that he was a Wehrmacht *hauptman*, who'd been wounded in the shoulder several weeks ago and had run out of morphine. "Does this hospital have any?"

And although he and his soldiers were retreating, they'd heard about the *Kanada* warehouse and wanted to see what valuable items they could find in it. "So why not let them? Since the hospital here probably has some morphine. "

Which it didn't.

Another group of retreating soldiers stopping by to loot the place. Geir reflected, resentful of the situation. Only this man's voice sounded familiar. Who was he...? Then it hit him. Klaus Warda, his non-commissioned field usher from the convoy and very dear friend.

"Klaus," he mumbled, opening his eyes. "You've left the convoy."

"Look!" Maxim bellowed in an excited voice. "Geir's coming out of his coma!"

Dr. Bach rushed over to him and took his hand. "We're so happy you made it!"

Geir's back was to the man he believed to be his old friend. And by not turning, he wasn't seeing his face. *Even if I am out of the coma, I feel a bit dazed.*

"I'm not Klaus *Warda*," said this Wehrmacht *hauptman*. "I'm Pieter Brucker. And I've never been on a convoy. But who are you and what happened to you? From the uniform next to your bed it's obvious you're in the SS."

"I got shot."

"By who?"

"A Russian."

"Here?" Brucker questioned, like he was genuinely astounded.

"Y...yes." Geir spoke in a broken whisper. "It was during the evacuation and there was a lot of confusion. And I can't remember why, but a good many of the prisoners had left when something made me head to the block near the forest." He stopped, giving it some more thought. "And that's when I saw it—"

"Saw what?"

"Russian soldiers handing submachine guns to the prisoners through the fence...and these prisoners had managed to hide and not go on the evacuation."

"Did you tell anyone?" asked Brucker, the awe in his voice making Geir feel like he'd done something wrong.

"I was wounded and in a coma," he said, turning and looking at the man. "But now that I'm out of it, I do need to tell someone."

A shadow crossed Brucker's face. "Is *Kommandant* Baer still in charge?"

"Probably not, since I suspect he's fled."

"More than likely. But since you're obviously not able to get up, I'll go find someone."

"I'd appreciate it."

The *hauptman* left quickly. Prompting Bach, Ana, and Maxim to crowd around Geir. "What are you going to tell this SS official?" Bach asked him.

Geir's first thought was to say, 'not sure,' but once he opened his mouth, he knew exactly what to say. "When I was in the coma I heard everything. I'm alive but my loved ones aren't. So my mission is clear. I have to save the nine thousand people still here."

Maxim shook his head like he was at a loss. "And just how are you planning on doing that?"

"I intend to stop them from cramming the majority of those people in the *Kanada* warehouse and Crematorium 5, before they blow up those places."

"Stop them?" questioned Bach, the plan clearly bringing him up short. "Impossible."

"But I saw the Russians handing some of those people submachines through the fence," Geir quickly reminded. "Which is the reason I got shot."

"Only in your dreams," said Ana, laying her hand on his forehead to see if he had fever." *Hauptman* Bischoff shot you."

Geir grinned faintly. "I know all that. But the SS here doesn't. And if they're stupid enough to round-up most of the prisoners, then they're going to find out they're not enough SS men left to take them on."

"That's true," said Bach, appearing to mull it over.

"Especially when I tell them there's a detachment of Russians in the forest," Geir added shrewdly.

"That is apparently part of a larger detachment close by—"

"—who are standing-by to invade this place," Maxim completed for him. "And if the prisoners open fire, these soldiers are liable to step in. So the SS needs to get out of the camp before these Russians show up."

"Why that's an excellent story." Ana brightened, starting to get excited.

"When I was going through my near-death experience, I was with my mother," Geir explained. "And she said when I opened my eyes, I'd know what to do in order to fulfill my mission here."

"Sounds like you've hit the nail on the head with your story, " said Bach. "Which makes me feel like the freezing weather outside has suddenly been replaced with sunshine. So let's hope one of the SS officials still here is headed our way to hear it."

Which one was.

"Lieutenant Weir, with me, wants to talk to you, *Herr* Gallen," said Brucker bursting into the first ward.

"I apologize that *Hauptman* Stocker, who's overseeing things, couldn't be here," remarked the lieutenant. "So if you'd be kind enough to repeat the story you told Major Brucker, I'd very much appreciate it."

Geir didn't hesitate. "You've got to leave at once—the Russians are *here*!"

"And you? What about you?" asked Weir.

"I'm to sick to leave. But since I'm thin like some of the prisoners, I'm wearing some striped pajamas."

Weir turned to Bach. "What's to stop you medical people here from turning him in?"

"Nothing. But he's given us some food bribes, and since we're people of our word, I've assured him we wouldn't."

Weir scowled at the doctor before glancing at Geir. "You're taking a risk—"

"Probably... but I'm too sick to leave."

"Too bad. Because your death will most likely occur when the Russians hang you."

"What's to stop you SS people here from leaving now?" Brucker questioned him.

"Evidence —" Weir paused to release a tremulous sigh. "That we've stayed behind to destroy."

"Like people?"

He nodded. "In the *Kanada* warehouse and Crematorium 5—"

"Then I'd suggest," Geir anted in, "that you focus on the one with the most evidence." He jabbed an index finger in the direction of the crematorium. "Then blow it up and get out of here. And since many prisoners now have submachine guns, it's out of the question to round them up and kill them."

"Crematorium 5 is at the top of the list," said Weir, also pointing a finger in its direction.

"The prisoners can talk, but without proof—" He paused briefly before changing subjects. "Still, *Herr* Gallen, aren't there camp files with information about the prisoners stored in the *Kanada* warehouse here?"

"Just a few," he lied. "With most having been blown up at Birkenau."

Weir stared at the floor. "Then it makes sense to blow up Crematorium 5 and get out of here."

"Which is what you need to impress on *Hauptman* Stocker before it's too late—"

"Don't worry, I'm headed to his office now."

The ward door swung open, and Geir was on the verge of sitting bolt upright, when he looked up and saw a Wehrmacht corporal holding a dummy. *A red-headed dummy. Exactly like Helmut said Gunther had described.*

"Can you believe what I found in the warehouse!" exclaimed the corporal. "This fellow talks—like maybe he has a battery-powered record player inside him. And he's telling me that he can do all the talking and make people think I'm a ventriloquist, which will make me money—"

"No! Stop—" said Geir, holding up a hand to deflect conversation. "That dummy has a gypsy curse on it. And if you don't leave it be, you'll end up getting killed."

The corporal laughed. "Now who in hell told you that?"

"One of our officers," said Geir, the corporal's lack of belief making him uncomfortable. "Who left with it and got blown up—along with some of his men."

"That's crazy." The corporal laughed again. "This dummy can't get blown up and be here. Which obviously means it's a different one—"

"Taking the dummy is a temptation hard to resist," Brucker interceded. "So if the corporal wants to do it, I don't see a problem."

"Your chance. So be smart and take my advice," Geir advised, eyeing both men sharply. "Or you'll end up regretting it."

But they made no response as they turned to leave.

After they left Bach asked Geir, "Since you're supposed to be able to able to hear everything around you, I know you heard our weeping—"

His breath caught painfully before completing the sentence. "Yes. A... about the great tragedies that befell our loved ones at Dr. Novak's hospital. Which is the reason I'm not worried about what the Russians might do to me."

Tears formed in the doctor's eyes. "Oh, Geir, you shouldn't feel like that. Even if you lost Hedy, Daniel, and the other friends and family you so dearly loved—" He stopped talking long enough to wipe he tears from his eyes. "And I lost Yelena after all we did to save her—"

"I'm sure when the explosion happened she was in Hedy's arms—the arms of an angel."

Their tears continued until Maxim reminded them about the lack of food that had been in the camp since the evacuations. When was the last evacuation, January twenty-first? "

"If my memory's correct," Ana answered. "And today is January twenty-fifth. Which is a long time to be without food."

"True," Maxim agreed. "So let's just hope the SS official here believes Geir's story, and he and the other SS men leave."

"Then the prisoners can start rummaging through the camp to see what they can find," Geir remarked.

"Tomorrow, January twenty-six, would certainly be a good day for the SS to vacate this place," said Bach. "Especially with the Russians at our door."

Maxim pointed a finger at the open window. "And if you listen to the echoes of their shots, you can tell they're getting closer with each passing hour."

And he was right. Because the very next day, January twenty-sixth, after blowing up Crematorium 5, all those in the SS departed.

"With me being the exception," Geir said.

Bach was elated. "They believed you, Geir. And didn't put any prisoners in Crematorium 5 when they blew it up."

"I'd like to think I had something to do with it."

"You did," said Ana, giving him a hug.

"I suspect history will say it was *happenstance* that nine thousand prisoners were left alive here." Bach said. "Which, sadly, from the looks of things, possibly twenty-five hundred dying later, from starvation, exposure, and disease. But all things considered *you*, Geir Gallen, were the one who saved the majority. With your made-up story of being shot by a Russian."

"When I saw the movie Helmut made of this camp, it caused Hedy and me great pain," he said, tears welling in his eyes. "So now **I** know that saving those people was my *destiny*. Because like my

mother said during my near-death experience, '*Once you open your eyes, you'll know what to do.*'

But still, what I don't know is why everyone I loved had to die?"

"Simply because," said Bach, "in the beginning in the garden, we know the world was poisoned by a serpent. And thus, began the conflict of God vs Satan. Which unfortunately is happening in the souls of each man and woman on this planet."

"S...something I've heard many times," Geir replied in an unteady voice.

"As I'm certain you have."

"Then why mention it?"

"Because you share the pain of the prisoners here who lost their loved ones too."

Bach hesitated before continuing, "Auschwitz is hell! And it's my belief that this journey you make out of hell with these prisoners, will be unique." He gave him an encouraging look as he placed a hand on his forearm. "My reason being that since you're the only *living* SS man who was in the Resistance, things will be different for you—"

"That they will," he cut him short. "Because my sorrow will end when I 'm hung by the Russians." "Not likely," Bach said, inhaling deeply before adding, "With the prisoners here loving you, like me, whom you saved. And hearing from me how you saved them at the cost of losing your loved ones, they'll flock to comfort you. So, please— try and focus on life for *yourself* rather than death." He gripped Geir's arm. "Knowing that such a focus will inspire many of these former prisoners to go back *to* their *Land* again."

"But how can I?" he asked, giving his head fierce shake. "When I feel so dead inside."

"By coming to realize that God has never completely destroyed all the Jews. And that all this death and destruction here, will shine a fresh light on life. A light which— I feel certain— will help to fertilize the seeds for the Jews to go and build a new Israel. "A brief pause fell between them. "Which is one of the great miracles of Jews that they can begin again after a tragedy or disaster. And those seeds you, Geir Gallen, have sowed for *life,* will reach out and touch a good many of those who've suffered so badly. Giving their existence a rebirth. As the magic of their centuries' old dream of the new Israel, blossoms into being."

"S...so that much of what is lost can be returned." Geir voice fractured as her recalled his mother's words.

"Which to me is God's way of intervening in these very turbulent and confusing times," said Bach.

"And like you've told me many times, Geir, your wife's happiness depended on doing for other people." "Her legacy to me," he remarked. "A wistful ache, but one necessary to her memory...meaning that I must now follow suit."

The rest of the afternoon progressed with a few wary prisoners beginning to search for food. "They find it hard to believe the Germans are really gone," said Ana, staring out the window at them.

"They will tomorrow." Maxim beamed. "Since some of us here will be on a hunt for food for the hospital."

"As close as they are, the Russians should be here tomorrow." Bach was quick to point out.

Geir lifted his head. "I'm not sure, but an officer in the Birkenau barracks joked about hiding some tins of food under some boards there. Of course this officer was always amusing us with his wild tales, so it may be nothing. Although I should go with Maxim and have a look."

"But you're not fully recovered," Bach reminded.

"If I can get out of these striped, prisoner pajamas and into some warm clothing, I can ride in the sidecar of one of the motorbikes, I feel certain the SS left behind,"

"Which I'll be driving," Maxim volunteered. "However, not wanting to take chances, we'll do it in the afternoon. Because that way, if the Russians arrive in the morning, you won't have to get out in this icy weather."

But when the morning of January twenty-seventh came, and there was no sign of the Russians, Maxim waited until afternoon before he brought one of the motorbikes around, from the place Geir had told him they were stored.

The weather seemed to be getting increasingly severe by the hour. And the temperature, although not as bad as Russia, made Geir shiver as if it were. Fortunately, most of the prisoners who were scavenging for food had taken the advice from Bach's remaining *block* companions and were wearing warm clothing, from the Kanada warehouse's abandoned belongings. But the shivering ones who hadn't secured any, apparently feared the Germans might reappear, from the way they kept looking from left to right.

When Maxim reached the officers' barracks at Birkenau on the motorbike, Geir went inside with him. "The officer said it was behind a board in the north corner," he informed him.

Which immediately prompted Maxim to take the chisel he had and remove the board. "Nothing." He sighed. "So this officer must have been joking."

"Must have been." Geir agreed, when a sudden commotion outside grabbed his attention.

"Ghosts!" came shouts. "Our dead have returned!"

"Something's happening out there," said Maxim. "So we'd best hurry and see what it is."

The former prisoners were standing at an open gate, connected to the barbed wire, where three men in long, white coats stood in the snow.

"Where did you people come from?" asked one of the men, frowning. He spoke in a language apparently unfamiliar to the prisoners standing close by."

"Not ghosts but Russian scouts!" Maxim exclaimed, a gleam of wonder in his eyes. "They've come at last!"

Maxim pulled the motorbike closer to them, and speaking in Russian informed the scouts who these people were.

Many of these former prisoners hugged the Russians and cried; while others got on their knees and kissed their boots and coat hems.

These soldier scouts didn't quite know how to act until Maxim explained this was a concentration camp with starving, sick prisoners. And immediately these scouts, the expressions in their faces looking like they'd stumbled onto something terrible, promised to return with troops and food.

Which wasting no time, they did.

However as they began to disperse the food, they were even more horrified by what they saw.

Prisoners too starved to eat the food they offered. Barracks encrusted with excrement. And piles of ash that had once been human bodies.

There were hungry children who had been part of Dr. Mengele's medical experiments. And when they spotted the soldiers they went over and exchanged hugs with them. "Cookies and chocolate," said Maxim, helping his fellow Russians pass them out.

Hospitals were needed on site, so the townspeople and Red Cross workers were called in to help.

"Nothing on this planet will ever be the same after Auschwitz," Geir remarked to Bach and Maxim.

Who were quick to add it was the first major Nazi camp that had come to light. And journalists were visiting it so they could tell the world about it.

Along with the healthier prisoners and Red Cross, these hospital people worked day and night to help the living and save the dying. There was a food shortage and limited supplies of medicine, but it didn't stop them. Geir offered to help, but Dr. Bach insisted his two wounds were still in the process of healing, so he wasn't strong enough to work. "You'll get your change later," he assured him.

The *Kanada* warehouse flabbergasted the Russians. Among many things there was such a large amount of women's dresses and coats, hanging beside racks with men's suits and coats, that the number was almost too high to count. But what really mortified the Russians were the seventy pounds of eyeglasses, the piles of prosthetic limbs, the pots and pans numbering ten thousand, and the fifty thousand pairs of shoes.

"Of the great number of people sent to Auschwitz over the years, only fifteen per cent if them were believed to have survived," a journalist wrote.

It wasn't long after this newspaper article appeared in a Polish paper that the Russian commander, with most of his troops still at Auschwitz, approached Geir in the hospital. "The people here are telling me you saved them. Which considering your wounds, your thin body, and prisoner clothing I find it odd—"

"Because he's one of us?" Bach interrupted

"No offense, but I'm not one of them," Geir quickly let it be known.

"Now, Geir, watch what you say," Bach cautioned.

"The commander needs to hear the truth. So, considering I now have no family, what the Russians decide to do to me doesn't matter

"He's had a difficult time," Bach broke in. "And took the two shots meant for me. Which explains his wounds. And reminds me of the old Jewish saying.' He who saves one life, is like he's saved the world.' He put his hand on Geir's shoulder in a possessive gesture.

"I took the shots because I was in the SS Resistance," Geir quickly said. "And there were four of us resistance fighters, who came here in late November to help the prisoners any way we could."

"I'm sure you've heard about the resistance in this camp," Bach reminded the commander. "Since some of your officers have seen our hidden BBC radio. Where we were able to listen for a few minutes before shutting it down."

The Russian commander frowned at Geir. "Were you in the Wehrmacht?"

"Yes." His eyes clung to the commander. "My friend and I were conscripted. And we hated what Hitler stood for. So while on a convoy troop, we had a Russian shoot us. Because, that way, we'd be crippled and not have to fight for something we didn't believe in."

"Well now," said the commander, shaking his head. "I never expected to hear that from a German."

Geir then went on to explain about *Hauptman* Bischoff shooting him. "But I lied to the SS and said I got shot because I saw the Russians handing the prisoners near the forest, submachine guns."

"And he sent word to those in the SS still here, to avoid the prisoners and get out," Bach added.

A slow smile spread across the commander's face. "Which apparently they did. With many of the prisoners telling my men that they feel like *you*, *Herr* Gallen, had something to do with the SS not blowing them up in the warehouse."

"Possibly...but since I can't be certain, I'm unwilling to take the credit."

"Doesn't matter you've earned their respect for your attempt. And, Bach, standing here, tells me you stashed the records of many of the SS war crimes in chests and trunks in the *Kanada* warehouse." Geir looked at the commander with a forced calm. "I did. So what's going to happen to me now?" "Nothing. After I write my report about your being an SS Resistance fighter. And since Dr.

Bach, Maxim, and you have all lost your loved ones, they think the three of you should stay together. So I'm discharging Maxim from the military and giving him permission to go wherever you go."

"That's a relief to hear."

"Think nothing of it since you've earned it."

When the commander left someone was playing a violin **in** the background.

Bach told Geir, 'One of the musicians you helped to save. And they'll all be staying here at Auschwitz with the Russians for awhile in order to care for the sick."

"What about Warsaw?"

"They'll probably go there later. Ana's family is there, and she says they, like us, can stay with them while we help in the Warsaw hospital. However after the war, when the Americans are in Berlin, then we'll return with you to your home."

"There are papers hidden behind some bricks in the cellar which will allow me to claim my father's money. So, that way we can live comfortably." He paused, hesitate to add, "Provided we can come by some money that'll get us to Berlin."

"Which we already have."

"What!" Geir exclaimed, shock hitting him like one of *Hauptman* Bischoff's bullets. "How?"

"Those SS men your friends killed had some bags of gems stashed in their pockets. Plus, you had some money in your pockets, even after you'd given Bischoff the American dollars and South African pounds. Which, believe it or not, he had on him."

"Money that certainly should get us to Berlin... but what about the gems?"

"We divided them among, you, Maxim, Ana, and myself. So we'd all have something."

"Then we should be good to go when the time is right." *But will the time every be right without my Hedy?* Geir seriously questioned. "I doubt it," he mumbled.

CHAPTER THIRTY-THREE

When the train Hedy, Alexi, and Daniel were on arrived in Minsk, they got off. Thanks to the penicillin Daniel and Yelena were doing much better. "We're spending the night here in a hotel," Alexi informed them, holding the little girl. "Since we're got quite a way to go before we get to out destination."

For a moment Hedy was paralyzed by his statement. "You mean we won't be living in Minsk?"

"No. We'll be living in Kiev in the Ukraine," he said as calmly as possible." The Ukrainian Soviet Socialist Republic, which is considered to be one of Russia's most prosperous areas."

"Kiev?" She was still aghast. In 1922 it had been taken by the Ukrainian Bolsheviks and was much deeper in the Soviet Union than she cared to think about. "And little Hansi will be there?" she finally managed to ask.

"She's been in living on an out-of-the way collective farm run by people, my cousin Natasha knew. And I might not have allowed it had Pauline not told me in a dream, 'Hansi will be safe there, even if it is in a war-torn part of the world.'"

"Which she was."

"Because the people little Hansi was staying with were talented. They not only grew barley and wheat, but the Russians knew the wives of these grain farming people were experts, when it came to canning vegetables such as cabbage, pickled tomatoes, potatoes, squashes, and beetroots. So as an experiment they helped them develop a place on the farm where they could *can* the produce they brought them—"

And then what?" Hedy asked.

They'd come back in a truck and deliver it to the places where the government said these canned goods were needed. But if this wasn't enough, their daughter, Svetlana Ivanov, had learned waffle weaving from a deceased aunt. Something that not only impressed the Russians, but the Germans as well. Which, I suspect, was the reason the farm was spared."

"What I'm thinking," said Hedy, impressed with the way these farming people had managed to save themselves.

"But getting back to your being in Kiev. You must have known the city well to know these farming people outside the city."

"I began my medical career in Kiev. Where at that time Natasha and Joseph were living. And they had friends there, many of whom worked in the hospital and promised me I could have a job any time I wanted one."

Hedy sighed. "Yet, you never told me Hansi was so far away."

"I didn't because the distance made it seem I was abandoning her. And besides, if I got killed those farming people would raise her—"

"Which you almost did at the chalet-hospital," Hedy interjected, "With those Russian Yaks overhead."

"True." He gave her arm a reassuring squeeze. "But if I remember correctly, Geir was in Kiev, was he not?"

"Briefly." The memory misting her eyes. "And in a letter he wrote me he didn't seem to find it unpleasant,"

"And you won't find it unpleasant either. Since I, Alexi Zeroff, gave my word that *you*, Daniel, and Yelena will be under my protection." He took her hand. "Because once again, I promised Geir at Christmas that I'd lookout for the three of you, along with little Hansi. And besides, a good many Poles hate the Russians like they do the Germans. And though, the Russians are their liberators, they're also their conquerors. So even if I'm Polish, my father had a Russian last name. Which will be difficult for me to remain in Warsaw. Because the partisans there, will now be fighting the Russians."

"I can certainly understand that," said Hedy, giving him a hug.

Their hotel was across the street from the train station, with a restaurant next to it.

It was a pleasant hotel. And since Alexi knew the people who worked there, they gave him two bedrooms with an adjourning door. "Daniel and I will be spending the night in a double bed. With Yelena between us." He reached for the little girl in Hedy's arms. "Since that way, she won't roll out." "Wise thinking" Hedy said, kissing Yelena's cheek.

They dined at the restaurant, with the owner's wife providing a high-chair for Yelena. The food served family style was the familiar beef stroganoff, cabbage rolls, and salad. Yelena had her milk, and Hedy didn't think the little girl would want much other than the stroganoff noodles but to her surprise, she did.

"*Want,*" she said using the word Daniel had taught her, as she pointed at the beef and cabbage rolls.

So Alexi put small portions on her plate, that made it easier for Hedy to feed her with a spoon.

Daniel enjoyed the food as much as Yelena. And everyone loved the sweet *pierogi* rolls, which was their dessert.

But what really caught Hedy off guard was that Daniel spoke a little Russian. "Where on earth did you learn it?"

"From my European business contacts in my travels," he said, smiling at her as he sipped his wine.

"Which lets me know you have a gift for language—"

"As I suspect you have too," Alexi intervened, touching Hedy's forearm. "Which I daresay, the Russian language records I intend to buy for you will prove my point." He tensed slightly. "Since speaking only German and English won't put you in a very good light with the Soviets these days."

"I don't doubt it for a minute," said Hedy, covering his hand with hers.

It was snowing heavily when they left the restaurant. So they walked slowly, careful not to slip on the ice as they took the few steps to the hotel.

The early morning weather was even worse than the night before. But after dining on some of the pierogi rolls and fruit juice Alexi had bought at the restaurant last night, it gave them the strength to cross the street to the train station.

A long ride with frequent stop. Hedy reflected as they moved deeper and deeper into the Soviet Union.

When they finally arrived at Kiev, Alexi called the hospital from the train station, and they sent a vehicle to pick them up. "Are we staying overnight at the hospital?" she asked.

But Alexi shook his head. "One of the doctors I wrote has found us a place to stay in an Edwardian-looking house like the one in Minsk. Which isn't that far from the hospital, so he's sending someone to drive us there."

Of course the house was communal living. Though two of its nurse residents had found apartments and would soon be moving out.

From the looks of Kiev's remains the war had taken its toll on the city, the way it had on the other cities the Germans had invaded. "I'm told the

Jews have been in the Ukraine for centuries," Alexi informed Daniel and Hedy. "And many were quite wealthy and brought a lot of culture to cities like Kiev. But sadly, Babi Yar or the *Old Wives' Gully*, is in a ravine nearby where a great many Jews were murdered—"

"With reports later reaching the Polish partisans," Daniel broke in, "that the number was at least thirty-four thousand. However, overall I'm hearing reports that a million and a half Ukrainian Jews were killed by the war."

"Horrible." Hedy cringed, just as their driver from the hospital stopped in front of the house.

"Where we'll be staying," Alexi announced.

Outside, it looked to be similar to both the boardinghouse in Berlin, and Alexi's residence in Minsk.

"With these houses having the same Dormer windows from their sloping roof," Hedy noticed, glancing at them before she went inside the house.

She wasn't expecting much. But, surprisingly, the house had a parquet floor, and it's ceiling murals and decorative rugs weren't faded beyond recognition.

"A pleasant beauty after the war-torn mess of the Ukraine," Daniel said, craning his neck to stare at the murals.

In the back was a small house that had once been servants' quarters where a woman, about twelve years older than Hedy, lived with her husband, who was missing a leg from the war.

The woman was named Galina. And she was such a good cook that the other residents had made an agreement to pay her to do the cooking and housecleaning.

"I was told it takes the burden off them to divide the time," Alexi remarked. "Since each resident is given a schedule when they're allowed to cook for an hour in the kitchen."

"Like the boardinghouse," Daniel remarked, clearly pleased. "Except we always had someone to cook for everyone."

"Such as me." Galina beamed.

"Yes, like you." Daniel grinned.

Galina adored children and immediately took to Yelena. "I married and had my children when I was quite young," she said, watching

Yelena toddle toward a large chair in the common room. "Although my son and daughter are living in Moscow, and we rarely get to see our grandchildren."

"Well, in a week or so my little girl will be joining us," Alexi informed her. "So, you'll have two children to help occupy some of your time." He handed her some money, then handed Daniel some.

"When Hedy and I are working at the hospital, you can help Galina look after the children."

"Not necessary." Daniel shook his head, handing the money back.

"I say differently," said Hedy, giving it back to him. "Your presence is necessary for the children. So Alexi and I insist you keep the money we give you."

"Everyone needs a little money he can call his own," Alexi reminded. "Which is why you must take it."

Mixed feelings appeared to surge through Daniel as he shoved the money in his coat pocket. "Will Alexi and I be sharing a room?" he asked Galina.

She nodded. "Until the other two residents move out."

Alexi leaned over and picked up Yelena. "Then she'll sleep between us until I can either buy her a bed or make one."

But he need not have worried because Galina knew of three baby beds for sale, which he paid her to buy.

Afterwards, she put twin beds in the room Alexi and Daniel shared—as well as the baby beds she purchased the next day. The third one would go to the country, for Yelena when she visited.

Hedy's room adjoined Alexi and Daniel's. So if Yelena cried, she could get to her as quickly as the men.

Alexi was in a hurry to get to the country and see little Hansi. Who like Yelena, would soon be two years old.

Although, a week passed before he got Sunday off at the hospital and was able to borrow one of its cars... It was not a happy day. News had come that Natasha's husband, Joseph, and his men, who'd rescued Hedy and Daniel from the chalet-hospital had all been killed in a German attack. And if this wasn't bad enough another source had reported that the SS, delivering its prisoners to Dr. Novak's freighter had decided to shoot them.

Poor information had put the partisans in the wrong place at the wrong time. And when they'd arrived the prisoners had been shot to death, with their bodies floating in the water.

Fortunately, the SS was taking its time about leaving. 'Lucky for the partisans word had it.

'Who immediately opened fire on them, killing all but a few.'

"Joseph and the prisoners." Hedy sobbed. Tears gushed from her eyes and Daniel's, as Alexi checked the chains on the hospital's car.

"Even with snow and ice everywhere, I think we'll be safe," he assured them, once he was back in the car.

He started up the engine but before taking off, he blotted the tears in Hedy's eyes and tossed

Daniel a fresh handkerchief.

"I gave Galina money to purchase food, wine, and vodka to put inside that large picnic basket, "Alexi remarked. "Because its collective farming, I don't like to impose on the family. So, I think it best to bring food we can share together."

"But do they know we're coming?" Daniel asked him.

"I sent them a letter— like I did the hospital— a month or two ago. And in it I advised them not to be surprised when I showed up. Since the way things were going, I wasn't sure of the date, but I'd definitely be in Kiev soon—so keep a lookout."

This collective farm where little Hansi lived was run by two families: the Turgenevs and the Ivanovs. And each family lived in a large log house with a thatched roof. "Two barns, some sheds, and another building that looks like a storeroom," Daniel remarked, with a broad sweep of his hand.

"Which doesn't appear to be that far from the houses."

Hedy was not impressed with the run-down look of the houses, but she tried not to let it bother her.

'Like I'm having to do most of what I'm seeing behind the Soviet Union's iron curtain.' She wanted to say. **But** deeming it unwise said instead, "Which house does little Hansi live in?"

"The first one." Alexi gestured. "And Egor and Iryna Ivanov are the husband and wife's names. With their oldest child, Svetlana, approaching twenty, or twenty-one. And their son, Yuri, eighteen or close to it."

Hedy's response to Alexi was a smile. "Since your Russian language records are helping me, I'll try and greet them in Russian."

"Good idea," he agreed, just as the car pulled up to the door on what was the yard's snow-covered, gravel path. "Though I would like Yelena and Hansi to learn English and German," he continued. "Since we Russians value people who can speak several languages."

It was around noon and the couple, fair-haired and green eyed like typical Ukrainians, were standing, bundled in coats on their tiny porch, waiting to greet them. "People usually come in trucks out here. But because we're in a car, they must have figured out it's *me*," said Alexi with a grin, as he opened the car doors for Hedy and Daniel.

Standing in the doorway a fair-haired young woman held a toddler's hand. *"Little Hansi.* So pretty with her blue-eyes and brown-hair," Hedy whispered to Alexi.

"Whom I'd love to smother with kisses," he remarked. "But I fear that since she has no idea who I am, I'd frighten her—"

"Dr. Alexi Zeroff," announced Egor, stepping from the porch's two steps into the yard." We're so very happy you made it out here."

Alexi shook hands with him and then introduced Daniel and Hedy.

"Step inside—please," said Ivanov. "It's too cold for a lady with a toddler to be outside."

The fair-haired young woman holding little Hansi was already back inside.

"What's your little one's name?" Egor asked Hedy.

"Yelena." She set her down before gesturing at little Hansi. "Why look, there's a friend."

Both of the children stared at each other as if thunderstruck. "Tell her hello, Hansi," urged the fairhaired woman. But the little girl stood stock-still, continuing to stare, before taking a step toward Yelena.

Finally, the two were face to face. "Hansi looks like she doesn't believe Yelena's real," said the fairhaired woman, who introduced herself as Svetlana.

Iryna handed a small, wooden duck to Hansi. "Show it to Yelena." But she hesitated, as if uncertain what she should do before she finally gave it to her.

"Like." Yelena said, turning it upside down, before handing it back.

Hansi then toddled toward the large, roaring fireplace with Yelena following. "From the looks of it," said Alexi, "those two will probably end up becoming best friends, like I've wanted."

Daniel, holding the picnic basket, set it on the large wooden dining table surrounded by eight chairs. "Alexi brought us plenty to eat so we could have more time to visit."

"That's good," said Iryna, "because I've just made some Borscht."

"The Ukraine's favored dish, Alexi informed Daniel and Hedy."

"But before Iryna serves her Borscht, let's send for the Turgenevs," said Egor."

"In case you didn't hear, they're my family now," said Svetlana.

There was a moment's pause before Alexi spoke, "Natasha mentioned something about it." "Svetlana and their son, Dimitri, married when he got drafted," explained Egor. "And they were quite young. But sadly, he was only in the army six months before a German shot him."

"Like Hansi's father," Alexi murmured. "Only he died stepping on a mine."

Hedy found the Turgenevs, who were also fair-haired and green eyed, to be as delightful as the Ivanovs. And their thirteen-year old son, Dusan, was quite helpful when it came to setting the table with Yuri.

Iryna laughed. "Those two are doing it because they're anxious for my Borscht.

"As I am too," said Daniel.

The soup proved to be as excellent as the pan-fried sliced chicken breasts in a large jar, with a piece of an old quilt around it to keep them warm. There was also sausage, boiled eggs, bread, cheese, and crackers. They were all finger foods, except for the German potato salad Galina had made from Hedy's recipe.

"Alexi is spoiling us with all this tasty food he brought," said Egor, reaching for a piece of chicken. "And for dessert he's even brought some chocolate cookies."

Yelena and Hansi drank juice as they ate their cheese, crackers, and the sliced chicken, which was Yelena's favorite.

And both Hedy and Svetlana watched as they ate their cookies and played. "Though toddlers, they're trying to show us they can run," Svetlana remarked, smiling at them.

But when Yelena fell and started crying, Hansi rushed over and kissed her cheek.

Alexi brightened. "Those two are acting like sisters, Hedy, isn't it wonderful?"

"It is," she agreed, before getting up and going over to help Yelena off the floor.

When everyone finished eating, Iryna took Alexi, Hedy, and Daniel on a tour of the house, and some of the outside buildings close by. "We also have some roaming cattle, chicken in coops, and dairy cows in the barn." Egor was pleased to inform them.

"Seems like you know what you're doing," Daniel praised him.

Hedy was especially impressed with the inside of the house. There were red-checked valances on most of the windows and a drawstring curtain, like them, below the sink.

The vanity in the single bath was attractive with a honey-toned wooden base. But what Hedy really admired were the extraordinary bedspreads in each bedroom.

"All hand woven by my aunt," Svetlana remarked proudly. "And two by me... but look at this." She opened an old tin box and removed a lovely woven belt. "Something my aunt bought that's from the nineteen hundreds. And it was made and worn in the Ukrainian Carpathians, with the person selling it to her not even knowing it was in the box."

"It's clearly a special piece with it symbols," said Hedy, touching them.

"Which highlight Ukrainian fertility and procreation," Iryna told her. "But follow me outside, and you'll see some more of what we do here." She indicated her visitors walk on a recently snow-cleared, board walkway to a storeroom that had been converted into a small canning factory.

Mrs. Turgenov reiterated what Alexi had told them about the farm being a government's experimental program...where a truck brought them produce to can in tins. And when the time was right, the truck would return and take the canned produce to various places to sell."

Daniel was especially intrigued and said that if the opportunity arouse, he'd like to learn how to can so he could help them with it.

"We can use all the help we can get," said Iryna, smiling. "But in the meantime we need to figure out where Hansi is going to live— "

"Hopefully with me," Alexi broke in.

"She will," Iryna remarked, the smile on her face blossoming. "Because, if you can find a place for Svetlana to sleep, she's going back with you."

Alexi's mouth curved upward as he turned to her. "We'll make sure you have a comfortable place."

"Hansi's getting along quite well with Yelena," said Svetlana. "And the two girls don't need to be separated. Any more than Hansi needs to be separated from me."

"But you have weaving work to do here, don't you?" asked Daniel.

"It's slower in the winter. So I'll go back to Kiev with you for a week. And the following week you'll return with me to the farm—"

"Wow! Me on a farm," Daniel interrupted.

"Yes *you* on a farm," Svetlana confirmed. "And we'll do this, until Hansi and Yelena are able to connect the two families and are satisfied with the arrangement."

"That's an excellent idea," said Alexi, nodding his approval. "Why didn't I think of that?"

"It'll all work out like it's supposed to be, "Svetlana assured him. "Which you'll soon come to realize."

Daniel smiled, as if thinking about it. "Especially since I'll be getting to spend time on this lovely farm."

⸻ ◆ ⸻

Sometime later when they were back in Kiev, sleeping arrangements were made for Hedy with Svetlana. "The nurses are moving to their apartment tomorrow," Galina informed her. "So after that there won't be all this room sharing."

The beds for Yelena and Hansi were in Hedy's room. And Alexi kissed Yelena before putting her in hers. "Me too," said Hansi.

"A pleasant surprise for you." Hedy smiled, watching Alexi kiss the little girl on the cheek.

It was getting late, so everyone got ready for bed. But before Hedy could join them, Alexi pulled her aside. "Circumstances being what they are in the Soviet Union, don't take this the wrong way. But I think for sake of ID clarification, you and your step-father, Daniel, should have Russian passports. "Alexi stalled briefly, before shifting the conversation. "Which in order to speed things up, means that you and I should get married in name only."

"Name only?" Hedy questioned, stunned by the offer.

"I know you'll always love Geir," Alexi said. "And that Daniel has left his money to the new Israel when it is born but—"

"The new Israel will need it more that we do," she interjected. "Which means we have to move on.

And since the women in my family go through the change early, I'd like to have baby before it happens to me."

"But you're still so very young." Alexi grinned. "That I doubt you'll go through the change any time soon."

"I won't. However, Daniel is all I have left of Geir. And since your twice my age and have been so kind to us, I'd like to have something left of you." She raised her head to his, before adding, "Should you die before me."

Alexi took her hand. "Which most likely I will—but oh Hedy," he gasped. "You're so beautiful, kind, and loving that nothing would delight me any more than being your husband and knowing I fathered a child of my own."

"Then the matter's settled," she replied as his arms encircled her.

"Y...you've picked up the aching heart I've dropped at your feet." He marveled, a moment before his lips devoured hers with a hungry, eager kiss.

And her cheeks, warmed with a blush, as she felt the hardness of his body pressing against hers. *Like my soul is attempting to reawaken.*

CHAPTER THIRTY-FOUR

Late August 1945

With the war over and the allies, now in charge of Germany and Berlin, Geir deemed it a good time to return from Warsaw to the boardinghouse, with Dr. Bach and Maxim. "The papers that will allow me to claim my father's money, are bricked in the cellar of my house in the American sector. So we have to hope and pray it hasn't been destroyed."

Which to his relief, it hadn't been. In fact, the door to the house was unlocked. "Someone in the military is probably living here," said Bach.

"Only one way to find out," Geir replied, pushing back the door. Although, to his astonishment, it looked like nothing had been touched.

"This is strange," said Maxim. "I would have thought the Russians would have looted the place."

"Anybody here?" Bach called.

But when no answer came, Geir suggested they go to the cellar. "It's Geir Gallen," he raised his voice. "And in case you're wondering why I'm here, I own this place."

"Geir!" came a shout from behind a wall. "Is it really you?"

"Fritz?" Geir questioned. "You're alive?"

"I was supposed to have died," he said, stepping out from the secret panel that had been created long ago. "But somehow, to everyone's amazement, I pulled through."

Geir hugged him. "I'm so glad you made it."

"Me too. But where's everyone?"

"All dead—"

"What!"

"These are the only people I have now." He turned to Dr. Bach and Maxim and introduced them.

"But how did this place survive the Russians?" Maxim asked.

"They were here. I could hear them talking, but I don't think they took much."

"It's been my experience they only take what they can carry," remarked Maxim. 'But what about the Americans?"

"I heard them talking too."

"Strange," Geir said. "Because if nobody took much of anything, it sounds like an angel was watching over the house."

"The Mercedes," said Fritz. "I kept hearing that word. So I suspect the Russians or Americans took it."

"Certainly couldn't carry that," said Bach.

Geir hugged Fritz again. "I'm sorry you had to be here alone."

"Doesn't matter, you were doing important work for the Resistance."

We did the best we could," Geir managed through his sadness. "But what about those papers sealed behind the mortared bricks next to the cellar's fireplace? I take it they're still there."

"They are. And I have some tools in my hideaway that will allow us to retrieve them right away."

"Then let's get started."

There was another brick next to it that looked like it had been added fairly recently.

"Greta and Hedy's jewelry, plus their sterling silver," Fritz said, running his fingers across it. "And a *will*." Daniel re-wrote while you were in Russia."

Geir smiled at him. "That I'm quite anxious to see."

It didn't take long to retrieve the *will*, jewelry, silver, and the roll of film about Auschwitz, with Helmut's document, in the metal boxes behind the mortared bricks.

Part of Daniel's *will* went to Greta, and the other part to Geir and his American wife, Hedy. The second metal box had Hedy's American passport, and her marriage license to Geir. "This will give me my father's money and allow me to get my American citizenship." Geir smiled, handing it to Bach. "And once I get my American citizenship, I'll be able to help you, Fritz, and Maxim get yours—along with Hayim and his wife, Judith, in Switzerland. Which means the six of us will *then* head to America."

"America—we never dreamed!" was all Bach and Maxim could exclaim.

"I give my word it will happen," Geir promised them. "And we'll stay in my father's chalet in Switzerland, where my friends Hayim and his wife, Judith, are living until we all *leave*. But first we have things to do here—"

"Like what?" Maxim asked.

"Like identifying ourselves to the Americans and letting them see the papers the Russians gave us. Which show we weren't working with the enemy."

"And the other things?" asked Bach

Geir ticked them off as if reading from a list: "Validating my father's *will*. Selling this house. Packing up here. Hiring a truck to move the stuff to Switzerland. And then, going there ourselves, after we've identified ourselves to the Americans."

"You make it sound easy," said Fritz.

"It will be," Geir assured him. "Because soon you'll see that truer words were never spoken."

Hayim's son in New York, Leo Glick, was an outstanding attorney, and Geir didn't see a problem in Leo validating Daniel's *will*.

A day passed, then another as they went about packing not only sentimental items, but whatever they could use. Otto and Hugo's clothes fit Bach and Maxim perfectly. And wearing them, they strutted around the house as they helped with the packing.

Geir packed all of Margit's clothes and pieces of her needlework, including everything that had belonged to Greta. Hedy's clothing and wedding dress were in the armoire in their bedroom, and he packed it gingerly, including her sketch board. Her furs, like Greta's, had been untouched by the invaders. "So in memory, I'll take them to NewYork with their jewelry, like I'm taking my aqua blue suit, lederhosen, and leather pants and coat." he remarked, after a contemplative moment.

"But as for my things—" Some of his model airplanes had been destroyed. However, he didn't care. His and Hedy's photo albums were in tact as was his play, *The Sorrows of Destiny*, he'd been in the middle of writing.

The items and clothing belonging to Daniel, Rudi, Volker, Charlotte, and their parents were packed also.

"We'll leave a good bit of this stuff in Switzerland," Geir told Fritz. "And from time to time I feel certain, Hayim Glick and Judith —who'll be living in New York with **us**— will vacation there. As well as his son's family, who're New Yorkers. So they'll be welcome to help themselves to some of this stuff."

But before Geir hired a truck to deliver the items to Switzerland, it was necessary that he, Maxim, Fritz, and Dr. Bach identify themselves to the Americans.

"Why you're practically an American citizen," an officer exclaimed to Geir. "And to think, according to this Russian report, you were working with us all along. So congratulations, you'll do well in America."

And sure enough, the day came sooner than expected when Geir and his five friends, boarded a ship bound for New York.

Leo Glick, Hayim's son, who looked identical to his father, would be meeting them. "Daniel's left you a fortune," he told Geir on the phone. "And I've spotted a large, exquisite house on Long island with a maid for the six of you... And the good news is that the place is only an hour away from Columbia University, where you, Maxim, and Fritz have indicated you want to get degrees in economics. However, does Maxim speak English?"

"I'm teaching him, and he's teaching me Russian," said Geir. "But regardless, I don't like the fact he'll be in school, while working as a medic alongside Dr. Bach."

"Why is he doing that?" Leo asked.

"So he can send money to his niece and her husband in Russia," Geir said, trying to bury his frustration.

"And you offered to send it, I'm sure."

"Naturally... but he feels like he's imposing on me."

"Then I'll have to talk to him about it and see what I can do," remarked Leo with an air confidence.

Except for Maxim's refusal to let them help him, until he could get on his financial feet, it seemed things were all coming together. But when the ship pulled into New York's harbor, Geir spotted the statue... green and holding up the torch of liberty. She brought tears to his eyes, the same as she did his friends. *Margit said I should have lived here all along,* the voice in his head reminded. *But then would I have met Hedy? A tragic loss. Yet, if I hadn't met her, I doubt those nine thousand people at Auschwitz would be alive...considering they were the destiny, I was meant to fulfill.*

Hedy was pleased at the way her life was going in Kiev. She and Alexis were happily married with a baby on the way. Something Yelena and Hansi were quite excited about it. "My twins," she would call the girls, giving them each a kiss on the forehead. "And even if you're not identical, I still consider you twins."

They were so anxious for the baby to arrive, that when asked if they wanted a little brother or sister, they would answer in a three word sentence. Because young as they were, it was still a little difficult to add more words to their sentences. "You're gifted children," Daniel told them. "And I'm going to help you add more words to your sentences."

And sure enough, he taught them to say, 'Mom says it's always nice to have a boy and a girl.

But what's really important is to have a normal, healthy baby.'

"You're certainly helping the girls to advance," Hedy praised Daniel. "Which makes me feel good."

When the baby arrived, Hedy was delighted it was a boy. Sveltana had asked if he might be named, Dimitri, after her deceased husband. And since Hedy, like Alexi, were fond of the name, they had no objection.

On the day Dimitri was born, Hedy fell asleep after nursing him and dreamed a peculiar dream.

It was odd because in it, Dimitri, as a young man, declared a book he held to be a treasure he'd found.

"Could this mean our son will become a writer?" she asked Alexi.

"Who knows?"

"Geir wanted to be a writer."

"I know," said Alexi. "And it's sad, because he didn't get to fulfill his dream."

Yelena and Hansi wanted to help with the baby anyway they could. So when Hedy and Alexi would bathe him, the girls would hand them the towels. They also wanted to hold him, but Hedy wouldn't let them unless she was in the middle of the bed with him.

The two girls would then get on each side of her. "Has to be like that," she'd say, "because if we drop him, he'll break."

Daniel told the girls he was like their grandfather, which greatly pleased them.

He was as happy with the children as Galina, who was teaching him to cook. "Never thought I'd feel about children the way I do," he confided. "But I dearly love them. And when the weather warms, the girls and I will spend a week on the farm. Where we three will find a way to help out and have fun doing it."

The only thing that disturbed Daniel was he couldn't tell the world about what he'd seen at Auschwitz.

"Don't worry," Alexi would assure him, "the world knows."

A hospital worker secretly listened to Radio Free Europe, so when Alexi asked him if word had ever got out about the camps, the man nodded." The American General Eisenhower insisted they be filmed, or otherwise future generations would say the camps never happened." This worker then went on to describe what had happened at Dachau. "The American military, ordered to liberate the camp, discovered to their horror, boxcars full of dead bodies. The SS capo was then shot in the face by one to the American officers—and that's when hell erupted! The

Americans began shooting the SS, and giving guns to the remaining prisoners to shoot them also.

War Crimes. Did the American military not realize this...? A question frequently asked. If they did they did, they didn't care. Though, General Patton did, and ordered the upcoming charges against the allied soldiers to be dismissed."

Daniel was excited to hear what Alexi told him. "But it still doesn't mean that when I approach the throne, I won't ask God why we had the holocaust—"

"And if you do," Hedy cut him short, "ask God or one of his angels, to send me a dream and let me know what our good Lord says."

"Don't worry, I'll do my best," Daniel promised, a gleam in his eye. "But one last question, Alexi. Do we know what happened to General von Paulus when Stalingrad fell?"

"Of course we know. He was made a field marshal the day the city fell—"

Anger swept across Daniel's face. "Damn it!" he interrupted. "I can't stop thinking that if Geir's convoy had made it to Stalingrad he could have been one of those soldiers living on one slice of bread per day, as someone reported was happening And he would have probably died or been taken prisoner by the Russians."

"Without a doubt." Alexi nodded. "But the rumor circulating is that von Paulus sided with the Russians when he was captured. And after the war, when he was released, he was said to have told them that he would be living in Dresden doing military research."

"But do you really think three million German prisoners were captured, like we continue to hear?" Daniel asked him.

"Yes. With yesterday's rumor claiming that a million have died since they were," Alexi elaborated.

Daniel cast his eyes downward. "As we know, war is hell. Something that makes me continue to regret that you and Hedy weren't allowed to give the medical assistance you offered, to some of those German prisoners. Since like we've said, there had to be those among them who thought like Geir and his friends, yet got conscripted and ended up at Stalingrad—"

"And even if these German prisoners didn't think like them," Hedy interjected, "you know as well as I do that Alexi and I took an oath which stated... regardless of our feelings... we'd give medical assistance to those suffering."

Alexi's face was suddenly grim. "Which I find exasperating, considering how the Soviets are ignoring these oaths."

⸻◆⸻

The years passed, and the girls were getting close to school age.

Hedy and Alexi read to them and told them stories. But the story they liked best was one about a relative of Daniel's— a girl named Lila Lee.

"Once upon a time in America, I met Lila Lee," Hedy told them. "She was three years old and looked like someone's doll with her blond hair. She was an only child, who lived on farm with her parents, Nathan and Marie. They were quite poor. And **her** mother had not been able to give birth to a baby, until a doctor told her that if she stayed it bed for nine months, it would happen. And sure enough, Lila Lee arrived..

All was well at first. But when the toddler, Lila Lee, drank gasoline, Marie and Nathan rushed her to the hospital in their truck. They didn't need a horn because Marie was screaming all the way—"

"Oh my!" Hansi interrupted. "Did she die?"

Hedy shook her head. "A kind-hearted doctor saved her. Although her parents had no money with which to pay him. Making Nathan more determined than ever to find an investment that would bring them a lot of money. Though, sadly, the years passed without much luck. Until a real estate lady showed him some land in Texas, that she predicted would become quite valuable. 'Buy it,' she urged Nathan. And he did. Several years passed, and true to the lady's prediction, the land was suddenly valued at a million dollars.

But unfortunately. Lila's mother died close to the time—then her father. Still, the money Lila Lee inherited enabled her to go to college and became a teacher. Which was her dream."

Yelena and Hansi were intrigued with the story and wanted to know what games Lila Lee played as a child.

Hedy mulled it over for a moment and then remembered. "Old Maid cards."

"We want to be like Lila Lee," said Hansi, nodding at Yelena. "Can we play that?"

"Well." Hedy sighed. "Once there may have been a similar Russian game, but to date, I haven't seen any Old Maid cards in Kiev. So, if you really want to play the game, I'll make the cards."

Which she did. *Beautiful cards.*

And though history claimed it was Victorian game played by adults, it was also enjoyed by children.

"We like the game too," Alexi and Hedy would say. "In fact," Hedy would add, "it's so crazy, it's fun."

When Dimitri got older, he was a handsome fellow with green eyes and dark hair— the same as Hedy and Alexi. And he would enjoy the Old Maid game until his sisters teased him. "You're going to end up becoming an old maid." They'd laugh.

"Impossible for a handsome fellow like you," Hedy would smile and say.

"I'm glad you think it, Mom."

He could never be angry with his two lovely sisters because they were taking ballet lessons and were becoming extraordinary ballerinas.

They had always admired a picture of Pauline in a ballet costume. "So naturally, we intend to become ballerinas," they liked to inform everyone.

The children were getting good educations but with no religious training. The reason being that religion was not discussed in the Soviet Union. Still, Alexi and Pauline had arranged for Hansi to be baptized, shortly after her birth.

Yelena too, had been baptized in Poland in an attempt to cover the fact she was a Jew. And since only old people went to church in Russia, Galina had taken Dimitri to be baptized.

Alexi and Hedy believed the children should have some spiritual development. And they took it upon themselves to be their teachers in that respect. So Alexi arranged for Daniel to explain Judaism to Yelena, which he was happy to do.

"We should know too," insisted Dimitri, with he and Hansi joining them.

They celebrated the new year as if it were Christmas, with a small tree decorated with cookies and chocolate. Gifts were exchanged with Daniel always buying lovely gifts for everyone from some of the money Hedy and Alexi gave him. And afterwards there was a wonderful dinner Galina prepared.

Dimitri was especially interested in the dream his mother had on the day he was born. "I'm going to find you a treasure," he'd promise her.

So Hedy, like Daniel and Alexi, usually gave him a book along with several other presents. "Do you think these books will tell me where a gold mine is located?" he would ask his Hedy each year.

But she'd just shrug and say, "There's always the possibility."

————— ⬥ —————

More years went by, with Hedy pleased at the way Yelena and Hansi— now in their early teens— were on the way to becoming noteworthy ballerinas.

Dimitri had his interests too, which centered around medics in the military. "I think we've influenced his medical interest," Alexi told Hedy. And she agreed.

Hedy encouraged Yelena and Hansi to follow their hearts. But each time they did, they'd say,

'We are, Mom, but they always lead back to you.' So they decided their future would mean they'd be nurses four days a week and dancers on the week-end.

It was during this time that Daniel died. A heart attack. He went quickly, with Hedy and Alexi holding his hands. "When God answers my question about why we had the holocaust, Hedy, I'll try and get *Him* to send you a dream about what *He* said."

Those were some of his last words.

The girls and Dimitri were sickened by his death, the same as Alexi and Hedy. Who knew better than to tell them Alexi was having some heart problems of his own.

He saw to it that Daniel was buried in a well-kept cemetery not far from the house. "And if something happens to me, I wouldn't mind being buried next to him."

"God forbid that something does," Hedy said.

She never really expected she'd have the dream about God's answer to Daniel's question. But one night as she lay sound asleep, an angel appeared. "Our good Lord says that when you're able to sail the seas in a wooden shoe, you'll have your answer about the holocaust."

Now that was really something. And when she awakened the next morning, she couldn't wait to tell Alexi.

"It sounds like the poem "Wynken, Bynken, and Nod," he said, a half-smile crossing his face. "Only their wooden shoe was a wee one's trundle bed."

For a minute Hedy was bereft of speech. "Do you think what the angel meant was that our lives are merely a dream—like Wynken, Bynken and Nod's experience was?" she asked, swept cold by the idea.

"In church I was taught we must live with faith, despite our unanswered questions," he said, squeezing her fingers affectionately. "Since we have limited minds that cannot expect to understand *God's*." He hesitated. "Though the aboriginal people in Australia *do* believe our life is a dream."

His unwelcome frankness made his half-smile fade. "And you believe them?" she asked, aware of the way his face had suddenly **changed**.

"No," he regarded her quizzically for a second." Because you'd be a dream, like the other good things in my life."

"Then maybe it's the bad stuff that's the dream."

"I'd like to think—" He stopped, gazing at her with a somber curiosity. "But perhaps this dream didn't come from God—"

"If not, then *who?*"

"Who?" he repeated, appearing to give it more consideration." The author of that long-ago poem you mentioned. Making me suspect you were quite possibly so anxious for an answer about the holocaust, that the memory of that poem helped you create one—"

"From my overly active imagination. " She grinned, her mind swimming.

"That's a lot better answer than believing the good and bad of our lives is merely a dream."

"Then I think that's the one we should accept," she said, reaching out and taking his hand.

Hedy was fortunate enough to have Alexi for several more years until, like Daniel, he had a sudden heart attack. Alexi was sixty years old and knowing Hedy would outlive him, had made certain to provide for her and the children.

These days Hedy only worked part time at the hospital, helping Yelena and Hansi, who were now nurses. "And ballerinas," they would exclaim. "Who've been lucky enough to perform in Moscow twice."

Dimitri was in the military and on his way to becoming a combat medic. "All seems to be going well with our children," she informed Alexi and Daniel as she placed some flowers on their graves. "And I know you're in a better world above— and not lying in this ground. But for now, it's the closest I can get to you. Which makes it easier for me to envision that a portal to heaven has been opened, and you can hear me." Then continuing, she let it be known, "Yelena and Hansi will probably marry soon, having met two young military men who were patients in the hospital... kind and handsome fellows courting our daughters."

She touched Daniel's tombstone. "One of the fellows reminds me a little of Geir—or am I just imagining it? Since Geir is lying in a mass grave, which makes me sometimes pretend your grave is his. So I hope you don't mind."

CHAPTER THIRTY-FIVE

New York

January 27, 1967

Geir entered the date in his journal:

"The day of the month the Russians arrived at Auschwitz. And I know I should write something about it, but I haven't—instead, I've floundered. Until someone told me that when boxcars, loaded with howling Jews, passed by German churches the choir director would make the church people sing louder to blot out the howling. Which made me know then, I had to write this poem."

"CLACKY-CLACK: A TRAIN IS ON THE TRACKS"

Clacky-clack the train goes by,

As people in boxcars are sent to die.

Clacky-clack the train goes by,

As further down murderers wait,

With rifles at a barbed wire gate.

Clacky-clack the train goes by,

As smoke from towers red with fire.

Darkens the blue, cloudless sky.

Clacky-clack the train goes by,

Until— finally—after this terribly long ride,

To the other side, it starts to slow,

As murders, ablaze in darkness at the barbed wire gate,

Fling back its heavy, boxcar doors,

Glare at the souls behind them like they're trash,

Then— motion them toward the flaming pyre,

That will turn them into ash.

*"**After** I finished this poem, I also knew it was time for me to write, The Sorrows of Destiny. Of course, it wouldn't be the play I'd started. Because it needed to be a book about the war, and my great love for Hedy.*

*　**And** it would include information about my being in the Wehrmacht and the Auschwitz **Resistance**. I would **also tell** the story of Hedy's death, when the hospital trucks were bombed to rubble by the Russians, **and** the patients and hospital workers died.*

*　The **years have come** and gone **quickly** in New **York**, with its bright lights and interesting places to visit. But never a day passes, that I don't think about the tragic deaths of my loved ones.*

*　Maxim, Fritz, and I finished degrees at Columbia University in economics. Afterwards I received training as a medical assistant and worked with Maxim and Dr. Bach at the hospital. Each person there I could help or save was in memory of someone, I wasn't able to save at Auschwitz.*

*　Fritz worked in investments with Leo Glick —**who considered** himself a stock broker as well as an attorney. He and his attractive wife, Beth, had adopted a Jewish brother and sister. Two of the many children the Jews from Palestine had **managed** to smuggle to England.*

*　Leo liked to brag that his mother, Judith, would take it upon herself to see our Long Island house, with **its** many suites where all of us lived, was **properly run**. A **boardinghouse** with no stairs, I would reflect.*

*　I no longer minded stairs. I was doing much better walking and climbing, since I'd had some more surgery on my foot-wound. Too bad Volker couldn't have had it. But then, he was in a better place and didn't need it.*

*The fifties was an age of world travel on jets. Which is why each year I insisted that the six of **ustake** a **trip together**...**something** I was more than willing to pay for. Traveling I felt, would help me find some pieces of my old self that were **missing**. **A**nd **possibly** help me overcome the writer's block I'd **developed** after the war. **Plus**, I didn't want to travel **alone**. **And besides**, who wouldn't want to see the world when the opportunity was handed to them? So off we'd go. We toured the US, **Canada**, and Alaska the **first two years**. And the next year we went around the world. After that it was Australia, Central and South America, and a photo shoot in South Africa. We toured western Europe too, along with Israel. I gave money to the Jews who'd been in the camps— as I knew Daniel would have wanted. But I never mentioned his name, since he'd stated in his will not to do so, **because** he didn't consider himself a good Jew.*

In 1962 Hayim died. Dr. Bach was sorry and did his best to console is wife, Judith. It eventually led to their being married. It was a lovely wedding with Fritz saying he'd never married because he was crippled and felt a woman shouldn't have to put up with that.

*Maxim and I felt the same way. However, we were so emotionally crippled from the war that I couldn't stand the thought of any woman but Hedy—like Maxim, **who** felt the same way about his**deceased** wife.*

*Were we living normal lives in **peacetime**? Not really. Life didn't seem as important to us as it once had.*

*I wanted to write, **yet couldn't**. I **was different**. And sometimes had difficulty recognizing my old self. Since as **someone** said, 'war can do that to a man **who's** lost the love of his life'. **Something** Maxim and I would talk about, admitting we were like that, **because** we **probably felt guilty for being alive, when so many we'd loved had passed.***

Of course, having married Judith, Dr. Bach didn't feel that way. And when Leo and his wife moved in with us, we shared some pleasant memories. However, when Judith died from a sudden illness a year ago, our good doctor vowed to never marry again."

⸺◆⸺

New York
January 27, 1968

A year later on this day, Geir wrote in his journal:

"To my surprise I wrote my book, The Sorrows of Destiny, in an amazingly short amount of time. And believe it or not, the first publisher I sent it to bought it.

The book was printed in the English speaking countries of Britain, Canada, Australia, and South Africa. And it sold quite well. I had now shared my story with the world and felt a great relief to have done so.

Of course it was dedicated to Hedy's memory. But I also wanted to dedicate something to Yelena's memory...our little toddler who died so tragically. So I decided to write a fable for her and put it in the back of my book.

Dedicated to the memory of my sweet little angel, Yelena— gone but never forgotten.

A Fable

The Shark That Walked On Land

A beautiful, young woman, Lanetta, loved on an island in the Mediterranean. She liked to surf and often went out at dusk with her surfboard.

All was going well until, terrorized, she spotted a huge **shark**, and lost control.

She blacked-out when this shark swept her up and took her ashore. But alas, when she opened her eyes and saw a handsome, young man in a black uniform, she couldn't believe it. He wore a cap on **his head with** a skull and crossbones on it.

"Don't be afraid," he said. "We sharks can stay on land for twenty minutes without breathing. So the Sea Wizard, with his magic sword turns *us*, his male sharks, into men so we can."

The young man's name was Kuhl, and as they talked, a strong attraction **developed between** them. But when twenty minutes was up, he had to return to being a shark. So they agreed to meet tomorrow at dusk, when she was surfing.

This time she wasn't scared when he came up. And they frolicked in the water, until a large, fishing vessel appeared. Onboard was an angry-looking man with a rifle who shouted something about a shark. Suddenly, Kuhl had a gunshot wound, so Lanetta quickly grabbed him...an act that astounded this angry-looking man. "He's a man and not a **shark**!" she cried. "So help me get him to the **shore**—"

This angry-looking man quickly began to aid him. And once on the beach, he removed Kuhl's bullet and patched up his wound. "My name's Eduard," he said. And he agreed to do whatever he could to aid the couple. "I'll even marry you, since I'm the captain of that vessel." He pointed, grinning at it.

But sadly, Kuhl could only be a man for a brief time each day. "What does the Sea Wizard make you shark-men do?" Eduard asked.

"Study the people on the islands," Kuhl said. "And some of us—but not me—capture them." And then he explained the hostility between these people and the sharks. "These people on the islands are rich from sunken treasures. And always eat the best fish, leaving the motley ones for the sharks. "So some of these men are able to trap these people and lock them in a cage, to be eaten later." But he quickly clarified that he only ate the motley fish and not the people. Because he felt sorry for them. And he would have rescued them had the Sea Wizard not **warned that** under his spell, any shark devising a way to open the **cage** would never be able to become a man again."

"Now that you've come into my life, I realize that I must do everything I can to save these people," he told Lanetta.

"But you might never become a man again," she reminded.

"Even so, regardless of our love, I'll have to try and save **them**—"

"Unless we can find a way to get around the Sea Wizard."

So Eduard, in his speedy vessel, took them to a huge cage where the people were imprisoned. But unfortunately, there was no way anyone could open it.

"Only the three men in white—**which** look like ghosts —have such power," said a female, **Romani** prisoner who called herself, Vada."

"And they're where?" Kuhl asked her.

"On that fiery mountain." She pointed at it. "They're fighting the Sea Wizard and his sharks, who can remain humans longer when he's with them. **Which** is enabling them to keep these men in white, from coming to rescue us."

"But I'm down here and not with him," said Kuhl. "So I don't have the power to remain human any longer than twenty minutes."

"True. But this key to the *Kanada* warehouse on the mountain, should help you do it." She handed it to him. "The warehouse has all of our things stored in it. One of which is a small, wooden dummy that can talk. His name is Chuck. However, he won't show himself until you say, '*Vada has sent me.*' She touched the key in Kuhl's hand. "And when this red-haired, wooden man appears, then bade him take you to the Sea Wizard and his shark-**men. Who** refuse to stop fighting these men in white, until they've killed them."

"But will I have time before I turn back into a shark?" Kuhl asked her.

"Oh yes," she assured him. "Since Eduard's speedy vessel will get you to the mountain quickly."

So Kuhl and Lanetta boarded it, urging Eduard to move at full speed.

When they got to the mountain, Kuhl made Lanetta wait on the vessel while he went into the *Kanada* warehouse and fetched Chuck. "We must hurry to the Sea Wizard," he told the little fellow. "Is he very far?"

"He's close," said Chuck. "So it won't be a problem."

The Sea Wizard was waving his magic sword and giving orders to his shark-men. However, when he saw Kuhl holding Chuck, and heard this little, wooden man talk, he was so amazed that he dropped his sword, **when** he reached out and took this little man from Kuhl.

The shark-men, staring, were also amazed and didn't notice that the Sea Wizard's magic sword was on the ground.

In fact, the Sea Wizard was so enraptured with **Chuck, he** didn't see or feel the heat from the ball of fire, rolling down the mountain at him. But **the** shark-men, feeling it, quickly headed to the water to become sharks again. "Without realizing it's for the rest of their days," remarked Kuhl.

"Kuhl!" Lanetta cried, rushing toward him.

Her haste made him suspect that she believed he would soon become a shark forever. "Which in order to save myself, I'll have to do," he lamented.

When suddenly, the three men in white appeared. One of them held the Sea Wizard's magic sword.

"This sword, stolen from us, has been hunted by our people for centuries," he informed Kuhl. "And now that we have it, just tell us your wish, and it will be granted."

"Wish!" Kuhl exclaimed, excitement coursing through him." Just keep me a man for the rest of my days."

Which they did...muttering an incantation, before touching each of his shoulders with the magic sword, like they were knighting him.

Eduard beckoned Kuhl and Lanetta toward his vessel. "Are you ready to get married now?"

And knowing they'd live happily for the rest of their days, they shouted, "YES."

⋯⋯◆⋯⋯

Geir wrote one Sunday afternoon:

"My publisher liked this fable so much that he believed it was one of the reasons my book sold so well. Which I'd like to think—"

"Are you writing another book?" Bach interrupted, stepping into Geir's bedroom-study.

"Just my journal."

"Which will probably get published **soon.**"

Geir yawned. "Possibly. But right now I'm too exhausted to think about it."

"**Then you should** take a nap." Bach grinned. "So I'd best leave."

"Guess you'd better before I fall asleep," Geir mumbled, crawling in bed after he left. "Because it

seems I *do* need a **nap**."

And closing his eyes he immediately fell into a deep sleep. How long he **slept**, he wasn't sure? But when someone tapped him on his shoulder, he opened his eyes. *Was this a dream?*

Then, he turned his head and saw a woman standing over him, who looked like his mother. *Am I dead?*

"No, Geir, but answer the phone!" the woman urged." Because that which has been lost is being **returned...**"**and then**, this woman vanished as quickly as she'd appeared.

So in his dream-like state, he picked up the phone. And when he did, a young man's voice came on the line. His voice sounded like it had an eastern European **accent—*However** that could be a bad connection,* *couldn't it?* Anyway, Geir could barely make out what the young man was saying.

"Who are you?" he mumbled into the phone

"Dimitri Zeroff— **Alexi's** son. And I'm calling to tell you that, **even though** my father is dead **like yours**, your beloved Hedy— **my mother**— is with me."

"Then I know I'm dead," Geir said. "And must be in heaven if Hedy's there. So tell me where she is so I can get to her."

"She's in Kiev."

"Kiev!" Geir made a distasteful face, recalling that five million Ukrainians died fighting Nazi Germany.

"Kiev's not heaven, it's the Soviet Union. So just who in the hell are you?"

"Her son—like I said."

"This is a scam. Because if you read my book, you'll know she didn't have a son—"

"When I was born Mom said she dreamed I'd find a treasure for her in a book. *Your book*—**that** I'm holding in my hand."

His tone of voice clearly invited a response. "It was only published in English-speaking countries," Geir pointed out. "So how'd you get it if you're in Kiev?"

"From an American man in the hospital, who broke his rib taking pictures at Babi Yar. And he asked me if I read English, which I do. So he gave it to me when he was discharged from the hospital—"

"Give me the phone," interrupted a female voice in the background. *When* suddenly, a voice he hadn't heard in over a **decade** came on the line. **Although** with **the poor connections**, he **had difficulty recognizing it.**"Geir, it's me, Hedy. And I know it's hard to believe, but your father, who died some years ago, Yelena, and myself weren't on those hospital trucks, Because due to a medical emergency, Dr. Zeroff was able to save us..." *Oh how I've **mourned** for Hedy.* **But** this **couldn't** be Hedy.

He **was** ready to explode. "I won't be put through this," he yelled. "You're mocking the **people** I love! And one way or another, I'll see you pay **for** it—"

His voice was *so* loud that an astounded Dr. Bach and Leo **burst** into his room.

"What's wrong, Geir!" Leo shouted.

"These people are mocking my deceased loved ones."

Leo quickly grabbed the phone. "Just who in hell are you?"

"Hedy Gallen Zeroff," came a quick answer. "And we were told Geir was dead—"

"Which he mentions in his book," Leo cut her short, "was like a near-death experience."

Bach, with his brows creased, shook Leo's shoulder. "Yelena,my niece—try and see if she's with her."

"I'm right beside her," said a young woman, who had apparently grabbed the phone.

"This is all a scam!" Geir continued to argue.

"Only one way to find out," said Leo. "Think of something, Geir, that you and Hedy would know, but no one else would."

But after giving it some hard thinking, Geir shook his head. "Nothing comes to mind."

Leo pondered it briefly before he said into the phone," Do you, Madam, know something that only you and this man—**you** claim to be your husband— would know?" He handed the phone to Geir.

"Yes. The wedding ring he wanted to buy me," she answered in a **strangled** voice. "But I refused to let him **since** he didn't have the money. So he insisted I give him a picture of a ring I

liked, that he'd have made for me one day. And he put it with our marriage license—"

Dawning struck! *No hiding my shock*—"Because by God, **it is** her!" Geir exclaimed. "So my mother was right when she told me that what had been lost to me, would be returned." At the other end of the line he could hear Hedy sobbing. "I love you, Hedy, always and forever!' He **shouted** with a **choking** cry. Dr. Bach **had tears** in his eyes too. "But mine are tears of joy at the thought of my little Yelena **being** alive."

"We're coming to Kiev tomorrow," Geir said. "Just tell us where you live and how to get there—"

"I'll have to tell you," Dimitri intervened, "because Mom's fainted."

"Then see to her!" Geir quickly said. "**Since** I'm not there to do it."

"Don't **worry, my** sisters are mopping her brow with a wet rag."

Leo took the phone from Geir. "Give us the information we need, Dimitri. Because even if it's Sunday, the Soviets at the United Nations will see me. **Since** from time to time, I give them free advice about the city."

He gave it to him without hesitation, with Leo promising, "I'll call you back the minute we know something."

Which he did.

CHAPTER THIRTY-SIX

The Events That Follow Are Taken From Geir's Journal

*"After that, when the connections were good, Hedy and I talked many times on the phone. And I learned with great sadness how Volker, Charlotte, Nicholas, and Rudi had died. I also let her know that Daniel's handwritten will had stated that if there were no survivors, the money would revert to the new Israel **when** it was born.*

*'I agreed with **Daniel** on that,' she said.' And was pleased to **learn from** you that you and your friends gave money to Israel... But what is more important to me **than** the money you gave the country is that you **survived** —for **which** I'm grateful to God.'*

*' Like I am **for** you. And I'm assured by the Russian embassy, that I'll be in Kiev by this time next week. As will as Fritz, Maxim, and Dr. Bach. **Of course, the four** of us **will** remain **American** citizens, **but we'll** be welcome in **Russia.'***

*'And I can hardly wait to see the **four** of **you**,' she never failed to say.*

*'**Neither can we**,' I'd tell her, 'a smile in my voice. 'Then I'd inform her about Leo handling the money.*

*'It's your money, **since** I didn't have any when we married...' **But** she wasn't willing to accept that it was hers, not mine. Then I'd remind her that Leo and his wife, Beth, would be coming the following week after my **arrival**, and **we'd discuss** the matter with them.*

Hedy was a Soviet citizen-the same as Dimitri and his sisters, who now had Ukrainian husbands.

*The Soviets were so impressed I was willing to live in Kiev **instead** of **New** York, that there was talk Life magazine would do a story about it... which seemed to please them.*

*Dr. Bach and Maxim were excited to be moving there with me, as was Fritz. 'Wouldn't Otto be surprised to learn I was ending my days in the Soviet Union,' **Fritz** was fond of saying.' But then I'd remind him that you, **Geir**, the good doctor, and **Maxim** are my **family** now. **So** I go where all of you go.'*

*Leo and Beth would continue to live in the Long Island house. **And** I encouraged them to allow their children and grandchildren to live there too. Also, there was the chalet in Switzerland, where they could vacation.*

*And since the couple would be coming to Kiev the following week, to see how we were doing, I asked Beth to take the picture of the ring Hedy liked and have one made like it. 'The rings of hers I've tried **on do** fit my fingers,' she'd said. 'So I'll bring the one you're having made for her when Leo and I come.'*

'Which, considering we'll be renewing our vows, I'll surprise her with it when we do.'

*'Also, you're bringing **her** the furs, family jewelry, and sterling silver,' Beth reminded. 'Which she and her daughters will probably love.'*

*'Another reason I'm so anxious to get to Kiev— **Yelena**, Hansi, and Dimitri.'*

'I know this week is passing slowly for us,' Bach said with a sigh. 'But our big day is just around the corner.'

*And I **thanked God... Not** caring **that** I might never **see** New York again, even if it did have better weather than Kiev.*

*Chest-high snow in places, I remembered. '**But** who cares,' I said as I stepped off the plane. The important thing was being with Hedy and her family. And hopefully getting to help out in the hospital where she and her daughters worked.*

*Some **reporters** were present with cameras. And some medical people were waiting to help Dr. Bach and Fritz, **since** they had canes and could possibly use assistance. Of course, Maxim and I were helping them too.*

'It's so cold, we wouldn't let the ladies come out," said a dark-haired young man who introduced himself as Dimitri. "So they're waiting inside.'

'You look like your father,' I told him, giving him a hug.

Bach, Maxim, and Fritz also hugged him. And together, like a chorus, we thanked him for all he'd done.

'Mom's inside, so follow me.'

*There was a bit of coldness inside, but it didn't stop me... **Hedy** who was before me Hedy whom I'd **believed** was dead…And reaching out to each other, we **collapsed** on a bench with some pillows.*

*Flashes from cameras followed as we embraced with the **memory** of our long-lost **love. We held** each other silently while these **photo flashes**, like bolts of lightning, were followed by our downpour of **joyful** tears. 'You look the same as I remember you,' I said.*

'And you do too.'

I brushed back the hair falling across my forehead. 'Except for the gray in my hair.'

'I've got streaks like that too,' Hedy said, removing her wool cap. **'But I think we're still skinny enough to get into our wedding clothes, I mentioned I was bringing—'**

'Look, Geir,' Bach interrupted, nudging me. 'Yelena.'

'Yelena?' I questioned, turning and staring at a coppery-haired toddler wearing a red, wool bonnet that matched the toe of her red shoe. I was astounded. 'Why she hasn't aged a day since I last saw **her**!'

'Not her, but I have,' said a coppery-haired young woman. 'I'm **Yelena, that** you dedicated the fable in your book to. And this is my little girl, Yelda.'

'And I'm Hansi and this is my little girl, Paula,' said a brown-haired woman. 'We didn't tell you about our children because we wanted to surprise you.'

'Which you did,' I said, hugging the two women.

'Our husbands are in the military and won't get leave until next month,' Hansi said. 'But they're anxious to meet you, knowing you saved my life and Yelena's.'

'My daughters had a double wedding,' Hedy informed me. 'And a year later had the two little girls they both badly wanted.'

'However, next time we're hoping for boys.' Yelena smiled.

More hugs and kisses followed, with the **toddlers** wanting kisses too. Hedy hugged Fritz and told him how thankful she was he'd lived. 'I've never been around children, which tells me it's going to be a new and exciting experience for me,' he said.

The weather was getting worse, so Dimitri suggested we all go back to the house in the bus provided for us by the **news reporters**.

'I'm anxious to see the house.' I told **Hedy**.

'Even if it's old with a **pre-war facade**?' she **asked**.

'I'll love it,' I assured her

Galina, the now widowed housekeeper, was treated as family. So we hugged her too.

She showed **Dr**. Bach, Maxim, and Fritz to their rooms, then pointed at the small house outback**,** which had once been **servants'** quarters. "I'm sleeping in the cellar because it's warm. **So** if anyone wants to join me, there's an extra *bed in it.' She reached out and took Yelda. 'She's sleepy like Paula, so I'd best put them to bed while all of you visit.'*

Hedy and I sat down at the house's big, round table. 'You look so like your father, Dimitri,' I told him. 'And it pleases me that a piece of him is still here.'

Hedy brightened. 'Like Daniel was a piece of you, Geir.'

She kissed me again as did Yelena and Hansi. 'God took our mothers,' said Yelena—

'—but sent your Hedy, an angel, to watch over us,' Hansi completed.

*Dimitri handed me Helmut's Grand Cross. 'Daniel gave it to me. But I know he'd want you to have it, like his **ring**...w**h**ich Mom keeps locked up for safe keeping.'*

And with tears threatening to fall once again, I took it. 'When I die this cross will be yours again— along with his ring.'

'You don't have to do that,' Dimitri insisted.

'But I want too.'

*Dr.**Bach** and Fritz, having **quickly** returned from their rooms, were thumbing through some photo albums with pictures of Yelena and Hansi dancing. **I was sitting next to Hedy, but Dr. Bach moved to the vacant seat beside me so I could see the pictures. Yelena and Hansi's** little girls were in some of the photos, with a note **that read**:*

*'**After** we finish dance **class** practice, we take our daughters' hands, turn them around, and then we bow **together**.'*

*The good doctor showed some of the photos to Maxim, **who** was **seated behind** him. **But** he **simply** nodded. **Since** having obtained permission from Hedy to have his Moscow relatives visit, he was on the phone talking to them. 'I sent you plane tickets, so now's the time to come,' **we heard him tell them.**

*I **got** up and **opened** my suitcase so I could hang **Hedy's** furs on the* coat*rack. Then, I opened my carry-on bag and laid out on the table, the **sterling silver** in cloth rolls, **along** with her jewelry.*

Yelena and Hansi were astounded. 'We'd be robbed if we wore that,' said Yelena.

'Then wear it around the house,' I suggested. 'Unless the four of us are asked by the Soviets to be in New York for a week on diplomatic business.'

'That would be interesting.' Hedy grinned, picking up her emerald-drop necklace. 'Because the girls could dance there—'

'**That** they could,' Bach intervened, holding up a photo. 'With these pictures telling me they're outstanding ballerinas. And if you get lucky, then maybe Dimitri, along with the girls' husbands, could come with them to New York as their military escorts.'

' We'd like that,' said Yelena, 'but changing the subject.' She went over to the coat rack. 'What about these furs hanging here?'

' They're old but in good shape,' said **Hansi** running her fingers over one.' So does anyone see a reason why we can't wear them here?'

'I've seen some women at the hospital wearing vintage furs," Hedy said. 'And to my knowledge, they didn't get robbed.'

I put my arm around Dimitri. 'It's getting close to bedtime, but before we say goodnight, I **want** to say that your father and my father were two extraordinary men. And since Hedy's told me they're buried close, then when the weather gets warmer, I'd like to get some nice flowers and go with all of you to pay tribute to them.'

'I'd like that,' Dimitri **replied**.

'And I'd also like to make a trip to the country and meet the people who took care of Hansi when she was a baby,' I **told** him, hoping we could do it soon. 'Hedy said Daniel was quite fond of them.'

'He **was.** 'Dimitri smiled. Then he** explained that when they visited, it depended on his getting the loan of a military vehicle from the hospital where he worked. 'And we always take large baskets of food, so as not to impose on the family.'

'I'll rent a bus with a driver,' I told him. 'And we'll have an indoor picnic at their place with all the food we'll be bringing. So, tell me, when's a good time to go?'

'Let's wait until Leo and Beth get here next week, 'Dr. Bach answered, before Dimitri could.

'And also my relatives. Who'll be here tomorrow and staying two weeks,' Maxim added. He turned to Hansi. 'She was just telling me, that Svetlana, who helped **raise** her, lost her husband during the war and never remarried.' **He** looked around the room at **everyone**. 'Same as I lost my wife. So Svetlana and I will have something in common.'

'When we're there Hansi and I usually clear a space and dance for the family,' said Yelena. '**Because** living in the country, they don't get much entertainment.' She pointed at a picture in the album of what appeared to be two family members.

'There **are** some new quilts on your beds,' said Galina, returning from having put the little girls to bed. She gestured at Bach, Maxim and Fritz. 'So go to your rooms and try them out, because come tomorrow Dimitri, Yelena, Hansi, and myself are preparing a lovely breakfast **for you**. **With** table settings that use the sterling silver that was **brought** here tonight.

'You didn't need to go and do that,' said Bach.

'Nonsense.' Galina replied, dismissing it with a shake of her head. 'I taught Dimitri and his sisters how to cook. Which means it's up to me to keep them in practice.'

'We've talked about it on the phone 'Hedy reminded, taking my hand as we prepared to head toward our bedroom. 'But are we ready for each other?'

I nodded. 'Even if it's almost like— once again— we're two virgins.'

Her grin was quick and warm, as if she was thinking of our pleasure to come. 'We made it the first time, and we'll make it again.'

'My thought exactly.'

When we reached our bedroom door I turned and kissed her. 'I'm glad you had Alexi, and that you came to love him.'

'We bonded—'

'—because you each had loves you'd lost.'

'I try not to grieve over our being separated for so long,' she remarked candidly. 'Since nine thousand Jews were **saved—as** was Yelena.'

'My destiny,' I reminded, looking at her without expression. 'But, tell me, was it worth it…? You taught me to care for others. **Which** prepared me for what I had to do.'

'Even if to our **great** misfortune, we **got** separated.'

'A **bone**-aching loss.'

She bit **down on her** lower lip. 'A misery which makes me wonder, if given a choice, would you do it again?'

'How could I not?'

'You couldn't.' She shook her head regretfully. 'Any more than I could.'

'God called us.'

'And we listened and did what he **said. And** our bond did not perish.'

'That dream about the wooden shoe you mentioned on the phone,' I said, redirecting the conversation. 'I've thought about it and decided that like you, it's only the bad part of our lives that's the dream— or nightmare. I don't believe **the aboriginal people**, **when they say** our life is just a dream.'

'A thought that gives me some relief,' she replied. 'It's just that I do regret I couldn't give you a child before I went into the change.'

'You've given me children—**but** not of our flesh,' I said, thinking about what extraordinary human beings Dimitri, Yelena, and Hansi were. 'Because what you've given me are the children of our souls.'

I smoothed my hands over Hedy's dark curls, like I'd done the first time. Then, we hugged each other so tightly, that it inspired us to shed our clothing quickly and topple onto the **bed...With** the ecstasy of joy we'd looked forward to immediately following.

'I always knew we were meant to be together,' she told me, like she'd done the first time.

Which prompted me to return the words I'd said **that** time— 'Of that I'm certain.'**And kissing her once again, my soul melted into hers.**

THE END

DISCUSSION QUESTIONS

1. What do you think about Hedy being jokingly called a mail-order bride? She and Geir fell in love at first sight. Do you think this often happens in such relationships? Why or Why not?

2. Do you feel Daniel did right leaving Geir to be raised by Margit and Wilhelm? Discuss your reasons for and against it.

3. What influences in Hedy's life do you feel could have made her such a caring person, determined to help humanity?

4. Daniel feels guilty for leaving Geir as a baby. Do you think he was justified to feel such guilt?

5. How do you feel about the Luftwaffe pilot who refused to fly the wounded to Minsk, until Geir gave him a diamond ring? Give possible reasons why the pilot might have been reluctant to help Germany's soldiers.

6. What do you think about Daniel sending Gunther to Spain? Daniel upheld the agreement he had with him but, should he or should he not have done so, since Gunther had committed crimes against humanity?

7. Daniel did not feel people would believe the holocaust, so he visited Auschwitz. Do he did right to visit the camp and see it for himself? What might you have done if you'd been in his situation?

8. What were your thoughts of Hedy's dream about the holocaust? Do you believe it reflected the Aussie Aboriginal idea that this life is just a dream? Could that be possible? Discuss reasons why it might or might not be.

9. Would Dr. Zeroff have become friends with Hedy and Geir had she not had her unique sketching ability? Give opinions.

10. Do you agree with Hedy's choice to remain in Russia? What other choices might she have had?

11. What do you think about Charlotte, after Nicholas died, running back into the hospital being bombed by Russian Yaks, shouting, "I'm going too!"

www.ingramcontent.com/pod-product-compliance
Lightning Source LLC
Chambersburg PA
CBHW061622210726
48287CB00001B/238